No Wake Zone

Linda Lovely

L & L Dreamspell
London, Texas

Cover and Interior Design by L & L Dreamspell

Copyright © 2012 Linda Lovely. All rights reserved. No part of this publication may be reproduced, stored in a retrieval system or transmitted in any form or by any means, electronic, mechanical, photocopying, recording or otherwise without the prior written permission of the copyright holder, except for brief quotations used in a review.

This is a work of fiction, and is produced from the author's imagination. People, places and things mentioned in this novel are used in a fictional manner.

ISBN: 978-1-60318-485-4

Library of Congress Control Number: 2012938328

Visit us on the web at www.lldreamspell.com

Published by L & L Dreamspell
Printed in the United States of America

Acknowledgements

I'll start with family. A special thanks to Mary Eunice Kennedy, curator, Iowa Great Lakes Maritime Museum, for help with Spirit Lake research. Lay any inaccuracies at my doorstep, not Mary's. Brenda Mann and Tammy Nowling, my Ph.D. nieces, deserve star billing for their attempts to explain complex biotech subjects. I hope enough of their wisdom rubbed off to sidestep major science gaffs. Thanks to my great nephew Duncan James Nowling for letting me attach his first and middle names to a main character. As usual, I'm grateful to my husband, Tom Hooker, and sister, Rita Mann, for suggestions on early drafts.

Major (Retired) Arlene Underwood, a dear friend since kindergarten, continues to provide anecdotes to help flesh out my heroine's Army experience. My long-distance critique partners—Maya Reynolds and Robin Weaver—and local critiquers—Donna Campbell, Danielle Dahl, Polly Iyer, Howard Lewis, Jean Robbins, Helen Turnage and Ellis Vidler—help me hone my craft and inspire me with their creativity. Thanks a million.

Finally, hats off to Cindy Davis, my editor, who has a keen eye for spotting grammatical errors and possible sources of confusion. Thank you to Lisa and Linda, L&L Dreamspell publishers, for their professionalism and dedication to producing quality work.

Note to Readers

While this is a work of fiction and all characters and events are fictional, Spirit Lake, Iowa, and the Iowa Great Lakes are very real and every bit as enticing as No Wake Zone suggests. Arnolds Park, a century-old amusement park; the Queen II, a classy double-decker tour boat; the Iowa Great Lakes Maritime Museum, located inside Arnolds Park, and the Tipsy House are honest-to-goodness, real-life entertainments. I love and highly recommend every one of them.

My thanks to Historic Arnolds Park Inc., the nonprofit umbrella encompassing Arnolds Park, the Queen II, and the Maritime Museum, for allowing me to use these settings as a backdrop for my mystery. For plotting purposes, I invented security routines and emergency procedures, law enforcement and medical examiner responses, and carved out jurisdictional boundaries. I know nothing about real-world security at Arnolds Park or the operations of the Dickinson County Sheriff's Department or the Medical Examiner's Office. I hope the true professionals in these organizations will smile at my follies and the fictional characters I've added to their staffs.

I cheated some descriptions of physical locations as well. For example, I lent Arnolds Park's Tipsy House distorting mirrors. The mirrors actually were part of Arnolds Park's old Fun House, torn down decades ago. While the Tipsy House has probably been remodeled during its life, the renovation described in the novel is purely a plot device. I also changed the dates and format of the annual Antique and Classic Boat Show. Don't go hunting for a Spirit Resort either, though it's evocative of many grand old resorts that have since passed into legend.

If you want to catch me in any other prevarications, come visit the Iowa Great Lakes and Arnolds Park. It's a trip worth making.

A huge thank you to Mary Eunice Kennedy and John and J.D. Kennedy for permitting me to borrow endearing traits, sayings and folklore associated with family members no longer with us. They give my characters humor, depth and spirit. If you find something likable in one of my composite characters, hats off to my kin. If you find something objectionable, hand me full blame.

With love to the Iowa Great Lakes.

Linda Lovely

Dedication
To
—Son & Mother—
Stephen Ross Kennedy,
1st Captain of the Queen II,
& Mary Deck Kennedy,
Nurse & Storyteller Extraordinaire

You are sorely missed. Thank you for your gifts of laughter, courage and love, and for the fond memories that kept me company while writing No Wake Zone.

One

"Miss, Miss—are the crab puffs all gone?"

I tightened my grip on the tray, wishing I held my Glock instead of a platter of tricked-out wieners. At the rate these folks snarfed hors d'oeuvres and champagne, they'd empty the galley before the midpoint in our afternoon lake cruise.

"I'll check, sir."

While answering the portly merrymaker, I spotted my cousin Ross in his crisp captain whites. His blue eyes twinkled, and his moustache quivered like a frightened chinchilla. What nerve. I'd tell him where to stuff his chuckle—and my frilly apron—the minute we docked.

Ross grinned. He'd shanghaied a junior helmsman for backup so he could kibitz now and again with the well-heeled guests. "Having fun, Marley?" he whispered as he slid by me.

He tossed off a two-finger salute and headed back to the wheelhouse. While Ross only pilots the Queen on special outings, today qualified. Jake Olsen, a tycoon the locals claim as one of their own, had chartered the double-decker excursion boat for a post-wedding reception.

When a waiter called in sick at the last minute, I agreed to fill in, never dreaming Olsen's newest wife—number three—would turn out to be Darlene Sherbert, an old college friend.

As I trotted down the metal stairs to restock my tray a blur of red and black snagged my attention. Windmilling arms. Splayed legs. A body thudded against the lower deck railing a few feet to my left and ricocheted. My mind flashed on the image of a limp rag doll. A geyser sprayed me with cold rain as the body tumbled into the lake.

Sweet Jesus. How long would it take Ross to stop the Queen? *Please, God. Not another drowning. Could I save him?*

I threw down my tray, toed off my deck shoes, and clambered over the railing. The water rushed by three feet below. I pushed hard with my feet for distance and dove.

Knifing into what felt like an ice bath, I gasped. Big mistake. Water flooded my throat. I fought to the surface, and coughed up some of the inhaled water. Tremors shook my body. Screams from the Queen's passengers blended with the seagulls' raucous cries.

I scanned the churning lake for a head breaking the surface, for a body, for anything human. Sunlight sparkling on the water blinded me. Was it a man or woman? The Queen's wake flung me upward, and I spotted the victim a few yards away. The floater vanished as I descended into the wave's trough. Head down, I swam toward the spot where a flash of red clothing last appeared.

When my hand touched skin, I stopped mid-crawl and raised my head. The Queen's wake made it tough to tread water. Had I gotten turned around? No. There he was. The man floated face down and bobbled like a cork. Well-toned arms stretched wide. A red silk shirt clung to his back, as revealing as plastic wrap. A swell flung him against me, and I seized a thick mat of white hair. My desperate yank flipped the body.

Heaven almighty. Jake Olsen.

Empty eyes told me I was too late. The man's eyelids drooped at half-mast as though he could no longer resist sleep. A thin rim of faded china blue circled dilated pupils—black, lifeless holes. Disconcertingly the eyes had pin-balled in opposite directions. It didn't matter. Jake's vision of this world was gone.

With an arm tucked across his chest, I cradled his head to keep his lips above water. Lifesaving 101. Though I hadn't been a lifeguard for thirty-plus years, it's something you don't forget.

Wasted effort. Jake wouldn't be organizing any more cruises or have a chance to introduce wife number four.

My scissor kicks and feeble one-armed sidestroke kept us afloat. I pivoted to keep an eye on the Queen. A low growl escaped the engines. How long would it take Ross to slow and make the seventy-five-ton vessel heel?

A lifeline buoy shot across the waves and skipped over the surface just out of reach. I kicked harder. Though I wore only thin slacks, a blouse and that damnable apron, the waterlogged apparel felt like chain mail. A desperate lunge brought the nautical ring within inches. Once my fingers snagged the rope netting, I looped my free arm through the buoy.

Now I simply needed to hang on and prop up Jake's head until help arrived. The frantic crew lowered a lifeboat. The dinghy swayed several feet above the lake's surface before it plopped down with a theatrical splash. After what seemed an hour, but was more likely two minutes, the lifeboat pulled alongside.

"We'll take him, Marley," shouted Carlos, a carnival roustabout Ross befriended years before.

"Are you okay?" he asked as he hoisted the body. "We'll pull you in next."

"I'm fine." My teeth clattered like castanets. I clung to the gunnels while Carlos and another crewman checked Jake's pulse and attempted to revive him. No dice. Carlos shook his head, then grabbed me under the armpits and hefted my body like a sack of potatoes.

Panting. I collapsed. As the rescuers rowed, I managed a final look at Jake's haunting visage before shifting my gaze to the idling Queen. A knot of nattily attired partygoers crowded the lower railing, while a parallel flock of wealthy gawkers elbowed each other for good balcony seats. Cell phones bristled like antlers among the herd.

Who are they calling—their brokers?

Then the realization hit—they were using the phones as

cameras. I turned away. But not before I spotted my friend Darlene. Standing alone. Arms crossed as she hugged herself.

My God. Her marriage had lasted one whole week. A sob caught in my throat. I knew too well how it felt to lose a husband. At least, I'd had sixteen years with Jeff.

I'm so sorry, Darlene.

As soon as the crew hoisted my soggy butt aboard the Queen, May claimed jurisdiction.

"You're a damned fool." May shook her head as she tightened the blanket around my quivering body. "Only an idiot would do a swan dive off the Queen. What if you'd hit the side of the boat or a log? We'd have two corpses instead of one. Damned fool."

My seventy-nine-year-old aunt talked tough, but after decades on the receiving end, I knew her fierce bark to be colorful bluff. The tremble in her fingers and warble in her voice said fear for my safety, not pique over my idiocy, prompted her latest tirade.

She loved me like a daughter. When Mom was alive, May offered to swap one of her three sons for my sister or me. That was Irish bluster. May Carr would do anything for her "boys"—now men creeping up on Social Security eligibility.

May shepherded me to the wheelhouse, away from the morbid circus surrounding Jake. I let my aunt fuss. Arguing took too much energy, though I didn't feel especially traumatized. Sitting around in wet clothes seemed a cakewalk compared to all too many of my experiences in the Army.

Though I'd retired from the military, I still worked, sort of. My part-time gig as a security officer let me travel when the spirit moved me. This tenth day of June, the spirit—an impressive one in the form of Aunt May—had moved me to Iowa and the haunts of my youth to help arrange a combo birthday party/family reunion. May took the opportunity to observe that I'd had ample time to recuperate from my tangle with Dear Island's psycho killer and my backside would spread to the size of Alaska, if I didn't get off it and do something.

When asked so sweetly, how could I refuse?

I glanced at my aunt. White hair as wispy as cotton candy and deep crinkles around her blue eyes reminded me she'd turn eighty in two weeks. That fact dismayed me as much as it amused her. A two-time veteran of open-heart surgery, she'd outlived four siblings and her own longevity expectations.

"Hell, people have tried to kiss me goodbye so often, they've got chapped lips," she quipped.

A cold bead of water meandered from my hairline down my back. I used the towel May had commandeered to give my short hair a vigorous scrub.

Jeez. My mind pattered about like an insomniac tap dancer. Guess it balked at focusing on the present. Who wouldn't want to block out Jake Olsen's walleyed death mask or Darlene's sobs? Yet Jake's death hadn't brought on the bone-rattling shakes I'd experienced two months before when I'd found a friend dead in a Jacuzzi.

Two big differences between the corpses. It appeared the Grim Reaper claimed Jake without a killer's helping hand, and the tycoon was almost a stranger. We'd shared one quick handshake at a gala event at the Iowa Great Lakes Maritime Museum after Jake praised Ross as the nonprofit's amiable leader. I'd instantly liked the philanthropist for that.

Still the image of Darlene standing alone at the Queen's railing made me shudder. Once we reached port I'd ask how I could help. We hadn't spoken since our brief reunion at the start of the cruise. After whooping with delight at seeing me, she'd whispered, "Some wedding reception. These people are all Jake's business cronies. You're my only friend here."

With a shake of my head, I tuned back into the conversations swirling around me. Radio in hand, Ross alerted various authorities about the accident. May pasted her cell phone to her ear and issued marching orders to her daughter-in-law, Eunice.

"Find some dry clothes, too," she suggested. "Marley looks like a drowned squirrel. Maybe sweats from Ross's locker. She'd never fit in your clothes."

Unfortunately, May was right. She called them like she saw them.

My aunt toyed with a clip-on pearl earring as she talked. "We need to keep the bulls separated from the cows. Let's set up the museum theater for Jake's guests and try to corral the reporters in the museum proper until we see what's what."

She paused, her forehead wrinkled in concentration. "Imagine the authorities will need a space, too. Maybe the boardroom? Oh, better order sandwiches from Yesterdays, and start some coffee."

May stuffed her cell phone back in a pocketbook large enough to double as a body bag and patted my hand as the Queen made stately progress across a six-mile stretch of West Okoboji. High speed isn't an option for a double-decker tour boat ferrying more than a hundred passengers.

"Do you honestly expect a reporter stampede?" I asked. "The local paper has what, a five-person staff?"

She speared me with a look. "You didn't see the vultures descend when that plane crashed over in Clear Lake with Buddy Holly, Ritchie Valens and The Big Bopper aboard. I was visiting folks over there at the time. Believe me, reporters will swarm out of the woodwork like termites. Jake's worth a billion."

I choked. "Holy kamole." I tried to watch my language around May. "After I met the man at that museum benefit, Ross told me Jake was wealthy. But he never mentioned Jake's bank account boasted that many zeroes."

Having set foot in Iowa twenty-four hours ago, I was way behind on lake gossip.

"Jake founded Jolbiogen and made fifty million when he took it public," May said. "Just the beginning."

I slipped off my wet socks and wrung them, creating a miniature waterfall. "A billion dollars. Wow. I'd be hard-pressed to spend a million."

"Well, kid, I hear Jake's family rolls up their sleeves to help."

My aunt often calls me "kid." While it may not be the most

accurate handle for a Midwestern-bred baby boomer, May's use of the moniker makes me smile.

When Ross put down his radio, my aunt tapped him on the shoulder. "D'you hear me talking with your bride? You need to radio Carlos. Tell the sheriff, we'll shepherd the passengers into the theater and attempt to bottle the reporter vultures in the museum proper."

"Already done," Ross said. "I also told Sheriff Delaney the boardroom was his. He wants to hold our passengers until he can get statements from everyone."

Beyond the wheelhouse window, Arnolds Park's signature roller coaster steadily grew taller. The amusement complex over a century old provided a home to both the Maritime Museum and the Queen II, a replica of a famed steamboat that plied the lake in the 1800s.

As Ross slid the Queen into her slip with studied grace, I surveyed the reception committee gathered on the pier.

"There's Gertie's ride." May pointed at a battered four-wheel drive truck. "She's parked beside the ambulance."

I knew Gertie. The county medical examiner played bridge every Thursday with my aunt. When May was Dickinson County Hospital's Director of Nursing and Gertie was a new hire, my aunt took the young nurse under her wing. Later, May encouraged her protégé to return to medical school. The addition of "Doctor" to Gertie Fuerst's name hadn't altered their friendship.

May chuckled at the assembly of official vehicles parked catawampus along the pier. "It'll be interesting to see who wins this pissing contest. My bet's on Sheriff Delaney. He's that string bean who looks like he withered on the vine. Not a man to underestimate."

A rangy six-footer stood beside an SUV with Dickinson County Sheriff emblazoned on the side. I watched as the sheriff shook a finger in the face of a state trooper who'd just climbed off his motorcycle. In the background, a cop leaned against a City of Arnolds Park cruiser. He'd apparently conceded jurisdiction and was content to observe the fuss.

"We don't get much excitement," May said. "Guess that trooper figured to get his mug on TV by responding to the death of a celebrity."

"What do you suppose killed Jake?" I asked. "A heart attack?"

"Doubt it was a heart attack." Having completed his docking duties, Ross joined in the speculation. "At our museum board meeting last week, Jake told me he'd just had a physical—EKG, cardiac scoring, the works. Passed with flying colors."

He turned toward May. "Yes, Mom, I know—some doctors don't know a stethoscope from an enema tube." Ross and I grew up listening to Nurse May grumble about know-it-all interns with book learning but no horse sense. In other words, idiots who paid nurses no heed.

"I'm sure we'll get the lowdown if Gertie's allowed to talk," May added. "Nobody saw wife number three give Jake a little push, did they?"

My aunt must have seen the dismay written on my face. She backtracked so fast her tongue practically performed a somersault. "Sorry, sorry. Sometimes my mouth outruns my brain. I forgot Darlene's an old friend of yours. I didn't mean anything. Just a stupid joke. Work in a hospital long enough and black humor becomes a bad habit."

Ross cleared his throat. "At least no one's going to accuse this wife of helping her husband overboard. Two of my deck hands swear Jake wandered off and was completely alone when he doubled up and pitched over the side."

A crewman jumped to the dock and secured the Queen's lines. At a neighboring slip, two Iowa Lakes Patrol officers tied their speedboat. The Queen had towed even more law enforcement in her wake.

As soon as the gangplank was set, paramedics hustled aboard. Hardly a minute elapsed before they wheeled Jake Olsen's body to the ambulance. A plaid wool blanket covered the body. Darlene trailed the official procession. "Can I ride with him? Please." Her voice broke, her pain evident.

"No, ma'am. Sorry."

The ambulance doors snicked shut, and the sirens emitted a few high-pitched burps to warn milling officials. A news photographer snapped pictures of Darlene staring after the vehicle as it peeled away. I lost sight of my friend when the sheriff clamped her arm and steered her toward the museum.

That's when I spotted a tall interloper amid the confusion on the pier. He stood ramrod straight, watching Darlene. With his face averted, I could only see his salt-and-pepper hair, styled not barbered. The way his suit molded to his body proclaimed it wasn't off any ready-to-wear rack. Definitely a Mr. Moneybags. He looked eerily familiar. I shuddered.

He turned to stare at the Queen, and my stomach clenched.

Quentin Hamilton.

What the hell is he doing here?

Two

"Quentin Hamilton." The very sight of the man had me muttering. "You pompous jerk."
Ross's eyebrows shot up. "What? You know him?"
"Afraid so. Sounds like you've made his acquaintance, too. Why's he here?"
May looked at me, then Ross. Her frown said she'd never heard tell of the man—a rare occurrence for a woman who'd birthed, nursed or sold real estate to most of Dickinson County. Ross smiled at May's consternation. "He's an out-of-towner, Mom. Doubt any members of your Spirit Lake intelligentsia have researched his bio."
I tapped Ross's arm. "Hey, cuz, you didn't answer—what's he doing here?"
He let out a long sigh. "His company provides protection services to a lot of bigwigs, Jake included. He was all over me before this cruise. Demanded a guest list. I politely told him to stuff it—he'd have to ask Jake. Hamilton got huffy. Said his clients were too important to be bothered with crap from some make-believe captain in a Halloween costume."
Ross scrubbed his face with his hand. Exhaustion shadowed his eyes. The day was taking its toll. "I reported the conversation to Jake. He laughed. Said Hamilton was an arrogant bastard, and he only used the security company because he owed Hamilton's father."
Ross nodded at me. "Okay, your turn, Marley. Was Hamilton some Army mucky-muck?"

"Not exactly."

I chewed my lip. How much should I say?

"During my stint at the Pentagon, Hamilton's firm, Thrasos International, sought a multi-million dollar contract to revamp computer security for Department of Defense facilities worldwide. I represented Army Intelligence on the taskforce that slogged through proposals. I couldn't believe some of the follies in the Thrasos bid."

"I think I know what's coming," Ross said. "You torpedoed the bid."

"Not exactly. General Irvine had that honor in a closed hearing well attended by government and military elite. But I sat at the general's elbow. The hostile reception shocked Hamilton, who seemed unfamiliar with his own firm's proposal. He was furious—expected business to be handed to him as a *droit de seigneur*. Since he could never accept the blame, he projected it onto me, a convenient scapegoat."

"So you've been getting dirty looks ever since."

"After the hearing, he cornered me in a deserted hallway, 'You,' he snarled, drawing out each vowel into a syllable of its own. 'You're finished. You hear me?' He kept his voice low, but it quivered with hatred. He told me no one in the military would touch me after he was finished."

"So he bullied you into retiring?"

"God, no. I made my decision before he issued his threats. To this day, my sole retirement regret is Hamilton's belief that he cowed me into a rushed departure."

I took a deep, calming breath and gave Ross and May a Cliff Notes version of what happened after the contract debacle. Hamilton lost a few million, but he used his contracts to bootstrap himself back into favor. To my mind, he still had too many former DAs, Special Ops soldiers, spooks and techie magicians at his disposal.

We watched Hamilton follow the sheriff and Darlene inside the museum. Suddenly I felt anxious for my old friend. She didn't need that dipwad bullying her. I wanted to get inside, find

Darlene and offer help—even if it was just a sympathetic ear.

As the last straggling passengers left the Queen, a couple of sheriff's deputies passed them on the gangplank, headed in the opposite direction.

"Guess I'd better greet our newcomers," Ross said. "Why don't you two go ahead to the museum? I imagine Eunice would welcome your help."

I shrugged off the blanket tucked around my shoulders and took May's arm. "Shall we?"

We crossed the wooden walkway onto the pier. When I glanced back at the Queen, sheriff's deputies had already festooned the top railing with police tape. The ribbons of orange looked more like bunting than markers of an accident or crime scene.

Somehow the festive image made Jake's death seem all the more macabre.

Eunice intercepted us before we reached the museum. "The volunteer docents and a couple of park security guards are keeping order. You were right, May. How did the TV, radio and newspaper folks get here so quickly? It's been what, half an hour since the accident?" She shook her head.

Eunice handed me a towel and a set of extra work clothes Ross kept in his office. Though he served as museum director, he put in plenty of time varnishing wood, painting signs and oiling gizmos. The paint-splotched sweatshirt smelled faintly of my cousin's aftershave.

She held a pair of worn tennis shoes by their laces. "I even scrounged these. Ross said you'd lost yours. You can change in the restroom and then come join us. The security guard at the theater will ask for a password. It's Hafer."

I smiled. What else? Ross's vintage Hafer runabout was his pride and joy.

"Thanks, you're a doll." I hugged her. "I'll be along shortly."

Since Godfather's Pizza was located a hop, skip and jump from the museum, the manager knew my kin well and volunteered to hang on to my soaked waitress duds for the duration.

Ross's sweatpants sported a drawstring waist and elastic at the ankles, while the tennis shoes were only one size too large. I have big feet. Still I felt a little like a homeless hobo as I entered the museum.

The pool of reporters had grown like bacteria in a Petri dish. As Eunice warned, they roamed the exhibit areas, sniffing for story meat. Luckily, my skuzzy apparel marked me as hoi polloi—common folk—not one of Jake's ritzy guests.

When I reached the theater entrance, the security guard eyeballed me with suspicion. But as soon as I whispered "Hafer," he motioned me inside.

After the door closed, the throng's whispers seemed to fuse into a white-noise hiss. Uncharitably, I decided the affluent were gathering gossip kindling to stoke next winter's cocktail-circuit fires.

No sign of Darlene. Probably cooped up with Sheriff Delaney. I did spot Aunt May mid-hubbub, making soothing noises and patting the shoulders of sobbing guests. Eunice, who's more than a tad shy around strangers, hid behind the refreshment table. A relieved smile lit her face when she saw me.

"Now I don't feel so out of place," she whispered. "Look how I'm dressed."

She wore a cotton rag sweater, jeans with that aged patina prized by kids, and not one iota of makeup. Eunice and her twenty-five-year-old daughter could star in a mother-daughter anti-wrinkle cream commercial.

"Hey, my fashion statement makes you look like a runway model. But don't worry. These people won't notice either of us. Serfs are invisible."

Few young faces appeared in the middle-aged to geriatric sea. While most were over forty, the guests tended to exude that prime-of-life glow that's a badge of the wealthy. Tucks, lifts, and liposuction expunged the consequences of gravity and two-martini lunches. Emollient bronzers polished cheeks with a warm glow. Flitting smiles revealed rows of straight teeth, so white they bordered on fluorescent.

I'd met a few of the Iowa "Who's Who" at the one gala I attended. I recognized the owners of a restaurant chain featuring low-fat buffalo steaks. An evangelist who performed lakeside baptisms for a TV following prayed over a small group of bowed heads. While I couldn't place any other faces, many looked news clip familiar.

The theater door squeaked open for another latecomer. Ross.

Oh, crap. Hamilton followed at his heels. A bas-relief cord in the man's neck thumped like an overworked piston. Not a happy camper.

Ross fast-walked toward us with Hamilton cemented to him and spewing invectives.

I wondered how my old enemy would react when he saw me. Had the past three years lessened his animosity? New bulls to gore and all that?

His gaze flicked over my face. Bingo. The gray eyes narrowed to slits. "Colonel Clark." He addressed me with a mocking bow. "What are you doing here?"

"No need to call me Colonel. I'm retired."

"I heard." He almost purred, quite pleased with himself. Yes, the dolt thought I'd run because he'd frightened me.

I declined to explain my presence. No sense contaminating Ross's situation by introducing our cousinhood. With a shrug and a cold smirk, Hamilton let it go.

He coughed. Hamilton's look seemed to blame me for whatever he'd hawked up. He turned to Ross. "Someone from my staff will be in touch."

He strode away as if on a presidential mission. My cousin and I remained silent until he was out of earshot.

"So what's that SOB want now?" I prodded. "Why are his people contacting you?"

"He's just trying to cover his butt. His company was on point when his billionaire client dropped dead. He's calculating how to shift blame if there's anything hinky about the circumstances."

Ross cracked his knuckles. "The asswipe told me he's conducting his own probe into 'Jake's accident.' He demanded background on Queen employees and zeroed in on Carlos. Hamilton is too politically correct to call him a gypsy, but he pigeonholed Carlos as an undesirable."

Ross grinned. "I couldn't help myself. Had to ask: 'Gee, didn't your people vet everyone ahead of time?' That really torqued him."

I shook my head. "Welcome to Hamilton's enemy list. Say, did Olsen have a Thrasos bodyguard aboard the Queen?"

Ross cut his eyes across the room to a muscled fellow standing at parade rest. "Yeah. That guy with the twenty-inch neck. He was in the head taking a leak and missed all the action."

My chuckle bubbled up before I thought better. When scowls swiveled our way, I sobered. These people had just suffered a loss.

I touched Ross's sleeve. "With all the excitement, I haven't had a chance to say how sorry I am about Jake. I know how much you liked him."

My cousin bit his lip. "Yeah, I did. We weren't exactly bosom buddies, but he sure was a friend of the museum. He loved the lakes as much as I do."

My aunt bustled over. "Ross, there are a bunch of limos outside. The guard tells me they're waiting to shuttle these people to Jake's house for dinner. I'm certain the widow won't want to play hostess. See if the drivers could take these folks to their cars instead."

Before Ross could run the errand, a sheriff's deputy entered and made a beeline for our group. "That's Pete Marshall," May said. "I was in the delivery room when he was born. Cared for his mother before the cancer took her."

The lawman leaned down and whispered in May's ear.

My aunt turned toward me. "Pete, this is my niece, Marley

Clark. Deputy Marshall here has a message from Sheriff Delaney. Apparently Darlene wants to know if you'll go home with her and stay the night."

I hesitated, then nodded. I'd want company in the same circumstances.

"Good," Deputy Marshall said. "Follow me. I'm to drive you and Mrs. Olsen home. The Sheriff said he'd be by later to get your statement. You were the one who jumped in after Mr. Olsen, right?"

"Yes," I answered. "That'll be fine."

Ross touched my shoulder as I turned to go. "Want me to pick you up at Darlene's house tomorrow morning?"

I smiled my thanks. "Okay, I'll treat. Breakfast at the Family Diner."

We settled on a nine o'clock rendezvous unless I called to reschedule.

As I left with the deputy, a scowling Hamilton pointed me out to a local. Was he trying to ferret out my Spirit Lake connections? How tight did he hold to his grudge? What was it Jeff used to say? "The smaller the brain, the bigger the need for revenge."

Three

Deputy Marshall escorted me to his official ride and handed me into the backseat. "Sheriff Delaney is bringing Mrs. Olsen."

He'd barely got the words out when the sheriff shepherded Darlene out the museum door. Predatory reporters circled like a wolf pack, ready to cut out the weak and rip them apart with questions sharp as canine teeth.

With a protective arm around her shoulders, the lawman cleared a path with repeated "get out of my way" commands.

A man shouted at Darlene's back. "How did your husband die? How much do you inherit?" Another voice piped in, "How will this affect Jolbiogen stock?"

Darlene looked shell-shocked. Tears dribbled down her flushed cheeks, and smeared mascara lent a bruised look to the skin beneath her eyes.

Until our surprise rushed reunion aboard the Queen, it had been thirty years since I'd seen Darlene in anything except sporadic Christmas card photos. I'd barely recognized her.

As a twenty-year-old, she'd been farmer's-daughter curvaceous, her strawberry blonde hair long and ironed straight. Now she was model thin with platinum-dyed hair feathered in a short pixie style. Only her luminous green eyes remained unchanged.

As the sheriff opened the car door for Darlene, he turned on the reporters and held up a scrawny, sunburned hand. "Mrs. Olsen just lost her husband—please extend a little courtesy."

Bless you.

Darlene scooted across the bench seat and wrapped me in a bear hug.

Sheriff Delaney leaned in. "I know you have private security, but I'll lend a patrol car to help keep the tabloid snoops at bay." His message arrived on tobacco-laced breath.

His gaze slid toward me. "Ms. Clark, I have some questions for you. I'll try to come by before it gets too late."

Delaney slammed the car door and the deputy sped away, official blue lights flashing, siren silent. The deputy didn't say a word. The sudden silence gave me chills.

Darlene bracketed my face with her hands and pulled my head close so she could whisper in my ear. "Oh God! It's so awful. We've only been married a week." A sob caught in her throat. "I can't tell you how much it means to have you here. Those people think I killed Jake." Her breath felt hot, fevered.

I squeezed her hand and kept my voice low. "Everybody knows your husband was alone when he went overboard. No one could think you had a thing to do with his death."

She bit her lip, straightened, and flicked her gaze to the back of our deputy-chauffeur's head. "I can't think straight," she murmured. "I'm numb."

Darlene's wary glance suggested she was reluctant to say why she might be a murder suspect with the law eavesdropping.

I changed the subject. "Have you talked to Jake's children?" Ross had mentioned the billionaire had a son with wife number one, and a daughter with wife number two. The siblings were almost as old as Darlene and me.

"I asked Sheriff Delaney to phone them. They didn't bother to attend our wedding and we're not exactly fond of each other, but I didn't want them to learn about their dad's death on TV." Her eyes narrowed. "They'll be here by nightfall. Carrion are quick to circle when there's fresh kill."

Uh-oh. The family dynamics signaled firefights ahead, and I had no interest in serving as peacekeeper. What had I gotten myself into?

"How about your daughter? Will Julie be here soon?"

"Tomorrow morning. You'll like her. The minute she finished her doctorate, Jake offered her a post-doc at Jolbiogen. Called her a kindred soul. He loved her."

Darlene massaged her neck. Her engagement ring's walnut-sized diamond trapped sunlight streaming through a side window and practically blinded me.

When she caught me gaping, her lips curved up in a wry smile. "Kind of obscene, huh? This ring's usually stashed in a safe. It's only the second time I've worn it. Jake said, 'humor me,' so I put it on. It's so big it looks like I pulled it from a box of Cracker Jacks."

My friend collapsed in her seat. "I was so shocked to see you today, balancing a tray of champagne glasses, no less. I remembered Captain Ross was your cousin, but never dreamt you were in the area or I'd have invited you to the party.

"Last I heard you were a Lieutenant Colonel working at the Pentagon and married to a soldier. So I assume you're not starting a second career as a waitress?"

This woman just watched paramedics pronounce her husband dead. How could she make polite chitchat?

"Hey, Darlene, we're friends. You've suffered a big shock. Forget social etiquette. It's not like we met by accident in a supermarket reaching for the same carton of eggs. You don't have to make conversation."

She shook her head. "I'm cried out. I just spent half an hour answering the sheriff's questions. If I close my eyes, I still see Jake smiling, toasting me with his champagne glass. A minute later he was gone. I need normal conversation…a few minutes of sanity. Humor me, please. Just talk. About anything but this afternoon. Tell me about your life."

"Okay." I tried to remember the last time I'd sent Darlene a Christmas card and realized she didn't know my husband was dead or that I now lived on a South Carolina island where I worked part-time as a security guard.

Hard to believe we'd once been so close we knew what the

other thought without a word being spoken. We'd worked together as cooks at Spirit Resort the summer before I started Northwestern University. The workers, all high school and college kids, lived in dormitory cottages. Darlene bunked next to me.

We'd hit it off instantly. She was two years older—a lifetime of experience when those years span the gulf between high school and college. Darlene was tall, blonde and, in the parlance of the day, built like a brick shithouse.

In Spirit days, she was feisty, swore like a sailor and led search-and-pilfer raids on Chef Rudy's stash of Kentucky bourbon. I adored her. During the school year, we traded campus visits and phone calls. A second summer of high jinks at Spirit Resort cemented our bond. Still it was the pre-internet, pre-Facebook era, and we only stayed in touch sporadically after the Army shipped me overseas.

As I told Darlene about my husband's death in a car crash and my day-to-day life on the Carolina coast, her fidgeting fingers stilled. My monologue seemed to soothe her. By the time I completed a comic digest update of my life, the deputy turned off the main thoroughfare onto a winding private road.

Less than five miles from Arnolds Park, Jake's estate fronted on West Okoboji, one of fourteen northwest Iowa lakes gouged out by retreating glaciers. Underground springs lent West Okoboji, the chain's deepest gem, its aquamarine hue and sticker-shock pricing.

Darlene sucked in a breath. "Goddamn bottom-feeders."

Two uniformed Thrasos guards had conceded squatting rights to reporters just outside the gate. However, the uniforms stoically defended the estate's perimeter stone wall and evergreen hedge. The Olsen home was invisible from the roadway. Of course, nothing obstructed the view of lakeside gawkers, who routinely throttled down outboards to sidle past the tycoon's spread.

As we approached the wrought-iron gates, a TV newswoman, excitedly motioned to her cameraman. His lens swung our way as our car idled, waiting for the gates to open. We slipped inside and a wall of greenery swallowed us. A moment later, the slate roof of Jake's fieldstone and glass castle popped into view. Guilty of scouting the Olsen compound in Ross's Hafer runabout, I recalled my aunt's offhand appraisal—"at least ten million" and her appreciative chuckle at Jake's shrewd land grab. He'd used multiple agents to scoop up five adjacent lots before anyone knew the buyer's true identity or what he might be willing to pay.

After razing houses in the center of the combined properties, Jake built a Frank Lloyd Wright-style fortress straddling two lots. The two lake homes flanking the manor were remodeled for his son and daughter. However, according to Ross, Jake's offspring preferred swankier watering holes to Iowa's meat-and-potatoes lifestyle and only visited on patriarchal command. The final piece of the Olsen compound made my history-obsessed cousin drool—a vintage cabin.

Gravel crunched and the police cruiser skidded to a stop. I snuck a look at my watch—ten after six. As the deputy helped Darlene from the car, I scrambled out my side. The day's warmth lingered, a welcome relief from the car's stale air-conditioned breath. Afternoon light bathed the stunning house in molten gold.

An older gentleman opened the front door the instant Darlene stepped on the porch. He wore black slacks with a sharp crease and a starched white shirt. The butler? Did anyone use that term anymore?

The man's words rolled out in a low rumble. "Please accept my condolences. Mr. Olsen was a fine gentleman. He'll be sorely missed."

His voice caught, and Darlene threw her arms around his neck. His eyes squeezed shut, and a single tear meandered down a cheek pitted by acne decades before.

"I know how much you'll miss Jake." Darlene stepped back, releasing the gentleman from her hug. "I'd like you to meet Marley Clark. She's an old friend, and she's not expecting Jeeves, so lose the Mr. and Mrs. nonsense. Marley, meet Harvey Krantz. He manages our lake property. Jake calls him Handyman Harve."

Darlene's face crumpled as she realized she'd spoken of Jake in the present tense—the world of the here-and-now he'd never occupy again. She closed her eyes, took a ragged breath.

Harvey's bushy white eyebrows bracketed the deep fissure of a frown. "Want me to talk to the caterers? I wasn't quite sure what to do with all the food."

His voice had lost all trace of its frosty formality, and I figured his relationship with Darlene came closer to fond uncle than obsequious butler.

"Oh, cripes," Darlene swore. "I forgot about the buffet. Don't worry, Harvey, we'll figure something out."

I trailed my friend through the great room. Her brisk pace barely gave me time to appreciate the West Okoboji view framed by a two-story wall of glass. Breezing through oversized glass doors, she led me onto a trio of stone patios spilling down the hillside.

The sound of gurgling water drew my eyes to a rock-edged waterfall. Its meandering course fed an endless-horizon swimming pool on the terrace below before burbling its way to a lakeside catch basin I'd spotted from a previous boat idle-by.

"Just look at all this food." Darlene waved a hand at a half-dozen buffet tables that practically sagged under the weight of accumulated delicacies. "It's a shame to waste it."

"How about one of the camps?" I suggested. "I'll bet the girls at Camp Foster wouldn't mind trading hot dogs and s'mores for a little lobster and cheesecake."

"What a great idea." A smile flickered across her face.

While working at Spirit, we'd discovered we were both alumna of Camp Foster, a Y camp offering canoeing, archery, horseback riding and dorm-style bunk beds. A fixture on East Okoboji for more than a century, the camp was every eleven-year-old tomboy's dream.

Darlene excused herself to arrange the food giveaway.

When she returned, she headed straight to the bar setup. "I figure we can both use a drink. You still a rum and Coke fan?" I nodded and Darlene chuckled. "Me, too. To Jake's chagrin, I never acquired a taste for champagne or wine."

Pouring with a heavy hand, she splashed rum over ice in two glasses before adding pop.

As the catering crew continued to bundle food, she led me down to the next patio level where we sank into poolside chaise lounges, sun-warmed and toasty. It would be almost nine o'clock before the sun set. We had hours before the night's chill crept across the lake.

Darlene stirred her drink with a finger. "It's not real yet. I can't believe Jake's gone. Three hours ago we were joking and laughing."

She reached over and her fingers skated over my cheek. "I can't believe you dove in after Jake. Thank you for trying to save him."

She retracted her hand and stared out at the lake. "Doc Swann, one of our party guests, said he figured Jake was dead before he hit the water. Probably an aneurysm." She looked up, her eyebrows knitted. "Was he dead? Did he say anything?"

I shook my head. "He was already gone. Whatever happened was mercifully fast."

Darlene stared down into her glass. "Good."

"Had Jake been ill?"

She took a generous swallow before answering. "A while back, he groused about eye fatigue. Then, he started getting short of breath for no reason. The company doctor diagnosed myasthenia gravis—MG. He got it under control and he's been fine ever since. My husband," she hesitated over the word... "My husband was such a bear about privacy, it's a wonder he even told the doctor he had a problem. Jake never wanted anyone to suspect he had any weakness."

"Do you want me to call anyone?" I asked. "Family? Friends? A minister or a doctor?"

Darlene sipped her drink. "As far as a doctor goes, forget it. I've been through this before. There's not a drug in the world that helps. Tomorrow I'll call our minister, but I don't want to see him tonight. I do want to go to the house and check in with Julie. Find out what time to expect her. Do you want to stay here or go in?"

"Here," I answered. "Is it okay if I take a walk?" Stone steps meandered toward an enchanting gazebo and flower garden. I could almost hear the buzzing of ecstatic bees.

"Of course, make yourself at home. I won't be long."

I ambled through the garden and stooped to smell a rose. The swing hanging from the gazebo ceiling was a pleasant surprise. I sat and rocked, staring at the tranquil lake. I knew all too well what it was like to lose a husband without a moment's warning. Darlene wouldn't have it easy.

❀

"Ready for another rum and Coke?"

Darlene's return startled me. I hadn't heard her footsteps.

"Sure." I took the offered glass.

As my fingers slipped round the icy refill, a shiver ran up my spine. Winds barreling out of Canada were hastening the mercury down its evening scale.

Darlene sat beside me. She tilted her head back, closed her eyes, and traced circles around the rim of the glass. She'd exchanged Donna Karan silks for roomy, well-worn sweats. Except for the paint splotches on my sweatshirt, we almost matched. She'd scrubbed away all traces of makeup, too. Stress etched delicate lines at the corners of her eyes. Up close, she looked haggard, almost our age.

"Julie says she'll be here by ten." Darlene's feet pushed against patio pavers to restart our swing's gentle rock. "I'm worried about her. Earlier, when I phoned to tell her Jake had died, I sensed she'd been crying *before* I broke the news. That's not like my daughter. I pressed her and got nowhere."

She turned toward me. "I forced myself to call Kyle and Gina—Jake's son and daughter—too."

"How are they holding up?"

"They may be half siblings but they both inherited a cold fish gene." Bitterness laced her tone. "Can't wait to bury him and cash in."

A vein pulsed at the side of her temple. "Kyle informed me he'd make the funeral arrangements. Said I was 'ignorant' of how to handle a funeral for someone in his father's social strata.

I might have conceded except Jake gave me written instructions. He was determined not to lie in state and have Jolbiogen employees file by like peons at Stalin's tomb.

"He donated his body to the Mayo Clinic and prearranged a simple memorial with our minister. I told Kyle to check with Jake's attorney, Duncan James, if he didn't believe me. That's when I got what Jake called his son's dry-ice anger—so cold it burns."

Crap. I knew Jake's Mayo bequest was a no-go. I'd checked the donation criteria for my mother. Bodies couldn't be emaciated, obese or autopsied. Autopsy saws were a certainty for Jake.

I groped my way to the heart of the matter as diplomatically as possible.

"Oh, Lord," Darlene moaned. "Can't Jake even have the final say about his body? Money and power don't mean shit when it comes to what matters. His kids never showed him affection. But they always walked the tightrope—spiteful but never quite nasty enough to endanger their precious inheritance."

Darlene stood. "Guess I'd better find Jake's letter. Are you still comfortable here or do you want to come inside?"

"I'll wait here."

I set my drink down and hugged myself, trying to ward off a chill as I visually inventoried the lakeside enclave. Paved paths connected the main house and the two houses that flanked it to the shared patios, swimming pool and a dock that stabled every manner of big-boy float toy from jet skis to a sleek, high-speed cruiser.

A flicker of light drew my eye. Jake's adjoining lots occupied a cove, and the curving geography brought the rough-hewn cabin on the estate's edge into clear view. I could swear firelight danced inside the deserted cabin. Probably a mirage—the sinking sun reflecting on the wavy antique windows.

Darlene's return interrupted my speculation.

"Here's Jake's letter." She handed me a sheet of textured linen paper, her husband's signature scrawled at the bottom. "He had a fallback plan. See what you think."

I scanned the notarized document. Should anything nix his

Mayo bequest, Jake wanted to be cremated and his ashes scattered without benefit of a graveside service.

He didn't mince words: *No funeral. One simple memorial service in Spirit Lake, which has given me a sense of belonging and peace.*

I looked up at Darlene. "Sounds straightforward."

"I think so, too." She took a ragged breath. Her hands trembled.

"You're exhausted. Why don't you lie down?"

She shook her head. "Not yet."

I was glad her daughter would be here by morning. I just hoped Julie didn't arrive with more troubles in her backpack.

My friend stared off into space. I knew that faraway look. She'd escaped into memory. "Julie's father died two years before I started seeing Jake," she said after a while. "You never met Mike. In college, he was two years ahead of me—a forestry major—but he signed on as a firefighter after graduation to stay near till I got my degree. That was supposed to be temporary. When I got pregnant, it became permanent. I worried about Mike every time I heard a fire engine. Then one day he died in a freaking car accident.

"I felt so angry. Julie was finishing grad school and shared an apartment with friends, and the memories were suffocating. I'd inherited Mom's old clapboard on Big Spirit so coming here seemed a logical choice. That's when I started the catering business."

"A good move?" I asked.

A smile flickered. "Yep, I called on Jake hoping for a share of his catering business. He used to throw quite the parties. Never imagined we'd end up together."

"What was he like?" I probed.

She sighed. "A real sweetheart. Jake treated me like the heroine in a romance novel. We'd fly to Paris for the weekend, or he'd whisk me to Rio for carnival. His kids never understood what he saw in me. I don't hobnob with the right crowd or have a standing appointment for Botox. Hell, I even chew my nails. But we laughed a lot."

"Laughter is one of your special gifts, Darlene."

Her shoulders slumped. "Another fairytale screeches to a halt."

When she turned to me, she sported the wicked grin I remembered as a staple from our college days. "Actually it's been a hoot to be cast as an evil, gold-digging bimbo. When you're past fifty, it's kind of flattering to be 'the hussy.' Kyle and Gina thought I'd cast a sexual spell over their father, when he dropped out of the party circuit."

"And did you?" I grinned.

"Of course. Handcuffs and whipped cream all the way." She smiled, then shook her head. "Jake was bored with the social scene. He preferred to stay home. We'd read, putter around the kitchen, watch old movies, go for a boat ride. Today's party was a special occasion. Jake felt obliged to appear in public with his new bride to keep the tabloids from starting rumors about us." Darlene flinched. "Dammit."

"What?" I followed her gaze to a young man charging our way from the house to our left.

"It's Eric—Jake's grandson. Dammit, I'm not ready to face him."

The kid—I guessed early twenties—bulled within shouting range. In other circumstances, I might have labeled him handsome. Jet black hair. Irises a remote china blue, just like his granddad's. Pale skin that would turn lobster pink after an hour on the water. At the moment, he reminded me of a vicious dog, bristling with hostility.

"You stinking bitch," he yelled. "What made you decide to kill him? That ten-carat diamond wasn't enough? You won't get away with murder."

Eric gulped air to fuel his tirade. I could almost feel his hot breath abrading Darlene's face. His hands balled into tight red fists, the exposed white knuckles looked ready to abuse. Fearing he'd escalate from verbal pummeling to physical assault, I slid sideways and stood. Edging behind him, I considered my options should matters deteriorate.

Darlene's face turned white as flour, bleached by fear. But her eyes flashed with anger. Past experience warned me she was about to blow. "I loved Jake, you little shit." Her clipped tone vibrated with controlled fury. "More than you. Jesus, your grandfather's body isn't cold and you're ranting about your inheritance."

Eric sneered. "What bullshit. You love money, period. I'll see you in hell before you steal more."

Time to interrupt. "You need to leave—*now*." I used my best up-yours, military command voice.

The surround sound surprised Eric. He hadn't noticed I'd scooted behind him.

He swiveled. "Who the hell are you? Another over-aged whore?"

This boy was not winning brownie points.

When he grabbed my arm, it made anything I did self-defense. I captured his forearm with my free hand. My thumb found the spot just below his elbow and dug in. His face went from pallid to pasty. Silently I thanked the sergeant who'd schooled me in pressure points and practical defense.

Eric tried to free his arm. While I didn't release him, I eased up on the pressure. "Are you ready to leave?"

He stared daggers at me and spat at Darlene's feet. "Guess you're hiring freakin' lesbo guards now. Well, she won't always be around. We're not finished."

I eased up more and he jerked free. The scene was so over the top I felt like giggling. Was he for real?

As we watched the irate man-child stalk away, neither of us uttered a word. When he disappeared from sight, Darlene sighed. "Eric thinks he inhabits a soap opera." She shook her head. "He's convinced life's dealt him a cruel blow. With Gina as his mother, there's some justification. But lots of folks have it worse. Poor Eric's twenty years old and can't touch a fifty-million trust fund till he's thirty. He's flunked out of four colleges, majoring in recreational drug use. This spring Jake tried to interest his grandson in Jolbiogen, brought him in as a lab tech. He lasted three months. Thought the job beneath him. Jake worried about the boy, but knew throwing money at him wasn't a cure."

"Your husband sounds like a gem," I said. "But I don't envy you his family."

"Jake told them he planned to write a new will. They're all sure I goaded him into it. Truth is, I don't give a flying rat's ass if I'm in Jake's will. Hell, I could sell this diamond and be set for life."

The value of expletives is often underrated. Letting loose with a few swear words seemed to help Darlene vent her frustration. Her shoulders straightened. Her eyes flashed.

A strong lady. Good thing. Whatever was—or wasn't—in Jake's will, Darlene faced tough sledding.

I did find her nonchalance about a billion-dollar estate hard to swallow. Darlene was a rare bird if she didn't covet a chunk of change for her daughter, if not for herself.

FOUR

I jumped when a hand gripped my shoulder. "Ms. Clark, we need to talk."

Sheriff Delaney's shoe-leather face hovered above me. His gray eyes looked anything but friendly. Darlene started to get up. He held up his palm in a stop motion. "This is official. If you'll come with me, Ms. Clark, I'd prefer we do the interview in private."

Little hairs on the back of my neck saluted. Holy crap. If the sheriff's squinty eyes were any sign, I'd joined the suspect list.

A popular Army acronym sprang to mind—FUBAR.

I followed Delaney back to the Olsen house where Harvey ushered us into a small study and shut the door. I headed for the red leather couch, automatically pulling one of the decorative throw pillows onto my lap.

The sheriff claimed a club chair next to the couch and took out a pen, a notepad, and a digital recorder. "Mind if I record this?" he asked as he set it on the end table between us.

"That's fine," I answered, trying to keep my voice from warbling. My throat felt parched and my nervous fingers toyed with the fringe on the pillow. I told myself I had no reason to be nervous; I'd done nothing wrong. But sweat glands and nerves seldom respond to logic. I knew that well enough from being on the questioning side of an interrogation.

"Can we begin with why you were on the Queen this afternoon?" Delaney asked. "According to my notes, you live in South Carolina."

I took a steadying breath. At least the first answer was easy. I explained I was on vacation, visiting May and Ross Carr, my aunt and cousin. I'd agreed to waitress last minute as a favor to Ross.

The sheriff scribbled a note, then pinned me with a cold stare. "Why weren't you on the guest list for the party?"

Huh? Where did that question come from?

"I'd met Jake Olsen once at the Maritime Museum. We weren't friends. He had no reason to invite me."

The sheriff's eyebrows lifted. "Yes, but I'm told you and Mrs. Olsen are long-time friends. Why didn't she invite you?"

"Friends who hadn't seen each other in literally decades. I had no idea she'd married Jake Olsen, and Darlene didn't know I was in town."

The sheriff tapped his pen on his notepad. "Okay, let's talk about your actions on the Queen. Did you serve any food or beverages to Mr. Olsen?"

The man was getting my Irish up. I felt my cheeks flame—an early-warning sign I'm angry. Was the sheriff suggesting I'd poisoned my friend's husband?

"Yes, I brought a tray of champagne flutes to a group that included Darlene and her husband. Mr. Olsen helped himself to a glass of the bubbly. Darlene took a glass from that same tray. As far as I know, no one else who drank the champagne fell over dead."

A small smile tugged at the corner of Delaney's mouth, pleased he'd ruffled me. Probably figured I'd say something stupid and confess in a fit of pique. I willed myself to calm down and smiled. I could play that game, too.

"According to eyewitnesses, Mr. Olsen finished the champagne you provided just before his collapse," Delaney said.

"How interesting." I looked directly into the sheriff's cold gray eyes.

"Yes, it is." My return stare didn't coax the sheriff to blink. "Now, tell me how you came to leap into the water just seconds after Mr. Olsen fell overboard."

"I was headed down the stairs to the galley when I saw a body fall from the top deck. I recently found a drowning victim—a friend. I couldn't bear the thought of someone else dying that way without making an effort to save him."

The sheriff kept his gaze locked on mine. "Save him, huh? At least two eyewitnesses seem to think your 'lifesaving' efforts pushed Mr. Olsen's head under water."

My fingers squeezed the pillow I longed to throw in Delaney's face. "Nonsense. The man was floating facedown when I reached him. I flipped him over and held his head above water until the lifeboat reached us. Unfortunately he was dead when I reached him."

Delaney looked up from his scribbling with a raised eyebrow. "What makes you so certain? Care to venture a guess on what killed him? Poison, maybe?"

"I haven't the faintest, Sheriff. Is that all? If you're going to play bad cop, can we do it later? I have a friend who just lost a husband. She needs me."

Delaney snapped his notebook shut and picked up the recorder. "Fine. I hope you don't plan to leave town."

"Not for two weeks. I'm staying with my aunt, May Carr. You can contact me there after tonight."

I stood and walked out without a backward glance. How did the sheriff come up with the notion I had a nefarious motive for my dive into the lake? Talk about ridiculous.

A possibility dawned. Not how, who.

Quentin Hamilton. He'd be all too happy to seize innuendo and make me a suspect.

I rejoined Darlene on the patio. We talked and watched the lake until darkness drove us indoors. I didn't share the sheriff's insulting questions. No need to upset my friend more. Jake was dead before I reached him. That meant no one could pin a drowning on me. And, even if he'd been poisoned, I couldn't buy that someone played champagne roulette to deliver the coup de grace.

Our footsteps echoed as we crossed the great room's ocean of marble tile. The caterers had long since departed. Harvey Krantz offered to linger, but Darlene shooed the butler home, insisting we'd be fine.

The stale, cold air made me shiver. Had Harvey lowered the thermostat earlier, anticipating a coven of sweaty celebrants?

"Can I fix you something to eat?" Darlene asked. "I'm not hungry."

I touched her shoulder. "I can fend for myself, just keep me company. I don't like playing mother, but you should eat a little something."

The kitchen boasted more appliances than an entire home economics lab—a doublewide refrigerator, a freezer, a Jenn-Air grill, two cooktops, twin ovens, a rotisserie that looked big enough to roast a large turkey, a warming drawer and a quartet of sinks anchored in acres of granite.

"Holy smokes." I chuckled. "Chef Rudy would shit his britches if he saw this layout. Well, maybe not. He'd miss his battery of deep-fat fryers."

While our old boss at Spirit Resort possessed a reasonable culinary range, his Sunday-feed-the-masses specialty was deep-fried chicken.

I rubbed my hands together. "Based on your kitchen toys, raiding your larder should be fun. Is this the pantry?"

Darlene nodded, and I opened a door to a walk-in treasure trove. Amidst stocked delicacies like artichokes and truffles, I found an abundance of mundane canned goods. "Ah ha, you rich folks do eat something besides caviar."

My kidding coaxed a smile from Darlene. After retrieving a can of Campbell's Tomato Soup, I added milk, and nuked two cups in the microwave. Then I scavenged cheese, sawing off a few hunks of sharp cheddar to munch with some crackers. I set a mug of soup in front of Darlene and joined her at the kitchen table. The steaming soup warmed my hands. My friend cradled her mug against her cheek.

She smiled. "Remember that Republican Women's Club meeting, when Rudy banished us to the freezer to carve an elephant out of ice? Thinking about it still gives me goose pimples."

"I seem to recall you made one of the elephant's appendages larger than his trunk. It was downright cruel how Rudy whacked it off."

My friend tilted her head. "I still say Jumbo was anatomically correct. You know those old ladies would have loved it. Maybe behind closed doors, but they would've giggled. But listen to me, calling them old ladies. We're their age now."

Darlene sipped her soup. "When we were twenty, I sort of figured old people—you know, fifty and up—didn't do it anymore. I never imagined we'd be fitting sex in between hot flashes." Her index finger traced the Iowa State logo on the red mug. "The first time I felt horny after Mike died, it came tinged with shame. But grief doesn't kill desire."

Amen to that. This spring, two years after Jeff's death, I received my own libido wake-up call. Nothing like a handsome forty-year-old homicide detective to rekindle banked embers.

"Think you'll stay in Spirit Lake?"

Darlene shook her head. "I don't know. I sold my catering business, and I can't imagine moping around this place with nothing to do."

"There's plenty of time to decide."

I didn't add that moping would require a fat bankroll. If she inherited this mansion, she'd better hope Jake left cash for taxes and upkeep—no mean feat on a multi-million dollar spread.

Chimes sounded, and Darlene jumped. "What the hell? Those security bozos weren't supposed to let anyone through the gates."

She walked to a kitchen intercom. "Who is it?"

"Quentin Hamilton."

She hesitated. "What do you want?" Her hand trembled. "Can't it wait till morning?"

"No. I need to speak to you now." His booming reply vibrated the intercom grid. He sounded peeved.

"Just a minute." She released the button. "Now I'm doubly glad you're here."

"It might be best if I hang in the kitchen. I don't exactly have a calming effect on the man. If Hamilton sees me, he'll become even testier."

"You know him?" Her eyebrows shot up.

"Afraid so. I'll explain after he leaves."

"Okay, but *please* listen in, and if I call out, charge in like the cavalry."

As Darlene ushered her unwanted guest into the great room, I skulked a few feet away, my ear plastered to the kitchen door. Hamilton didn't waste time on condolences.

"My men will be here first thing tomorrow to secure Jake's papers. You need to show them every place your husband kept important documents. And I need a complete guest list for your party."

Darlene jumped in. "That's not going to happen." Her tone suggested gritted teeth. "I will not let a bunch of strangers paw through Jake's personal things on your say-so. If *I* happen to find any Jolbiogen documents, I'll let Tom Brooks know.

"And why do you need a guest list, Mr. Hamilton? I don't want you harassing Jake's friends. Frankly, I can't see how any of this is your business. The sheriff's investigating the accident. I had to put up with your pompous ass when Jake was alive. I don't now. Get out of my house."

"As the *grieving* widow, I thought you'd be happy to cooperate." Hamilton's voice dripped with sarcasm. "Since you've refused, it's my duty to share my impressions with the sheriff regarding you and your daughter."

"Marley, would you join us, please?" Darlene raised her voice. "I want Mr. Hamilton to see I have a witness in case he makes more threats."

I stormed in like a thunderclap, the kitchen door swinging wildly in my wake. I wanted to deck him.

Hamilton's jaw quivered. "Stay out of this, Colonel Clark. I don't know how you're involved, but I'm going to find out. Maybe you helped your friend cook up this little sendoff for her husband."

"Get out." Darlene made her demand in a controlled voice. "Now."

He marched to the front door and slammed it as a punctuation point. For a moment, we stood dumbstruck.

"Well, that went well," I said.

Darlene turned to me in surprise and then laughed. A second later, I joined her. Our laughter grew until tears rolled down our cheeks.

Steam escaping from the day's pressure cooker.

In Darlene's cheerful kitchen, our laughter ebbed and a feeling of gloom descended.

"I can't believe his nerve," she muttered. "Jake retired three months ago. What papers could possibly justify Hamilton coming on like a storm trooper? And why bring my daughter—and you—into this?"

She shook her head. "Hamilton's never disguised his opinion of me. Thought Jake was slumming. I cooked for a living and graduated from Iowa State, not *Haa-vuud*."

She cocked an eyebrow. "So tell me. You've apparently crossed swords with the butthead. Should I be plain mad or worried?"

I offered a brief synopsis of my encounters with Hamilton.

Darlene raked a hand through her pixie-cut hair. "There's no way Tom Brooks authorized Hamilton to pull this."

"You mentioned him before. Who is he?"

"Jolbiogen's president. He's worked with Jake forever, almost from day one."

"Call him," I suggested. "Ask him to put a choke chain on Hamilton."

I gave Darlene more detail on Thrasos International. Hamilton knew he needed big names in his stable to dazzle corporate America. He used family clout to recruit retired Army generals, FBI and Interpol specialists, computer and technology gurus. The firm not only offered protection for bigwigs, it built a reputation for making problems disappear—the kind of problems companies and governments don't want public.

Darlene's fingers fastened on a saltshaker. She twirled it back and forth. "What kind of problems?"

"A foreign official trying to extract a bribe in exchange for a mega-bucks contract. A CFO suspected of insider trading. A security breach inside a DoD contractor's organization."

I paused to consider the types of secrets Jake's firm might hire Thrasos to hush up. "Jolbiogen's a pharmaceutical firm, right?"

Darlene nodded.

"That opens other possibilities. Maybe some gang in Chechnya is counterfeiting pills and selling them as genuine Jolbiogen cures. Patients swallowing harmful fakes isn't good for business. Or maybe someone's selling trade secrets."

My friend frowned. "I know Jolbiogen has a big military research contract. Jake said the project made him nervous because something horrific could happen if the research fell into the wrong hands. He never talked specifics, but it had something to do with DNA sequences."

Darlene's eyes widened. "Do you suppose that's it? That Jake kept documents about that research here, and that's why Hamilton's being such a bastard?"

"I honestly don't know. That man doesn't need a reason to be a bastard." I stood. "We're not going to solve this tonight. Let's go to bed. You have to be exhausted."

She nodded. "I am tired though I doubt I'll get much sleep."

An unwelcome thought popped into my head. "Do we need to worry about Eric pulling some stunt tonight?"

She hesitated. "I always activate the alarm."

Sensing a note of depression in her tone, I regretted mentioning Eric.

She tapped a key on an alarm panel. "If a door even cracks open, the guards swarm. Don't roam outdoors once the house is locked. Last fall, Julie ventured out and found herself facing three drawn guns. Security's tight. Unfortunately, that applies to everyone but Hamilton."

Darlene led me upstairs to an exquisite guest suite. A large bay window offered a panoramic lake view. An inviting down comforter graced the elegant four-poster bed.

My casual perusal froze when I spotted my very own suitcase on the bedside luggage stand.

Darlene followed my gaze. "Oh, Harvey arranged for someone to run to your aunt's house and pick it up. I thought you might have prescriptions or want clean clothes for morning."

The gesture would have been sweet if she'd asked. Instead it left me uneasy. I had no plans for an extended stay.

"Thanks." I forced a smile. "It's always nice to sleep in my own PJs."

"It's the least I could do. Make yourself at home. You should find everything you need."

She flicked on a light in the adjoining bath. Lace-edged towels hung with military precision, and soaps carved into miniature fish perfumed the vast marble sanctuary. A far cry from the accommodations I offered guests. When visitors surprised me, I crossed my fingers they wouldn't notice the free-range dust bunnies roaming the floors.

"It's lovely. If you need me—or my snoring rattles the walls—shake me awake. I sleep like a log."

"Goodnight." Darlene hugged me. "Thanks again. I'd have gone nuts tonight without your company."

After she left, I set a bedside alarm for seven a.m. Ross was due to pick me up at nine, which would get me out before Darlene's daughter arrived at ten.

While the bed beckoned, the hypnotizing view drew me to the bay window. Curled up on the window seat, I drank in the West Okoboji scenery. A full moon floated on the horizon, painting a pale silver path across the velvet lake. Pastel in-ground lights transformed trees and bushes into exotic, disturbing sculptures in the lush landscape.

Was there a glimmer of light in the deserted cabin, or was my imagination on speed? I didn't even know if the relic had electricity. Might be worth checking out tomorrow afternoon when I promised to return and help with funeral arrangements.

Reluctantly, I abandoned the view. Snuggling beneath the down comforter, I sighed with pleasure. Tomorrow had to be an improvement. First I'd take steps to erase my name from the list of murder suspects. Then I'd see if I could get through the rest of the day without a surprise corpse.

FIVE

A violent shudder wrenched me awake. My heart pounded as if some grunt just screamed "incoming." My fright arrived compliments of a nightmare—Jake tried to drag me underwater, his walleyed stare strangely at odds with his grasping hands.

I wrapped myself in a throw and huddled by the window. The nightmare slowly receded as the crimson sun performed its alchemy, transforming the leaden lake into liquid gold.

Though it was barely six o'clock, I tiptoed downstairs. Darlene sat in the kitchen, elbows on the table, head in hands. She glanced up, eyes puffy, and offered freshly brewed coffee. She looked as if she could use a little space to pull herself together.

"Mind if I go for a short run while the temperatures are cool?"

"No problem," Darlene answered. "I'll call the guards."

An exercise junky, I get downright cranky if I fail to jog for several days. My temper shortens and lethargy takes root. Okay, I'm a pain in the butt. Whenever I reached this stage, my husband, Jeff—a fitness agnostic—handed me my running shoes and shoved me out the door.

Since my knees now scream for mercy when I mount stairs, I don't run as far or as often. But this morning I yearned for the mind-numbing release of a sweaty run. I stretched half-heartedly and saluted Darlene from the doorway.

"Be back in under an hour—unless Hamilton instructed the Thrasos riflemen to use me for target practice."

Darlene smiled. "They know to expect you. Just head to the front gate."

I slipped out the sunroom's French doors. The guard on the front gate directed me to an opening in the stone wall. The day had dawned as a beauty—for anyone who didn't love Jake Olsen. Freshly cut pines lent an astringent scent to the wooded landscape. It whisked away my nightmare fog.

I hoofed over side roads to Spirit Lake's Spine Trail, a paved stretch of abandoned railroad right-of-way that's a Mecca for walkers and bicyclists. The section I chose followed a dry creek bed. Green fields flanked the path. The chatter of birds and the crackle of last fall's leaves provided a soothing soundtrack.

Aunt May introduced me to the trail after her second bypass. When doctors insisted she exercise, she mapped a two-mile walking route with McDonalds as a pivot point. May's strolls included a half-hour McMuffin layover. I turned toward the Olsen estate with visions of steaming coffee and breakfast burritos dancing in my head.

The roar of a motor startled me. Was I near a spot where the path crossed a road? No. The sound grew louder. Wonderful. Some jackass had decided to race a motorcycle down the footpath. The "no motorized vehicles" signs at each entry were hard to miss. Another bastard who thinks he's exempt from the rules.

I couldn't see the idiot yet, but the growling engine said he'd pop into view any second. Better safe than sorry. I stepped off the path onto a patch of dry brush.

The biker shot around a corner. Twenty yards away. The asswipe had to see me. Why didn't he slow?

Instead of swerving away, he seemed to take aim. His wheels straightened, heading straight toward me. What the hell was he holding—a stick?

I dove farther into the brush. "You imbecile!" I screamed just as his left arm swung in a looping circle. My shoulder screamed in pain as his baton landed a glancing blow.

My throat wasn't injured. I fired a stream of cusswords at the biker's broad back.

My heartbeat slowed. Bastard. I'd call in a report for what it was worth. Not much the sheriff could do. The bike had no plates, and the psycho wore a full helmet. Dressed head to toe in black leather, only a thin strip of his twenty-inch white neck revealed itself. Hardly enough for an I.D.

I picked myself up. Felt my shoulder. Bruised, no breaks, no dislocations. A few bramble scratches on my legs and arms. Permanent damage zip. No point mentioning the incident to Darlene. Enough shit was raining on her head.

The guard opened the footpath door without fanfare. Approaching the house, I shifted from jog to a cool-down walk. As I entered the sunroom, a male voice put me on alert. A beep ending a recorded message.

"Have a good run?" Darlene asked, her voice husky. She batted away a tear. "I've been listening to answering machine messages. A few tore me up. Jake's secretary sobbed."

I poured coffee and sat beside Darlene, who pushed a plate of Danish my way. Her cell phone trilled. "This number's unlisted. It's probably Julie." She snapped it up. "Hello."

"Mrs. Olsen, this is Dr. Fuerst, the medical examiner." Darlene's cell was on speaker, letting me eavesdrop on the crisp, no-nonsense voice. "The sheriff gave me your private number. He said you wanted to know as soon as we finished the preliminary autopsy. You're free to make funeral arrangements."

Darlene squinted at her phone and hastily hit a button. "Sorry Dr. Fuerst, I accidentally put you on speaker. Was it an aneurysm or a heart attack?"

My friend frowned. "I'm sorry. I don't understand."

I could only hear her side of the conversation, but Darlene's white-knuckled grip suggested unwelcome news. "Can't you just tell me what you found in the autopsy? Why do I need to talk to the sheriff first?"

A brief pause. "All right. Thank you."

Darlene lowered the phone. "Oh, God, the M.E. says Jake's cause of death is *suspicious* so she can't discuss the autopsy without Sheriff Delaney's okay. She'd only confirm that Jake didn't drown."

She walked to the sink and tossed her coffee down the drain. "Dr. Fuerst says the sheriff will drop by this morning. What do I do until then? Sit around and wring my hands? I have to know what happened to Jake. I'm calling Delaney now."

Returning to the table, she pulled a business card from her purse, and dialed. "Sheriff Delaney, please. Darlene Olsen calling." She closed her eyes, bit her lip. "No, that's okay."

The widow put down the phone and slumped into a chair. "His office has no idea when he'll be back. I didn't bother to leave a message."

I patted her arm. "According to Aunt May, Sheriff Delaney's a take-charge guy. He won't leave you hanging. Want me to call Ross and tell him I need to stay longer? I can wait until Julie comes."

"No." Darlene sucked in a deep breath. "I'm fine. You'll be back this afternoon, right?"

"Right."

Her smile never reached her eyes. "Since the sheriff seems in no hurry, my arrest doesn't appear to be imminent." Darlene's dark humor had a sharp bite. "I'll be the prime suspect if Jake was murdered. Kyle and Gina will see to that. And there's not a damn thing I can do to stop them."

No point adding that the sheriff had nominated me as co-conspirator.

Darlene's shock at the news seemed genuine. She'd believed Jake's death was due to natural causes.

She sighed. "Time to buck up and plan the funeral. I'll call Reverend Schmidt first. Today's Saturday, right?"

Her bravado and relative calm impressed me. "Since Jake's to be cremated, I imagine any day this week would work. Would Wednesday give out-of-towners enough travel time?"

"Sounds fine," I answered.

As I waited for my ride, our talk turned to funeral rituals—all those busywork formalities that postpone the nitty-gritty of grieving until we're alone. Having buried parents and husbands, we both knew the process. I helped make a list. Send obits to newspapers. Check. Search old address books to contact friends. Check. Select guest registers and crematory urns. Check. Pick hymns and psalms.

"Mom died in the hospital." Darlene shuddered. "Dad asked me to take burial clothes to the funeral parlor. After agonizing an hour in front of her closet, I selected a dress. Then I grabbed a slip in case the dress was too see-through, you know? The funeral director took my offering and looked at me like something he wanted to scrape off his shoes. 'Didn't you bring underpants or stockings?' he asked. 'And where are her shoes?'

"I was floored. Mom always nagged me about wearing ratty underwear—'What if you're in an accident, dear?' I wanted to scream that Saint Peter wasn't going to inspect Mom's undies." Darlene rolled her eyes. "Lord, I've never told another person my deepest, darkest secret—that I buried my mom without underpants."

I tried to stifle my laughter, but built-up stress defeated me. I brayed like a mule, and Darlene joined me in a laughing jag, the kind that tends to coincide with a loved one's death. The laughter—often wildly inappropriate—bubbles up from some deep psychic well we can't cap. Maybe it helps us keep our mental balance as we stare death in the face. I simply knew my sides hurt and hiccups lay right around the bend.

"Oh, Darlene," I choked out. "I'm lucky Mom willed her body, and Jeff was cremated. I'd never have thought of underwear. Hey, promise to leave me braless. If someone digs me up in two thousand years, I want 'em to think I was uninhibited."

Walking toward the wall of windows, I sucked in deep breaths to regain control. The old cabin snagged my attention. "You know I thought I saw lights in that cabin last night."

"Probably landscape lights reflected in the windows," Darlene replied. "No electricity. Jake told me the cottage intrigues Ross.

Take a peek inside if you like. Though I should warn you it's full of cobwebs. Creepy. Jake even claimed it had its own ghost."

"I may take you up on that later. What time should I come back?"

"How about four o'clock?"

I jotted down phone numbers for May and Ross so Darlene could reach me if her plans changed. I remained one of the six people on the planet who refused to buy a cell phone. After twenty years of being at everyone's beck and call 24/7, I refused to be tethered to a phone.

I checked my watch. "Wow. Ross will be here in no time."

❂

Declining help from a Thrasos guard, I wheeled my suitcase to the same hidden door I exited for my run. Set behind leafy camouflage, the door allowed foot traffic to pass through the stone perimeter that flanked the fancy wrought iron gate.

My timing proved perfect. In seconds, Ross's silver Chevy Blazer kicked up dust as it turned off the highway and wound down the lane. The guards motioned my cousin to execute a U-turn as I stepped through the guarded portal. Wary of lurking reporters, I shoved my suitcase in the back and jumped in the front seat.

"Thanks for picking me up."

Ross glanced at me. "No problem, Cuz. You promised breakfast. How's your friend holding up?"

I fastened my seatbelt. "Doing okay, given what she's facing." I told Ross the preliminary autopsy suggested homicide.

His eyes didn't stray from the road, but his jaw tightened. "I haven't seen all that many dead folks, but Jake's eyes sure looked weird. But how could it be murder? Folks on the upper deck said he started coughing and excused himself. A minute later, he had some sort of seizure and fell overboard. Everyone swore Jake was alone."

I took a deep breath and slowly exhaled. "Sheriff Delaney considers me a suspect."

"What?"

"He seemed to think I had ample opportunity to doctor the champagne I served Jake just before his swan dive."

"Delaney's off his damn rocker," Ross huffed. "I'll phone the son-of-a-bitch. Hell, you didn't even know you'd be serving drinks until an hour before we left port. This is preposterous."

I ran a hand through my hair. "Agreed. Maybe I'm paranoid, but I suspect Quentin Hamilton added my name to Delaney's Most Wanted list." I opened the window a crack for a breath of air. "Oh, and the sheriff claimed a couple of eyewitnesses said I held Jake's head underwater. Guess the theory is I drugged him, then dove in to make sure he wasn't breathing when your crew fished him out."

Ross stood on the brakes. My body shot forward, tightening my seatbelt like a corset. My cousin's face turned scarlet. "Are you kidding? That's insane."

"I'm more angry than worried. Even if Hamilton's whispering in Delaney's ear, his innuendoes won't hold up."

My cousin loosened his stranglehold on the wheel and we rolled forward again. "Who was with Jake when you served that champagne?"

Closing my eyes, I scrolled through my memory bank. "Darlene and that tele-evangelist Reverend Eliot. Another woman, too, with permed hair a weird orangey shade. I flashed on Orphan Annie when I saw her."

"Vivian Riley." Ross didn't think twice about his I.D. "She's a friend of Jake's son, Kyle, and his missus. Vivian was in Eunice's high school class. According to my wife, the woman's an airhead."

Ross slid into a parking slot on Main Street. As we walked to the Family Diner, he jingled the keys in his pocket. A frown made his eyebrows practically shake hands. I quit jabbering to give him think-time.

While I'm always happy to spend time with Ross, his company this morning was especially welcome. During our formative years, the two of us—the babies of our respective families—ranked below spit in our siblings' worldview.

Over the years, our childhood survival alliance strengthened despite distance and divergent lifestyles. I loved Ross like a brother. Sure, we teased the hell out of one another. Yet if he'd told me he'd murdered someone, I'd bring a spade and ask what size hole. We had each other's backs.

Waves of knee-buckling aromas assaulted me inside the Family Diner. The aroma of sizzling sausages and cinnamon buns ambushed my fragile resolution regarding sensible caloric intake.

Ross punched my arm. "You're not going to order something wimpy like a poached egg, are you?"

His attempt to lighten my mood worked. "No way, I could eat a whole cowboy."

He waggled his bushy eyebrows, though he knew the object of my lust was a pile of hash browns topped with a cheese omelet and smothered with lumpy country gravy—every lump concealing a spicy sausage nugget.

We claimed an empty table. Once we'd secured our very own coffeepot, I launched a new topic, one that didn't hint I might be in line for iron bracelets. "What happened at the museum after Darlene and I left?"

Ross tucked his napkin into his shirt collar. "Limos spirited away each batch of guests as the sheriff dismissed them. By the by, some news crew filmed you and Darlene entering the Olsen estate. At first, they identified you as 'a friend,' but they had your name by the eleven o'clock news. The reporters were desperate. The only celebrity they could corner was *moi*."

I smiled. "You couldn't resist, could you? Did you work in a plea for donations?"

Ross's face fell. I instantly regretted my motor mouth.

"Jeez, I feel like a ghoul. I hope nobody thinks I used Jake's death as a fund-raiser. I just said he was a wonderful friend of the Queen and the museum and that we'd all miss him."

Ross paused. "Had Jake known his time was up, he'd probably have voted to spend his final moments on Lake Okoboji."

"Ah, but there's the rub. It may not have been Jake's time. It looks like someone cheated and pushed the clock hands ahead." The conversational turn got me thinking about the convenient timing of Jake's death. Just when he'd decided to pen a new will. "Darlene mentioned her husband talked to a local lawyer about a new will—one he probably hadn't signed. Do you know a Duncan James?"

"Sure. He's on the museum board. Moved his law practice from Ames three years ago. He's in our general age bracket. Divorced. Lady volunteers at the museum go gaga when he comes around. Can't understand it since they can swoon over me any day." He arched an eyebrow. "Eunice toyed with the notion of fixing you two up. Interested?"

I smiled. "It's my policy never to date a man prettier than me. Besides, most hunks our age date babes, not boomers. You say he's from Ames? Wonder if Darlene knew him when she lived there."

Our breakfasts arrived and we tucked into the impressive stockpiles of fat and carbohydrates. "Tell me again about the history of that old cabin on the Olsen estate."

I figured the prompt would keep Ross yammering through breakfast and beyond. When we were kids, his aversion to book learning earned veiled threats from his mom. Hard to believe he now devoured any book, letter or diary he could lay hands on—provided it dealt with the Iowa Great Lakes. He loved recounting tales about Indian uprisings, robber barons and ghost stories.

His lips hitched up in a grin. "Boy oh boy, I'd love to have that cabin as an annex to our museum."

Like a Jim Carey disciple, Ross could instantly transform his rubber-like face to reflect boyish glee, and he had Jerry Seinfeld's gift for timing. The one-two punch made his love of the lakes contagious.

"Clarice Hunter haunts that cabin. She drowned in 1928 when the Miss Lively sank. Clarice's beau saved himself, left her to drown. No one knows exactly how she got trapped. The boat went down at a spot where the lake's one hundred feet deep. The wreck wasn't recovered until scuba divers happened on it by accident."

He waved a forkful of biscuit. "The day after she sank, Clarice's body floated into the bay near that cabin. Newspaper accounts speculated her foot wedged under a seat, sentencing Clarice to a very unpleasant death."

"So why haunt that cabin?"

"She and her boyfriend rented it with two other couples. She's searching for the friends and lover who abandoned her."

"I can see why she'd be a little crotchety. I won't hold any séance if I take a look inside."

Ross reached for his wallet. "I know you said you'd buy, but it's my treat today."

I pushed my clean plate across the tattered oil tablecloth with a whimper of satisfaction. "I'm surprised May didn't join us."

"Mom seldom eats breakfast out. Claims she needs time to read the obituaries and make sure her name's not there. She starts a little slower, but she should be raring to go by now." Suddenly his smile evaporated. "Don't tell Mom that Sheriff Delaney thinks you're a suspect. She'd have a coronary—or he would after she cut out his tongue."

Six

Since May's a tad hard of hearing, Ross rang the buzzer repeatedly before opening the door with a spare key wedged under a flowerpot—traditional Iowa security.

"Come in, come in." May's disembodied voice floated from her boudoir. "Just got out of the shower. Won't be long—no sense gilding the lily."

Ross wheeled my suitcase inside. "Want it in the guest bedroom?"

"Sure. Thanks."

He lifted the suitcase onto a cedar chest and headed back to the living room. "Think I'll read the sports section. Didn't have a chance earlier."

Goosebumps sashayed up my arms. May cranked her air-conditioning to sub-zero. Weren't older ladies supposed to like heat? Unzipping my tote bag to grab a cardigan, I spied Steve Watson's package. Ross would get a kick out of a little show-and-tell.

Steve, an old Army buddy, runs a "Defend-U" Internet business. While he doesn't sell machineguns, hand grenades or other weapons of mass destruction, he provides everything from bear repellent to Klingon "fantasy" weapons for people fearing terrorists, aliens, wild hogs or Goth teens. He relies on me and other retired vets to field test his gadgets.

I walked to the living room and dumped my beta testers at Ross's feet. "Want to see my newest toys?"

My cousin peeked over his newspaper. "A cell phone? Thought you were as rabid about them as I am about jet skis."

I laughed. "These are gadgets from my friend with the Internet store. The cell phone's a disguised stun gun. That perfume atomizer holds pepper spray."

Ross chuckled. "What's with the gas mask, gloves and binoculars?"

"Worried about anthrax in your mail? Bio gloves are the answer. The binocs are night vision goggles—all the better to spy on neighbors. Not sure about the gas mask."

A note from Steve was tucked in with the goodies. I read it aloud: *Marley—Finally found a cell phone to your taste. P.S. Does the gas mask bring back fond memories?*

Ross arched an eyebrow. "Huh?"

I smiled. "We tested chemical warfare battledress at Fort Bragg. The suits had two defects: one, you couldn't pee; two, the built-in com systems made everyone sound like Donald Duck on helium. Orders were unintelligible. We had to resort to charades."

My cousin rolled his eyes. "Sorry I missed the fun. Sounds right up there with belly-crawling through swampland."

"Guess I'd better find a discreet location to try out these gizmos. Your mom doesn't need neighbors phoning the cops about a gas-masked mad woman. I unnerved them enough taking my Tae Bo routine on the balcony."

I stuffed the gloves, mock cell and atomizer in my shoulder bag and returned the bulky gas mask and night vision goggles to my suitcase.

A phone rang. By the time I re-entered the living room, May had the receiver plastered to her ear. She cupped a hand over the mouthpiece—"It's Darlene"—and handed me the phone.

A short cord afforded no privacy and May and Ross made no bones about eavesdropping. I tried to ignore them and keep my side of the conversation cryptic.

"Uh huh. Uh huh…You're kidding!…How could they get lab results so fast?…Does the sheriff have a suspect?"

The receiver wasn't back in its nest before May insisted on details. "Was Jake murdered?"

No point stonewalling. May and Ross would unearth the

answers with or without my help. Spirit Lake's a small town.

"According to current theory, someone filled Jake's Visine bottle with something called cyclogel. When he put drops in his eyes, it shut his lungs down. Jake suffered from MG, an autoimmune disease, so he was especially vulnerable."

My cousin leaned forward. "Wait a minute. This is Spirit Lake not L.A. We have no magical CSI lab to provide instant results. What gives?"

"The results aren't official. Jolbiogen's CEO offered expedited lab analyses. The M.E. gave Jolbiogen autopsy tissue samples, swabs from Jake's champagne glass, and samples from a Chapstick tube and Visine bottle, the only items in Jake's pocket. Gertie also sent samples to the state lab for parallel testing. It'll be weeks before the official results come back."

May's forehead wrinkled. "Cyclogel. Well, I'll be. Pretty ingenious, getting the victim to do himself in. Took me a minute to work it out. Never would have if I hadn't taken care of a couple MG patients. "

Ross sighed. "Okay, Mom, stop looking like the cat that swallowed the canary. What are you talking about?"

"Optometrists use cyclogel to paralyze and dilate patients' eyes. That's why Jake's pupils looked so big. Did Jake use eye drops a lot?"

"He had allergies." Ross shrugged. "Always carried a bottle. But back up—are you saying optometrists can kill patients with this stuff?"

May harrumphed. "Keep your britches on, I'm getting there. Marley said Jake had MG, a disease that tends to afflict men over fifty."

I held up a hand. "But Darlene told me Jake's MG was under control."

My aunt gave me "the look" and I shut my trap. May didn't cotton to audience cue cards. As a nurse, she'd spent years translating medical mumbo jumbo for dazed patients. Sooner or later, she'd dumb down an explanation for us.

"MG fries muscle receptors. It shrinks the number of healthy ones available to respond when the brain sends a message, like reminding the lungs to breath. Undiluted cyclogel would muddle communication with the remaining receptors. When Jake's muscles failed, his lungs quit. No air. Asphyxiation."

Ross tugged on his moustache. "Would a dose of pure cyclogel have killed someone who didn't have MG?"

May shook her head. "Doubt it. The killer must have known about his illness."

My stomach clenched. That narrowed the suspect list. "Darlene said Jake was rabid about keeping his illness a secret."

May's eyes narrowed. "Someone could have taken a gander at his medical file, or Jake might have confided in a Jolbiogen researcher looking into autoimmune disease research." She lasered me with her baby blues. "Then again, Marley, your long-lost friend could be involved."

She held up a hand, anticipating my protest. "People change. I'm not saying Darlene did it, but you need to butt out. You're tempting fate spending time with her before Sheriff Delaney looks into this mess. Even if she's innocent, I'd bet dollars to doughnuts someone in Jake's family of vipers is guilty as sin."

I was sorely tempted to blurt out that Delaney's suspect list included me. Maybe that little tidbit would remind Aunt May suspects are innocent until proven guilty. I kept my mouth shut. No point arguing. I'd yet to change one of May's opinions. Not that I wasn't equally pigheaded. Darlene needed a friend. End of story. I'd keep our afternoon date.

May lowered her recliner footrest and pushed to her feet. "I know that look, Marley. You're going to ignore me so I won't beat a dead horse. But it's less than two weeks to my birthday and our overdue family reunion. Can you still drive me to Gull Point and take a look at the banquet menu before you go gallivanting off to the Olsens?"

"You bet."

Ross saluted his mom. "Guess I'm dismissed. I need to get

cracking on our Antique and Classic Boat Show. We've signed one hundred entries and I need to figure out what boat goes where." He cut me a look of devilish glee. "Every one of them deserves the red carpet treatment reserved for ye old mahogany missionaries."

I returned his grin. "Yes, I remember your motto—'If God had wanted plastic boats, he'd have grown plastic trees.'"

"Right you are, Cuz. I fully intend to bamboozle the winners into showing off their wooden darlings in a rotating permanent exhibit."

Aunt May sighed. "Lord help me, I suckled an idjit. How in blazes can you shoehorn more boats in that museum? You have to leave room for things women like—old photos, swimsuits, antique beach toys."

"Don't worry, Mom, that's why they pay Captain Ross the big bucks. We just need a new exhibit wing." He paused half way out the door. "Say, I promised Eunice to remind you both about dinner at the Outrigger. Six o'clock okay?"

"I can't swear I'll make it," I answered. "I'm due at Darlene's late afternoon. I may not finish by six."

Aunt May rolled her eyes. "A mistake," she grumbled. "You're being a danged fool."

❖

Assuming my customary chauffeur duties, I headed May's Buick toward West Okoboji and Gull Point State Park. The midmorning sun beamed at full wattage, boosting the temperature inside the vehicle to broil. May jacked up the air. Not a day for rolled-down windows. Strong gusts shook the car. The arms on the town's Picasso-esque windmills twirled in a blurred frenzy.

Ross seized on blustery days like this to educate tourists about Spirit Lake's perch atop a Great Plains ridge. The location makes the Iowa Great Lakes nirvana for summer sailors and a boon to insulation contractors come November. The area's windy status also helped secure grants for two of Iowa's first windmills.

Today's westerly blasts were not auspicious. A big storm

brewed over the plains. That meant we were likely to be watching natural fireworks come dusk.

As we turned on Highway 86, I glanced at May. A comment Darlene made about her first husband troubled me. Maybe I should ask another widow's opinion.

"Darlene said she was angry after her first husband died. I sensed she truly was mad at Mike—not fate. Were you angry at Uncle John after his death?"

May doffed her glasses and polished away. "Felt sorry for myself, mad at being left alone. No one in her forties expects to be widowed. But angry with John? No. He certainly didn't want to leave the boys or me. 'Course, struggling to make ends meet left little time to wallow in emotions."

She paused. "Do you know how Darlene's first husband died? Maybe he did something dumb that helped him wind up in a coffin. Could be he fought with Darlene, stormed out, ran a stop sign. Stupidity might make a widow feel anger along with other hurts."

I nodded. "Makes sense." Out of morbid curiosity, I'd look up a news account of Mike's death.

As we approached the park, May studied her planner. "I've already reserved Gull Point for our Friday fish fry but I need to check out the lodge's kitchen."

May's reunion plans also included a Saturday picnic, a Sunday cruise aboard the Queen and a finale banquet at Village West for sixty people—a number inflated by "shirt-tail relations."

Though May was a relative-by-matrimony, I loved her as much as any blood kin. So had my mom. As working mothers in a June Cleaver era, they had plenty in common.

For years, my bond with Aunt May seemed flash-frozen. Whenever we visited, we slipped into adult-child roles and reminisced about the good old days. Then, once Alzheimer's claimed Mom, we conversed as adults, giving our relationship a deeper dimension.

As May poked around the lodge kitchen, I strolled down

to the sandy beach. The stone buildings and arbor of bur oaks looked just as they did in tintypes taken before I was born. I could almost see the ghosts of reed-thin Grandpa Carr lighting his pipe, his stout wife anchoring a picnic tablecloth as winds stirred whitecaps on the lake.

"Hey, give the woolgathering a break," Aunt May called. "Come give me a hand with some measurements."

Our Gull Point mission complete, we stopped by Mrs. Lady's for lunch—hand-dipped ice cream—then popped into O'Farrell Sisters to order homemade pies. At our last stop, Village West, we picked up menus from a chatty group-meeting coordinator and my aunt inquired after three generations of her family.

"Now be sure to give my best to your grandmother," she sang out as we reached the door. She didn't add "the big twit" until we started down the stairs.

I rolled my eyes. "May, you're incorrigible."

"If you can't say something nice, don't say anything—until you're out of earshot."

After buckling her seatbelt, she slumped against the headrest and sighed. "I'm too pooped to pop. Time for a wee bit of shuteye."

May slipped into her bedroom for a nap; I sauntered down the hill to fetch her mail from the community mailboxes. The haul proved predictable—AARP specials, optometrist bills and antique catalogs.

"Colonel Clark. I need to speak with you." The thirty-something speaker loped across the lawn with an athlete's easy grace. I envied her long strides, if not her height—over six-feet. We'd never met. I'd have remembered the angular face, patrician nose, and red-gold hair. Arresting.

The Colonel salutation and a nondescript sedan parked catty-corner from the condo entrance tipped me off. Military or law enforcement.

She flipped open her badge. "Sherry Weaver, FBI. Could you spare a few minutes? Maybe we could sit in the shade and talk?"

"Okay." She'd raised my curiosity and my guard.

She led the way to a shaded park bench. "Hope I didn't startle you. I needed to catch you in private." She stopped, licked her lips and started again. "I'm looking into Jake Olsen's murder."

Most folks get nervous when an authority figure braces them. Even innocents think, "What did I do?" I wasn't immune. A quiver of fear tightened my throat, but the FBI agent seemed even jumpier.

"You're taking over the investigation from Sheriff Delaney?" I asked.

"Not exactly. We're keeping the FBI and military roles quiet. I've been on the case three weeks. We hope to wrap up our investigation discreetly before the press gets wind and complicates our investigation."

"You're kidding, right?" I laughed. "Reporters already outnumber tourists. But I'm confused. Jake died yesterday. Yet you say you've been investigating for weeks. Was he getting death threats?" Then her military mention hit home. "And how's the military involved? True, I've been retired two years, but I don't recall Congress rescinding the prohibition against military involvement in domestic investigations."

"Granted, the situation's murky." She pushed her hair back from her face. "Let's start over. Do you remember Laura Young?"

I nodded. Sure. A brainy Pentagon attaché. The young lieutenant didn't make a huge effort to hide her sexual orientation. Never bothered me. I liked Laura, admired her work ethic, valued her intelligence. What she did in her bedroom was her business.

Weaver smiled. "Laura and I live together. She now works for one of the beltway bandits, an Intel consulting firm. When I mentioned your name came up in this investigation, Laura told me how much General Irvine respects you. She suggested I talk with him about bringing you in. The general agreed." She licked her lips. "We know you're friends with Darlene Olsen, and we need your help."

I felt my face flush. "Sorry. You have the wrong person. I won't take advantage of a friend's trust—even for the FBI or my old boss. And you still haven't explained the general's involvement."

"No, no. You have it all wrong. I think Darlene's innocent—her daughter, too. Our investigation isn't focused on Jake's murder. At least, it didn't begin that way. I specialize in intellectual property theft and corporate espionage. The FBI's coordinating with the military because the Jolbiogen theft involves research that has bioterrorism implications."

My head spun. I was in Spirit Lake, Iowa, not some War Games room. "You lost me."

Agent Weaver squeezed my arm. "If I say more you're bound to secrecy, you can't tell Darlene—or anyone else—about this bioterrorism investigation."

Not keen on making open-ended promises, my reply wasn't instantaneous. "I understand, but I'm not promising to help."

The FBI agent bit her lip, nodded. "That's fair. Jolbiogen and other researchers have been using a common cold virus to deliver drugs that target specific genes inside the body. It's a promising way to switch off rogue genes specific to illnesses like cancer. However, the military recognized the research had its scary side."

"Good God, are you saying the process could be reversed and used to activate rogue genes?"

Weaver's head bobbed in ascent. "Just let me finish. Imagine what might happen if our enemies adapted the technique to deliver viral or bacterial pathogens—ones targeted to kill people with a shared DNA sequence? Let's say we're fighting in the Middle East, our enemies could unleash a virus with fatal pathogens programmed to activate only if the host bodies had a DNA sequence common to people of European descent."

The little hairs on my neck quivered. "They can do that? Decode ancestral DNA to target specific populations?"

"Yes," Weaver answered. "Each person's DNA provides a key to his ancestry. Research with African populations proves it's possible to use DNA to pin ancestry down to the tribal level. The Nazis would have had a field day. No need to round anyone up."

My stomach clenched. Good Lord, no wonder the military

engaged. "So what kind of contract did the military give Jolbiogen?"

"They asked the company to build a portable detection system that uses DNA samples to identify any pathogenic agent and the gene sequence set as its target. Three weeks ago Jolbiogen discovered a security breach in the lab where Darlene's daughter works. The missing research described its prototype detection system. It also listed formulas for a group of deadly pathogens the prototype had been unable to detect."

My jaw dropped. "You're saying someone could use those formulas to concoct a virus cocktail designed to wipe out selected ethnic populations?"

She nodded. "Right, and our inability to quickly determine the nature of the attack could cost thousands of lives."

"Where does Jake fit in?" I asked.

"I'm convinced Jake discovered the thief. The day he died, he called and asked for an urgent face-to-face meeting in Spirit Lake. He refused to say more on the phone."

The FBI agent paused to scan the landscape, added recognition of our chat's covert nature. No wonder she was nervous. Conversations like this weren't in any FBI playbook. I had no need to know. I couldn't tell a viral pathogen from pine pollen, and I'd never laid eyes on Darlene's daughter, Julie.

How did Weaver and General Irvine expect me to help?

"Okay, you suspect Jake's death is linked to the theft. Surely no one believes Darlene and Julie are bioterrorists. They certainly wouldn't have killed Jake."

Weaver didn't answer for several seconds.

"That's the theory my boss is pushing. Jake caught Julie selling secrets so mother and daughter murdered him. I'm not buying, but Quentin Hamilton's more persuasive than I am. His company handles Jolbiogen security, and he's heading the internal corporate investigation. The theft was definitely an inside job, and Hamilton likes Julie for the crime."

It wasn't hard for me to picture Hamilton pontificating. "The fact Hamilton's pushing the theory tells me it's bullshit. The guy's a snake—always looking to slither for cover. His theory's a red herring, meant to distract from the fact the theft occurred on his watch. Does he claim to have any actual evidence?"

Weaver shook her head. "Only a shaky motive. Thrasos conducts heavy-duty background checks on all new hires. A grad school classmate of Julie's blabbed about the young woman's affair with a fifty-year-old professor, a left-winger, who's since dropped out of academia. He now works for some European think tank."

The agent huffed out a breath. "Hamilton contends Julie stole for her radical lover, who's gone psycho. I think it's a crock. By all accounts, the short-lived affair ended two years back. There's no indication Julie shared the guy's worldview. Plus, why would she pull a stunt like that when her mother was marrying Jolbiogen's founder? From all reports, mother and daughter are quite close."

"So why tell me? What do you want?"

"Just keep your eyes and ears open. If you learn anything connected to Jake's murder or the theft, call General Irvine or me. Though I don't like coincidence, I can't rule out the possibility Jake's murder isn't connected with the theft. Someone might have killed him for a different reason."

Weaver handed me a card with two private cell phone numbers scrawled on the back—hers and General Irvine's.

Reluctantly I pocketed it. "Okay, but I'm damned uncomfortable. This cloak-and-dagger crap makes it all too easy for Hamilton and his dunderheads to ruin reputations without a lick of evidence."

"We'll share information with local authorities in a couple of days," Weaver replied. "General Irvine flew in as soon as he heard about Jake's death. The general isn't convinced Hamilton's investigation is on track. Once the computer forensics work's finished at Jolbiogen, we'll brief Sheriff Delaney."

The agent's eyes locked on mine. "I hope we haven't made a mistake confiding in you. My head will roll if my boss finds out. I think he's bucking for a lucrative consulting gig with Hamilton's company when he retires."

"I don't break promises." We shook hands. "And I don't betray friends."

❖

My head throbbed. I wished I'd followed May's lead and taken a nap. My trip to the mailbox killed any illusion I'd soon return to a relaxing family vacation.

I changed into suitable attire for my afternoon sympathy visit—beige silk blouse, loose peasant skirt and sandals. I heard May stirring. Naptime complete.

I caught her pawing through her purse. "I'm almost late for my weekly hair appointment. You can drop me by the beauty parlor and take the car. I'll walk home. It's only two blocks. Ross will drive me to dinner if you're not back in time."

Newly cataract-free, May had zero problems driving in daylight if she didn't have a willing chauffeur. Nighttime was a different matter. Nonetheless, I declined her offer of the Buick and insisted she take the car. The woman would never fork over money for a two-block taxi ride and I didn't want her schlepping home in a thunderstorm.

She turned at her front door. "You be careful now, Marley Clark." She fixed me with a stern stare. "Stay long enough to be polite and skedaddle. I expect you for dinner."

When it suited, Aunt May reneged on our adult relationship and treated me like a willful child. My reaction was equally predictable. At age fifty-two, I'd simply learned not to say the words out loud.

I'll do as I damn well please.

Seven

"Hot diggity. Do I get to drive through the gates?" My destination tickled my cabbie.

"Maybe." I shrugged. "They've battened down the security hatches to keep reporters out. I may be asked to walk in from the gate."

And I might get soaked.

Ominous black clouds massed on the horizon like army troops readying an attack. It wouldn't be long before thunder growled its battle cry.

As the first fat drops splashed on the windshield, a Thrasos guard scanned an approved visitor list. He instructed the cabbie to drop me at the mansion and return at once. He sounded like a bored automaton reading a Monopoly card, "Go to jail. Do Not Collect $200." Regardless, he made my driver's week.

Harvey, the consummate butler, opened the carved oak door and rumbled a greeting. "Mrs. Olsen is in the great room. She asked me to show you right in."

The Mrs. title warned me—Darlene had company. Down the corridor, strident voices echoed from the great room. My nose twitched at the cloying aroma of the sympathy bouquets crammed in the entryway. Wonderful.

"This is preposterous," a loud voice asserted. "You were married to my father less than a week. Talk about motive. This ridiculous document will never stand up."

I hung back, queasy about entering the verbal melee. Harvey trudged onward. I attempted to mimic his unflappable demeanor. The volume of the conflagration lowered. Had they heard our footsteps? Once we breached the great room's entry, conversation halted.

Darlene rushed to hug me. "I'm so glad you came. Let me introduce you. Marley Clark is a dear friend from college days. You probably know her cousin, Captain Ross, or maybe you've met her aunt, May Carr—she's a legend at Spirit Lake's hospital."

After dispensing with my pedigree, Darlene introduced the room's occupants, starting with daughter, Julie. Wearing raggedy jeans and a faded University of Okoboji T-shirt, she looked like a carbon copy of her mom at twenty—a green-eyed, blonde bombshell with attitude. On cue, she popped up with a hundred-watt smile and a firm handshake.

Jake's daughter Gina came next. Lanky beige hair framed her jaundiced face, while loose flab creased in folds around knees that unfortunately poked beneath a too-short skirt. I knew Gina was in her early forties. She looked older than her step-mom. When introduced, she blinked rapidly and wheezed a tad louder. No other sign of intelligent life. It wasn't necessary to smell the brine to know the lady was pickled.

Gina's amorphous bulk provided a startling Jack Sprat contrast to her husband's anorexic frame. An iron-gray moustache punctuated Dr. Robert Glaston's hawkish face, while a surgically-precise pink part divided his sooty hair. The good doctor mumbled a "nice to meet you." Light glinting off his wire-rimmed bifocals made it impossible to see his eyes.

Gina's son Eric was absent. Thank God for small favors.

Kyle Olsen sat beside his half-sister, Gina. Gray streaks accented his styled chestnut hair. The racing stripe color shift made his waspish face look narrower. A sloped forehead kept his eyes in shadow, a natural cavern.

He held his head still like a cobra poised to strike. I stifled an intense desire to shudder. Kyle didn't offer to shake hands. "Quentin Hamilton warned me about you. This is a family meeting. You're not welcome."

"I invited her," Darlene snapped. "This *is* my house."

I braced for fireworks when another member of the tableau jumped up. "Delighted to meet you, Marley. I'm Duncan James. Darlene told me how much your friendship means. We had family business, but it's finished."

I wanted to kiss the stranger even before my brain kicked in with a what-a-hunk report.

The man sandwiched my hand between his warm mitts, and gave an encouraging squeeze. "I'm pleased to count your cousin as a friend, and I've met your captivating aunt."

Ross had told me the lawyer was in his fifties. There were few signposts of age. Little crinkles bookmarked dancing blue eyes. I surmised his curly hair had been cheeky red before a sprinkling of silver toned it down to copper. Devilish seemed the best adjective to describe his grin.

The movie "The Sting" sprang to mind. As an impressionable teen, I'd mooned over actor Robert Redford. Duncan reminded me of the film's cocky scoundrel a few decades down the road. A damn shame Eunice hadn't arranged that blind date.

"Nice to meet you, Mr. James."

He smiled. "Please, it's Duncan."

Kyle leapt to his feet. "We didn't come for social hour." I could practically hear his teeth grind. "Darlene, you'll hear from our lawyer. Gina. Robert. Are you coming?"

"Yes, yes of course," Dr. Glaston stammered.

As Glaston levered his wife out of her chair, Gina swayed. When her heavy ballast finally shifted, the woman wobbled forward. He trailed his wife, carrying her respirator.

No one uttered a word until the threesome vanished. I expected the massive front door to bang. The whisper-like snick signaled Harvey had shepherded them out. Maybe there's a role for a butler—or bodyguard—if you have relatives like Kyle.

"Thank God, they're gone. What an afternoon." Darlene collapsed in an easy chair. "I don't know about anyone else, but I'm ready for a drink." She laughed. "Marley, you'll think I'm a lush, but whenever Kyle enters or leaves a room, it's Miller time."

Harvey materialized to take drink orders. After Darlene requested a rum and Coke, I added a why-the-hell-not ditto. Julie asked for a Coors Light, which prompted a "me too" from Duncan. No one seemed able to summon the energy to be inventive or terribly sociable.

Duncan crossed to the wall of windows. "Looks like we're in for one crackerjack of a storm."

Sprinkles freckled the glass. Sheet lightning pulsed in the distance, and bright reflections flowed down the windows like light in a lava lamp. Though the pyrotechnics ignited too far away for audible thunder, I felt sure Ross had radioed the Queen's captain to haul his keister back to Arnolds Park. He was terrified the tour boat might be damaged in a pop-up thunderstorm.

Darlene sighed. "Any storm will be anticlimactic after Sheriff Delaney's bombshell. I can't believe someone murdered Jake. With eye drops no less. Delaney said the M.E. concluded the cyclogel killed Jake because he suffered from MG. Since I'm the only one who admits knowing about his illness, I'm—taa daa—the lone suspect."

"That's ridiculous." I tried to inject astonishment into my response even though the FBI agent had given me a preview of coming accusations.

"Tell Marley about the search," Julie prodded.

Darlene gnawed her lip. "Sheriff Delaney asked to search our house. Said he didn't have a warrant but wanted to keep things quiet. I agreed. I had nothing to hide. 'Course I didn't plan on his deputies cleaning out my medicine chest. They even confiscated my hormone replacement pills. If my hot flashes return before I get a refill, they'll get to see true homicidal rage."

My friend's flash of sass signaled she was far from cowed.

Darlene sighed. "They fingerprinted Julie and me. Said they

needed our prints to exclude them from any unidentified prints in our bedroom or bath."

Harvey dealt out the drinks. Now that the Olsen offspring had departed, he'd reverted to his fond uncle persona. "They fingerprinted me, too." He laughed, then rolled his eyes. "I suggested that any notion that 'the butler did it' was a true cliché."

Darlene chuckled. "Join us, Harvey. Bet you could stand a drink."

"Thanks, just the same. I'll have mine later. And I won't be toasting that prick Quentin Hamilton."

"Yeah, sorry you got caught in his crosshairs," Darlene said. "Hamilton reprised his grand inquisitor role after the sheriff left. Badgered both Harvey and me about documents. I told him to take it up with the sheriff, who'd already searched the house stem to stern."

She ran a finger around the rim of her glass. "Hamilton's decided I'm too stupid to have killed Jake all by my lonesome. He's hinted Julie's the brain behind some devious plot. He grilled her about work. I warned Julie not to answer the dickhead. He's evil. She wouldn't listen."

"Oh, Mom." Julie groaned. "I confirmed what the bastard already knew. He hoped I'd lie. So I told him, yes, I have access to cyclogel. And, yes, security is loose as a goose for all kinds of substances in our lab. We stock lots of nasty concoctions—stuff far more deadly than cyclogel—and I could waltz out with samples any time."

Darlene sighed. "Did you have to add it would be tough for a stranger to steal cyclogel from your lab?"

Julie bit her lip. "It's true. We don't display cyclogel, snake venom extracts or mushroom toxins like produce at a fruit stand. A thief would have to know where to look. He'd better know what he's doing, too. I won't touch puffer fish toxin without double gloving."

Darlene shuddered. "I hate this. How safe can it be?"

Her daughter rolled her eyes in an exasperated pantomime.

Darlene shrugged. "Hey, if condoms break, so can rubber gloves."

"Too bad I didn't arrive sooner," Duncan said. "I'd have put an end to the questioning."

"Well, at least you were here to keep the other heirs from skinning me alive." Darlene raised her glass in a salute. "I still can't believe Jake signed a new will the day before we married."

Good grief. I'd walked in on the reading of the billionaire's last will and testament.

A smile tugged at the corners of Darlene's mouth. "Boy, was Kyle steamed. Gina may have been pissed, too, but it's hard to peer through her alcoholic haze."

My jaw dropped. Given the bitter protest, it appeared Darlene hit the inheritance jackpot. Though it was none of my business, I was dying to know how all the heirs fared.

Duncan interrupted my higher math speculations. "Marley, you can let Ross know the Maritime Museum is a beneficiary. Jake bequeathed the old cottage on the estate plus funds to feature it in a new museum wing. He also established a trust for capital improvements, acquisitions and operating funds."

I grinned. Wow. "Ross will be thrilled. I can't wait to see it. My cousin's sure enamored."

"Want to take a look now?" Darlene asked. "If so, better head out before it starts raining in earnest."

"Mind if I join you?" Duncan asked. "I've been curious about it ever since Jake told me he was leaving a ghost to his favorite nonprofit."

I glanced out the window. Wind gusts bent the large bur oaks like reeds. "We'd better be quick. Anyone else interested?"

After Darlene and Julie begged off, Duncan and I hustled out the French doors and onto the sun porch. I staggered as a gust of wind caught me full force.

Duncan took my arm. "Steady there."

We scurried across the flagstone patio and down the cottage path. "Do you have a key?"

"Don't need one," Duncan replied. "Jake never locked it. The estate's patrolled and, from what I hear, there's not much to steal."

I was glad we walked side-by-side. The wind literally whistled up my fanny, ballooning my loose peasant skirt above my derriere. My figure's not too bad, but the skirt-over-head look is seldom chic. I wasn't eager to model my Hanes cotton undies for just anybody.

Chubby raindrops plopped on my head as we scurried up creaky wooden stairs to the cottage's wide wraparound porch. The porch screen boasted more holes than mesh, and flies swarmed in platoon strength.

"Ouch!" I swatted a portly one feasting on my calf. "Forget about fish biting before a storm. It's the Iowa flies that become ravenous."

"Maybe they won't be so vicious inside." Duncan opened a door fashioned of eighteen-inch wood planks. Filtered through decades-old windows, the outside light lent a greenish tint to the musty interior, which seemed several degrees colder than the air-conditioned manor.

Duncan and I weren't the only recent visitors. The broom leaning against the doorjamb was gift-wrapped in cobwebs. It appeared the floor had been swept, though no one tried to air the place. Dust motes danced in smog-like layers. A kerosene lantern and matches sat atop a cockeyed table missing one leg, and a burned match rested in a tin ashtray. Was that the light I'd seen last night?

"Don't think I'll ask for the decorator's name." Duncan's gaze swept over the parlor's furniture. Rusty iron springs in a fifties-era glider poked through ripped plastic slipcovers. Orange flowers bloomed on a chartreuse field. "I sort of doubt these pieces are original." He chuckled. "Even Ross would have a hard time finding redeeming artistic value."

In the kitchen, the tattered remains of café curtains clung stubbornly to a rod above the stained porcelain sink.

"That's funny." I pointed at water puddled in the sink. "Given the rust on those faucets, it's hard to imagine the hook-up working."

Duncan attempted to turn a faucet. It might as well have been set in concrete. We both glanced at the ceiling. Dry as a bone.

"Maybe someone brought in a bucket of water to wash up," he speculated.

"Possible. Or a gardener could have used the sink to mix pesticides." I pointed to a pair of thin disposable gloves sitting a yard from the sink.

While my fellow explorer left to check the two bedrooms, I opened cupboards. The upper reaches held a few chipped cups and saucers in the same Currier & Ives pattern Mom secured with Green Stamps when I was a toddler.

The front door banged loudly, and I jumped. Take it easy, just the wind. When the hairs on the back of my neck refused to return to parade rest, I turned.

Eric loomed in the doorway. The smell of liquor preceded him. Out of habit, I'd tossed my handbag over my shoulder as we left the house. I groped inside for my cell phone-stun gun. Never hurts to be prepared.

"You're trespassing." He staggered forward. "Get the hell out, or I'll throw you out."

I eased the stun gun into my palm and held it up like a talisman to ward off evil. I was about to warn Eric that it was, indeed, a stunner, when the kid rushed me.

"You're not going to call anyone," Eric growled. His charge ended as quickly as it began. He collapsed and commenced a horizontal jitterbug. Then he stilled and his face went slack.

"Shit. Shit. And triple shit." I knelt and felt for a pulse. Fast but steady. He'd fainted. Probably the alcohol-shock combo.

I hadn't meant to zap him. In fact, I was fairly confident Eric buzzed himself during our tussle. Still, my mock Ma Bell indisputably had Eric down for the count.

I looked up and saw Duncan, arms folded, leaning in the doorway. His lips twitched. He thought it was funny. "I ran to your rescue when I heard Eric bellowing. I presume you simply decked the brat and he remains among the living? Of course, if it comes to it, I could testify it was self-defense."

"It's a stun gun." I held up my make-believe cell. "He should revive quickly."

Duncan surveyed the spilled contents of my purse. "Any other surprises?"

The litter on the floor included my faux perfume atomizer. Thank heavens my bag had been too small to accommodate the gas mask and night-vision goggles. Duncan probably thought I had Rambo aspirations.

"Given what I know about your cell phone, I have to ask—perfume or..."

"Pepper spray," I answered sheepishly. "I don't usually carry this stuff. I'm just testing these for a friend."

He chuckled. "Even more interesting."

Eric moaned.

"Why don't you head to the house," Duncan suggested. "Might be better if you're gone when he comes around. I'll explain I saw everything. He has only himself to blame. Only his pride's been hurt."

A bolt of lightning lit the room like a camera strobe. An almost instantaneous bang shook the cottage's foundation. I didn't need a second invitation to skedaddle. Outside, a wall of water marched across West Okoboji. I ran, knowing the sporadic drops were about to become a torrent. I gained the threshold of the main house just ahead of the deluge.

"Well, you made it under the wire," Julie welcomed me. "Where's Duncan?"

"He'll be along in a minute." I hoped I was right. Surely Eric wouldn't feel peppy enough to threaten anyone else.

I looked around. "Where's Darlene?"

"Mom asked me to apologize. She developed a whopper of a migraine. I urged her to go to bed."

I nodded. "I'd have a migraine, too, if I'd had your mother's day. I'm so glad you're here, Julie. I'll check in tomorrow. Your mom knows how to reach me if there's anything I can do."

I glanced at my watch. Five-thirty. Amazing how time flies when you're decking asswipes.

"Looks like I'll be able to meet my family for dinner. That'll please Aunt May. Now all I have to do is coax a taxi to brave the storm and pick me up."

"Don't even think about a cab. I'll give you a ride." Duncan had slipped in the French doors unnoticed and dripping. "Besides you might get into more mischief without a chaperone."

Julie looked a question at Duncan, who laughed. "Marley didn't mention she just KO'd Eric with a stun gun."

Julie whooped with delight. "I can see why Mom likes you so much."

The explanation that my knockout was accidental didn't lessen Julie's pleasure.

Duncan took a squishy step on the tiled sun porch. "Stay put," Julie said. "I'll get towels. You look like a drowned rat."

Before she could fulfill her promise, Harvey arrived with a stack of fluffy towels. Duncan took one and vigorously buffed his head and arms. Then, he slipped off his loafers and removed his dripping socks.

"We keep some clothes upstairs for house guests," Harvey offered. "Try the closet in the second bedroom on the right."

Duncan shook his head. "Nah. I'm not sugar. Won't melt. Besides I've offered Marley a ride and I don't want to keep her waiting."

"I can call a cab." Duncan's look told me a taxi wasn't in the cards. I smiled. "I don't mind waiting while you change. It may give the storm a chance to blow by. There's no sense trying to drive for a few minutes. Visibility is zip."

"Go ahead, Duncan," Julie urged. "Don't ruin the leather seats in your cute convertible. Besides, Marley and I haven't had much of a chance to chat."

With two women weighed against him, the attorney conceded.

Once he disappeared, I asked Julie about her Jolbiogen research. While I'd have posed the same innocuous questions without a nudge from the FBI, I felt a niggling of guilt about pumping my friend's daughter for intel.

Julie told me she'd earned her doctorate in biochemistry from Iowa State. After Jake read her doctoral thesis, he offered a post-doc at Jolbiogen and assured her it was strictly on merit. The opportunity thrilled her.

"My lab head Kendra Jacobs is great. I love my work. We're on the cutting edge. There's only one fly in the ointment. Kendra reports to Dr. Glaston, who tries to micromanage. Unfortunately he's not smart enough to carry Kendra's test tubes."

Julie bit her lip. "He keeps looking for some flaw in my work—any excuse to can me. That goes double since his demotion. Dr. Glaston used to report directly to Jake. Now he's slipped two rungs down the executive ladder. That didn't improve his disposition."

I heard a cough and turned. "I'm ready, if you don't mind being seen with me." Duncan gestured toward his bare legs. Borrowed khaki shorts left his alabaster limbs naked. He padded down the stairs barefoot, carrying his soggy loafers in one hand and bagged wet clothes in the other.

He looked adorable. I know, I know—most men would punch someone for calling them that. But they'd be more receptive if they realized how far a lost puppy-dog look could go toward getting them laid. Women are suckers for cute.

"Couldn't find any long pants that fit." He slipped on his wet loafers. "I could pass as Casper's cousin. Guess I should get more sun. Marley, if you're ready, I'll pull the car around front. Harvey lent me a big umbrella so I won't get soaked again."

The curtain had come down on the lightning and thunder theatrics. The rain fell gently. I hoped it wasn't just intermission.

Julie waited with me until Duncan's BMW convertible pulled up to the front door. Harvey materialized like magic and covered me with another umbrella as I dashed to the car. I slid into the passenger seat dry as toast.

Eight

"Am I taking you to May's condo?" Duncan asked.

"No, I'm meeting the family at the Outrigger. Hope that's not out of your way."

"Perfect. My condo's right around the corner by Brooks Golf Club. Have a boat slip, the fourth tee out my back door, and not a lick of yard work. What more could a man want?"

I considered a comeback—"Hot sex?" But not knowing the gentleman's sexual proclivities, let alone his sense of humor, I bit my tongue. Instead, I asked, "Anything exciting happen after Eric rejoined the conscious world?"

"Nope, amazing how a few thousand volts of electricity will settle a fellow down. I doubt he'll mention the incident to Gina or his stepfather. I helped him realize he'd come out the villain if he spread the story."

"How well do you know Eric?"

"Only by reputation, one he lived up to today. Jake described him as a hothead and doper. His granddad felt sorry for him growing up with an alcoholic mother and a weasel of a stepfather. Jake hoped he'd outgrow both drugs and his belligerence. I wouldn't bet the farm on it."

I decided to pry into Duncan's past. "I understand you moved here from Ames. Did you know Darlene or her husband there?"

He kept his eyes on the road, nary a glance my way. The reply wasn't immediate. Did his jaw muscles twitch?

"Mutual acquaintances introduced us, but we weren't friends.

I got to know Darlene once I joined Jake on the museum board. Jake and I golfed and fished—guy stuff. And I got an occasional party invite when they needed a spare male."

I didn't doubt the handsome divorcé was in demand for parties. If I threw a shindig, he'd get my invite. Yet my cynical side warned some disgusting personality trait lurked beneath his charming façade or he already had a significant other he failed to advertise.

Though tempted to pepper him with more questions, I suspended my interrogation. I've been told curiosity is not my most endearing trait.

He swung his convertible into an empty parking spot at the Outrigger and turned toward me as he switched off the ignition. "How often do you hear you're a Sigourney Weaver look-alike?"

I groaned. "Those stupid 'Alien' movies. In the Army, my lieutenants sent off for posters with a bald Sigourney holding a big-ass gun. They drew little balloons over her head filled with supposed quotes from yours truly. Things like 'Colonel Clark eats aliens for breakfast.'"

Duncan laughed. "I wasn't thinking 'Alien.' Sigourney played glamorous roles, too—with hair. She's beautiful, and so are you. I'm a sucker for curly hair and big brown eyes."

My breath caught. "Thank you." Exercising great restraint, I let the comment lie. My husband crabbed about my inability to accept a compliment without making a flattery-nullifying comeback. "Just let people pay you a compliment," he urged. "Would it kill you?"

My answer: "Maybe."

I felt tongue-tied. It appeared traffic on Attraction Street might be moving in both directions. The realization floored me and complicated my innocent fantasies. A mere two months had passed since my surprise romp with a younger man. It had ended with smiles, not tears. We'd sworn to remain friends—maybe friends with benefits whenever our long-distance paths crossed. Yet there were no commitments. So why did my attraction to Duncan bring on a frisson of guilt?

"You have a devilish smile," he added. "It seems beyond your control. When your humor gets the upper hand, the edges of your mouth curve up, your eyes twinkle, and, wham-o, you're smiling. Like now."

I laughed. "It's your fault. Now I know why you're a lawyer—your silver tongue—or is it a forked one?" I grabbed the door handle and prepared to bolt. Though I enjoyed his company, I didn't want to trap Duncan in a Good Samaritan role that required door opening or other gentlemanly gestures. "Thanks. I really appreciate the ride."

"Not so fast. I'll walk you in. It's drizzling and Harvey insisted I keep an umbrella. Besides, if I don't pay my respects to Miss May, I'll get my comeuppance next time we meet."

My family always sat at the same circular corner booth so I had no difficulty locating them. May, Ross and Eunice chatted as they looked over the specials. Good, I hadn't delayed the proceedings.

Aunt May glanced up. "Glad you could make it." She caught sight of Duncan and her smile brightened. "And look who you brought as a dinner companion. My, my, your taste is improving, Marley."

"You're too kind, May," Duncan said. "But I'm merely a chauffeur. I only dropped in to say hi. Wouldn't dream of horning in on a family dinner."

Those words sank Duncan's chance of flight. He'd had a slim window of opportunity to claim he was en route to an important meeting. That escape hatch had slammed shut. May's eyes twinkled. Oh God, she'd entered matchmaker mode.

"Horn in?" my aunt purred. "Did you hear that? Ross, tell your friend he must join us." She patted the bench seat. "For heaven's sake, sit down. Don't make an ass of yourself."

Ross and I looked at each other. "Better sit," we agreed in stereo.

May's "don't make an ass of yourself" line had been honed into a multi-purpose weapon. It always threw unsuspecting opponents—and, sometimes, alert ones—off balance. Every time

Mom and May argued over a restaurant check, my aunt trotted it out. In turn, Mom harrumphed, "I don't know why I'm the ass, when you're making a spectacle of yourself."

The repartee had become family folklore. Duncan, however, was unprepared, and May triumphed easily. He slid into the booth beside me. Our bare legs briefly brushed. The glancing touch ignited my overactive imagination.

After my husband died, I'd not so much as kissed another man for twenty months. Then, a handsome detective took me by storm. The affair, though brief, had reprogrammed my libido. Now my naughty neurons could fire with machinegun speed. My alert mental-health censor warned my id was up to no good. Didn't help. My breath caught as I pictured us together.

I felt my face flush and hoped no one noticed I'd colored from my erotic daydream. Everyone seemed focused on their menus—except Duncan. His frank, approving appraisal caused more warmth to rush in multiple directions. Crimey.

Impervious to the heat being banked in side-by-side human furnaces, May, Ross and Eunice nattered on about wine selections and cholesterol counts.

After our drinks arrived, Duncan shared the good news with Ross, spelling out Jake's bequest of the cottage and the creation of a trust for the museum.

Ross rubbed his hands together. "Wowzer. I never dreamed Jake would be that generous. Now I really can schmooze with those antique boat owners next weekend."

Duncan held up a hand. "Don't start spending money—even mentally—until the will goes through probate. One or more heirs may contest. However, if all the lawyers act in their clients' best interests, they'll advise against a fight. Contesting ties up everyone's money, escalates expenses, and shrinks the proverbial pot of gold."

"So who's unhappy enough to duke it out?" May piped up.

I wanted to know, too, but felt it indelicate to ask. There are definite perks to being eighty and not caring a whit about people's opinions.

Duncan smiled and waggled a finger at May. "I can't disclose other beneficiaries or the terms of the will. But I can tell you that Iowa probate law lets any surviving spouse elect to 'take against the will.' That option grants the widow or widower one-third of the estate, even if the survivor isn't mentioned in the will. So, no matter what, Darlene's guaranteed one-third of Jake's estate. The fact the marriage lasted seven days is moot."

Ross exercised his fingers doing a bit of math. "If Jake's worth a billion, Darlene'll inherit—oh, my God—thirty-three million and 300,000 in change."

Not too shabby for someone who used to sling hash with me at Spirit Resort.

Duncan squirmed. "Let's change the subject. I really can't say more."

Eunice took pity on our dinner guest. "I saw you last week at that Minnetonka auction but had to leave early. Did you buy the musket you were eying?"

"No. Too pricey, and it had defects."

The chitchat revealed my dinner companions were passionate antiquers. Duncan, a hunter, favored antique weapons. Ross scouted for marine memorabilia. May and Eunice waxed eloquent about furniture finds. Me? Unable to tell aged schlock from treasure, I kept quiet.

Realizing I had nothing to contribute, my aunt called a halt. "Marley, tell Duncan what you did before you retired." She patted my arm. "My niece was a colonel in military intelligence no less, and she speaks Polish and Russian."

She turned toward Duncan. "Were you in the Army, too?"

"Yep, two years between college and law school. I lucked out with a posting in Germany—Bad Kreusnach."

I smiled. "Small world. I was stationed at the same base."

After determining our tours were a few years apart, we expounded on the joys of wiener schnitzel, apple wine festivals, flowers spilling out of window boxes, and how one's adrenaline revs into overdrive when hurtling down Alpine slopes or cruising the Autobahn.

May sported the same smug look of satisfaction she wore after a real estate closing.

Our check arrived and so did new rumbles of thunder. Intermission was over. Time for the main storm event.

"Ross, why don't I give these young ladies a lift?" Duncan nodded at May and me. "That'll give you a chance to make sure the Queen's bedded down. Things are getting mighty frisky."

"What a nice offer." May accepted before Ross could reply. "I've always wanted to take a ride in your convertible. It looks cute as a button. Too bad we won't have the top down."

Two blocks from May's condo the deluge erased the world beyond the windshield. Sitting up front with Duncan, I peered through the curtain of water, vainly searching for some hint of a yellow centerline.

"Should we pull over?"

Duncan shook his head. "No shoulder here. I'll take it nice and easy."

He even managed an occasional question to restart May's patter and keep her calm. I'd have been too busy swearing and strangling the wheel.

"I see lights at the condo entrance, May." Relief colored Duncan's tone. "Looks like we made it."

Duncan grabbed the nearest parking spot, a few feet from the entrance to the four-unit cluster. He swiveled in his seat and smiled at my aunt. "Soon as I get my umbrella open, I'll come round the car for you. Then I'll return for Marley."

"Don't be silly. It's a three-second dash."

Though Duncan and I exited the car in unison, he reached May's door before mine closed. He claimed one of her arms and I took the other. We moved with the speed and grace of a six-legged, arthritic bug. While Duncan's umbrella gallantry sheltered my aunt, horizontal rain gusts soaked both her escorts.

Inside the vestibule, May shook a few drops from her London Fog raincoat, patted her hair and chuckled at her bedraggled guides. "I got the better of that deal. Being old has its rewards. Come in, come in, Duncan. Least we can do is fix you an Irish coffee. Can't drive anyway. Might as well relax until it lets up."

Thunder crashed and the lights flickered. "I'll find candles in case the lights go," I said.

Little rivulets of water forged paths down Duncan's freckled cheeks. "Maybe a towel is a higher priority than candles," I said. "But unless you want to strip and don May's raincoat, we can't offer the Olsen's change-of-clothing options."

He grinned. "Don't want to impersonate a flasher. I'll just towel off best I can."

After supplying a towel and a hodgepodge of candles, I filled the coffeepot with water. "May, want decaf or regular?"

"Doesn't matter, kid. The whisky'll knock me out. Can't hold my liquor like I used to. Doesn't mean I want my drinks watered down. Now there's a bone of contention with my sons. I keep telling the little stinkers I'd rather have one stiff drink that tastes like something than three diluted excuses."

May snuggled into her recliner while Duncan lit candles, making the coffee table look like a votive altar. I puttered in the kitchen, assembling a tray of Irish coffees and a plate of May's famous brownies—their secret an icing layer thicker than the cake.

Meanwhile my aunt entertained with tales of how she'd snared the room's antiques. While the best-loved pieces came from her grandmother in Missouri, she was quite partial to finds she'd haggled over and won for a fraction of their value.

May seemed full of piss and vinegar. Yet, as soon as I served the drinks, she yawned theatrically and professed exhaustion. Yeah, right. She retired with her coffee in hand. As soon as Duncan left, she'd tiptoe back, wide awake and pester me for details. Did he see through her, too?

Moments after she toddled down the hall, thunder clashed with ear-splitting fury. All lights extinguished, shrinking the living room to an intimate envelope of flickering candlelight.

"Be right back," I said. "Want to make sure Aunt May's not stumbling around in the dark. Last thing she needs is to fall and break a hip."

I grabbed a candle, cupped my hand to shield the flame, and hurried down the hall. "May, is everything all right?" I knocked. "Want me to bring some candles or help you to bed?"

"Don't be a ninny. I keep a flashlight on my nightstand. I'm not in my dotage."

I returned to the living room. A broad smile lit Duncan's face. May's sass tickled him. He patted the cushion beside him on the couch.

"Ross told me you were a widow." His blue eyes searched my face. "I'm sorry. I'm divorced and even though the parting was sheer relief," he hesitated, "it's hard to adjust to being single. Dating after so many years is hell, isn't it?"

The warm whisky and candlelight nibbled at my inhibitions.

"Yeah, when you're over fifty, it's tough to keep a straight face and claim 'I'm saving myself for marriage.' Nowadays the trick is to find a socially-acceptable way to exchange certification that you're HIV-free."

"Darn, I forgot to put mine in my wallet," he quipped. "Tomorrow I'll show you mine if you show me yours." He added softly, "You really should get out of your wet clothes."

Duncan touched my arm through the beige—and, I suddenly realized—almost transparent blouse molded to my breasts. Worse yet, the damp silk advertised my arousal. Might as well have taken out an "I'm horny" billboard. Even the most discreet gentleman would notice.

"Right you are," I choked out. "Back in a jiffy."

Mortified, I sprinted toward the guest bedroom, shed my wet clothes, and slipped on shorts and an oversized velvet pullover—thick enough to camouflage any eager salutes by my girls. Returning to the living room, I chose the chair adjacent to the couch. Away from temptation.

"Hey, come closer so we can talk without waking your aunt. I won't bite."

Unable to think of a comeback, I surrendered. A hand-crocheted afghan rested on the back of the sofa. Duncan draped it around our shoulders. A cozy cocoon. The candles sputtered down to nubs as we talked. I glanced at my watch—five after midnight.

"Do you know what time it is?" I asked in disbelief.

"Past time to do this." He brushed his lips over mine. They felt warm, insistent.

Okay, if Duncan had a fatal flaw, it wasn't his kiss.

The fantasy I'd squelched in the restaurant forced my heart into double time. I imagined his body sliding against mine. In my flight of fancy, Duncan's dog tags swayed.

Where had the dog tags come from? Get a grip, Marley. Are you nuts?

Since Jeff's death, I'd bedded exactly one man—and I hadn't collapsed into Braden's arms like a rag doll the day we met. Had that spring fling short-circuited my brain? When Braden left the South Carolina coast to return to Atlanta, we released each other of any romantic commitment. Still I felt obliged to ease off the gas pedal.

My brain dismissed the yellow caution light to focus on the teeth nibbling my earlobe. My reservations melted faster than chocolate chips in a double boiler. I think I refrained from purring. His hands sauntered lower, heating the skin beneath the velvet. My fingers joined the dance as I threaded them through his curly hair. Our tongues twined in exploration.

Duncan lifted his head and broke the embrace. A space opened between us. Cool air raced in, raising goosebumps on my heated skin.

"Sorry, Marley. Don't know what came over me." He trailed a finger down my cheek. "I'm fifty-five years old not a rutting teenager. I don't want to give May a stroke by propositioning her niece on her living room couch." He stood, pulled me to him, tilted my face to his. His thumb trailed along my cheek. "Can I call you? Tomorrow? I promise to be more romantic."

I squeaked out a ladylike, "sounds great" and squelched my desire to say, "the hell with romance, I'm ready any place, any time."

I was on vacation, old enough to know better, young enough not to need a pacemaker. Life was good. Inside our candlelit cavern, our encounter seemed more fantasy than reality.

My brain argued it was good our necking halted a mile short of my erotic daydream. Reality never lives up to fantasy, right?

Yet I sensed I'd have been quite content with Duncan's reality. Who needs swaying dog tags?

NINE

A phone rang, loudly and insistently. I groped the bedside table to still it. Oh, I wasn't sleeping in my own bed. The bell tone cranked above humane decibel limits was in May's room, not mine. The ringing ceased.

It was pitch black. The alarm clock's fluorescent numbers flashed 5:05 a.m. No one calls at this hour unless it's an emergency.

Was it some family crisis? I threw on a robe. My knock opened Aunt May's door a crack. Phone to her ear, she motioned me inside. "You're kidding. They're both dead?" Her eyes went wide, all trace of sleep gone. "The sheriff's there, right? Yes, yes, I'll put Marley on."

May handed me the phone and sagged against her pillows. She looked so fragile, her skin almost translucent with the veins at her temples visibly throbbing. Without benefit of a comb's camouflaging efforts, her pink scalp played hide-and-seek through her wispy hair.

"Marley, it's Darlene. I know I'm putting a real burden on an old friendship but could you come to the house? Now? I called Duncan, too. I'm petrified."

A small sob forced a pause. "The sheriff's next door. They're taking the bodies away."

"Bodies?" I interrupted. "What bodies?"

"Sorry, my brain's scrambled. I told May, not you. Gina and Robert—the Glastons—are dead. Eric came home snockered and registered something wasn't right. Lights burning at four a.m. in both his mom's bedroom and his step-dad's. He stumbled upstairs and found them dead. I'm really scared."

I clutched the lapels of my robe and shivered. "I'll come right away." My promise earned a stern look of disapproval from my aunt. "Give me half an hour, but I'll be there."

May started her harangue before I hung up. "Are you crazy? Bodies are stacking up like cordwood, and you mosey into the fray like it's a Sunday school picnic. Has to be some Looney-toon. I know, I know. You think you can take care of yourself, but nobody's safe around crazies."

"May, calm down, the sheriff's there—heck, probably the whole Sheriff's Department. No killer is going to try something right under Delaney's nose."

"Then answer me this." May pinned me with a stare. "How did the Glastons get murdered with private cops scurrying around like cockroaches and a security system worthy of Fort Knox?"

Excellent question.

I shrugged. "Maybe it was a murder-suicide. The couple didn't exactly impress me as America's sweethearts."

The upside of May's excitement? No questions about Duncan. The reprieve gave me hours to prepare for her grilling and decide how I felt about the unexpected mutual attraction.

I kissed May's cheek. "I'll be careful. Promise. Go back to sleep. Odds are I'll be home before breakfast. Is it okay if I take the Buick? What time do you leave for church?"

"The service starts at ten. But my neighbor can give me a ride. Go on, take the car."

Despite my hurry in dressing, I took more care with grooming than the emergency warranted. I damn well knew the reason.

Would our first post-amorous meeting feel awkward? I hoped not. Even if last night's heat proved the proverbial flash in the pan, it was nice to know a sturdy match could light my out-of-warranty pilot.

✿

The estate's gates stood open. An ambulance rolled past in the opposite direction. Its leisurely pace confirmed its destination—Spirit Lake's now busy morgue. A pewter-gray sky cast a funereal pall over the landscape. The rain had halted and puddles glinted like black ice beneath the security lights.

I pulled up and waited for the Thrasos guard to approach. I'd spoken to the same sentry when I left on yesterday's run. He remembered me. A glance at his clipboard and he motioned me ahead. "Please park to the right, Mrs. Clark."

Waaaay back, when first inoculated with feminist furor, I corrected folks, let 'em know it was "Ms." not "Mrs." Never bothered nowadays. Political correctness means nada. Either people think women have brains and deserve independent status from the men in their lives, or they don't.

Happily, my husband belonged to the first camp. We'd married late and neither of us could fathom why marriage should change my identity or last name. God, I loved Jeff and missed him. Nothing ever touched that compartment of my life. Not friends, not family, not a lover.

A gaggle of official cars cluttered the Glaston driveway. The catawampus parking angles testified to the hyped-up state of the drivers. Only one vehicle sat outside Darlene's mansion. Duncan's convertible.

The door opened before I could ring the bell. Julie welcomed me with a light-as-a-feather embrace. "Come in."

The young lady wore what appeared to be her uniform of choice—baggy britches and a T-shirt, hot pink this time. I followed her to the kitchen.

Darlene sat like dejection's poster child at the end of the butcher-block table. The floor-length robe wrapping her slim frame didn't disguise the wilted posture. Puffy eyes and reddened cheeks testified to a lengthy crying jag. She stared vacantly at the table, while the hand at her throat worried the edges of her terrycloth robe. She glanced up, started to stand.

"Stay put." I came round and kissed her forehead.

Duncan greeted me with a lift of a coffee mug. "It's not Irish, but let me get you some." A brief smile carried to his eyes. "Glad you're here."

His fingers grazed the back of my hand when he handed me the mug. A little tremor reminded me what those fingers had been up to a few hours ago.

Darlene lifted her head. "I wasn't fond of Jake's daughter or her husband. Frankly I disliked them. But I never wanted to see Gina and Robert dead."

"How did they die?" I asked. "Does anyone know?"

"When Eric called 911, he triggered the security alarm," Duncan said. "Thrasos bodyguards swarmed to the scene. As soon as the sheriff turned up, he sent a deputy to check on Darlene and Julie. When I arrived, I pumped the deputy for details. He said both bodies were stone cold, probably dead for hours."

Duncan swiveled his coffee cup to and fro. "The Glastons slept in separate rooms. They found Gina in her bed, her respirator clamped to her face, and Dr. Glaston sprawled in a heap at the foot of his bed. If the dual deaths hadn't screamed foul play, the guard said he'd have figured heart attacks."

Recalling Eric's rage-contorted face made me wonder. "Could Eric have killed them?"

"No." Darlene sighed. "Gina was his mom. Eric's a hothead, not a cold-blooded killer. I can't see it—even if he was hopped up on some drug."

My friend paused. "At least Julie and I won't be suspects this go-round. Sheriff Delaney got an earful from Kyle. He claims Jake's new will prompted me to kill my husband before he came to his senses. I have no incentive to kill Jake's children. These new murders will expose his ravings as pure crap."

Duncan's hand covered Darlene's and gave it a little squeeze. "I wouldn't say boo about the will. You do benefit from Gina's death. It ups your share of Jake's fortune."

Darlene's eyes widened, and she yanked her hand free. "What? Surely Eric inherits his mom's share. This is ludicrous."

Duncan shook his head. "The will stipulates Jake's beneficiaries must survive him by at least thirty days to inherit. If anyone dies earlier, the deceased person's share reverts to the estate to be divided among survivors."

"Why did Jake put that in his will?" Julie looked puzzled.

"In case there was a bad accident involving several family members," Duncan explained. "If some heirs lingered briefly on life support, Jake didn't want their shares to become windfalls to 'money-grubbing leeches.' His words. Specifically, he didn't want Dr. Glaston waltzing away with dollars intended for his flesh and blood."

"Good heavens, does that disinherit Eric?" I blurted.

Duncan shook his head. "Jake didn't neglect his grandson. Eric claims a multi-million-dollar trust fund when he turns thirty. That trust is outside the will, and the trustees can advance money for any good reason—say, college or buying a house. The boy's also a beneficiary in this will. His share will increase with other survivors. Plus Eric inherits the remainder of the trust Jake set up years back for Gina."

Julie pushed back from the table. "The will doesn't have a damn thing to do with the Glaston murders. All the heirs inherit millions. What kind of idiot risks killing two people for a few more million? They can't spend it rotting in prison. Besides, Dr. Glaston didn't inherit. Why kill him?"

"Good points," Duncan said. "Just wanted to warn you the new murders don't pare down the suspect list. The beefed-up security also argues against a stranger as killer, though maybe the electronic security system will confirm you and Julie were both here when the Glastons died."

He nodded at Julie. "Too bad you told the sheriff Dr. Glaston wanted to fire you."

Duncan absently tapped a finger on the side of his mug.

"Darlene, you should hire an attorney. Immediately."

My friend's brows knitted in confusion. "Aren't you my attorney?"

He massaged his temples. "I'm an estate attorney. I know beans about criminal law. I doubt Sheriff Delaney will jump to any conclusion. He's too independent-minded to be bullied by Kyle or Hamilton. But it's only prudent to be prepared. I'll find you a good criminal lawyer."

I'd been pondering motives. "Suppose the Glastons knew who killed Jake and planned to talk. If so, the killer had nothing to lose. He couldn't be put to death twice."

Darlene's hand flew to cover her open mouth. Shock. Time to disengage my motor mouth. "Sorry, Darlene. When I get excited, I blurt things out without thinking."

"It's okay." She exhaled. "I didn't call you and Duncan to be coddled. If Sheriff Delaney even hints Julie and I are suspects, I'll hire a criminal lawyer."

"I wouldn't wait," I put in, "even if the sheriff acts like your best buddy."

I longed to blab about Hamilton's pressure on his FBI liaison. That was a far bigger worry than the local constabulary. My tongue practically bled as I kept my promised silence.

"You might consider hiring a private investigator," Duncan added. "The sooner somebody uncovers the real murderer, the sooner you're in the clear—and safe. Until we figure out why it's open season on the Olsen family, I'll worry plenty about both of you."

Darlene shot a horrified look at her daughter. "My God, what if the killer comes after you?"

She knocked over her coffee as she leapt up. "Julie, I want you to go away—far away—until things settle down. Duncan, can you find a safe place to hide her?"

Julie put her hands on her hips. "Calm down, Mom. Don't be ridiculous. I'm staying."

"We'll see." Darlene swiped at the puddled coffee with a napkin.

I remembered that someone had been in the cabin. "Sheriff Delaney ought to give that old cabin a once-over. Someone's been using it, maybe the killer. Yesterday Duncan and I spotted disposable gloves on a counter. Maybe the murderer wore them when he mixed up some little surprises to knock off the Gastons."

Darlene bit her lip, nodded. "The cabin would be a good hiding place."

The doorbell trilled. Duncan answered it and ushered the sheriff and Deputy Marshall into the kitchen. When Delaney spotted me, his frown deepened. My presence didn't delight him.

Both men accepted Julie's offer of coffee and claimed vacant chairs. Though the blush of sunrise warmed the kitchen windows, the faces around the table looked gray, exhausted.

"We need to get statements," Delaney began. "I posted deputies on the grounds for your protection. If you want to go anywhere, they'll escort you."

Duncan frowned, opened his mouth to speak. Delaney held up a hand. "Don't get all lawyerly on me, son. This isn't house arrest. I'm not trying to step on anyone's rights. But this has gotten way out of hand. I wouldn't be doing my job if I didn't try to protect Jake Olsen's remaining heirs."

Darlene spoke. "Fine by me. I'm frantic with worry about Julie's safety. I'll welcome any protection you offer."

The sheriff nodded, pulled out his pen and a recorder, and asked Darlene and Julie how they'd spent the evening. He didn't bother to quarantine them for questioning. Probably figured if any of us were in cahoots we'd had ample time to synchronize stories.

Mother and daughter claimed they never left the house after eight p.m. Unfortunately they only had each other for alibis. When the storm took a breather between six and eight, Julie soaked for a while in the poolside Jacuzzi. Once the storm renewed, she hunkered down with her mother, who'd shaken her migraine and wandered downstairs.

The women said they saw nothing unusual through the home's vast windows, except the storm's awesome lightning display. While the house lost power, a backup generator—part of the estate security package—kicked the lights on within minutes of the initial outage.

"The guards called to make sure we were all right when the power went out," Julie volunteered. "I answered the phone. That was around nine-thirty."

The sheriff turned to Darlene. "Tell me about the health of the deceased."

She frowned. "Everyone knows Gina was an alcoholic. She had liver disease and asthma attacks. Robert popped pills regularly. I don't know why. We weren't close."

Finally, the sheriff focused his attention on Duncan and me. The look wasn't friendly when he asked our whereabouts. Duncan said he dined at the Outrigger with my family, squired May and me home, and stayed until shortly after midnight.

I substantiated his story, though I failed to mention May could only vouch for our whereabouts until nine-thirty. After that, my aunt was sawing logs.

I saw no reason to expound on our entertainment.

Once the sheriff closed his notebook, Duncan suggested the cabin search. He described how we'd tramped through the place and gave a neutral account of our encounter with Eric.

Delaney's jaw clenched. No tealeaves needed to read his mind. If the cabin was a crime scene, we'd botched any evidence of value.

"Where's Eric?" Darlene asked.

"He took ill—shock I imagine," Delaney said. "A deputy delivered him to his uncle's house. His aunt said she'd call a doctor."

I hadn't met Kyle's wife, Olivia, but sympathized with her sight unseen. Nursing Eric wouldn't be a barrel of laughs, but I'd prefer it to sitting down to dinner with her beady-eyed hubby.

"One more thing." The sheriff held Darlene's gaze. "We don't know what killed the Glastons. Not a mark on either of 'em. We're guessing they ingested some killer chemical, just like Jake. They didn't use eye drops, but there's more than one way to poison a victim. Be careful what you eat and drink. Hell, if I were you, I'd clear out of this house."

Delaney arched an eyebrow. "We can escort you to a hotel if you decide. Meanwhile, I'm gonna remind everyone—this is a real, live murder investigation. You will not tell anyone outside this room about our conversations or share details about this case."

As the sheriff added this last pronouncement, his eyes bored into mine. Was I being paranoid? Nope. Sheriff Delaney was acquainted with Aunt May. Maybe he'd even experienced her devious and effective interrogation methods.

Or did he suspect I had a pal with the FBI?

Duncan walked me to my car. "Hope I didn't scare you by rushing things last night."

I grinned. "I'm a charge-ahead type myself. Guess it's my Taurus birthright." My attempt at a seductive smile short-circuited when I realized my breath must smell like stale coffee.

He tucked a wayward curl behind my ear. "I realize we're on call for Darlene, but maybe we can steal a few hours for ourselves. How about dinner at my place? Say, six? I can pick you up at May's."

"Sounds wonderful. I don't know May's plans so it's probably better if I just drive myself. Can I bring anything?"

He cocked an eyebrow. "I'm a big fan of dessert."

A blush sauntered up my neck. Duncan's eyes said he wasn't talking strawberry shortcake. "I'll bring dessert—the chocolate variety."

A Cadillac fishtailed to a stop beside us, putting an end to our teasing banter. Hamilton jumped out and slammed his car door. Great. Darlene was in for more laughs.

"Where's the sheriff?" Hamilton barked. "I need to speak with him."

"He just left," Duncan answered.

"Dammit. Why wasn't I informed? Are Darlene and Julie inside?"

I felt my Irish rising. "The sheriff just finished talking with them. Let them be."

"Stay out of my way." Hamilton enunciated carefully. Ice

frosting every syllable. "I warned you. My company's in charge of security, and I don't have to put up with your idiocy. Maybe I should instruct the guards to do a full-body search each time you visit."

"Peachy," I answered. "Nice to know your guards are good for something. They're pretty lame at stopping killers."

Hamilton's hands tightened into fists, and Duncan shouldered between us. "Let's stay calm. Remember Darlene is one of your clients, and Marley's her friend."

Before Hamilton could fire a rejoinder, Duncan turned to me. "Marley, don't you have an appointment this morning? Go. I'll handle this."

His gaze flicked from me to my car. The visual cue urged a rapid departure. I nodded. He'd protect Darlene and Julie from the arrogant bully.

"Right, see you later."

I pulled away, keeping one eye glued to my rearview mirror. Both men stood a tetch over six feet. Nose-to-nose, Hamilton yammered at Duncan, who'd adopted the classic arms crossed over chest stance. A self-imposed straight jacket arguing restraint?

Even absent the soundtrack, I could guess the source of Hamilton's ire. His own Thrasos employees had failed to call him the minute two new corpses popped up. Multiple heads would roll for that oversight.

My mind seesawed between murder and romance. I repeatedly punched the replay button on Duncan's warm lips. That memory cushioned the shocks that seemed to come with every visit to the Olsen estate.

It was not quite nine a.m. when I yoo-hooed loudly and used May's spare key. An irritable pout greeted me. Good thing I'd kept my promise of an early return.

"Well, well." May closed the 'A' section of her fat Sunday *Des Moines Register*. "I didn't expect you to finish counting body bags so quickly."

Before she could launch into Q&A mode, I let her know that Sheriff Delaney had sworn everyone to secrecy. "I can't talk about the murders with anyone."

My aunt rolled her eyes. "I'm quite certain Sheriff Delaney didn't mean me. The old buzzard knows I've never blabbed about police business—not child abuse cases or rapes or suicides. Saw them all in my twenty-five years at the hospital. Always kept my mouth shut."

I sighed. "May, forget it. I'll give you one tidbit, no juicy details. Here it is—what the authorities know doesn't amount to a hill of beans."

Collapsing on the sofa, I tried a conversational feint. "In my humble opinion, the investigation's headed up a blind alley. Because Jake had so damn much money, everyone's fixated on his will. But money's a far-fetched motive for the Glaston murders." I toyed with a throw cushion. "Somebody ought to be noodling around with other possibilities. Does anyone have a grudge against the entire Olsen clan?"

May sat straighter, and her eyes brightened. "Plenty of folks hate all of them, including that son-in-law Glaston. Jolbiogen sucked the blood out of one local business like some giant mosquito. Then there's that botched drug trial. Six people died from liver failure—one a teenager—before Dr. Glaston pulled the plug. A civil negligent homicide suit is still lingering in the courts."

"Wow. I vaguely remember. About three years back?"

"Yes. Jolbiogen got a regulatory slap on the wrist. Stock prices dipped a few bucks. Didn't hurt the Olsens one whit. When you're rolling in it, you can afford a long-term view."

"You mentioned a local business. What happened?"

"Jolbiogen bought a local start-up that employed fifty people—a big deal in our tiny burg. Folks were thrilled. Figured big brother would pump in capital, create more jobs. A few locals borrowed money to buy land near the lab. Thought they'd strike gold when the expansion started. Jolbiogen closed the lab, kept four employees. Boom. It only wanted the patents."

My fingers fiddled with the fringe on the throw pillow. "Think the sheriff will check out links between the murders and Jolbiogen?"

May harrumphed. "Delaney looks like a hayseed, but he's no dummy. He'll turn the Jolbiogen mess over to the state police or Feds. He'd better with three dead bodies."

My aunt eyed my casual attire and frowned. "Stop talking and start scrubbing. We leave for church in fifteen minutes."

TEN

As we stood for the opening hymn, I wondered when May became a regular churchgoer. In my childhood, Sunday was the day Uncle John cooked mounds of fried eggs, bacon and toast, while May sipped coffee, kibitzed and planned everyone's day. Her agendas seldom included church.

I smiled recalling the Sunday May whisked me to a rickety clapboard church after I stubbornly insisted I had to attend Sunday School to earn a white Bible. That reward for two years' perfect attendance still claims a place of honor on my bookshelves.

Unwilling to risk holy wrath, May checked newspaper listings and deposited me at the earliest option. When she picked me up, she was eager for details. "Do those holy rollers really shout and roll in the aisles?"

The pastor's voice rose. "It is easier for a camel to go through the eye of a needle, than for a rich man to enter into the kingdom of God."

The well-heeled parishioners around us squirmed as the minister meandered through parables about people tested by wealth. The fidgeting lessened slightly when he noted that being too poor presented its own spiritual hazards.

Had Jake's death prompted the themes?

As we stood in line to greet the preacher, a large hand settled on my shoulder. "Good to see you, Colonel."

I looked up into General Irvine's lined face. "General Irvine. What a surprise."

Aunt May nudged me in the ribs. No way to get around an introduction. The general bowed slightly, held her hand, smiled. He claimed he had business in Omaha. Since he had some free time, he'd driven over to see first-hand the lakes region I'd raved about.

The old boy laid it on thick, but I had to give the wily old coot his due. Though his Mississippi accent no longer dripped molasses, he could still ooze Southern charm. The general could abduct me at gunpoint, and Aunt May would wave bye-bye, murmuring *what a nice gentleman.*

"I won't keep you," General Irvine closed. "I'm meeting a colleague. Maybe we can grab a cup of coffee later, Marley. Give me a call." He slipped a card into my palm and disappeared. I glanced at the note before tucking it into my purse.

Today. 1400 hours. Spine Trail, Mile 4. Come alone.

Why was General Irvine here? Weaver said he was focused on trying to figure out which terrorist group had taken possession of Jolbiogen's stolen bioweapon recipe. I'd assumed his involvement in the murder investigation was tangential.

I drove May to Walmart where we bought silk flowers for our visit to Lakeview Cemetery and Uncle John. Once a rural graveyard, the cemetery now sat a stone's throw from the buzz of Highway 9 traffic. My uncle—an inveterate Jaycee booster—probably cheered.

With May's arm linked through mine, we shuffled over uneven ground to the hilltop grave. May's name and birth date already etched the joint headstone. Only the "Died" date waited to be carved. Years of nursing gave my aunt a matter-of-fact acceptance of death. "There are things a lot worse than dying," she reminded whenever someone passed peacefully.

But, oh how I'd miss the crusty curmudgeon, my last family link with her generation.

May turned up the bronze vase attached to the headstone. "Wonder how many times I've come here to talk to John?" She fiddled with her arrangement of lavender lilacs, red tulips and lily-of-the-valley sprigs. "I know it's silly. I can speak to John from my heart anywhere. But it's a comfort to visit. We've held some long conversations, I'll tell you—though I imagine he still complains he can't get a word in edgewise."

She chuckled. "I've told John everything that's happened with my boys, you and Kay. But, oh kid, it saddens me to think of all the pleasures he missed—the wonders life offers to compensate for cranky joints and cataracts. He'd have popped his buttons bragging on you."

My throat tightened. "I'm sure he's enjoyed your stories. Remember how Uncle John answered that neighbor who asked if he tired of hearing you tell the same tale? 'Why not at all, I'm always anxious to hear how things turn out—May's stories never end the same way twice.'"

The oft-repeated anecdote coaxed the expected smile from May.

Walking toward the car, I spotted a vehicle parked on a gravel loop off the main service road. Motor running. It wasn't there when we arrived.

I scanned the graveyard. No sign of people paying respects at family plots. The tan car's darkened windows precluded a look inside. I felt the hairs rise on the back of my neck, then chastised myself. For heavens sake, who'd bother to tail me to a graveyard? Or was it General Irvine?

"So what shall we do for lunch?" I asked.

"Oh, dear. I plain forgot my open house at Pillsbury Point, a stone and log beauty near where Vern & Coila's Restaurant used to stand. The house wasn't built when you waitressed there."

She rummaged in her purse for her date book. "Have to park my fanny there from two until five. Shouldn't complain though. If they get anywhere near the asking price, I'll be flush. Come first snowflake, I'll jaunt down to South Carolina to visit you."

I smiled. "I'd love that. But, May, you still haven't told me where to head—home or a fast-food dive?"

"Hy-Vee." Her answer came an instant before the turn. "You order us sandwiches from the deli, while I buy nibbles for the open house."

"Sounds like a plan. I needed to pick up a few groceries, too. This will save me a trip."

"We out of something?" May asked.

Okay, time to evict the bagged cat. "Duncan invited me for dinner. I'm bringing dessert."

"Well, well, his invite includes me, right?" She elbowed me. "You should see your face. I'm kidding. You could do worse, Marley Clark. Nevertheless, be careful. I've heard tales about these sex-crazed divorcés."

She hoisted her eyebrows. "By the by, what time did Duncan leave last night?"

"Look for a parking place," I suggested.

Not that busywork would derail May's curiosity for long.

❁

After helping Aunt May organize her open house, I threw together a Death by Chocolate trifle. While relying on store-bought brownies, chocolate mousse, Cool Whip and Heath bars, I took time to soak the brownies in Kahlua. I have a few culinary scruples.

Employing Hy-Vee as my prep chef halved my kitchen time, leaving ample leeway to keep my date with General Irvine. If our visit was short, I also planned to drop in on Cousin Ross and pay my respects to Spirit Resort's skeletal remains. My reunion with Darlene had triggered an itch to check out our old haunt. If the grounds were as deserted as advertised, my reminiscing could include a little Tae Bo and a few weapon tests.

At two o'clock sharp, I entered the Spine Trail at the Mile 4 signpost. General Irvine scanned the trail in both directions to make certain we were alone. He'd stowed his church smile. "This is bad business, Marley. Guess you figured I didn't come to Spirit Lake to pay my respects. According to the CDC, a dozen seasonal workers have dropped dead on farms just south of here. They all caught colds, then died within twenty-four hours. Their symptoms suggest they're victims of a bioterrorism cocktail."

"Oh, my God. Why would a terrorist target farm workers? It makes no sense."

"Probably a field test. They wanted to see how quickly the cocktail worked and if deaths would be limited to people with a targeted DNA sequence. All the victims are Hispanic. If they consider their little trial a success, they could decide to launch in earnest anytime. But we still don't know who 'they' are, what population group they're targeting, or where they'll strike."

"How can I help?"

"I'm not sure. Maybe your contact with the Olsen woman and her daughter will provide a lead."

General Irvine grabbed my forearm and squeezed. "Marley, I recognize that quiver in your jaw. You're upset. If the stakes weren't so high, I wouldn't involve you. But I'm hoping you can ask Julie a few questions without tipping her—or anyone else—off. I don't think the girl's involved, but if she is, we can't afford for her to warn her buyers we're on their tail. If Julie's not involved, she may still give you some information that would point us in the right direction."

❧

Wanting to scrub my mind of the potential horror a terrorist could wreak, I ran flat out. Sweat coated me head-to-toe by the time I unlocked Aunt May's condo. After a quick shower and a snack, I headed to the Maritime Museum.

No need to phone Ross before dropping by. He'd be up to his elbows in chores designed to reassure skittish boat owners that their vintage watercraft would be treated like royalty.

I turned into Arnolds Park, and nostalgia overwhelmed me. Despite inevitable changes, the amusement park remained comfortingly familiar. The grand dame held onto her majesty through her periodic facelifts.

How many hours had I spent riding the tilt-a-whirl and trying to ram and slam my sister and cousins before they could wedge my bumper car into a dark, embarrassing corner? May had chauffeured me to dozens of dances at the Roof Garden, including the night Gary Lewis and the Playboys rocked the place. Gary Lewis called me out of the audience to sing with them and kissed my cheek when the song ended. Would I be as thrilled today at winning the lottery?

Ross spotted me as I pulled May's Buick into the lot and motioned me over. Ross and Nels Jacobs, a carpenter who volunteers at the museum, were engaged in an animated discussion.

"We need something dramatic." My cousin's hands danced as he drew imaginary entrances for the boat show. "I'd love to put a few boats on pedestals. But how in tarnation could we hoist them?"

Nels cocked his head to the side. "The road crew has a pretty big forklift."

My cousin's eyes sparkled. "Oh, yeah."

Ross turned to me. "You remember Nels, right?"

I shook the carpenter's leathered hand. "Don't let me interrupt. If you're busy, I'll drive over to your house and chat with Eunice."

"She'll be here any minute." Ross consulted his watch. "Nels and I are about to take a late lunch. He's made me happy as a clam. Says he can build exactly what I want. Let's get some pop and sit by the lake a spell. Too nice to be cooped up inside."

We sauntered down to the boardwalk, and Ross bought a round of soft drinks while Nels staked out a table under a giant umbrella.

Last night's passing storm had scrubbed the sky a crystal blue. A rainbow of spinnakers curved across the lake as sailboats played the zephyrs on West Okoboji.

Ross slid a large to-go glass in front of me. "Mom filled me in on your dawn romp. The Glaston murders are topic *numero uno*. When TV crews couldn't get inside the Olsen estate, they used the Queen as a backdrop for live updates."

I shrugged. "Surprised they didn't opt for a waterfront stakeout. The lakeshore bordering the estate is public property."

"Took 'em a while to manage logistics. The last Queen cruise ran into an armada anchored off the Olsen cove—mostly numbnuts who don't know how to drive a boat. Gus over at Parks Marina is flat out of rental boats. Asked if I'd rent my Hafer. Said media types were offering hundreds for any boat."

Nels jumped in. "Guess that safe room didn't do them folks any good."

My cousin and I shared a look. Huh?

Nels picked up on our bafflement. "Dad helped build it. Made his living framing houses in Sioux City. They used his South Dakota construction crew to build the safe room. Didn't want locals who might blab." He stopped and grinned. "Guess Old Jake should have asked if the workers had relatives in these parts."

"What are you blatherskiting about?" Ross asked. "What safe room?"

"In the Glaston house. A year after Jake bought that property someone tried to kidnap his grandson. So he retrofitted his daughter's house with a hidey-hole. Wanted his kin to have an ace up their sleeves if some no-goodnik got past the private cops. Carted everything in from out of town so no one 'round Spirit Lake would know. 'Course back then Jake had cause to keep things hush-hush. Locals were real riled at Jolbiogen for shafting that local lab."

Ross tugged on his moustache. "I'm impressed. Jake was mighty good at keeping secrets. I never heard any gossip about the construction. In our little burg, that's saying something."

Was Sheriff Delaney equally clueless? I wondered if my newfound FBI friend or General Irvine would consider this a valuable inside scoop. Surely some member of the Olsen clan had already disclosed the hideaway's existence.

I frowned. Jake's penchant for secrecy made his choice of a local attorney seem out of character. "If Jake was uptight about locals knowing his business, I wonder why he asked Duncan James to prepare his will?"

"That was his wife's idea," Ross answered. "Jake was set to use some hotshot estate planner in Des Moines when Darlene championed Duncan. Once Jake thought it over, he agreed."

"That's funny,"—actually I didn't find it at all amusing—"I had the impression Duncan was Jake's friend not Darlene's."

"So?" Ross shrugged. "Jake needed someone versed in Iowa probate law. Darlene had to know Duncan was Dickinson County's only estate planner. No need to be buddy-buddy with the guy to suggest he'd be more convenient."

Eunice squeezed my shoulder, then leaned down and kissed Ross's cheek. "Hi, guys. Did I hear Duncan's name? Am I missing out on juicy gossip?"

My cousin gave his wife a mock salute. "The admiral has arrived. I'm officially outranked."

Eunice slipped into the chair beside me. "Have fun with Duncan after we parted?"

"He's got a great sense of humor." I didn't mention his liplock skills. "We're having dinner tonight."

"Oh boy, romance is in the air." Eunice grinned. "Captain Ross always wanted to officiate at a wedding aboard the Queen. 'Course you've got to give him time to get certified."

I laughed. "He's certifiable, all right."

My cousin ignored me. "Reverend Ross—it has a certain ring to it."

I rolled my eyes. "Stop already. I have enough fits with May milking me for details."

"Okay, you're off the hook." Ross stood. "We have displays to build. Eunice, didn't you want Marley's opinion on an exhibit?"

The exhibit turned out to be a collection of old-fashioned beach toys. A donor had offered the museum an antique sand shovel painted with a likeness of the original Queen and a century-old tin pail embossed to give a busty mermaid perky size-D cups. Though Eunice asked my advice on placing the acquisitions, it was only a polite gesture. She had an artist's eye. I have trouble matching my socks.

While fussing with the display, Eunice made a few lame attempts to ferret out my level of interest in the eligible attorney before we settled into our usual routine, swapping stories about May's rambunctiousness.

Crossing my fingers for luck, I voiced my hope I'd be equally ornery at age eighty.

I left a message on Darlene's cell. She returned my call in a flash.

"How are you holding up?" I asked.

"I feel like a prisoner. When I go to the toilet, a deputy leans on the doorjamb. He can report every fart if he's so inclined. I've a notion to cook beans. I'm in my bath with the exhaust fan cranked to warp speed for a little privacy. I want the deputies for Julie's sake, but having minders gives me indigestion."

"Has Hamilton pestered you again?"

"Nope. Duncan, bless him, waylaid the dipwad and fibbed that I'd taken to bed due to exhaustion. He stressed that as far as Olsen security was concerned, I was his new boss. That pissed Hamilton off, but what could the blowhard say?"

"Hooray for Duncan." I wanted to kiss him. "You need to start shopping for a new security service and nudge Jolbiogen's president to do the same. The Thrasos track record doesn't exactly inspire confidence."

I wished I could mention the firm's failure to safeguard military secrets on Jolbiogen's turf.

She sighed. "I'd love to fire Hamilton. But that would just escalate the conflict with my stepson, Kyle. He'd scream that I was playing fast and loose with his family's safety—especially after his sister's murder."

"Any other new developments?" I asked.

Darlene said she'd entertained plenty of visitors, including FBI agents and a toxicology team from Atlanta's Center for Disease Control. "The sheriff admitted he's out of his league," she said. "It looks as if the FBI will claim jurisdiction. Something about a serial killer."

Son-of-a-Glock, the FBI had stepped out of the shadows even though the military had yet to stand up and be counted. Too bad the jurisdictional shift didn't promise to make Darlene's life easier. "The CDC took samples of residue on Gina's respirator," she continued, "and swept the estate looking for other contaminants."

"So they think Gina was poisoned when she used her respirator?"

"It sounded like it. I overheard one guy describe a toxin that's lethal in almost any form—inhaled, swallowed or absorbed through the skin. Victims die within a few hours of exposure. Based on that tidbit, Julie suspects the murderer used a mushroom toxin. She keeps one in her lab."

Uh-oh. Another finger pointed in the young researcher's direction.

"Julie tags the stuff—think she called it phalloidin—with a red or green fluorescent molecule. She says if authorities test samples from Gina's liver under a special light, they'll know for sure if someone used a tagged phalloidin. The cells would glow."

"How long will the tests take?"

A sigh punctuated Darlene's silence. "I warned Julie to keep her mouth shut. I can't shake this heebie-jeebie feeling someone's trying to pin these murders on us. Why help them? What if tests prove the stuff came from Julie's lab?"

I frowned. Darlene wasn't thinking straight. "If your daughter suggests the tests, it won't look like she's trying to hide a connection to her lab. Sooner or later, the authorities will discover Julie uses the stuff—if, indeed, that's what killed the woman."

A chill raced up my spine. Had we blabbed too much? Could Hamilton be eavesdropping on Darlene's calls? He had the technology and zero ethics. Not wanting to hand the snake more ammunition, I didn't mention the safe room. I wouldn't put it past Hamilton to plant evidence if he gained access before the FBI.

"Can you come over for supper?" Darlene asked.

"Sorry, no. I already made other plans."

I didn't mention Duncan, even though my reticence mystified me. Years ago Darlene and I had shared intimate details about our love lives. Why did I sense my budding relationship with her attorney might prove sensitive?

Leaving the museum, I turned May's Buick toward Big Spirit, a vast, shallow lake capable of summoning up tsunami-sized waves whenever stiff winds blew north to south. Just beyond the Gingham Inn Restaurant, I made a mental note to take the right fork next time I ventured north. I wanted to see how many baby fish now swam in the Spirit Lake Fish Hatchery's raceway incubators.

Ross and I visited the hatchery during the spring spawning season. In the musky, cave-like sanctuary we'd watched guys dressed in slickers milk sperm and strip eggs from strapping specimens. Outside we strolled beside the spillway connecting Big Spirit and East Okoboji. Fattened by Minnesota snowmelt, a torrent of water rushed full force through the narrows.

Walleye—a fish that thinks like a salmon but lacks its death wish—choked the passageway. They numbered in the hundreds, twenty- to fifty-pounders valiantly attempting to leap up the cascade. Never again would I doubt Okoboji fish stories.

The wistful faces of anglers, banned from fishing in the vicinity, amused us. Had any of those spectators slipped back in the dead of night to gaff a trophy fish? Was there a parallel with Jake's murder? Perhaps the killer had seen the billionaire and the Glastons as fat fish flashing their silver and wriggling out of reach? Maybe money, not bioterrorism, was the motive.

Beyond Spirit Resort's stone entry pillars, few touchstones hinted at the property's one-time glamour. Pilings that once supported a dance pavilion cantilevered over the water, and cracked concrete stairs led to a shallow beach. I spotted no other remnants.

Even in Darlene's and my day, Spirit Resort had begun its descent into seedy. Built in the 1800s, when castle-like resorts were the rage, the stuccoed walls, mullioned windows and clay roof tiles looked majestic. I'd seen Ross's collection of photos.

Unfortunately, the fortress-like walls repelled most renovation efforts—from enlarging the size of guest rooms to introducing twentieth-century plumbing. Over time, the dark interior became an incubator for mold, and hallways oozed a musty perfume.

While several developers floated ambitious schemes to

transform the sizeable acreage, none materialized. The buildings were razed and the state bought the grounds, even though its location off the beaten tourist path hindered its popularity.

Fine by me. I had Spirit Resort all to myself.

I made a beeline for the beach. As cooks, we prepped food for all three meals in the morning, which freed our afternoons to soak up sun and splash in the lake. I discarded my tennis shoes and waded into the cool water. Smooth, rounded pebbles massaged my soles. Eyes closed, I could almost hear the squeals of delighted kids splashing in the cove.

To plump my summer earnings, I taught swimming. The venture afforded mad money I spent guilt-free on junk food, Arnolds Park rides, putt-putt golf, and other teen lures—if we weren't lucky enough to have dates pick up the tab. Yes, we were feminist hypocrites. What can I say? My consciousness hadn't been fully raised.

An unpleasant memory niggled. Darlene and I double-dated with two Ivy Leaguers. During the matinee portion of our outing, the college boys were funny. After dark, they guzzled beer like soda pop. My date suggested a stroll. Intending to move from first-base to home plate, he pinned me against a tree. I didn't fret. I'd handled drunks before.

Then I heard the scream. Darlene.

I pulled free. A keening sound followed a hiss like air escaping a punctured tire. I spotted Darlene. Her chest heaved. Blood ran from her nose. Her college date writhed on the ground, knees to chest.

She grabbed my hand. "We're out of here."

We plunged through a thin strip of woods. Angry shouts trailed us. We stumbled onto the lake road and hitched a ride with an elderly couple.

Back in our dorm, Darlene rattled out a story in machine-gun bursts of rage.

"The son-of-a-bitch tried to rape me. Called me a cock tease. Said I'd signaled all night that I'd put out. I told him he had his signals crossed. When he punched me, I slapped him. He hit me—harder. So I rammed my knee in his nuts, tried to shove 'em up through his nostrils. Wish I'd killed the bastard."

Her dagger-like stare dared me to disagree. "I'm not kidding. Any man who hurts a woman like that deserves to die."

I discounted her outburst as hyperbole. Did my friend have the flinty core it took to kill? What could make her feel someone deserved to die? A threat to her daughter?

I waded toward shore. A loud pop. A geyser erupted to my right. Another pop. Water exploded on my left. Holy crap, someone was shooting at me.

I glanced toward the embankment, saw sun glinting on metal. A rifle. A third pop. Water rose two feet in front of me.

Damn, damn, damn.

I dove. Held my breath. My kneecaps scraped sand. Too shallow.

My belly flop gained me nada. I now resembled a half-drowned ostrich, instead of a sitting duck. Still a juicy target. I staggered to my feet, slogged forward. A chunk of concrete, left behind when the cantilevered pavilion collapsed, promised shelter.

I splashed into place, hunkered down. A scan of the ridge revealed no sign of a shooter. A bird twittered. His song and my heavy breathing the only sounds.

Was the gunman waiting for me to abandon cover?

My teeth chattered. Long minutes crawled by. Should I shiver in the water until dark? Then, what? Would nightfall make things better—or worse?

A deep, calming breath. Okay, think. If the shooter meant to kill me, he was one piss-poor assassin. Maybe the potshots were meant to scare not kill. *Keep a good thought.*

I scrabbled up the bluff. Barefoot. Another pair of shoes sacrificed. Dirt attached to my sopping clothes like iron to a magnet. Mud's good camouflage, right?

My head popped above the edge of the embankment. A tan car idled alongside mine. It shot forward, flinging gravel, hell-bent for the main road. Mud conveniently cloaked the license plate. I plopped on the grass.

Now what? I could get to a phone, call Sheriff Delaney. And tell him what?

The lake swallowed the bullets. Recovery unlikely. And why would Delaney bother searching? The only thing hurt was my dignity. He had bigger problems. Plus I was a suspect. I scuffled along the bank area, searching yards in every direction from the shooter's perch. No shell casings. Nothing. Footprints erased by a piece of brush.

Was it the same car I'd spotted at the cemetery? I couldn't fathom why anyone would want to kill me. I wasn't one of Jake's heirs. I knew next to nothing about the bioterrorism threat.

Quentin Hamilton? Though I hated the man, his M.O. was innuendo and character assassination, not spilling real blood.

Maybe Agent Weaver would have some clue why I'd been nominated as a shooting target. She could pass the news along to General Irvine, too.

I squeezed water from my shirt and the hem of my shorts, opened the car trunk for a beach towel, and dried off as best I could, eager to get while the gettin' was good.

Being alone on Spirit's isolated bluff no longer seemed a bright idea. I hadn't brought a gun on vacation—only carried when I worked as a security officer. Thanks to Eric, I knew my cell phone stun gun worked. Was the pepper-spray atomizer a winner as well?

I pulled it from my bag. Pressed the trigger. A few drops dribbled out. I fiddled with the nozzle, checked the wind direction, and sprayed again. Incapacitating mist. Great, but only if my would-be shooter decided to get up close and personal and stood downwind.

With eyes peeled for the tan car, I folded the towel on May's car seat to keep it as dry as possible. Should I beg off Duncan's dinner invitation?

Damn, my vacation was getting complicated.

ELEVEN

Ensconced in dry clothes, I fetched May from her open house, showing my aunt more teeth than a Desperate Housewife hiding a cabana boy in the closet. Luckily, she hardly glanced my way. Too busy making notes about prospect follow-ups. Her intuition hadn't penetrated my fake cheer. Good. No need to worry her.

I was worried enough for both of us. Still several notches down from hysterical. I'd talked to Weaver, who had no additional insights. After we ran through a few scenarios, she agreed the shots were meant to warn not maim or kill. Someone wanted to scare me off from helping Darlene.

Unable to manufacture a single reason why the shooter would object to my eating chocolate with a handsome attorney, I showered, dabbed perfume in spots that had suffered an extended cologne drought, and slipped into a silky red blouse and slinky black slacks.

In the sexy underwear department, the best I could muster was black as the color du jour for my briefs and Barely There bra. At least my pull-on, pull-off knit bra offered no hook-like obstacles, though haste could result in unsightly tangles, a sort of squashed, single-breasted pirate look.

Okay, I confess. I hoped chocolate and a few beers might make my clothes fall off. I lusted for a little heavy breathing not inspired by gunfire or dead bodies.

Though I looked forward to the evening, I was prepared to cancel if there was even the slightest chance someone was following me. I drove around Spirit Lake for half an hour, dodging down alleys and making U-turns. I even pulled into a grocery store parking lot, walked to the store and peered out from behind a pillar to see if a tan car with dark windows lurked anywhere in my vicinity. The spy craft made me feel a bit foolish, but it convinced me I didn't have a tail. Still, I parked in the golf club's parking lot and hoofed it the last block and a half to Duncan's front door. Not a single car in sight. If someone spotted May's car, I hoped they'd decide I was getting a bite at Bud's Pub inside the golf club.

Balancing a bowl filled with my Death by Chocolate trifle against my hip, I freed a hand to ring his doorbell. A second later, he seized control of my dessert and my lips. I think he set the trifle on a table. I know he quickly freed both hands. Perhaps getting shot at whetted my appetite. I was hungry for whatever the barrister planned to serve. Like tongue.

Duncan's hands slid up and down my arms. He pushed back. "Welcome."

I laughed. "Think I got that."

He looked past me to the street. "Where's your car?"

I rolled my eyes. "That's a long story."

"Well, you can tell me over dinner," he said. "It's almost ready. I'll slip your dessert in the fridge."

I declined wine, noting my allergies to both red and white varieties. After handing me my requested alternate—a beer—he opened a bottle for himself.

"I may not be directly in the line of fire, but I can still use a drink," he said. "Darlene's problems get uglier with each passing day."

"Amen to that." Since we'd met, twenty-four hours had yet to elapse without the discovery of a dead body—or two. "Since you mentioned being in the line of fire, I need to tell you about my afternoon. You may want me to disappear."

Duncan's forehead creased as he listened to my Spirit Resort tale of a hidden gunman taking potshots at me, and how I'd tried to ensure no one followed me to his house.

"Hopefully if they spot the car, they'll think I'm at the bar at the golf course."

"It sounds like someone just wanted to put a scare in you. But I understand your caution. I'm not worried though. Let's enjoy our evening. Take a break from tragedy. No mention of gunman, murder or death through the main course."

"You won't get an argument from me."

He took my hand and led me to a walled patio where a dozen citronella torches flickered. I figured they were as much for mosquito protection as ambience. Duncan seated me then brought out a large bowl of Caesar salad. My muscles gradually unknotted as we sipped our beers and nibbled greens.

We chatted about everything and nothing. I learned his twenty-six-year-old daughter Kelly, an only child, worked as a landscape architect in Austin, Texas, and was engaged to a podiatrist. "She was away at college when my wife and I separated." Duncan glossed over the details of his marriage breakup. "I should have become suspicious when my wife suddenly started buying slinky underwear." His smile didn't reach his eyes.

When he didn't elaborate, I changed the subject, reminiscing about my first visits to Spirit Lake to see Aunt May and Uncle John. From there we segued into genealogy, and I discovered his mother, like my own, was Irish and traced her relatives to County Cork. "Hey, maybe we're long lost cousins," I said.

His hand snaked across the table, and his fingers trailed along my arm. "Okay by me so long as it's the kissing variety."

My pulse took a hop, skip and jump. I felt pretty certain we'd soon see each other's birthday suits.

My nervousness made no sense—more like a teenager than a middle-aged female who'd read "The Joy of Sex" in bed with her husband and experimented with a variety of positions. Before we settled into our comfortable long-term routines, Jeff and I had been game to try most everything that did not mandate pretzel-like contortions. The purposely-shocking addition of ice cubes had been tested only once.

Duncan stood to clear the dishes. "How about a boat ride?

Then we can arm ourselves with spoons and attack your dessert. It looks delicious."

"I'm not sure that's a good idea—being out in the open like that. What if I'm a target? I don't want someone to miss me and hit you."

He laughed, but there was no twinkle in his eyes. Duncan understood I was serious. "Hey, you may be in more danger in my presence than I am in yours. If someone wants to cut Darlene off from her support, I'm a target, too." Duncan draped a loaned windbreaker around my shoulders. "Let's head down to the dock. Sit a spell. If there are no boats in sight, I think we can assume no one's stalking either of us."

Lingering sunlight didn't stop a sharp temperature drop. At the community docks, Duncan surprised me when he stepped onto what he called his "geezer craft"—an eighteen-foot pontoon boat with a sensible, no-wake, no-hurry fifty-horse motor.

"Had you figured for a sporty deck boat." I chuckled. "You know the wind-in-your-hair, plane at mach speed variety. Waterskiing on weekends. A buxom babe bouncing on the fore deck."

"You have me all wrong." He rapidly blinked his eyes in mock innocence. "As far as speed and water skiing goes, I've been there, done that—before arthroscopy surgery on my knees. Now I enjoy puttering around on the water, hoisting the occasional cold one, and actually hearing what my guests have to say."

Given his retort did not refute bouncing babes, I wondered how many girlfriends he'd wooed aboard his "geezer craft." I'd wager a harem. Who cared? At the moment, I had his undivided attention.

We sat on the pontoon boat as it gently bobbed in place. After fifteen minutes without a single boat scouting Duncan's cove, he convinced me we could shove off. After steering toward the Arnolds Park pier, he pivoted one hundred and eighty degrees to give us grandstand seats for the sinking sun. The shimmering lake mirrored every nuance of the kaleidoscope sky. Rich hues of red and gold seeped into the depths of the lake and became one with the fluid weave.

The sun made its final pirouette, and the sky deepened to indigo. Stars winked like fireflies across the heavens. Since the moon had yet to make its appearance, only stars and twinkling shore lights pierced the lake's shadowy cloak. Our low-wattage running lights did nothing to pollute the peaceful scene. Duncan notched up our cruising speed.

"Not sure I'd feel safe piloting at night," I said. "Come sun up, I know the landmarks to dodge shallows and rock piles, like that nasty one off Pocahontas Point. At night, it's harder to get my bearings. Arnolds Park's lighted roller coaster gives a faithful point of reference, but it's hard to judge distances away from the Park."

"Good thing I'm driving." He smiled. "I love the lake at night. So quiet. Not many pesky wave-runners. Know where we are?"

I squinted toward shore. Colored lights danced over a miniature waterfall. "Just outside the Olsen cove. I recognize the waterfall."

He nodded. "Sure doesn't look like a crime scene, does it?"

My gaze meandered along the shoreline. "You said opportunity is one reason Darlene and Julie are suspects. Sure it would be hard for an outsider to access the estate on land, but I could swim ashore easily."

"True. But what happens once you're on shore? You still have to neutralize house alarms and slip past guards on patrol. How do you know the Olsens or Glastons won't catch you fiddling with their Visine bottles or respirators? Sorry, but at the very least our killer has inside help."

My shoulders slumped. "Guess a SEAL-style assault is a little far-fetched."

I meant it. Unless the killer used the Glaston safe room as a comfy hideaway. Though tempted to ask Duncan if he knew about the room, I felt queasy betraying the second-hand secret. Jake had gone to great lengths to keep locals ignorant. I had no business spouting off until I spoke with the FBI and Darlene.

While we'd avoided murder as dinner conversation, our visit to the cove reopened the topic. "What happened after you got rid of Hamilton?"

"I had about two hours to myself before Darlene called with a new emergency. Wanted me to sit in on an interview with an FBI agent."

I held my tongue. Didn't ask, "How's Sherry?"

"I checked the Fed out," he added. "Her name's Sherry Weaver. Though young, she's built one hell of a reputation. Credited with catching a scientist who smuggled nuclear secrets out of Los Alamos. Seems to have her head screwed on straight."

"How'd the interview go?"

"The agent asked Julie about her research and quizzed her about some mushroom toxin the FBI suspects killed Gina. Julie handled herself well. Very matter-of-fact. Her lab uses the toxin. She even suggested an autopsy routine to pinpoint the source of the toxin."

My shoulder muscles relaxed. I was glad Duncan had subjected Weaver to a background check. Boy, was I slipping. That should have been my first action.

"Julie was smart to cooperate," I observed. "Darlene told me about the toxin. Any word as to what might have killed Dr. Glaston?"

Duncan guided his boat into his assigned slip. "Glaston took pills for a heart condition. Once again, Jolbiogen expedited some lab work. Blood work showed a mega dose of Viagra. Triggered a massive heart attack. Doctors don't prescribe that stuff to people with bad tickers, so it's doubtful he self-medicated. I don't mean to be disrespectful, but it's also tough to imagine Dr. Glaston wanting to pump up his penis to schtupp Gina."

My mental picture of the Glastons *en flagrante* was the opposite of erotic.

Duncan killed the engine. I stepped off and tied the ropes on my side to cleats fore and aft as he secured his bumpers.

"So did Weaver have a theory about how the killer tricked Glaston into taking Viagra?"

"Yep. Pills were ground up and dissolved in the bottle Glaston used to pour his nightcaps. The agent didn't bother to quiz Darlene or Julie about access to Viagra. Too easy to get an Internet prescription or steal pills from a friend's medicine cabinet."

He met me on the dock's center aisle and slipped an arm around my shoulders. When his fingertips skimmed my shoulder, my brain almost abandoned the Olsen puzzle. Yet I didn't feel I was eligible for recess until I'd finished my homework. Maybe Duncan could offer some plausible motives that I could pass along to Weaver.

"Have you come up with any motive beyond greed?"

"Money's always a safe bet. Guess I'll stick with it. But the who eludes me. Even if I weren't Darlene's attorney, I'd rule her out. She and Jake seemed genuinely happy. Had she wanted to dispose of her husband, she's smart enough to plan a less public and splashy—pardon the pun—demise. And Darlene only stood to gain a few million extra by killing the Glastons. Not much in the scheme of things. I'm convinced all three murders are related. As to Julie—she'd never do anything to hurt her mom."

I glanced at Duncan. "If inheritance is the motive, how about Eric or Kyle? Eric was mad as a hatter that his grandfather refused to back some harebrained music scheme, and I understand Kyle's relationship with his dad was strained."

Duncan chewed his lip. "Eric's too impulsive to intricately plot three murders. Kyle? Now he's the archetypical schemer. But why kill his own dad? He's not the type to commit a crime of passion, and he's not hurting for money. He has millions. If he waits a few years and Jake dies of natural causes, more millions fall from the sky. No way would Jake disinherit his only son."

Duncan shook his head as he opened the gate to his condo's fenced patio. "Patricide is very rare. No, I can't see it."

His assessment made sense. "Guess you're right. Where's the motive for Kyle to murder the Glastons? Gina's his half-sister, and her husband inherits nothing—even if Gina dies. No earthly reason to kill his sister and brother-in-law."

With appetites renewed by the chill air, we demolished generous servings of my rich trifle. Then Duncan circled the table and pulled back my chair. I stood. His palms cupped my face. He tilted my head, and our lips met. A hint of sweet chocolate. A promise of something sweeter with a touch of spice.

He backed me into the kitchen cabinets. While one of his hands migrated lower, the other fumbled inside a kitchen drawer. He pulled out an apron.

"Want to change into something more comfortable?" He laughed as he handed me an apron. Its red type proclaimed "I'm The Boss In The Kitchen." Duncan arched an eyebrow. "Wear this—and nothing else—and you can boss me all you like. I won't mind a bit."

"What happens if we move to neutral terrain, say, your bedroom?"

"I still follow instructions pretty well." Duncan's eyes bore into mine. "I aim to please."

He took my hand. I followed.

We halted beside the bed. He unbuttoned my blouse, one button at a time, taking care to kiss each new inch of exposed flesh. Duncan's hands snaked beneath the elastic waistband and my slacks shimmied to the floor. He knelt before me. Cupping my bottom, he clasped me to him. His hot breath sparked an inferno of desire.

This man needed no instruction. I ran my fingers through his curly hair.

God. Yes.

An hour later, Duncan brushed a sweaty curl off my forehead. "Want a shower? We can soap au pair or I can use the guest bath."

"Separate but equal showers," I replied. "My body can't stand any more excitement at the moment."

Leaving the bathroom, I noticed an oversized picture frame covered one of the bedroom walls. The photo collage charted daughter Kelly's march to adulthood from a four-year-old's gap-toothed grin to a teen's spunky victory leap near a soccer goal.

Arm-in-arm with a girlfriend, Kelly looked as if she loved life. I took a closer look at the friendship shots. The same towhead appeared with Kelly in half a dozen pre-teen and teen photos. Why did the friend look so familiar?

Oh, God. It was Julie. Darlene's daughter had been Kelly's best friend growing up in Ames, Iowa.

That meant the parents had more than a nodding acquaintance with each other.

So why did Duncan lie? Claim he didn't know Darlene before Spirit Lake? When kids are inseparable, parents have no choice. They know each other.

Suddenly, I felt ill—weak in the knees and in the head. Duncan walked into the bedroom, toweling his wet hair.

"I have to go now."

Duncan dropped his towel. My abruptness a shocker when he'd been expecting post-coital cooing.

Like a rockslide, my words tumbled out, spilling with no pattern. "I'm bone tired and Aunt May is certain to wait up. Let's hope we both get a good night's sleep with no new murder wake-up calls. Thank you for a wonderful evening."

"Do you really have to leave so soon?" Duncan's crinkled forehead signaled his confusion. "I thought we'd have a nightcap on the patio."

"Sorry, I'm too tired." I offered no further elaboration.

He frowned. "Well, okay. I'll walk you to your car."

We walked in silence. I unlocked May's Buick and Duncan opened my door. His goodnight kiss tilted more toward formality than passion. He'd definitely picked up on my confusion and mood swing.

"I'll see you tomorrow at Darlene's house. You'll be there, right?" he asked.

"Yes, I'll see you tomorrow." I closed my car door.

As I drove away, I watched him recede in my rearview mirror. I was glad to be alone. Dammit, I knew Duncan was too good to be true. Why did he lie? Exactly what kind of relationship did he have with Darlene? Had she urged her rich husband to use an ex—or current—lover to rewrite his will?

"Get a grip," I mumbled aloud. "Your imagination's in overdrive."

But I didn't like lies. They made me damn suspicious. Time to dig a little. Even if I learned things I'd rather not know.

❖

May woke from her easy-chair doze when I opened her front door. "Have a nice time, dear?"

"Yes, a good dinner and a nice cruise on the lake."

May's gaze seemed distant, distracted. No follow-up questions. She took off her glasses and rubbed the bridge of her nose. "I was dreaming. It was so vivid, kid. I was on our family farm in Missouri, riding my pony. I waved goodbye to Mother. She stood in our doorway, a lilac shawl draped over her shoulders." My aunt took a deep breath, let it out slowly. "I swear I could smell the cinnamon from one of her apple pies. I walked down the path and found my brother, Fred, and Father in our vegetable garden. Fred grinned to beat the band, like he might explode with a secret. He looked so handsome, nearly grown up, just like I remember him at fifteen. He never reached sixteen, you know. Fred drowned in that terrible flood, trying to get livestock to safety."

"Oh, May, I'm sorry. How sad."

"Seeing Fred didn't make me sad." She slid her glasses back on. "I felt happy. It's been seventy years since I laid eyes on my big brother. Funny how your mind works. Half the time, I can't recall why I've opened my refrigerator. Yet my dreams replay childhood vignettes like they took place a blink ago." May stood. "Guess I should head to bed. Maybe I'll have an even better dream with my head on a pillow."

Too keyed up to sleep, I powered up my laptop and logged on. While May didn't have wi-fi, a neighbor did. Time for a nosey-parker look into Darlene's past, beginning with the death of her first husband.

I called up Mike Nauer's obit and searched the Ames news archives for the prior week. Darlene's husband had died instantly when his five-year-old Camaro tangled with a tree. Broad daylight. Two in the afternoon. A single-car crash. He was traveling on one of Iowa's gravel county roads—the kind that bears Bingo call letters like A-1 and V-22.

How had Mike found a tree? Those country lanes bumped through cornfields. As a rule, the only shade trees clustered around farmhouses and sat far back from roads with their roiling clouds of tractor dust.

Then came the kicker. Mike wasn't alone. A single passenger—Sheila James, 46, of 819 Franklin Street, Ames, Iowa. She was taken to the hospital, treated for minor injuries, and released. The newspaper reported Mike's blood alcohol level had been .11— well above Iowa's DUI limit—when he lost control of his vehicle.

I held my breath as I cross-referenced the address for Sheila James. Sure enough, four years ago 819 Franklin Street had been the residence of Duncan James, wife Sheila, and daughter, Kelly.

Why was Duncan's wife driving down a country road with an intoxicated Mike Nauer at two on a Tuesday afternoon? I had a sudden inkling why Darlene's grief for her husband of twenty-six years was side-dressed with anger.

The Ames news accounts failed to tell me what I really wanted to know. Were Mike and Sheila illicit lovers? Or was it just as reasonable to assume Mike and Sheila were wronged spouses meeting to plot revenge?

The fact that Duncan and Darlene lied about their past connection troubled me. The falsehoods seemed awfully lame, given how easy it was to unearth their tie. Perhaps Duncan's claim that he hadn't been *friends* with Darlene was a literal truth. Yet they'd certainly been more than nodding acquaintances.

Too bad Google can't search people's souls.

I had other avenues to explore. You don't reach the rank of lieutenant colonel without participating in court-martials. I'd served as an Article 32 investigating officer—the equivalent of a one-man grand jury. If nothing else, I knew how to research and grill witnesses.

My troubled conscience fought my drooping eyelids. Sleep eluded me. Was I being a self-centered snoop? My mantra of justification did not serve as a total balm. No matter how you cut it, spying on friends is a breach of trust. Such serious insults usually destroy relationships. Darlene was a friend, and Duncan and I had certainly connected.

Should I just ask Darlene or Duncan to explain?

Maybe I would.

Twelve

Sun poured through the sheers covering May's guest room windows. The nightstand clock confirmed my suspicion. Nine-thirty. The morning half gone. The smell of hazelnut coffee and Aunt May's cheerful off-key hum got me moving. I'd tossed and turned most of the night, but my pleased senses suggested I'd awakened on the right side of the bed. Showered and dressed, I padded into the living room barefoot.

"Hello, sleepyhead," May chirped. "Thought I'd have to call the fire department to roust you. Anna will be here in half an hour. I thought she'd have to make the bed with you in it."

Anna Huiskamp had been my aunt's biweekly cleaning lady for fourteen years. May claimed she liked to be home when Anna dusted her antiques. The truth is, my aunt enjoys mining her housekeeper's vast gossip reservoir. In a two-week cycle, Anna cleaned upwards of fifteen houses, scattered throughout the community's neighborhoods—from Milford's Maywood to Big Spirit's Marble Beach. That made Anna ringmaster of an impressive, albeit relatively good-natured, rumor mill.

I'd just finished my first cup of coffee and wolfed down a piece of toast smeared with peanut butter when the doorbell rang. Figuring it was Anna, I wiped crumbs on my shirttail as I sauntered to answer.

Sherry Weaver towered and glowered behind the door. "We need to talk—alone." No pretense of a make-nice greeting. The lanky FBI agent scanned the room beyond me for signs of life.

"I assume your aunt's here. We'll go for a drive."

As I framed my uppity reply, May popped into view. "Hello?" My aunt bustled forward to welcome the newcomer, hand extended, a smile playing across her face. "Have we met?"

"No, ma'am." Weaver shook hands. Clearly, she'd hoped to avoid meeting anyone. "I'm with the FBI. I need to speak with your niece about the Olsen investigation."

"Well, come in, come in." I recognized my aunt's glee at a prime snooping opportunity. "Make yourself comfortable. How about coffee? It's fresh."

"No thanks." Weaver obliged my aunt by sitting, although her behind teetered on the edge of the couch. I could tell the Fed hoped to fly the coop at her first opening.

The doorbell sounded, and I reprised my butler role. This time the person behind door number one was expected. Anna, my aunt's affable cleaning lady, barely cleared the threshold before wrapping me in her husky arms. She squeezed hard enough to offer chiropractic realignment. A lifetime of milking cows had endowed the burly farm wife with weight-lifter forearms.

"Marley, you're a sight for sore eyes!" Her high-pitched giggle prompted a smile. "I'll bet it's been a year. Where you been hiding, eh? May's roped you into helping with her eightieth wingding, has she?"

The cleaning lady peered past me and spied Ms. FBI looking as though a corncob had been shoved up her derriere.

"Oh, m-m-my," Anna stuttered. "Sorry. I'm interrupting. You should have shushed me. Shall I come back later?"

"No, I was just about to put on shoes. Ms. Weaver and I are going for a drive."

My pronouncement drew a look of relief from Weaver and consternation from May. You win some, you lose some.

Weaver led the way toward her utilitarian coupe at a brisk trot. "Know someplace off-the-beaten track where we can be sure our talk is private?"

"Several." I gave directions to the Kettleson Hogs Back area, less than two miles from Spirit Lake's sleepy downtown.

Ross and Eunice introduced me to the wildlife sanctuary and its flock of trumpeter swans. Like my cousin and his wife, these feathered white giants appeared to mate happily and monogamously for life.

Weaver didn't say another word until we'd parked and exited the car. "I've never seen birds like that. They look prehistoric. God, their wingspans must be eight feet. What are they?"

"Trumpeter swans." I turned up my volume to compete with the birds' raucous cries, which seemed to vibrate the air. From our bluff-top perspective, we could see—and hear—a dozen breeding pairs weaving their elongated necks as they glided through the marshy shallows below.

"Let's walk." Weaver's motions crackled with pent-up energy or maybe frustration. However, she took another moment to survey her surroundings. "What is this place?"

I shared Ross's explanation of kettleholes, depressions formed when great ice chunks tore away from retreating glacier parents. As the orphaned ice clumps slowly melted to oblivion, they left steep bowls that later filled with rain and snowmelt.

Weaver asked no follow-up questions. "I'm disappointed you haven't phoned me, except to report that someone shot at you."

Okay, so much for nature, we were down to brass tacks.

"The Glaston murders make matters look worse for your friends. Dammit, the general and I need your help. Jolbiogen's testing suggests the killer used cyclogel and phalloidin to murder Jake and Gina. Julie's lab stocks both."

Weaver pushed her red-gold mane away from her face. "There's more. One of our hotshot computer specialists pulled disturbing emails from Julie's laptop. She told everyone her affair with Dr. Valberg was over, but her emails—deleted ones teased out of cyber trashcans—tell a different story."

I held up a hand. "You sure they weren't planted, then erased, knowing nothing ever really disappears?"

Weaver sighed. "It's possible. The erased messages don't

include any shoptalk about gene therapy and the military project. But, my boss finds the very existence of an ongoing dialogue troublesome. He claims they were communicating in code. Right now, technicians are examining phalloidin molecules from Gina's liver to see if they're tagged with the fluorescent Julie uses. If there's a match, her noose gets a little tighter."

I sighed. "Oh, come on. If Julie were guilty, would she have suggested a test to incriminate herself?"

"Maybe she's being clever...figures her candor will make us consider a frame."

"Well, that's my bet." Though somewhat troubled by my recent sleuthing, I still thought Hamilton's theory of Julie as a bioterrorism collaborator was pure crap.

"That's why we're talking," Weaver reminded. "Give me something to work with here."

I remembered the disposable gloves on the cabin counter. "Did those gloves test positive for the toxin used to kill Gina?"

"Yes," Weaver answered.

"Any usable fingerprints?" Like most TV-educated criminologists, I'd watched "CSI" and imagined myself a forensic genius.

"We couldn't lift prints. Apparently, the killer double-gloved—wore a second skin of plastic inside. The discarded gloves were the outer pair."

Weaver's explanation sent a shiver up my spine. Hadn't Julie advocated double-gloving?

I veered to a different subject. "The murderer seems well acquainted with the victims' health problems. Who had access to their medical files?"

"Anyone with a hairpin and a little nerve. Jolbiogen has a fulltime doc on staff. He provides free physicals to executives and their families. Complete medical information about Jake, his daughter, son-in-law—hell, the whole Olsen clan—is stored in a standard-issue file cabinet with a dime-store lock. The companion electronic files sit on the mainframe under the password RX. A decent hacker could grab the data in seconds. One of our guys is trying to trace any recent downloads. I'm not holding my breath."

"Did Jake's file include the MG diagnosis?"

"Yes. But, Marley, I didn't come to hear myself talk. Have you learned *anything* that might help me? And I mean anything. Hamilton's pushing hard for the FBI to arrest Julie for espionage and murder, even though the circumstantial evidence is fairly flimsy. He has to know an arrest would downgrade our investigation. If Julie's innocent, the real killer will have more time to cover his tracks."

"Not to mention the price Julie would pay in terms of mental anguish," I huffed. "Is there really enough evidence to arrest her?"

"Not until the phalloidin tag tells its story. Then, maybe. It depends how Julie answers questions about her lover. She needs to walk me through every move since she first hung up her lab coat at Jolbiogen. Her coworkers and lab director vouch for her. While I think she's a scapegoat, I can't afford to be wrong. I have to turn her life inside out and shake."

"Well, when you're through browbeating the young lady, I have a lead you can follow." I told Weaver about the Glaston safe room.

"I'll ask Eric how to get inside," she said. "If he pleads ignorance, I'll hunt down the architect. Meanwhile I'll keep the house off limits to everybody except investigators."

"Do me a favor and make sure that includes Hamilton. The man has an axe to grind."

I chewed my lip and wondered why I felt compelled to keep my trap shut about the lie Darlene and Duncan told about not being friendly before Spirit Lake.

Was I a total idiot? Friendship arm-wrestled my common sense and won. I wouldn't fuel the fires of suspicion until I gave my friend a chance to explain. Stubbornly, I clung to the hope Darlene could provide a reasonable account, and I'd be able to laugh off last night's wild speculation about a nefarious plot starring devious, greedy lovers.

"Has General Irvine made any progress on the murder of those farm workers?"

"No. The people who own the farms don't recall seeing any strangers around before the folks got sick. The general's coordinating with Homeland Security. We have the government's whole alphabet soup involved now."

❖

Entering May's condo, I almost collided with Anna as she performed her vacuum aerobics. Engrossed in sucking dirt from the plush wall-to-wall carpet, the woman jumped and screeched like a banshee.

"Oh, my," she gasped and powered down the upright Hoover. "You 'bout gave me a heart attack."

Rake-like vacuum tracks on the carpet and a thin sheen of sweat above Anna's lip said she'd reached the climax stage of her cleaning routine. Like a veteran stock car, Anna's chassis was unimpressive and pockmarked with dings, but it hid one heck of a souped-up engine. Solid, reliable, and fast as the wind. Potential clients begged to earn a spot on her two-year waiting list.

As the vacuum's whiney song faded, my aunt reclaimed her living room roost.

"Oh, Marley. Didn't hear you come in, but how could I over that racket? Just wait till Anna tells you the scoop on the Olsens."

Despite an insincere—"Tell her, Anna"—my aunt never gave her housekeeper a chance to open her mouth. "Kyle's mother is back in town and staying with him!" May blurted.

I shrugged. "Not exactly shocking news. Kyle just lost his father. Why wouldn't his mother visit?"

My nonchalant reaction clearly disappointed May.

"You forget." She clucked. "Nancy was wife number one. The bad egg. Jake caught her cheating when Kyle was a toddler. When he confronted her, she split and abandoned Kyle. Didn't want visitation rights. Imagine she's been stewing in her own juices ever since. If she'd kept her panties on, she'd be loaded. Instead she doesn't have a pot to piss in."

"You suggesting that Nancy materialized to grab a little cash? Possible. Then again maybe the woman's changed. It's been what, forty years since she was unfaithful? Maybe she returned to ask Kyle's forgiveness. Saw Jake's death as an opportunity to reenter her son's life."

May rolled her eyes. "Boy, have I got a bridge to sell you."

"I know nothing about motives," Anna chimed in. "I just clean Kyle's house every Tuesday. Usually not a soul's around. Easy money, though it's creepy. Olivia, Kyle's wife, knows I don't work on the Sabbath, but she called and asked me to come Sunday. Wanted her house spiffed up ahead of Jake's funeral."

Waiting for Anna to sidewind into her story, I gave Kyle's reconciliation with his long-lost mother more thought. The more I considered it, the odder a reunion seemed. Kyle didn't strike me as emotionally needy or forgiving. There had to be something in it for Kyle—something beyond a warm, fuzzy feeling. I voiced my opinion.

Anna vigorously nodded agreement. "I've never seen Kyle so much as give his wife a peck on the cheek. Yet there he was scurrying around his mum like a doting dachshund. Bizarre. Looks like Nancy is putting down roots, too. She's cozied up in a guestroom with all her bags unpacked. What with Eric barricaded in a room down the hall, the Olsen house is filling up fast."

"How's Eric doing? Can't say I'm enamored of the young man, but I'd have to be awfully hard-hearted not to feel sorry for him, losing his mom and granddad in the space of two days. He has to be hurting and scared."

Anna shrugged. "Who knows? I never saw him. Olivia told me to skip cleaning his room. But I saw enough of Nancy and Miss Olivia to know there's no love lost between them. They acted like stray cats pissing to mark territory. 'Course I always thought Kyle treated Olivia more like mother than wife. A little friction between those females could produce one beaut of a blaze."

"What's Nancy look like?" May emerged from the conversational sidelines with an inquisitor's focus. "The woman must be late sixties, maybe seventy. Bet she's no seductress now."

"Remember, Lilith, Frazier's icy wife on 'Cheers'?" Anna

asked. "Nancy could be her mum. Hair dyed coal black and pulled tight in a bun, eyebrows tweezed to a razor's edge, almost albino skin. Looks like she's done herself a favor there. Whatever she's been up to, she hasn't done it in the sun, so her face isn't a wrinkled prune like mine."

"Did Nancy seem pleasant?" I wanted to get a fix on the being inhabiting the wrinkle-free, late sixties' wrapper.

"How should I know?" Anna grumped. "Most clients treat me like family. Not the Olsens. I'm not talking about old Jake, just the junior Olsens and Glastons. Viewed me as a servant, plain and simple. Invisible. Nancy and Kyle talked a foot away from me, and he never so much as introduced me."

"You're sure it was Nancy?" May piped up.

"Yeah, Kyle introduced her to Reverend Schmidt, when he paid a sympathy call. Came to console Eric. Real Christian, seeing as how Kyle's and Gina's families never once warmed a church pew in Spirit Lake. Kyle told the reverend Eric was sedated, not up to any visitors."

"Anna, you're a fount of information." May beamed with proprietary pride.

"I have an unrelated question about the Glaston house," I interrupted. "You've spent lots of time inside, Anna. Ever notice anything odd about the rooms or layout?"

"Odd how?" She arched her eyebrows. "It's odd to me when someone pays a million bucks for a mansion and visits once in a blue moon."

"Never mind." I shrugged. Didn't want to give the housekeeper—or my aunt—too many clues. With their well-honed powers of deduction, I feared one of them would figure out my inquiry had to do with a hidden chamber. "I met an architect who mentioned that house had a few design eccentricities, that's all."

May's sharp look radiated skepticism, but she didn't dispute my claim.

Anna chuckled. "The Glastons put in an elevator a few years back. Mighty strange in a two-story house. As my mother liked to say, 'Just cause you've got a hole in your arse, don't make you a cripple.' Walking up a flight of stairs puts a little apple in your cheeks. That addition ate up a lot of space. One second-floor bedroom shrank to the size of a postage-stamp. Guess they needed room for all the mechanical what's-a-whozits to run the lift."

Bingo. Sounded as if the Glastons could take their elevator to a very private space. I'd relay that tidbit to Weaver.

Anna glanced at her watch. "Have to run." The housekeeper gave my aunt a parting hug. "Now remember, May, I'm giving you a free cleaning the week you turn eighty. My birthday gift. We'll have this place spic-and-span for your well-wishers."

Anna bussed May's cheek, while my aunt pressed folded bills into her housekeeper's hand.

"You girls behave now," Anna called as she left.

Once the door closed, May remembered I'd departed with an FBI agent, been AWOL for over two hours, and had not reported my conversation. "Now, let's hear why the FBI wants to chat up my niece." May claimed her easy chair and expected me to issue a full report.

"Just a background check," I fibbed. "The FBI is talking with everyone and anyone who happens to be friendly with the Olsens."

May didn't believe me. I could tell. However, even Midwest matriarchs understand there are some restrictions on their need to know.

May regarded the ringing phone with dread. Phone calls of late had not delivered cheery tidings. On the third ring, she snatched up her cordless, answering with what I recognized as forced jollity. "Carr Residence."

A pause, followed by a genuine smile. "Well, of course, you want to see the house again. No one in their right mind is going to pay three-quarters of a million without a little tire kicking. Yes, yes, I'm sure there's room for haggling. The sellers are motivated. Eager to move south. Want to be nearer the grandkids. Un-huh. Un-huh."

Pause.

"Well, I can't tell you what to offer, but they won't let you steal their home either. They're sitting on a true Okoboji gem. What with the way property values are skyrocketing in Pocahontas Point, I'll bet someone snatches this honey up before week's end." In full schmooze press, May started reeling in the live one on her line. She ended the call and chuckled. "Looks like you're on your own for a bit."

She kept talking as she walked toward her bedroom, expecting me to follow in her wake. "I'm meeting a couple from Minneapolis. They're smitten. What do you plan to do today?" She frowned. "I supposed you'll make your daily pilgrimage to the Olsens? Oh, incidentally, Anna told me there's a sale at Evans. You know the store on main. You really ought to buy a nice dress for Jake's visitation."

My aunt's version of a subtle hint.

"Okay, I'll buy a new dress."

I sighed as I leaned against the doorframe. Unless an unrelated male invaded her territory, May never closed the door or gave a nod to modesty—hers, mine or anyone else's. Maybe she feared she'd forget what was on her mind if she waited politely for guests to vacate a shower or exit a bedroom before she spoke her piece. More likely, Nurse May had seen enough bare hineys that clothing seemed optional when she was in conversation mode.

May perched precariously on the edge of her high four-poster bed, with only nylon panties and a bra anchored in place. She rolled up knee-highs as we talked. For all the world, she looked like a pudgy soccer player, standing arms akimbo before a stuffed closet, trying to settle on a lucky color for today's pants suit.

Since turning seventy, May wore pants everywhere except church and funeral parlors. My mother, who never wore slacks prior to my teen years, curtailed her skirt wear about the same time. That's when the two women went on a trouser-buying binge. Mom bought slacks of any color so long as they were navy. Aunt May's selection could shame a peacock.

"Say, pick me up a bra at Evans, will you?" May asked. "You

know the Playtex 24-hour one I like with the wide straps."

"What size, May?"

"I'm thinking a 36 long." May laughed at my look. "I'll settle for a 36 C though."

I laughed appreciatively. "Believe me, there's no way I'll ask your panty size. Hey, why don't I invite Eunice and Ross for dinner tonight? We've got all the ingredients to make chicken divan. I'll whip up the casserole and set the oven to turn on at five if neither of us is home."

"Oh, I'll be back. Either I'll have a sales contract buttoned up by three, or I've landed another wishy-washy buyer who's afraid to pull his wallet out of his pants."

"Good luck," I said. "I'm off to Evans. See you later."

"Thanks, kid," May called as I waved good-bye.

❧

Downtown Spirit Lake is a five-minute hike from May's condo. Though clothes boutiques had sprouted like mushrooms along the network of highways connecting Okoboji region lakes, Evans Department Store clung to life in a compact downtown that featured a vintage movie theater, bakery, drugstore, bank, the county courthouse, and a smattering of the inevitable law offices. Was Duncan's office downtown?

Inside, Evans looked much as it had when I was a girl, except now the dummies were decked out in clothes designed to appeal to residents climbing the upper peaks of the fifty divide.

"That's very becoming, Mrs. Olsen." The saleswoman's flattery floated out from behind a rack of clothes. I hurried to see the recipient of the compliment.

An anorexic mouse preened before a mirror, smoothing the black sheath's bust-line tucks against molehill bosoms. The prospective buyer's hair was the distressed brown of a molting squirrel and featured the same bristly texture. Her eyes blinked rapidly behind expensive, but unflattering, designer frames. The avant-garde glasses made the woman's small eyes seem to recede into her head, like objects seen through the wrong end of a telescope.

Had to be Olivia Olsen, Kyle's beanpole wife. From what I'd heard, she'd be loathe to set foot in a Spirit Lake store that catered to commoners. Must be desperate to find black duds for the gauntlet of funerals. Conservative black outfits aren't easy to locate in a summer resort and, what with the need to bury three in-laws, Olivia had plenty of wearing opportunities.

The saleswoman was Faith Iverson, Eunice's antiquing Questers friend. Faith smiled when she recognized me. "Oh, hi Marley, I'll be right with you."

The greeting snapped Olivia to attention. Kyle's better half gave me the same horrified look she'd give a cockroach audacious enough to scamper across her polished floor. With my anonymity shot, I thought, "what the hell," introduced myself and offered condolences.

"Thank you," Olivia muttered. She whipped her head away so quickly I thought her twig-like neck might snap. Not eager to banter about weather or the odd family murder, are we? I wasn't about to let my treed quarry escape.

"I hear you're looking after your nephew. How is Eric?"

"As well as can be expected," she snapped, "considering he just lost his mother, grandfather and stepfather, and some idiot attacked him with a stun gun."

Touché. We both knew the identity of the aforementioned idiot.

"I understand you have more company," I purred. "How nice that Kyle's mother could join you."

Olivia recoiled as if I'd doused her with ice water. In fact, she let out a "yip" before covering her faux pas with a snippy "yes." The physical response communicated real data—Nancy's presence was a personal affront she'd hoped to keep secret. Before I could fire another round of verbal artillery, Olivia bolted for the safety of the dressing room.

I glanced over at the flummoxed saleslady, sorry to have nixed a commissioned sale for the hardworking bystander. Nonetheless, I congratulated myself on my bravado.

I'd confirmed Anna's observations: One, Nancy had moved in with Kyle. Two, Kyle's wife wasn't happy. Three, Eric remained in residence with the Olsens. And, four—well, that point really needed no confirmation—I would not win a popularity contest with that branch of the Olsen clan.

Olivia's fifty-yard dash from the dressing room to Spirit Lake's main street impressed me. Figuring Miss Olivia might press assault charges if I tried to speak to her again, I pretended interest in a ragtag group of half-priced garments.

To make up for Faith' lost commission, I bought a staid navy suit and a gray print skirt and blouse that I could pair with the black jacket always tucked in my suitcase. Of course, I also purchased May's bra, 36 long.

Thirteen

Fresh from my downtown adventures, I rewarded myself with a little sin—twin chocolate cookies with icing smooshed in between—and iced tea, invited Ross and Eunice to dinner, and switched on the radio for company while I cooked. With the volume jacked up for May, the blaring newscast almost bowled me over.

This just in—a new development in Spirit Lake's billionaire murder spree. Sources close to the investigation say Jake Olsen, former CEO of Jolbiogen, his daughter and son-in-law may have been killed because they discovered the identity of a master thief stealing biological research commissioned by the military.

A week before Olsen's death, the Department of Defense called in the FBI to help investigate the theft of research materials from Jolbiogen—research that could be used by terrorists to launch a targeted biological attack. Dr. Robert Glaston, Jake Olsen's son-in-law, oversaw the lab conducting the military research.

Dr. Glaston and his wife were killed within forty-eight hours of Jolbiogen's billionaire founder. They were murdered in the Glastons' second home in the family's secluded compound on West Okoboji. Exotic toxins were used to poison the victims.

The FBI is questioning Olsen's stepdaughter, Julie Nauer, a Jolbiogen employee, about the theft and subsequent murders. Olsen married the researcher's mother, Darlene Nauer, less than a week before he was killed.

We'll bring you more breaking news as this story continues to unfold.

My heart pounded. I slammed my fist onto the kitchen counter with enough force to rattle May's spice set. I dialed Darlene's cell. Busy signal. Crap.

May's phone rang. I picked up. "You heard?" Darlene snapped. Then she let loose with a string of curses, hurling them at everyone she could think of—local reporters, Quentin Hamilton, Thrasos International, the FBI, and Sheriff Delaney. I wondered how she could go so long without taking in air.

When she sucked in a breath, I jumped in. "Where are you? What's happening now?"

"I'm holed up in my bedroom, waiting for two FBI agents to finish interrogating Julie. They wouldn't let me stay with her." Darlene sobbed. "Those morons can't believe Julie would help bioterrorists. Why would she? She loves this country—and her job. You wouldn't believe how often she's told me so. And we're certainly not desperate for money. Even before Jake came along, we were doing okay. Please come over. I need to vent in person."

Darlene's tirade stepped up my pulse rate one more notch. "Give me an hour."

By the time a taxi dropped me at the Olsens, my emotions had seesawed into a queasy equilibrium. I was cool and collected—well, collected anyway. I understood Darlene's distress over Julie and her desperate need for a friend. My shoulder was available. But I also promised myself to ask—straight out—why Darlene had lied about her relationship with Duncan. I damn sure felt entitled to an explanation.

Harvey was ushering Reverend Schmidt out when I arrived. As I exchanged "nice to see you" pleasantries with the pastor, I wondered if he'd trot across the lawn to the junior Olsen residence for his next sympathy call. If so, Olivia and Eric would surely give him an earful about my devilish proclivities.

Julie sat alone in the great room. My tongue glued itself to the roof of my mouth. I had no idea what to say.

"Marley, come on in. Mom will be down in a minute. She's on the phone with Larsson's Funeral Home. Or maybe you don't want to be left alone in a room with an alleged serial killer. Hell,

I'm right up there with Lizzie Borden, except I've found tidier ways to kill. That's why I spent four years in grad school—so I wouldn't get blood on my axe."

Her scrunched up face and tight fists telegraphed her battle to fight tears.

"I'm sure the FBI will try to put a stop to such groundless speculation."

Julie slumped, head in her hands. "Don't count on it. I'm sure the next newscast will tell everyone how I'm a sexual degenerate who sleeps with old men. I'm capable of anything. Even helping terrorists kill thousands of people without firing a shot." Her chest heaved. "I'm a real virtuoso—a one-woman crime wave."

"You're obviously upset. Do you want me to leave?"

"No, no. It's nice to see someone willing to look me in the eye. The poor reverend tried but couldn't quite hang in there. You could see the questions in his mind: Did she really kill her stepfather? Am I talking to a monster?"

I sat next to her on the couch, put my arm around her shoulder. "Well, you're here and not in custody. That wouldn't be the case if there were evidence to back up the media innuendoes."

Julie's shoulder shook. A sob escaped before she straightened. "Actually, there is incriminating evidence—just not enough to cart me away in handcuffs. At the rate someone's manufacturing stuff to frame me, I'll hang in no time. Hey, they almost have *me* convinced I'm guilty."

With her fist extended, Julie freed one finger each time she ticked off a potential nail in her coffin. The young woman began by admitting a brief graduate school affair with Dr. Derek Valberg, a fifty-two-year-old professor. "Dad had just died. I went a little crazy. He was married, with a daughter older than me. Not my proudest moment. I bailed out as soon as I learned how far he leaned to the left."

Julie was adamant she'd had no contact with Valberg since he'd left Iowa State University and signed on as a consultant with some European research outfit. "The emails on my PC. I can't explain them. I never sent them. Whoever wrote them knew enough about me to make them sound convincing. How did they do that? How could they access my hard drive? There's even a UPS record showing I shipped a package to Gertrude Valberg—Derek's daughter, who lives in LA."

"Did the FBI talk with the professor and his daughter?"

"Yes, Derek supports my no-email claim, and his daughter insists no package was delivered. Of course, that's what the FBI would expect them to say—guilty or innocent. My bet is the Feds may even find traces of the fabricated correspondence on Derek's computer, once they jump through all the international hoops to gain access."

"You really believe this is an international conspiracy?" I tried to keep skepticism out of my tone.

"That's exactly what I believe," she snapped. "And they're very, very good. Jolbiogen has tested the phalloidin used to kill Gina. It came from my research stash. And the FBI dug up a pair of phalloidin-dusted gloves with my fingerprints inside buried beside the old cottage."

She shuddered. "Someone's gone to a lot of trouble to set me up. My guess is they took a pair of gloves I'd discarded at Jolbiogen and buried them there. The UPS package listing me as 'Sender' was shipped two weeks ago, well before Jake's murder."

My lord. Julie was in a shitload of trouble. "Who do you think is behind this? And why? Do you have any ideas?"

"If Dr. Glaston weren't one of my alleged victims, his name would zoom to the top of my list. He hated Mom and me. Didn't try to disguise it. Plus he regularly visited my lab. But I'm relatively sure Glaston didn't kill his father-in-law and wife just so he could dose himself into oblivion and lay the blame on me."

"No other candidates?" I asked.

Julie sprang up from her seat and paced. "Once I rule him out, I have no clue. It's someone clever. Someone who has it in for me—or Mom. But I can't think of a single enemy at Jolbiogen. Maybe I'm just an unlucky patsy with all the right qualifications."

"What about Kyle or Eric? No love lost for your mom and they both work at Jolbiogen, right?"

She walked to the window, pressed a palm against her glass cage. "Kyle and Eric despise Mom and me. So, yes, they're possibles. Eric briefly worked as a Jolbiogen lab tech, but I doubt his old badge would let him in the building. Kyle never descends from his ivory tower to see what the peons are up to. I doubt he could find my lab, let alone know how to lay his hands on those toxins."

An alternate theory occurred to me. "Perhaps the FBI has it half right. Maybe the thief works in your lab, and Jake figured out his identity. After the thief killed Jake, Dr. Glaston tumbled onto him so he had to kill again. If that's what happened, framing you might not be personal—maybe you are just a convenient pawn."

Julie turned back from the window. "But the set up began *before* Jake was killed. It wasn't an afterthought. Besides, how did this evil colleague make his way onto the estate—or know where to go and what to do once he got here?" She crossed to the couch and collapsed. "I don't think anyone from our lab—except yours truly—has ever driven through the Olsen gates. The FBI is checking alibis for every person with lab access, but so far only my alibi sucks. I was here for the Glaston murders, and Mom was present when Jake died."

"I don't think I like where this conversation is headed."

Julie and I both jumped at the sound of Darlene's voice. "Sounds like we're back to the 'mother and daughter had opportunity and motive' nonsense Quentin Hamilton's pushing. That lead FBI agent—Sherry Weaver—admitted he's the one pointing a finger our way." Darlene crossed the great room and took a chair across from us. "I'd like to give him the finger and then some. The creep's been pocketing our money to protect us, and simultaneously knifing us in the back. He's getting his walking papers today."

Despite newly added strain, Darlene looked spiffier. Perhaps she had one good night's sleep between yesterday's five a.m. body bag count and today's finger-pointing newscast. Wearing hip-hugging peach Capri pants—pedal pushers to anyone my age—and a short matching top, the widow looked wired, not tired. Each gesture that raised her top showed off her trim, evenly tanned midriff. Darlene's short cap of platinum hair glistened in the afternoon sun.

Julie stood. "I'm exhausted. Think I'll lie down for a while." Lethargy seemed to have sapped the young woman's energy. Her retreat up the winding staircase almost looked like a slow-mo replay.

Julie's need for solitude was understandable. While family bonds give us the strength to pull through periods of grief and peril, constant togetherness stifles.

Who doesn't need a personal timeout to preserve sanity?

Alone, I expected Darlene to hash over the murder scenarios or hurl more scatological insults at her enemies. She surprised me with an immediate plea to help her review plans for Jake's visitation and memorial. A phone call from Larsson's Funeral Home had left her uneasy.

"They're expecting hundreds of people. I have so many balls in the air; I know they'll crash on my head any minute. Just talk me through the funeral arrangements. Tell me if I've overlooked anything."

I chewed my lip. Nope, couldn't do it. I was incapable of acting as Darlene's sounding board while this big black cloud hovered over our friendship. There was no good way to bring it up, and delay wouldn't help. I needed to admit my prying and ask for an explanation.

"Let's go outside. I'd like a breath of fresh air." For this conversation, I didn't want to risk eavesdroppers—even Harvey, a presumed pillar of discretion.

Darlene tilted her face to the afternoon sun as it peeked from behind scudding white clouds. "This feels wonderful; I've been cooped up too long."

The breeze was light, its scent tangy. We sank into cushy poolside seats on side-by-side chaises. Apparently, the absence of suitable sound-bite activity coupled with high boat-rental fees had prompted the news hounds to sniff for leads on terra firma. The departure of the floating news armada returned the aquamarine lake to gentle tranquility.

"Darlene, I don't know where to start, but there's something I have to ask."

"Well, damn, Marley, spit it out. You needn't stand on ceremony with me. You look like you're going to tell me someone else died. For once, I'm pretty sure everyone's accounted for."

"It's about Duncan—"

"You're lovers, right?" She laughed at my startled expression. "Hell, I didn't need a crystal ball to predict that. Not with the smoldering looks between you two. I saw the chemistry, just couldn't forecast the reaction time."

Darlene's grin looked genuine. "You're okay with that?"

"Why shouldn't I be? You're single. So is Duncan. I like both of you. Why wouldn't I be happy?"

I licked my lips and limped on. "Both you and Duncan misled me. At his house last night I saw photos of his daughter Kelly and your Julie—photos that spanned a decade. They were best friends for years. You and Duncan had to be more than nodding acquaintances in Ames."

"Did you ask Duncan to explain?"

"No, I just mumbled my excuses and ran."

She sighed. "You're right, we have some history but not the kind you're picturing. The four of us—Mike and me, Duncan and Sheila—were friends. Since our girls went everywhere together, we saw each other regularly."

Darlene stared at her hands and twisted her wedding ring back and forth. "When Mike died, police came to my bakery to deliver the news. Mike had the day off, told me he'd be golfing. When the cops said Sheila was a passenger, I was confused. What were the two of them doing out in the country on his golf day? I thought maybe one of the girls had a problem and they took a drive to discuss it."

"But that wasn't what happened?" I prodded.

"No." Tears leaked from my friend's emerald eyes. "That car accident killed Mike and my illusions. When I cleaned out his locker at the firehouse, I found love letters and hotel receipts. I still don't know why Mike was stinking drunk when he cracked up the car. Worse, I don't know why he stopped loving me."

Darlene gave into full-scale, body-racking sobs. I felt miserable reviving this old torment when she had so many fresh ones. Yet I needed to finish, to cauterize my suspicions. "So why did you lie? If you and Duncan were innocent bystanders, why not admit you knew each other in Ames?"

She straightened, swiped at the tears on her cheeks. "We sort of backed into it. I didn't want Julie's final memory of her dad to be as a cheater, so I asked Duncan to forego mentioning Sheila's affair in his divorce. He agreed.

"The girls think Mike and Sheila got together to plan a surprise birthday party for them—their birthdays are five days apart. Sheila realized it was in her best interests to play along."

I frowned. Darlene's story still didn't explain the need to prevaricate. "Sorry, but I still don't see any reason for you to lie about your relationship."

"Duncan and I became quite close just not in a romantic way. When I moved to Spirit Lake, I encouraged him to move, too. He felt strait-jacketed in Ames. Neither of us wanted to talk about our past. We figured if we said we were old friends, people would pump me for information about his ex and his divorce. And they'd ask him about my husband's car accident. You know how it is in a small town. It just seemed easier to pretend ignorance.

"There was never, ever anything romantic between us," she finished, "though we talked a lot our first years here. We were hurt and lonely. Professing ignorance of each other's pasts didn't hurt anyone. Our girls thought we were daft, but they shrugged it off. Neither lived in Spirit Lake. They didn't care."

Curiosity prompted my next question—one that was none of my business. "Did Jake know you and Duncan were close?"

Darlene shook her head. "No. When Jake first introduced us, I feigned surprise at meeting an Ames transplant. Never had the nerve to backtrack. I was afraid I'd look like a deceitful jerk. I never told Jake about Mike's betrayal either. Duncan's the only one who knows the whole story." Darlene's eyes met mine, her look questioning. "Are we okay? Do you understand how I got sucked in?"

I nodded. "I guess."

In my opinion, she'd owed Jake the truth. I couldn't see how an initial white lie would have tarnished her image in Jake's eyes. And it seemed downright wrong for her to encourage her husband to hire Duncan as his attorney under the circumstances. However, I'd made enough mistakes to know I wasn't qualified to second-guess someone else's conscience.

Darlene reached over and took my hand. "We're still friends then?"

"Yes." I squeezed her hand. "We're still friends."

A thought struck me from out of the blue. Perhaps Jake wasn't ignorant of his wife's relationship with Duncan. If Thrasos did extensive background checks on new hires, wouldn't the firm have dug into the background of his potential mate? And his new attorney?

"Darlene, you need to tell the FBI what you've told me. Casually mention you've known Duncan for years. I'd bet anything Quentin Hamilton had his minions dig into your past before your marriage. If I'm right, he'll spoon-feed the info to someone as soon as there's some way he can make it look damning. The man has a hard-on about incriminating you and your daughter."

Darlene's eyes widened. "Jake would never have asked Thrasos to investigate me."

"Maybe not. But Kyle and Hamilton are buddies, right? Kyle isn't a pauper. He could have paid for the background check, or asked Hamilton to bury his spying in Jolbiogen's corporate bill."

"Goddamn. I hate the idea of that arrogant jerk dissecting me like an insect," she said. "Thrasos International will be off this estate by the end of the day."

"Don't forget about damage control with the FBI," I urged.

"I won't." Darlene stood. "Let's go back in the house. I still need help with the funeral arrangements."

Fourteen

In the sunroom, Darlene waved me to a seat before walking over to a large paisley-covered ottoman. Raising the cushion that served as its lid, she extracted a half-finished knitting project and a new skein of yarn.

"I'm making this for cousin Tina's first grandchild." She held up the start of a baby afghan. "Mind if I knit while we talk? It relaxes me. If I don't do something to keep my hands busy, I'm liable to start smoking again—and it's been twenty years since I quit."

The afghan captured a rainbow of hues. "It's beautiful. Wish I had the patience."

"Did you see Jake's obituary in the morning paper?" Darlene asked.

"Yes. Very nice. But I was a bit surprised to see you're holding the Tuesday visitation at Larsson's Funeral Home. Weren't you planning to have it here?"

"The sheriff and FBI vetoed that. Security reasons." Her knitting needles clicked. "Frisking anyone kind enough to pay a sympathy call seemed a little tacky. Guess the authorities figure there's still a slim chance Julie and I might be victims rather than killers. Delaney doesn't want to be responsible if more people die."

Made sense. I nodded. "Good decision. Larsson's is big and set up to handle a crowd."

"Yep, it's also neutral territory. We can stake out one corner, and Kyle, Olivia and Eric can take the opposite one. That'll leave a demilitarized zone between us for noncombatants."

Darlene's industrious fingers flew.

"Still might be a good idea to pat down Jake's relatives for weapons," I said. "I had a run-in with Olivia today. What a donnybrook. Seems she shares Kyle's rather dim view of you and your friends—me in particular."

Darlene glanced up from her knitting. "Where on earth did you see Olivia? She normally avoids any place she might encounter—how shall I put it?—riffraff like you."

Figuring my tale of department store intrigue would cheer Darlene, I recounted how I'd stalked Olivia after I heard her voice. My friend shared my merriment right up to the moment I described Olivia's reaction to my dig about Kyle's mother being in residence.

"What did you say?" Darlene dropped her knitting and clamped onto my arm, her grip a vice. "Nancy is living with Kyle?"

"Yes." I'd assumed Darlene knew. Obviously I was wrong. "When Anna Huiskamp cleaned May's house today, she mentioned that Nancy had moved in with Olivia and Kyle."

"Dammit! Jake detested that gold-digger. Said the woman lacked any maternal instinct or sense of decency. He kept little Kyle because he didn't think any child should be raised by an uncaring slut. Jake loved the boy, even though he knew Kyle wasn't his."

Darlene blushed scarlet and squeezed my arm with a wrestler's fervor. "Marley," she pleaded. "Promise you'll never repeat that. Jake wanted that secret buried with him. He raised Kyle, loved him as a son. He never wanted Kyle to learn he wasn't his flesh-and-blood. Jake figured Nancy would never tell the boy differently."

"Of course I won't tell."

My mind reeled. Perhaps a scorecard would help me keep track of all the secrets tumbling around in my brain.

Darlene sighed, picked up her yarn and searched for a loose starter strand to unravel the new skein. "How odd." She tugged on a slip of tightly folded white paper stuffed into the yarn. Her eyebrows shot upward. "It's Jake's handwriting."

A series of indecipherable emotions flickered across her face as she scanned the note. "What the hell? Here, read it." She thrust the paper with its big, loopy handwriting toward me.

Dear Darlene – If you're reading this, our marriage was too damn short. I didn't want to involve you. Unfortunately, there's no one else I can count on. I need you to hand deliver a package to Sherry Weaver—she's an FBI agent—one you can trust. Don't tell anyone about this note until you have the package. And don't try to retrieve it if you think you might be followed. Lord help me, I don't want to put you at risk.

The location of the package is our final Spirit Lake treasure hunt: Though far from the San Andreas fault, the floors rattle and roll. At the top, cars whiz past your head yet spell no danger.

I tucked the parcel in a gutter—fitting. Please be careful.

Have a wonderful life, my love. Jake

I couldn't freakin' believe it. Ye gods. Another damn riddle? Two months earlier, a psychotic killer forced me to help decipher a brainteaser to retrieve his missing property. Eyes closed, I shook my head. I wanted no part of another riddle chase.

"Why the hell didn't Jake just tell you where to find the damn package?"

My outburst sounded like a rebuke. The idea of a riddle tied to more murders angered me. I struggled to tone down my ire. The game wasn't Darlene's idea. "Why didn't Jake hand the evidence over to the FBI when he hid the package? Maybe then he'd still be alive."

"Damned if I know." Darlene raked a hand through her short hair. "Weaver told me Jake called her the day before he died. Hinted he'd tell her everything after our party. He must have had his reasons. As far as the riddle goes, Jake must have decided it would be tough for anyone else to decipher his note. An insurance policy if someone found the note before I did."

I stood, expecting Darlene to follow suit. "You and Julie finally caught a break. This note could lead the FBI right to Jake's killer. You're going to call Weaver, right?"

My friend picked her knitting back up. "I don't plan to tell a soul."

Her vehement tone shocked me.

"One, I haven't the foggiest where Jake stashed the damn package. Two, I'm not about to call the FBI until I see what's inside. Someone's trying to frame Julie and me. For all I know, the FBI's in bed with them. They're certainly cozy with Hamilton."

"Don't be crazy—"

"Crazy! Who's to say the real killer hasn't beat me to Jake's hiding place? Maybe he's swapped Jake's evidence for manufactured crap that makes Julie or me look even more guilty. I'll be damned if I'll give the FBI more reasons to waltz us off to jail."

I held my hands up, palms out. "Whoa. Don't let paranoia overwhelm common sense. Granted someone is trying to distract the FBI, but even Jake trusted Weaver."

"I'll call her—eventually." Darlene's eyes met mine. "But not until I know what's what—until I see what's inside that package with my own eyes."

How to reason with her? "What if you never figure out Jake's hiding place?"

"Oh, it'll come to me," Darlene muttered. "It's somewhere we went together. Jake wouldn't hand me a puzzle I couldn't solve. Not when it's so important. The clue makes it sound as if the building's set close to a roadway—cars whiz by. My first thought was an overpass. Too bad Spirit Lake doesn't have one."

"Hey, there's one collection of buildings that almost fits—the shops near the Emporium. They sit on a sloped side street. The rooflines of the shops are almost level with the road behind them."

Darlene's puzzled look prompted me to press on.

"We used to stop at a coffee house near Arnolds Park. You know, our generation's version of a karaoke hangout."

"Yeah, I'm with you." A fleeting smile crossed her face. "But that's not Jake's hiding place. We played this game often enough to learn each other's idiosyncrasies. He's pointing me toward a landmark, not a group of buildings. It'll come. I just hope it's soon."

I bit my lip, thinking. "Well, if it's an historic building Ross can help. Is it okay to give him a clue? He and Eunice are coming to Aunt May's for dinner tonight."

Darlene nodded. "Ross knows Spirit Lake better than anyone and he knew Jake. But how could you get his take without telling him about the note. Don't forget, Jake's dead—and so are the Glastons. I don't want someone else winding up with toe tags because of me."

I wholeheartedly agreed.

"I'll tell Ross about the riddle game you played with Jake and mention you found a clue he'd saved for your next outing. If Ross unravels the riddle, we can decide what comes next."

On the drive home, I considered how much Jake had trusted Darlene. You didn't confide a lifelong secret like Kyle's bastard paternity on a whim. Nor did you reach out from the grave with clues about a murderer unless you had absolute faith in the recipient.

Both acts increased my confidence. I'd done the right thing asking for an explanation about her relationship with Duncan. She'd renewed my trust in our friendship.

As I opened Aunt May's front door, a cloud of inviting aromas enveloped me. A foundation fragrance of chicken divan underpinned a mouth-watering perfume of apples and cinnamon. The homey smells went a long way toward restoring a sense of normalcy.

My aunt was nowhere in sight. "I'm back," I sang out.

May's white perm popped up from behind the kitchen counter. She'd been bent low, peering in the oven. The stove's heat painted her cheeks with blush, and she beamed like a cherubic grandmother—though she'd bop me if I said so.

"Look out, Marley, here I come," May exclaimed gleefully. "I'm nouveaux rich and plan to spread the wealth. My buyers accepted the offer. That's the fastest I ever made twenty grand. Oh, and Duncan called. He left a message earlier, then we chatted when he called a second time. He sounds real anxious to talk. Why don't you give him a buzz before Ross and Eunice arrive?"

Great. How was I going to explain my behavior to Duncan? No way would I bring up his ex-wife's affair with Darlene's husband. He'd tell me when and if he ever felt comfortable sharing that hurt. Of course he might feel entitled to an explanation for my manic behavior.

Duncan answered on the second ring. He sounded pleased to hear my voice. "I hoped we'd get a chance to talk today," he said. "Is everything okay? Or did I commit some unrealized faux pas? You sure left in a hurry."

"No faux pas on your part. My apologies. I'm out of dating practice and these murders make me uneasy. I just lost it. Apparently you handle stress better than this old retiree."

"Well, old-timer—" I could hear the smile in his voice. "I'm glad we're still friends, and I hope lovers. You know, lovemaking is supposed to reduce stress, not add to it."

"Hey, no complaints." I laughed. "Maybe I just need another adjustment. You know chiropractors often need multiple visits to work their wonders."

"Ah, now there's a thought. Should I read up on massage therapy? If I didn't have a fundraiser tonight, I'd promise a massage—a very deep one. How about scheduling a treatment for tomorrow? After we call at the funeral home, we'll both be ready for stiff drinks and—"

"Maybe you shouldn't finish that sentence on the phone." I laughed. "It sounds like we're on the same therapy page."

Duncan's good cheer lightened my mood. "See you tomorrow."

Ross and Eunice arrived just as I returned to the living room. Ross started talking before we finished the prerequisite round of hugs.

"Set the table. No lollygagging," May ordered. "I'm so hungry I could eat a horse."

"You may have to if Marley cooked," Ross joked.

Eunice and I responded with simultaneous noogies to my cousin's biceps.

He grinned. "Hey, don't hurt yourselves."

Our dinner conversation stayed lighthearted. First, May regaled us with how she'd sweet-talked her buyers into beefing up their contract offer, then persuaded her clients, the owners, into making an attractive counter in a single afternoon.

Next Ross entertained with an update on his latest research project. "'The Iowan' asked me to write a piece about the Iowa Great Lakes during our golden era—you know the late 1800s. So I got to rummaging around in our archives and found this incredible eyewitness account."

Ross pulled drugstore reading glasses from his shirt pocket to quote directly from a scrap of yellowed newsprint. "This fellow talks about 'empty champagne bottles being piled like cordwood' and an eighty-dollar-a-plate banquet. Remember, this is more than a century ago, I'll bet that would mean eight-thousand-a-plate today. The author says yacht owners hauled their boats in from around the world just to race here. And he claims there were 'fish so plentiful they were caught for sport and buried by the boatload.'"

"Good grief, Ross." Eunice rolled her eyes. "You're frantic with the antique boat show, I can't believe you're off on a new crusade. Can't you finish one project before you start the next? Does sleep fit anywhere in your schedule?"

"Sleep is for winter." My cousin grinned. "Have to make hay while the sun shines—and while I have the ear of my good buddies who own antique boats. I talked a doctor from Estherville into putting his boat on display for six months. He said he hoped his wife never found out he paid more to restore that boat than he did for her facelift, tummy tuck and boob-oplasty."

Eunice and I played appreciative audience for our two favorite hams. The laughter wasn't forced. Finally, a suitable lull over apple crisp allowed me to casually share Jake's riddle. I'd barely gotten it out, when Ross shook his head in mock sorrow. "Marley, Marley," he crooned. "How you disappoint me. The answer should have been a slam-dunk. Let's take a stroll down memory lane. You're nine. I'm ten. We're at Arnolds Park. We press our greasy noses against Mrs. Nelson's shop window long enough to hoodwink her into free samples of saltwater taffy. Now, we're off on a new adventure. Mirror, mirror on the wall…"

"…who's the fattest of them all?" I completed Ross's sentence triumphantly. "Of course. The Tipsy House. It fits perfectly. In one section, the floorboards are on roller-bars and you feel like you're crossing a suspended bridge mid-earthquake. Inside some mirrors make you look tall and skinny, while others make you look squashed and fat. After you wind your way up through all the crooked rooms and slanted floors, you come out on the roof. Those roof-level cars Jake mentioned are roller-coaster cars. They zoom right past on the ride's last curve. Thanks, Ross, you're a genius."

"Always nice to be recognized." Ross dipped his head in statesmanlike acceptance.

"But, isn't The Tipsy House closed?" I frowned at my sudden recollection. I'd seen the workers repairing it on my last stroll through Arnolds Park.

Ross nodded "Yeah. Jake must have planned this treasure hunt for July. The Tipsy House was supposed to reopen Memorial Day. But the carpenters ran into unexpected wood rot. The manager hopes the attraction will open for the Fourth of July holiday crowd. He asked me to brainstorm promotional ideas."

"Is it locked up or could I get inside?" I asked.

"Are you planning a little B-and-E just to reminisce? The Tipsy House wasn't even your favorite. You always dragged me to that House of Horror, where the stupid little train chugged around and skeletons and headless corpses popped out on every bend. For some reason, you loved to have the bejeebbers scared out of you."

"Not any more." I laughed. "It's a lot more fun to scare the bejeebbers out of others."

"Tell you what," Ross said. "I want to stop by the museum on my way home, and Eunice will be fussing at me the whole time to hurry so she can walk our girls before their little Sheltie bladders explode. How about we let Eunice motor straight home to walk the dogs, and you drive us to Arnolds Park? A new batch of antique boats came in today. They're temporarily parked in our shipping and receiving area, I want to do a little inventory. Should take me less than an hour. Then, if The Tipsy House is unlocked, we can go visit. Maybe you can help me come up with a humdinger of a reopening theme."

May stood to start clearing dishes. "Now don't the both of you go prancing around in the dark and pratfall on some rust-caked construction debris. I'm not in the business of stitching you two up any more."

"It's okay, Mom." Ross rubbed his hands together with glee. "Marley can bring her night-vision goggles, give 'em a real field test. Always wanted to see how those things work."

"I suckled an idjit," May grumped. "Eunice, your dogs have more sense than these nitwits."

I was fairly confident May had a point. However, I had no intention of lassoing Ross into a nighttime excursion that could be dangerous. On our way there, I'd keep my eyes peeled for a tail. Then, once Ross was engrossed in his pet project back of the museum, I'd sneak out and reconnoiter on my own. If he said it would take an hour, it probably meant two—he always lost track of time when he was in his element.

Should I call Darlene? No it was stupid to blab about my plan on an open phone line. As long as I could make sure Ross and I weren't followed, the dead of night really was the ideal time for me to take a gander with no one being the wiser.

That's one good thing about spur-of-the-moment decisions. They're impossible to predict. My paranoia retreated. No one had tailed me to Duncan's house. No one had followed his boat.

Soon I'd be able to tell Darlene whether or not Jake had actually hidden anything at The Tipsy House.

Fifteen

On the drive, I regularly checked the rearview mirror for headlights. At one point, when I thought a car followed us too long, I pulled off into a strip mall.

"What are you doing, Marley?" Ross asked. "Uh, this isn't the museum."

"Just had an itch I had to scratch." I fumbled behind my back and scoured my shoulder blade with my fingernails. Ross rolled his eyes.

The suspect car sped by, its radio blaring rap music. A tattooed arm hung out the open passenger-side window. Not a likely candidate as a stealth tail. I pulled back onto the road. No cars at all behind us.

Beyond the lighted entry, Arnolds Park lay in shadows. Until the tourist season jumps into full gear in mid-June, the rides and attractions close at eight p.m. The exodus transforms the space. An echoing emptiness supplants the laughter of children giving the darkened space the feel of a "Twilight Zone" episode where all the townspeople vanish while the heroine sleeps.

Ross waved at the guard on duty as we parked May's distinctive Buick in the greenish light pooled beneath a towering streetlamp. Since Arnolds Park clean-up crews don't report for duty until six a. m., one lonely security officer rules the night.

"Does he have a set patrol schedule?" My part-time work as a security guard piqued my curiosity.

"Doubt it," Ross answered. "Think his whereabouts are

controlled by coffee consumption and his need to pee. Not much action."

"Is he armed?"

Ross chuckled. "No. Our guards don't encounter many hardened criminals. Not much to steal. Primarily they battle graffiti artists and college kids plotting to steal signs for dorm rooms. What twenty-year-old doesn't covet a bedside poster that reads 'Thrill-A-Minute Roller Coaster Ride' or 'Get Your Hot Dogs Here'?"

I laughed. "Okay, Arnolds Park guards don't need SWAT training."

The skinny sentry ambled our way. A police baton and radio hung from a worn belt and the weight threatened to drag his droopy drawers below crack level. Good thing his job didn't call for the added gravity pull of a gun holster.

"Working late tonight, Captain Ross?" the elder-guard asked. I pegged his age at late sixties.

"You got that right, Jerry," Ross answered. "I want to fiddle with my boat displays while I have some quiet. No interruptions. You keeping a close eye on those dandies for me?"

"Sure am," Jerry answered. "You've got some real honeys. Wish I could afford one."

Ross nodded. "Me, too. This is my cousin Marley. Say, don't get spooked if you see activity at The Tipsy House later. Marley and I played there as kids. I'm going to give her a busman's tour of renovations and brainstorm some ideas for promotion."

"Fine by me. Just don't break your necks on my watch. The general manager would have my hide. Don't know as we're insured for nighttime mishaps. There are no lights, you know."

"We'll pack a flashlight and be careful," Ross answered. "Won't be in there long either."

I'd joined Ross on evening excursions before. A true night owl, his energy level peaked after midnight, and he enjoyed visiting when he could survey his museum kingdom unimpeded.

Figuring Ross would be occupied for at least an hour before

he'd want to go exploring, I decided I had time for a quick visit to the web before I snuck out. I commandeered one of the museum's computer terminals and scanned two archived stories: one on the Olsen murders, the second, a business retrospective on the Jolbiogen empire.

Two interesting tidbits emerged. One of those "rumor on the street" type columns speculated Jolbiogen's new president planned to elbow out Dr. Glaston to make room for his own protégé. Did that give Glaston incentive to steal?

And Kyle held a Master's Degree in chemistry. Since he was a marketing exec, I'd assumed a non-technical degree. His education meant he could find his way around a lab, even if he visited infrequently. Presumably, he could handle cyclogel and phalloidin, too.

I closed down the computer and looked to make sure Ross was still behind the museum. I grabbed the flashlight and tiptoed toward the door. I cast one more look back before I opened the door, ran smack into Ross, and yipped in surprise.

"A little on edge, are we?" Ross asked. "Guess you didn't expect me to come out the back and in the front. I was just checking some storage options if more boats come in."

My cousin noted the flashlight in my hand and, probably, the sheepish look on my face at being caught in sneak-out mode. "Okay, cousin, somebody's got some 'splaining to do," he added in his best Desi Arnaz impression. "What are you up to?"

Busted, I confessed.

"Why didn't you say something before?" Ross asked. "That explains the sudden itch that forced you to pull off the road. No one followed us, right?"

"No. I don't think we were followed," I answered.

"Then let's rock and roll, Cuz." His blue eyes danced with mischief. "You have a flashlight, let's get your night goggles."

"You sure you want to go? Aunt May will murder me if anything happens to you."

"I'm sure," Ross answered. "This is the perfect time to do a little reconnoitering and you shouldn't go in there alone. I know the place better than you. Get the danged goggles."

"You realize we can't use the flashlight and goggles at the same time? A flashlight would blind anyone wearing goggles."

"Duh. Of course, I know," my cousin replied with mock huffiness. "I may not have served in the Army, but I'm a brilliant student of military tactics."

Ross had lightened my mood and lessened my paranoia. Now our mission felt more like a lark than a black ops incursion.

I chuckled. "Yes, I'm aware you've poured over accounts of every flipping Civil War battle. But we're talking night-vision goggles, not a Blunderbuss."

"Pardon me." Ross harrumphed. "The Blunderbuss was popular in the Revolutionary War not the Civil War, Miss Smarty Pants."

"Okay, okay." I laughed. "Kiss my Blunderbuss. Let's get this sortie underway."

The Tipsy House, a narrow bell-tower-style building, sat half a football field from the museum. As we strolled toward our destination, night winds blew empty candy wrappers along the vacant concrete. The rustling litter suggested the scrabble of little rodent feet. I shivered.

The intentionally crooked door of the Tipsy House was tucked into the wall furthest from the road. Still street lamps spilled enough light into the recessed niche for us to see it wasn't truly boarded up. A lone two-by-six covered the gaping hole where a rotting doorjamb had been pulled free. Sitting on nail hangers, it offered no challenge. Ross lifted the lumber, and we ducked inside the cavern-like darkness.

"Want to lead or follow?" I asked. "The leader gets the flashlight. You can try the night-vision goggles on the way down."

"I'll lead," Ross answered. "I was here a couple of weeks back. Jake and I poked around after a board meeting. Said he marveled at the effectiveness of its simple illusions."

The whole premise of The Tipsy House is sleight of hand—or

more accurately visual misdirection. While the building's floors do, indeed, incline, it's the weird, cockeyed angles of walls and ceilings that give the impression you're going up when you're going down. This prompts stomachs to lurch and balance to fail while navigating the maze. Throw in distorting mirrors, skinny halls, and balls that appear to roll uphill, and the recipe's complete for a bout of vertigo.

These gimmicks posed no mental menace until Ross quit focusing the flashlight on the floor and began brandishing it like a "Star Wars" light saber. As the roving spotlight jumped from one of the structure's out-of-kilter features to another, my stomach danced a soft-shoe. The musty smell, with its tacky paint overlay, and stifling heat didn't help. Sweat sprouted on my scalp and beaded on my forehead.

We'd traveled more than halfway up the tower, when Ross halted at a six-foot-wide mirror to study our munchkin-like reflections. We looked like Sleepy and Dopey smooshed by a bus. Our images rose a mere three feet but covered a good five-foot span. Waves in the mirror added a rippling, underwater effect that didn't help my nausea.

"Who says I wasn't born to play pro basketball?" Ross laughed as he splayed the flashlight beam across the mirror.

None of my Carr cousins are taller than five-foot-ten. Not a problem except they'd wanted to play basketball. As teens, their vertically-challenged stature caused lament each season. "If only" they were a few inches—or a foot—taller...

My aunt always sniped, "You picked the wrong gene pool. Play ice hockey."

May, ever the advocate of playing the cards you were dealt, tolerated no whining.

A silky caress brushed my cheek, and tiny furry legs sauntered down my back under my shirt. I yelped before I could stop myself. Trying to reach my back, I launched into ungainly spinning, jumping jacks. I hate spiders.

Let me repeat—I hate spiders.

Ross startled and dropped our flashlight. It rolled across the floor and conked against a pipe with a metallic ping. Instant blackout.

"Damn," Ross cursed. I barely heard him over my own whimpering. "You scared me to death. What's wrong? You sound like someone's torturing you."

"A spider's crawling down my back," I whined. "Get it off me. Now." I turned my back and lifted my shirt. "Brush it off, pleeeese."

Like a blind man, my cousin groped in the darkness. Holding my shoulder with one hand, he roughly flicked the palm of his other hand back and forth against my back like a stiff broom.

"You got him. Thank God. Wish I could see the hairy monster to squash him."

"What a wimp," Ross teased. "And you think women ought to be in combat."

Had Ross been visible, I'd have slugged him. Debate about the potential combat role of women was a given when I visited the Carr household. I strongly suspected Ed and Woods, my Air Force alumni cousins, raised my hackles for pure sport.

"Don't step on me," Ross said. "I'm on my knees looking for the danged flashlight. Got it." A series of clicks told me the flashlight had quit working.

"Well, fearless leader," I replied. "Now you get to wear those nifty night goggles."

I freed the goggles from around my neck and fumbled them to Ross. In return, he shoved the defunct flashlight into my hands.

"Still want to climb to the top?" Ross asked.

I shrugged, then realized he couldn't see the gesture. "We're halfway. No sense turning back. Once we get to the top, the exit is a no-tricks straightaway, right?"

"Right. Oooh, this is cool." Ross said. "I really can see. Grab the back of my belt. I'll tell you what's ahead so you're ready. Oh, boy. We're at the start of the rolling floor section. Ready?"

"Go for it." I hooked my fingers through his belt. "Your belt's secure, right? I'd hate to de-pants you."

Three steps on the heaving floorboards and I lurched left, throwing Ross off balance. "I need to let go. If I don't, I'll fall on my keister and pull you down with me. Just tell me if I should go straight or turn."

"Straight," Ross instructed.

My heart pitty-patted as I stumbled along in the rolling blackness. The beads of sweat on my forehead now felt like icicles. Once my feet returned to solid—though tilted—flooring, my whole body relaxed.

"Wow, is this cool," Ross declared. "Amazing the detail these goggles pick up, even though the color's leached out. Everything's tinged a grayish green. I feel like I'm on a deep-sea dive."

"Shhh." I found Ross's shirt and tugged ferociously. "I heard something."

We stood stock-still. Creaks and groans, the protest of aged wood, echoed in the dark.

"Just the Tipsy House settling," Ross said. "The building's older than we are. It's supposed to creak."

An out-of-place noise sounded. A footfall. Was it behind us? It sounded close by.

"Did you hear that? Someone's here," I whispered. "Look behind us. Can you see anyone?"

"Not a soul," Ross answered in a conversational voice. After my whisper, his volume boomed. "That spider spooked you. What did we say when we were kids? 'There's nobody here but Hazel, and she's nuts.'"

Maybe my imagination had run wild. Not the first time. Guilt at work? The minute we entered the attraction, my conscience telegraphed second thoughts about recovering Jake's package without Darlene's permission.

I tilted my face up and sucked in cool air. Stars floated where the stairway opened to the roof. Moonlight filtered into the opening. Ross lowered his goggles. An invigorating lake breeze wicked away my sweat and paranoia.

Though a few structures intervened, our rooftop perch revealed dancing moonlight on a sliver of West Okoboji. In the foreground, the undulating roller coaster with its crisscrossed scaffolding supports looked like a giant Tinker toy.

I scanned the roof and saw the elbow where a gutter once emptied into the downspout. The actual gutter was gone. Probably being replaced. Had Jake's package been hauled away with the trash?

I groped inside the elbow. "Do you see anything else that could be considered a gutter?"

Ross walked around the perimeter, stopped to admire the silhouette of his museum and remarked how landscape lights might jazz up its nighttime façade.

Eureka. My fingers closed on a slick piece of plastic. I yanked. A sealed sandwich bag with paper inside. I hoped it wasn't some lazy worker's lunch remains. Not enough light to scrutinize my Cracker Jacks prize. The appraisal would have to wait until we returned to electrified civilization.

"Any luck?" Ross's question ended in a loud "ughh."

My cousin sank to his knees. A man in a dark ski mask stood over Ross, preparing to deliver another blow. I screamed to distract him.

"Hey, you don't want him." I brandished my sandwich baggie on high. "You want this!"

His bludgeoning arm dropped to his side. Ross teetered on his knees.

What now? Tae Bo skills or no, the guy outweighed me by seventy pounds or more, had at least one weapon and sported his own night-vision goggles.

If I survived, I'd tell my friend Steve the night-vision market looks profitable.

The guy could definitely out-see me, and the breeze would carry the pepper spray in my pocket right back into my face. I'd given Ross my stun gun. The defunct flashlight in my hand wasn't much of a weapon.

Fight or flee? No choice. I had to run so the thug would follow and let Ross be. But where? The hulking ape stood between me and the rooftop exit. The downspout dangling from rusty rivets would never support my weight.

Shit, one choice left—not an appealing one to a person who wants a safety harness to climb on a stepstool. If I had to choose between spiders and heights, spiders would win fuzzy feet down.

Quit stalling. If you don't go, he'll kill Ross.

Shadow man stomped my way. I glanced toward the roller coaster, calculated the distance to the vee of the nearest crisscrossed support. No more than four feet. Maybe less. I'd jumped farther in basic training. In sunny daytime. Without a stalker.

I tried to pocket the baggie. No dice. I'd turned my pocket inside out when I'd yanked it free. I shoved the plastic between my teeth and clamped down. Okay, two hands free.

While a quick prayer seemed apropos, all that came to mind was "now I lay me down to sleep..." I settled for "Lord help me," threw the flashlight at the Darth Vader look-alike, and took a running leap.

Womp. My stomach hit the beams full-force. My lungs emptied at impact. I'd almost overshot my target. My butt hung over the vee on the Tipsy House side of the structure, my chest and arms dangled on the opposite side. Stunned I lay bent in half like a rag doll. *Move.*

I hugged a section of the beam with both hands, pulled my behind through the opening. I'm no scrawny Barbie doll, and every ounce of my frame exerted a pull toward the too-distant earth.

Calm...down...breathe...deep.

Panic subsided as survival instincts kicked in. I wrapped my legs around a support beam like a wrestler determined to squeeze his opponent senseless. A desire to avoid the two-story drop provided a strong incentive. Secure for the moment I spared a look at the Tipsy House.

The night sky outlined my bullyboy pursuer. He stood near the edge of the roof, rocking to and fro. He seemed undecided about making the leap. Maybe he wouldn't follow. His arm straightened. A bright light exploded. Splinters grazed my cheek.

I screamed, and the baggie fell. Damn.

Not my immediate worry. My problem was the bad guy's

decision to shoot now and chase later. Thank God, the heavy beams offered some protection. I wiggled to put as much of my flesh as possible behind solid wood.

Another gunshot pinged. A sparkler-like display bloomed beside my head. The bullet had hit one of the metal bolts holding the roller coaster supports together. Holy crap. My adrenaline zoomed into overdrive. I grunted and kicked. My body channeled decades-old obstacle-course training.

I shinnied monkey-like down the rough beams and dropped to the ground. My sides ached from breathing like an overworked bellows.

The man's feet pounded down the Tipsy House stairs. Fee, fi, fo, fum. What now? Maybe I could outrun the guy, but I couldn't outrun a bullet. I needed a weapon or a place to hide. I wanted to find the blasted dropped baggie, too, but searching was hopeless in the inky darkness. Later—if there was a later.

I spotted a construction dumpster, grabbed its lip and levered myself inside. I gritted my teeth waiting for a bevy of rusty nails to puncture my body. I settled intact. If he looked in, I was dead. He had to be outside by now. On the prowl.

I held my breath as long as I could stand it. Then took a shallow, measured breath. A flashlight roved the space above my head.

"Captain Ross, is that you? Are you okay?"

The security guard. Jerry? I had to warn him, even if it gave away my location.

"Jerry, get down. There's a nut out there with a gun. He whacked Ross on the head. He's close by."

"Whoever he was, he's gone. He snatched something off the ground and high-tailed it toward the exit when he saw me. When I heard gunshots, I came lickity-split."

"Thank God," I said.

Jerry helped me clamber out of a nest of painters' debris. I felt woozy and lightheaded and smelled of mineral spirits.

"Glad he ran," I added. "He must have figured you were armed. Let's get Ross."

SIXTEEN

Ross shambled out of The Tipsy House, holding a hand to the back of his head.

"Are you okay?" I asked.

"I think so. But I'm going to have one heck of a knot."

I turned to Jerry. "Could you loan me your flashlight and stay with Ross a second? I'll be right back."

A quick search of the area where the baggie fell to the ground turned up nada. I'd lost it. Dammit. At least Ross and I were alive to fight another day.

As I returned, I heard Jerry talking into his radio phone. "Yes, Sheriff."

Uh-oh. I hadn't thought ahead to cops. Nobody—Darlene, Weaver or the general—would want me blabbing to the local constabulary about messages from the beyond.

Jerry clipped his radio back on his belt. "Told the sheriff we'd wait for him down by the pier where we can sit a spell," he said.

"Not a good idea. I need to drive Ross to the emergency room and get him checked out."

"Sheriff Delaney won't be happy if you leave," Jerry said.

"He'll understand," I lied. "Tell him what happened. We surprised a park intruder who thwonked Ross upside the head and took a couple of pot shots at me before he fled on foot." I seized Ross's arm and gently propelled him toward the car. "Oh, tell Delaney the guy was dressed in black and had a husky build. I'd put him at six-three, six-four. Didn't get a look at his face."

A tightly-edited version of the truth. It simply left out the good parts—The Tipsy House, the guy's ski mask and night goggles, the missing sandwich baggie with its note from the grave, and the fact that the thug had surprised us, not the reverse.

It's hard to surprise a stalker. But I could swear no one had followed us. How did he find us?

Jerry grumbled that we were leaving him in the lurch, but his fondness for Ross won out. He didn't want to be responsible for any delay in getting Ross a medical once-over. While I squabbled with Jerry, Ross tenderly fingered the base of his skull. He didn't utter a word.

"Tell the sheriff we'll call in the morning," I added, "if we think of anything to add."

Ross kept his silence until I started the car and pointed it toward Dickinson County Memorial Hospital.

"Guess I should thank you for jumping off a building to distract my tormentor. I saw you wave something at him. Worked like a red cape with a bull. So was it Jake's package? Do you have it?"

I shook my head. Sheepishly, I admitted dropping the sandwich bag in my freefall. "Jerry saw the thug pick something up before he ran off," I finished. "Whatever was in that baggie is gone."

"Well that sucks." Ross moaned. "My head feels like it's going to explode. Delaney will be madder than a pissed-off hornet when he finds out what happened. And I have to live here."

At the hospital, the ER doctor, who knew the captain well, pronounced him fit. "Just a nasty bump on the noggin'—no need to give you a free bunk tonight." After eyeballing the cuts and scrapes I'd sustained communing with life-size Tinker toys, he engaged in a little torture by iodine.

"You two play nice now," the doc joked. We'd given him a lame stepped-on-a-shoelace account of our injuries.

As we walked down the hospital corridor, Ross unclipped the cell phone on his belt. "I have to phone Eunice. Let her know we're en route. She's sure to be fretting."

I grabbed his wrist. "Let me make one call first. You may need to tell Eunice we'll be a bit longer."

I pawed through my purse for the card with Weaver's cell

phone number. Ross rolled his eyes, but lent me his phone. Though I'd promised Darlene I wouldn't talk to Weaver until she'd retrieved Jake's package, that ship had sailed. Now more than ever, Darlene needed help, and I planned to get it for her whether she liked it or not. I didn't care if she told me to go to hell.

The FBI agent answered with a groggy, "Hello." Before I finished my spiel, her voice became celery crisp. "I want to talk to you and Darlene—now. I mean this minute. I can't believe you did something so stupid. Head over to Darlene's and bring your cousin. Don't call Darlene. We have FBI agents on the gate. I'll tell them to expect you. I'll probably beat you there."

Ross phoned Eunice and told her we were fine but had to attend an impromptu FBI meeting. My cousin counseled his wife not to worry—fat chance—and promised full details once he got home. He also prepped Eunice to fabricate a wholesome tale should May phone looking for me. I didn't want to wake Aunt May just to tell her not to worry. A call like that was sure to backfire, setting off two-alarm anxiety. If my aunt did happen to discover me missing, we reasoned she'd dial Ross's cell or his home phone first.

Our telethon complete, we drove to the Olsen estate with Ross keeping a lookout for any suspicious vehicles following us. Nighttime traffic proved nonexistent. Spirit Lake's a family resort with little in the way of titillating wee hours entertainment. The streets tend to remain deserted until four or five a.m. when early-rising fishermen limber up their rusty pick-ups and rattle to the nearest piers.

Weaver waited at the gate. Her scowl communicated an extra foul mood. She motioned to the guards, then climbed in the back seat of our car. The gates creaked open.

Neither of the men on duty wore the spiffy Thrasos International uniform—a loden green jacket with a gold key embroidered on the breast pocket. "Are all the Thrasos security guards gone?" I asked.

"Darlene fired Thrasos," Weaver answered. "When Hamilton

told her she didn't have the authority, she called the sheriff. Said she wanted everyone off her property, including Kyle and his family, and she expected the sheriff's department to back her up."

"Bet that went over well."

Weaver's lips curved up in a brief smile. "Five minutes later, Sheriff Delaney got a call from Kyle. Guess Hamilton thought Jake's son could run interference. Kyle gave the sheriff an earful about his right to protect his house and family from his murdering stepmother. The sheriff decided the law was on Darlene's side. The only entrance to the compound runs through land owned solely by Jake. The sheriff said he figured it belonged to the widow until he was notified otherwise."

"So it's a Mexican standoff?"

"Delaney told Kyle he had three options. Move to a hotel. Head back to Omaha. Or build an access road on his slice of property. Heaven knows there may be a road-building crew here before sun-up. Delaney also asked the FBI for help. Said he didn't have more men to spare and he refused to bear the responsibility if someone else was murdered. I can justify security here, at least until the funeral."

Realizing my questions had sidetracked her, Weaver stared daggers at me. "I'm almost as thrilled with you as Kyle is with his stepmother. What the hell were you thinking? You were a colonel. Army Intelligence, my ass. I thought you had more sense."

"Think again," my cousin muttered sotto voice.

It would take a while to return to Ross's good graces. With Weaver, it could take a century.

Weaver knocked repeatedly before Darlene ushered the three of us in. She'd thrown a robe over silk pajamas and hadn't bothered with slippers. Despite her dress, she looked wide-awake and hyper. "What the hell is going on? It's two in the morning."

Darlene led us to the kitchen where she set coffee mugs on the butcher-block table. She uncorked a bottle of brandy and offered chasers for the hot brew. "Julie's still asleep. Does she need to be here? Lord knows she can use some rest."

"Let her sleep," Weaver replied. "From the gist of Marley's tale, I only need to scream at you two."

I recounted the evening's escapades. When I explained how my go-it-alone search-and-seizure idiocy had lost information that might have identified the killer, Darlene's face turned crimson.

"How could you?" she demanded.

Weaver ignored the outburst. Her scorn encompassed Darlene as well as me. "Why didn't one of you call when you found Jake's note? That's evidence. Following Jake's clue was my job, not yours. We may have lost our only chance to nail the killer thanks to your paranoia."

Weaver glared at Darlene. "The note's disappearance sucks you into deeper quicksand. Lord help me, but I'm inclined to believe you and Julie are innocent. However, my boss will say the rich bitch hired someone to steal evidence that would have incriminated her."

"What a crock." Darlene snorted. "Jake never would have left a note for me if he thought Julie or I were involved."

"True." Weaver's voice was ice. "That doesn't mean he was right. He's dead. Could be his evidence merely pointed at your accomplice. That's how my boss will explain it. You arranged for the proof to vanish so the trail wouldn't boomerang in your direction."

"Oh, for cripes sakes," Darlene shouted.

"Hey lady, don't yell at me," Weaver countered. "If you'd called, we wouldn't be having this conversation. Now go get that damned riddle before it disappears. I need to authenticate it."

When Darlene left to retrieve the paper, Weaver returned her attention to Ross and me. "You guys unraveled the riddle at supper, right? So, how did our mystery man know The Tipsy House was Jake's hiding place? If he tailed you everywhere, what made him launch a full-scale attack when he did? His assault seems reckless unless he had reason to believe you'd retrieved what he was after."

The FBI agent made an excellent point.

Ross's forehead wrinkled. "Right, how did he know? Marley swears no one tailed us, and the mugger made no attempt to follow us into the museum. So why did he tag along at The Tipsy House?"

Even Weaver went quiet.

I returned her stare. "A bug? Seems improbable, but I don't have a better explanation. Let's say someone listened in on our dinner conversation. If our murderer suspected Jake squirreled away evidence, he might have put two and two together from my blatherskiting about a final riddle."

Ross shook his head. "You're saying someone bugged my eighty-year-old mother's condo? Hard to swallow. But if you're right, why didn't the joker just grab the package and scamper away before we arrived? He had a two-hour head start."

I shook my head. "He didn't know where to look. That's why. I never mentioned there was a package, let alone that it was stuck in a gutter. Without that tidbit, he could have searched The Tipsy House for hours and come up empty handed."

Darlene returned with Jake's note clutched in her hand. "Great, I just heard the tail-end of your conversation. If someone bugged May's house, they're probably listening to us right now."

"I can assure you they're not," Weaver said. "Our agents did a sweep when we took over from Thrasos."

"Did you find bugs?" I asked.

Weaver nailed me with an exasperated look. She didn't answer. "We'll check May's house," she said. "Don't worry about contacting the sheriff. I let him know we're taking over the investigation."

Weaver stood. Her body language signaled dismissal. I wasn't ready to leave. Not until a few of my questions were answered. "Have you searched the Glaston safe room?"

"No." The FBI agent shifted from foot to foot. "Darlene said she didn't know about it, and Kyle and Hamilton pleaded ignorance. Every time I call to talk with Eric, his uncle claims the young man is sedated and sleeping. I'll track down the architect tomorrow. If that fails, we can do a search. I doubt it'll gain us anything though. If only the Glastons knew it existed, it's doubtful the killer ventured inside."

"Want to find out?" I asked. "The woman who cleans house for the Glastons gave me an idea. Should only take a few minutes to see if I'm right."

"What's your hunch?" she prodded.

I shared Anna's observation that a second-floor guestroom had lost a passel of square footage when the Glastons installed an elevator. "I'll bet the safe room's accessed directly from the elevator. That would be a sound design, offering a quick route to safety from the first or second floor."

Weaver yawned. "I'll look into it tomorrow."

"Why not now? None of us is going to sleep. We're too wired. Aren't you curious?"

Weaver agreed, but put her foot down at all four of us trekking to the Glaston house. More people meant more chance to muck-up evidence. Ross and Darlene would wait while Weaver and I took a gander.

The outside air felt colder than forty degrees. The biting wind had not chased the clouds away. Zero cracks in the overcast canopy, no hint of moonlight. We stumbled along the path. The estate's soft landscape lighting was better suited to romance than sure footing.

Looking down at the rough stone path, we almost blundered into a black-cloaked intruder. He'd come within five feet before Weaver deciphered his shadow and drew her pistol. The man scurried along a feeder footpath that crossed our main walkway.

"This is the FBI. Identify yourself—now," Weaver challenged.

I froze, heart racing. My eyes, poorly adjusted to the blackness, pulled few details from the specter's image. The man loomed over six feet. Jeez, was he wearing a cloak? I blinked. Okay, his clothing wasn't quite so ominous—a black slicker with a hood cinched against the rain.

The dark form straightened. "Lower your gun, you idiot, or

I'll see you fired so fast your feeble brain swims." I instantly recognized the snotty tone.

"I'll lower it once I'm sure you're not carrying," Weaver barked back. "Assume the position, Mr. Hamilton. Kindly lean on the tree beside you and don't move a muscle."

"Consider your actions carefully." The silky voice stretched out the words. "There's nothing I'd like better than to instigate a fat civil lawsuit. If I were you, I'd forget any hopes for a government pension. I lunched with Director Swanson last week. Of course, you've probably never met the head of your FBI."

"You can't bully me, so can it," Weaver replied.

I cheered her chutzpah, playing with fire. I didn't doubt Hamilton's claim of influential friends, maybe even the FBI director. I crossed my fingers her record would protect her.

She completed a quick pat down and holstered her weapon. "What are you doing here?" Weaver didn't back down. "Thrasos was relieved of all security responsibilities at the estate. The sheriff passed that message to you personally. The estate is off-limits to everyone except FBI and family."

"So what's she?" Hamilton pointed at me. "I hadn't heard Jake had gone Mormon. I thought he only married one whore at a time."

I longed to jump down Hamilton's throat with my own zippy, curse-laced repartee. But Weaver seemed quite capable of reaming this guy's butt on her own. "Marley's here because I invited her," Weaver replied.

"And I'm here because Kyle Olsen invited me," Hamilton spat back. "I'm not some broken-down security guard. I'm in charge of security for Jolbiogen, and Kyle Olsen asked me to retrieve corporate documents from the Glaston house. We don't want any more secrets falling into the wrong hands."

Weaver didn't flinch. "You can tell Kyle Olsen the FBI has assumed responsibility for the contents of the Glaston house. We'll make certain any papers remain secured."

"Not reassuring," he purred. "Let me go about my business,

or I'll take this up with your boss. I have his blessing."

"I'll wait to hear it from his lips," Weaver said.

"You're unbelievable." Hamilton's voice rose. "Perhaps you're not very bright. My men did most of your homework. We handed you the case against Julie on a platter. Motive, emails. Good God, woman, what are you waiting for? A signed confession?"

"I just plod along at my own pace. I'm a suspicious cuss. Never accept a gift until I've unwrapped it and given it a few pokes."

"I hope no one else dies while you're poking," Hamilton said. "I checked in with the agent on the gate. Told him I had FBI approval. If security were still Thrasos International's domain, your man would have notified you, and we wouldn't be having this cock-up."

I decided Weaver shouldn't have all the fun. "If your visit's so legitimate, why skulk around alone in the middle of the night? You could have asked Agent Weaver to accompany you while you secured papers anytime in the last twenty-four hours."

"I don't have to answer questions from you." Hamilton spun on his heel.

Weaver called after him. "Maybe not, but I'd like to hear your answer, too."

He never responded, never looked back. He walked away, confident Weaver wouldn't resort to force to stop him.

"What's he up to?" I mumbled.

Weaver thumbed her walkie-talkie and arranged for an agent to escort Hamilton from the compound. "Wonder how long it'll be before my boss calls." She sighed. "Five minutes? I'm not helping my career."

"Might as well finish this treasure hunt." Weaver extracted a key from her pocket and unlocked the Glaston's front door. Inside she made a beeline to the elevator. She'd been there before. I trotted behind.

Weaver punched a button for the second floor. When the lift stopped and the door slid open, we began our search. The bedroom to the right had a sizable amount of unaccounted for square footage directly behind the lift.

We climbed back in the elevator and ran our hands over the ornate paneling on the right hand side. Nothing. We puzzled over the control panel and tested the buttons. They performed as advertised. Frustrated, we held down buttons in varied combinations and sequences. The elevator jerked like a peripatetic puppet at our conflicting commands.

After ten minutes of trial-and-error, Weaver found the open-says-me, pushing all of the Braille embossed pressure pads in concert. The right panel disappeared as a motorized pocket door glided open with whisper-like perfection.

Weaver and I ducked into the confined space. The elevator panel slid shut. "Hope it proves as easy to get the hell out of here," she muttered.

The cubbyhole resembled a large walk-in closet with padded benches attached to one wall. Room for six people in a pinch, if they weren't claustrophobic. The space held a small desk, too. Weaver donned gloves to rifle through it.

"A damn peculiar place for a desk," she said. "I searched Glaston's home office. It's ten times the size of this coffin." She picked up a paper. "I recognize the doctor's writing. He kept papers here."

While Weaver snooped, I scanned the cubbyhole's interior. An almost invisible seam threaded through a section of the tiled floor. In one area, the gray grout looked extra glossy. I touched it with my finger. The wet-looking substance was a putty-like plastic. "Weaver, I think I found a trapdoor."

The snug fit hid it in plain sight. With a little maneuvering, I lifted the lid to the stowaway space. At first—and second—glance, the contents disappointed. A few pieces of antique jewelry lay beside a single sheet of folded paper and a cloth-bound journal.

With gloved fingers, Weaver shook the lone paper by a corner to unfold it. "It's printed on Jolbiogen letterhead. A summary of DNA test results. It must be connected to the stolen research."

Looking over her shoulder, I read the header: "Results, DNA Trial, May 10." The document listed thirty subjects by patient number—no names. No mention of pathogens or targeted gene sequences. Under conclusions, it said patients 1333 and 1342 had the same father, and patient 1300 was the father of subject 1355.

"Sounds like paternity testing. Why squirrel it away in a safe?" I wondered aloud. "Can the FBI's computer gurus search Jolbiogen files to match these patient numbers with names? That might help us figure out why Glaston kept it."

"There is no us," Weaver reminded. "I'm looking into this. You're butting out. I'll talk to our forensic guys, but they already have a full plate tracing possible hacks into top-secret research and Olsen family medical files. Whoever the Jolbiogen thief is, he—or she—certainly knows how to play a computer keyboard."

Weaver opened the journal. "Looks like Dr. Glaston's personal journal. We'll leave everything as we found it. After our crime scene specialists process the scene, I'll read the journal, see if it offers any clues."

A button to call the elevator sat in plain view. Weaver pressed it. The panel slid open and we descended in ghostly silence to the first floor. Neither of us spoke during our uneventful stroll back to the main house.

"It's about time." Darlene stood. "What did you find?"

Weaver briefed them regarding the desk contents but conveniently omitted our encounter with Hamilton. Guess she didn't want to rile Darlene more.

"Okay, it's late, and I have work to do," she concluded. "First task is to get Jake's note analyzed and verify he wrote it. Please, don't even think about any more sleuthing."

The agent left, and we fell into a funky silence.

"Guess we should go, too." Ross and I edged toward the door.

"Please stay just a couple minutes more." Darlene walked over to a credenza covered with snapshots. "I spent the afternoon poring over scrapbooks to pull together a tribute to Jake, one that focuses on happier times. I'd like your opinion, Ross. The funeral director said he'd mount the snapshots on a magnetic board before tomorrow's visitation."

We studied the photos. In them Jake morphed from a rakish college student into an adoring new dad. In middle age, he performed duties as the proud ribbon-cutter for Jolbiogen's headquarters. In his seventies, he sported a carefree grin as he looked adoringly at Darlene. The pictures offered nary a clue about who would want this man, his daughter and son-in-law dead.

"Jake was a good man." Ross bit his lip. "Sure hope they find the bastard who killed him."

Amen, to that. And I hoped they did so before anyone else turned up dead.

Seventeen

Jake's body floated just out of reach. I could tell he was dead, but his animated hand busily scribbled messages on a piece of paper. The page remained blank. Invisible ink.

"What are you trying to tell me?" I demanded.

A disembodied voice answered. "I told you. You lost it."

A loud pounding prompted me to cover my ears. "What is that?"

Jake fixed me with his wall-eyed stare and refused to answer.

The image dissolved. The banging grew louder. I woke. Someone pounded insistently on Aunt May's front door. My monster headache intensified the racket.

Where was May? I hurried into her bedroom. Bed neatly made. She'd decamped for the day. I snatched a hot pink velour robe hanging from a hook, zipped it, and headed to the door. Hemmed floor-length for my aunt, the robe hit me mid-calf.

"May? You here?" I called en route. Silence.

The door offered no peephole or safety chain. "Who is it?"

"Weaver."

Though muffled by the closed door, her schizophrenic speech pattern—a Southern drawl spoken with an allegro cadence—identified her.

I cracked the door open. "Come in. What time is it?"

"Eleven o'clock. Your aunt left five minutes ago. It seemed a good time to chat. Get dressed. We'll take a drive."

Recalling that May's house might be bugged, I didn't quarrel—

though I longed for a kitchen detour and strong coffee. Instead I vamoosed to the bedroom and threw on a short-sleeved sweatshirt and jeans. I returned in two minutes flat. Brushing my curly hair isn't obligatory when I'm on a clock. My husband always swore he couldn't tell any difference between my combed and uncombed locks.

"Let's do it," I said.

Sliding into the front passenger seat, I got a pleasant surprise. The agent had requisitioned two large coffees. Steam curled tantalizingly from sipping slips cut into the Styrofoam mega mugs occupying the holders between the seats.

"Thanks." I reached for the nearest cup.

Weaver put the car in gear and rocketed away. A wave of hot coffee sloshed out the top. I didn't complain. "Is everything okay with my aunt?"

"Far as I know." The FBI agent glanced over at me. "She got a call from her real estate office, mumbled something about leaving you a note, and took off. Based on her phone conversation, she slept soundly. Had no idea you didn't return until the wee hours."

"Are *you* bugging May's apartment?" I demanded.

"Yes. Remotely." Weaver shrugged. "A scan told us someone else had bugged the condo remotely—and that someone didn't have a court order. So we put a fishing boat in your cove. His tuner picks up voices in the condo just fine. It's not that we don't trust you and your family. We just felt it prudent to hear what our eavesdroppers were hearing so we could anticipate any action."

"My lord, I can't believe someone bugged May's house."

"Didn't surprise me. We disabled a half-dozen bugs at the Olsen estate, and we're jamming to prevent any long-distance monitoring. So they went after a softer target. Anyway this is good news. Now we can script what we want your eavesdroppers to hear."

Weaver's *good news* didn't thrill me. "I'm not acting out any script that drags May into danger."

The FBI agent's chuckle didn't signal amusement. "You're

awfully righteous for someone who plunked her cousin in a shooting gallery. But no, we won't do anything to endanger your family." When she looked over, her eyes narrowed. "Will you please sit quietly and sip your coffee while I bring you up to date?"

Her dressing down didn't sit well. She'd recruited me with General Irvine's blessing. The woman acted awfully uppity for a pipsqueak who was fifteen years my junior and needed my help. Do they teach arrogance in FBI school?

I gritted my teeth. Maybe she had reason to be perturbed. I hadn't exactly been acting my age.

Weaver filled me in on the frantic activity that took place while I sawed logs. It started early morning, when experts examined the contents of the safe room vault. The clothbound journal proved an evidentiary goldmine. Jake's son-in-law definitely penned the self-congratulatory tome. In it, Glaston boasted how easy it was to filch the military research. He also crowed about the deal he negotiated with buyers. Unfortunately, he didn't identify them.

Weaver pulled onto an overlook at the Kettleson nature preserve and shut off the engine. "Now that we know Glaston was the seller, General Irvine's working his contacts. Not your problem. Before you start asking questions, let me finish."

Exhaustion shadowed her eyes. Not the time to spark debate.

"Glaston wrote a cryptic entry about his 'fair-weather friends.' Said they'd served their purpose and were in for a nasty surprise once he was safely away. He added it was too bad he wouldn't be around to see the high and mighty fall. Not a big leap to believe his collaborators killed him."

Weaver opened her car door. I took the cue, exited and rounded the car. The trumpeter swans seemed less vocal today. Weaver slouched against the fender.

"Glaston's journal let us pick up the money trail," she said. "The good doctor salted away two million in a Swiss bank account. His journal indicated ten million more would be wired after his buyers conducted a successful 'field test.'"

"The farm workers infected with that toxic cocktail?" I asked.

"That's our guess. Unfortunately, Glaston's foreign bank account was emptied and closed the day he died. The first installment vanished. We're guessing the man's accomplices double-crossed him. The good doctor had a new ID—passport, driver's license and bank accounts—in a safe deposit box with his plane ticket. He definitely planned to bolt."

A pair of trumpeter swans took flight, an effortless escape. Glaston hadn't been so lucky.

"Why did he take the risk? The man lived in the lap of luxury. His wife stood to inherit a fortune that makes twelve million seem like peanuts."

Weaver kicked at the gravel in our pull-off. "Mrs. Glaston's liver was shot, and asthma and alcoholism precluded a transplant. He feared his wife would kick the bucket before Jake. If that happened, his lifestyle would implode. He wasn't named in Jake's will, and Gina's trust directed the remainder to her son. When Glaston learned Jolbiogen's new president planned to shoulder him out, that was the capper."

Whoa. About time. The FBI could finally exonerate Julie and Darlene. "So Jake found out about the theft and Glaston killed him?"

"Maybe." Weaver stared into the distance. "Or the doctor's accomplices killed Jake first and then the Glastons."

I stretched. "At least Julie and Darlene are in the clear."

"Not quite." Weaver straightened. "While we know Glaston was the master thief, my boss has nominated Julie and her mom as his 'high and mighty' co-conspirators."

"What a crock! They had a mutual-hate society. They'd never have helped Glaston."

"Unless they were blackmailed. Hamilton's provided a tidy new theory—Glaston blackmailed the mother and daughter into cooperating. The women killed Jake when he discovered the conspiracy, then they did away with their blackmailer so he couldn't fix the blame on them. Hamilton's almost convinced my boss—his best buddy—that 'marrying money doesn't change trailer trash.'"

Sensing my pending tirade, Weaver jerked her arm up like a cop stopping traffic. "Save your breath. I don't buy it either, but I need a compelling rebuttal. Glaston left no clues to identify his accomplices or his buyers. We need to set a trap."

We? What happened to there being no *us*?

The FBI agent described a plan to draw out the real killers. The goal was to convince them Darlene had found a second riddle, identifying another site where Jake had stashed evidence. I'd confide this tidbit to Ross while we chatted in May's bugged living room.

Weaver said my conversation should emphasize four points. One, Darlene had turned the new riddle over to the FBI. Two, Weaver had placed her under guard. Three, suspecting a leak inside the agency, Weaver had decided to go solo to retrieve the missing evidence. Four, neither Darlene nor Weaver had entrusted me with any clue about the note's contents.

"That should goad the killers into coming after me." Weaver sounded gleeful. "But you have to make it clear no one else knows what the riddle says. I have to be the sole target."

The plan seemed rife with personal risk for Weaver. I told her so. She waved her hand dismissively. "I've taken precautions. No one else will be in any danger."

Her conviction sent a shiver down my spine. It sounded an awful lot like my justification for allowing Ross to tag along on my jaunt to the Tipsy House.

After Weaver deposited me at May's condo, I checked the front of the refrigerator, our family's never-fail bulletin board. A note from my aunt said she'd collect me for lunch at twelve-thirty. Egad. All of fifteen minutes to get ready. She'd also ordered me to cogitate on banquet menus for her wingding. A meeting with the Village West coordinator was set for two p.m.

I showered, dressed, and entered the vestibule just as May swung by. "Hi, Marley. Get your fanny in gear. We're burning daylight."

Actually there wasn't much light to burn. At least the drizzle wouldn't hurt my wet hair.

May's gaze snagged on my finger-combed hairdo but she swallowed any comment. "Thought the tearoom would be nice."

The renovated Victorian proved a cozy spot for lunch. We both ordered the daily special, a cup of creamy mushroom soup with lemon-laced chicken salad on a crusty croissant.

May fanned out the banquet selections across the unused portion of our table. She'd completed her initial cull, relegating most "heart healthy" selections to the dustbin.

"Hell's bells, this is a party, not a Weight Watchers' coven. People can get back on their diets after we celebrate."

Detrimental though it may be to the longevity of the Carr and Woods tribes, this diet-delay philosophy is deeply ingrained in family tradition. It's trotted out for any and every celebration from Mother's Day to thank-goodness-it's-Friday.

Okay, I subscribe. Good food is one of life's greatest pleasures. I surrender easily to eggs benedict, crispy onion rings and cheesecake. That makes exercise my main strategy to keep from weighing in on freight scales. The thought made me shudder. I'd actually seen a military doctor at Fort Bragg herd a pendulous, pregnant dependent onto a freight scale.

Hmmm. Maybe I'd fit in a run after lunch.

Our Village West meeting went swimmingly. May sweet-talked the group planner into an added "local" discount. By two-thirty, we were back home. When May retreated to her boudoir for a power nap, I opened a book, a mystery set in Rome. After rereading the same page twice, I closed the paperback. The Spirit Lake murders were far more intriguing.

Maybe if I organized my thoughts I'd discern a pattern, or at least find a clue. I tore a piece of paper from May's grocery pad and drew columns.

I headed the first column: "People with motives to murder Jake." The second column read: "People with motives to murder the Glastons."

In column one, I scribbled Glaston's name. Then flipped my pencil, eraser ready for action. If Glaston was inclined toward murder, why not kill his father-in-law right out of the starting gate? Once he ensured his wife would outlive her dad, he only needed to wait till Gina kicked the bucket. No need to mess around stealing secrets.

I started to erase his name and stopped. Instead I wrote "fear of exposure" beside it. Perhaps Jake confronted his son-in-law but gave him a grace period to turn himself in. That could have pushed Glaston into murdering Jake.

Okay. Column two, people with motives for the Glaston murders. I tapped my pencil a full five minutes, while I chewed my bottom lip raw.

A double cross? Perhaps Glaston's accomplices were willing collaborators who murdered him only after they discovered his plan to burn them. Was Glaston supposed to share his proceeds from the sale?

Below double cross I penciled in "blackmail" and doodled "opportunity."

The Glaston murders spoke volumes about his fellow conspirators. They'd filched phalloidin from Jolbiogen. Insiders? They knew how to handle it. Training? They'd accessed the Olsen estate.

Three people met all the criteria—Eric, Kyle and Julie. Well, maybe there was a fourth. I knew next to nothing about Nancy, Jake's first wife.

"Great nap." Aunt May yawned theatrically as she wandered into the room. I put down my pencil, pocketed the paper with my doodles.

"I'm going to jump in the shower," May said. "You'd better get cracking, too. Ross and Eunice are picking us up for Jake's visitation in half an hour."

❁

The funeral home foyer reeked of flowers. I fidgeted in line waiting my turn to sign the guest register. May handed over a pen, and I scrawled my name. The inked pages indicated we were latecomers. That made the sparse gathering inside the large reception area a surprise. Thirty people tops. The early arrivals hadn't stayed long.

A stout man hurried to greet us. "Do you remember, Sam Larsson?" Ross whispered in my ear. Without my cousin's prompt, I wouldn't have known Sam from Adam. The plump mortician bore little resemblance to the mischievous boy I'd known.

My eldest Carr cousin and Sam were inseparable in high school. Whenever the Larsson mortuary was vacant, my cousins and I bowled in the sanctum. With chairs folded away, our featherweight plastic balls sailed over the polished hardwood floors.

"Good to see you, Ross." The mortuary's owner stuck out his hand. Ross introduced me. Sam gave a slight formal bow. "Nice to see you. I recognized you, right off."

Sam's eyes darted left. He frowned and excused himself. "Afraid I have to act as a bouncer today." He hustled toward a woman in a pink pantsuit.

"She's a reporter," Ross whispered. "Not one of the locals or summer stock."

Dwarfed by baskets of flowers, a photo board occupied the space usually reserved for a mahogany casket. Where were Darlene and Julie?

On the right side of the room, a knot of people shuffled forward, and my friend's blonde hair popped into sight. A solid hunch prompted a look left. Bingo. Jake's blood relatives occupied a stronghold along the wall opposite the widow and stepdaughter.

Hmmm. The enemy cast offered a surprise. While Kyle held the position of first batter-up for handshaking, the woman beside him wasn't his wife. Coal black hair swept away from the matron's pasty face. Anna's description was dead-on. So this was Nancy, Kyle's much-maligned mother and Jake's first wife.

Where was Olivia? Had I chased her out of the dress shop before she could buy a suitable black frock?

Eric slumped next to Nancy. He looked zonked. Drugs for sure, who knew if they were the prescribed variety. I'd seen soldiers stoned on Percodan as well as pot. The boy's blue eyes failed to focus as the parade of mourners snaked by.

Kyle's head remained rock steady, while his beady eyes darted in all directions. Every few seconds, they cut to his nephew. Was he afraid the boy would do something to embarrass him? Or was he genuinely concerned about Eric's mental state?

Ross herded our family delegation toward tables mounded with crustless tea sandwiches and book-ended by punch bowls. So far I'd escaped Kyle's roaming gaze.

"Let's wait to give our condolences until there are fewer people with Darlene," Ross suggested as he helped himself to punch.

Eunice, May and I followed his example. While we sipped, Kyle huddled with Nancy. Their body language and whispered dialogue fascinated me. Totally ignored by Nancy, Eric might as well have been a mannequin. Of course, since he was the grandson of Jake's second wife, Eric was no kin to Nancy. No wonder the woman evidenced no desire to clutch the boy to her bosom.

My attention shifted to the photo display. A fair number of mourners dawdled there. If current protocol held, the visitors would soon vanish. Even the profusion of finger foods wasn't enough to hold people in the tension-filled room long.

I nudged Ross. "Didn't any of Jake's hotshot business associates come?"

He shook his head. "Sam says they'll fly in tomorrow for the formal service."

A glance toward Darlene and Julie revealed a break in the action. "Let's pay our respects."

Darlene prolonged the hug fest, clinging to each of us as if she feared we'd disappear. Uncomfortable, May, Ross, Eunice and I trotted out all the old chestnuts about the loss of loved ones. Each cliché encased its own sad kernel of truth.

Once a new wave of arrivals appeared, we sauntered to the Olsen photo tribute. Eunice and May, who hadn't seen the photos, commented on the good times they documented. When my relatives opted to soldier on and offer condolences to Jake's blood relatives, I took a cowardly left to the punch bowls. While Eric looked more comatose than angry, I had no desire to precipitate a brawl. Better to let sleeping dopers lie.

I staked out an oasis of empty folding chairs, and soon, my aunt and cousins joined me. We talked quietly as we sipped more of the tepid punch. I'd promised to stick around and give Darlene moral support whenever there were breaks in the hand-pumping action.

"Did you find out why Olivia's absent?" I asked May.

"Kyle claimed she felt poorly and stayed home to rest up for the funeral," she answered in a stage whisper. "Bet she's peeved about Nancy invading her domain. Don't blame her for snubbing her newly unearthed mother-in-law."

As Aunt May dissed Nancy, I studied the woman. Her pale skin, willowy build and sculpted hairstyle called to mind a Japanese doll. The waxen ex-wife slipped back from the entourage, retrieved a purse, and rummaged inside. Looking for a tissue?

Nope. Her head swiveled in Darlene's direction. Checking to see if she was being watched? Nonchalantly Nancy strolled to the photo collage. She studied it for a long moment before tacking a square addition in the right-hand corner. A snapshot? Memento or curse?

A shoulder squeeze interrupted my visual snooping. Duncan's smile—a wolfish one—captured my full attention. He greeted my kin with genuine enthusiasm.

"I need to pay my respects," he said. "I'll be back."

Would my chivalrous attorney run both sides of the grief gauntlet? Or would he be as chicken as me and skip Kyle's mourner camp?

I tugged on his sleeve. "Would you stop at the photo tribute and take a close look at the picture in the lower right-hand corner?" The add-on piqued my curiosity. "See who's in the shot."

Duncan awarded me a puzzled look. "Okay." He strode briskly toward Darlene.

Another member of the museum board greeted Ross, and the two reminisced kindly about the deceased.

My attention shifted to Duncan. He embraced Darlene and, in turn, Julie, speaking briefly with each before moving to the photo display. He leaned in for a close look at several shots, saving my request for last. Assignment completed, he demonstrated his chivalrous nature by shaking hands with Kyle. He even greeted Eric, who sullenly stuck out a paw.

By the time he poured punch and moseyed our way, my curiosity had passed simmer and reached boil. Duncan pulled a chair close to mine and whispered in my ear. "How about we wander into the annex and find a vacant coffin? Seems sort of a shame people don't get to enjoy all that smooth silk when they're alive and kicking. Course I have something other than kicking in mind."

His hot breath made my ears burn and the hairs on my neck prickle. I punched his arm. A flush of heat warned me my cheeks had turned scarlet. Had my aunt and cousins detected my discombobulation?

"Okay wise guy," I whispered back. "You need to stop reading zombie erotica. Just tell me about the photo."

Duncan's grin accompanied his shrug. "Not much to tell. It showed Jake and another man taking a little boy fishing. Kyle I suppose. The tyke held tight to a fishing pole. A young Nancy stood in the background waving goodbye."

I frowned. "Nancy tacked that photo up a few minutes ago. Maybe it's symbolic. That's around the time she kissed her son goodbye for good. I'd love to know what compelled her to add it."

Hushed voices drifted in from the foyer and Agent Weaver and Sheriff Delaney entered. The law enforcement duo went straight to the front of the room. Weaver split left. The sheriff peeled to the right.

Weaver clasped Kyle's arm and maneuvered him away from his mother. The agent's somber demeanor telegraphed bad news. Kyle's poker face didn't change.

The sheriff used a similar tactic to quarantine Darlene. He bent his head, brought his mouth near her ear. His lips moved, and Darlene shrieked. Delaney tucked an arm around her and guided her to a chair. The funeral director hustled over with a glass of water.

The pantomime left me clueless. "What now?" I asked Duncan. "Do you know?"

He shook his head.

Darlene massaged her temples, stared at the floor. Julie sat beside her and patted her shoulder.

Kyle spoke to his mother and Eric. Weaver waited at a respectful distance.

"Murderers!" Eric screamed.

The news—whatever it was—jolted him out of his catatonic trance. He shook a fist at Darlene and Julie. "Murderers! I'll get a gun. You're dead, you hear me. Dead!"

He'd barely issued the threat when two men in suits—FBI agents?—hustled him toward the front door. Kyle and Nancy scurried behind Eric and his official bouncers. The room grew silent as a tomb. The audience stunned speechless.

"What in the Sam Hill is going on?" May demanded.

"I don't know, but I plan to find out," Duncan answered.

Before his long strides could bring him face to face with the sheriff, Delaney took center stage and cleared his throat. "Ladies and uh, gentlemen," he stammered. "Sorry for the disruption, but Mrs. Olsen, uh Olivia Olsen, has been rushed to the hospital. Her husband…uh, Mr. Olsen, and his family have left to be with her.

"Mrs. Olsen—" he waved in Darlene's direction—"this Mrs. Olsen says she appreciates your thoughtfulness in um, honoring her husband's memory. Due to the uh, unfortunate circumstances, Mrs. Olsen has decided to reschedule the memorial service. It will not be held tomorrow. Uh, thank you for your understanding."

While the tongue-tied sheriff tried to differentiate between Mrs. Olsens, Duncan took a seat next to Darlene. Her eyes never left the floor as he spoke. Clearly a receiving line would not reform. Duncan cut a grim look my way before making his way to Sheriff Delaney.

Julie tugged her mother upright. An agitated Sam Larsson shepherded the women toward the protection of his back office. At least that would remove them from public display. I spotted the ugly-in-pink reporter. She'd snuck back amid the hubbub. She had to be delirious at her good fortune. She could now give first-person accounts of the family's reaction to the latest Olsen tragedy, including Eric's "murderer" outburst.

My throat spasmed as a burning sensation worked its way upward. Sweat beaded my forehead. Nausea. I tapped Ross's arm. "I have to get some air."

A broad porch wrapped three sides of the funeral parlor. Despite the roof's protective overhang, a cold mist shrouded the decking. I leaned against the railing. A steady drip pinged beside me, overflow from full gutters.

I gulped cool air. The nausea receded. Darlene and Julie had to be reeling from the tsunami of death and tragedy.

I straightened and turned to go back inside when Hamilton's angry voice stopped me. Who was the lucky recipient of his latest tirade?

"You happy now, Weaver?"

Though I couldn't see him, Hamilton's voice crackled with fury. He was right around the corner.

"You had enough evidence to arraign Julie, if not Darlene," he continued. "I *am* a lawyer, I know. Any judge would've said 'yes' to an FBI request. But, no, you stalled, and now we have another corpse. What's your plan? Wait for every innocent connected to this case to have a toe tag so you can arrest whoever's alive? I'll tell you right now who'll be left breathing—that conniving harlot and her daughter."

Weaver barked back. "What is it with you, Hamilton? What makes you hell-bent to stick your nose in my case?"

"Why waste my breath? Thank heavens your boss has a brain. I'm confident new evidence will link Julie or Darlene to this latest murder. I hope you're competent enough to find it." Hamilton bulled around the side of the mortuary and almost knocked me flat. "Dammit, it's you. Still trying to run interference for your murdering friend?"

He didn't wait for an answer.

Weaver joined me at the porch railing. We watched the man march off.

"Gets under your skin, doesn't he?" I asked. "Like a chigger. Wish there was a salt and Campho-Phenique cure for that pest."

The FBI agent massaged her neck, slowly rolled her head to undo the kinks. The murders were getting to her, too. "This gets stranger and stranger. If you overheard Hamilton's yell-a-thon, you know Olivia's probably dead by now. Looks like she was poisoned with the same stuff used on Gina Glaston's respirator.

"It's bizarre. Olivia had sweaty feet—we're talking buckets—and sprinkled foot powder in her shoes every day. Someone substituted phalloidin for her regular talc. It was absorbed into her system through her soles. Olivia started feeling woozy about the time the family left for the visitation. She told them to go ahead. An hour later, one of my men checked on her. When she didn't answer the doorbell, he broke in, found her unconscious—all but dead. Her pulse was thready and erratic when the ambulance whisked her away."

The news floored me. "Why kill Olivia? Could somebody have meant to kill Kyle and screwed up the attempt? A bad guess about who used the foot powder."

"Not a chance. Olivia kept the powder in her private dressing area."

"But why Olivia? I'd bet my Army pension she was no conspirator. It may be impolite to speak ill of the dead, but the woman was a nitwit. She wouldn't have known a military secret from a raspberry douche. No way she'd have enough gumption to kill someone."

"Hell, I don't know." Weaver gripped the railing tighter. Her gaze followed Hamilton's car as it shot out of the parking lot, spitting gravel at an elderly couple trundling down the sidewalk. "Maybe Olivia heard or saw something she wasn't supposed to. I plan to re-look at anyone who's come near the Olsen estate. Thrasos kept a visitor's log—at least for front-gate arrivals."

I didn't comment. Dripping water—ping, ping, ping—filled

the silence. Finally the agent asked me if Ross had agreed to join in her bait-the-murderer skit.

"I haven't asked yet. No time alone. I don't want Aunt May to find out her condo's bugged or that we're laying a trap for a serial killer. She'd freak. I'll pull Ross aside today. We'll schedule the play for morning."

Weaver's eyes bored into mine. "Be careful. The Olsen family seems cursed. I'm sure this massacre's tied to Jolbiogen, but the killer's shown no scruples about slaughtering bystanders. My guess is that Olivia Olsen and Gina Glaston are dead because they stumbled across something. Not to sound melodramatic, but you may have come across the same information and don't even realize it. Be extra cautious."

"Hey, I'll let my feet sweat, and I have no plans to powder my underarms for the duration." My attempt at a joke earned no smile.

The FBI agent turned toward the mortuary's front door. "I'm not sure what to do with the Olsen heirs—those left among the living. I don't want anyone to return to billionaire's cove tonight. For all I know, our killer's planted more biological booby traps. But finding two safe houses on a moment's notice won't be easy. Most cottages are rented for the season, and motel rooms are too public and hard to secure. And I plan to make damn sure our Hatfields and McCoys aren't within ten miles of each other. This killing spree is going to stop."

Weaver patted my shoulder before she walked away. Now *that* made me worry.

EIGHTEEN

Back at my family circle, Duncan held everyone's attention. "Sheriff Delaney says Olivia was poisoned. She isn't expected to pull through."

Eunice's hand flew up to her mouth. "Will this nightmare ever end?"

"Darlene's beside herself, worrying about Julie," Duncan continued. "I invited them to stay with me tonight. They shouldn't go back to their house."

Time to interrupt. "Agent Weaver agrees. She's trying to line up some lodging that will keep Kyle and Eric as far as possible from Darlene and Julie. She's looking for anonymous safe houses. Your condo doesn't quite fit the bill."

"I have an idea." May motioned us into a tighter football-style huddle. "An out-of-town owner just asked me to put his house on the market. It's secluded, way up on Big Spirit—no next-door neighbors—and it's vacant. Five bedrooms, fully furnished. No one knows it's available but me. I can tell your FBI friend where to look for the spare key."

I nodded agreement. "Sounds perfect. I'll bet Weaver will jump at the offer."

"Darlene's really frightened," Duncan added. "Given that many bedrooms, I'll offer to keep them company. Marley, how about joining us for dinner? Make it seem more normal."

"If you say yes, Marley Elizabeth Clark, you're a lunatic or suicidal," Aunt May erupted. She didn't bother to lower her voice to the funeral parlor's muted conversational level. Several heads swiveled our way.

"I'm counting four people dead or dying," my aunt hissed in a quieter voice. "Now, I'm all for helping these folks hide where a killer's less likely to find them, but why tempt fate? This killer strikes with impunity, day or night. All that razzmatazz security hasn't been worth a tinker's damn. For all we know, the killer's an FBI agent."

I tried not to smile at May's ire. Her flare-up would burn itself out once she saw her outburst wasn't yielding results.

She turned on Duncan. "I'm disappointed in you, too. Thought you had better sense!"

Duncan didn't say a peep. Good judgment.

"What's the sheriff's role?" I asked, trying to get the conversation back on track.

"The FBI's asked him to assist with logistics and community PR," Duncan answered.

I nodded. Smart move.

"Ross, can I borrow your cell phone?" I asked.

My cousin unclipped it. I walked to a deserted corner. Weaver answered on the first ring.

"What is it? I haven't made it ten blocks." Her tone sounded flat, weary.

I described May's new listing and added that Duncan and I might join them for dinner and possibly the night, if she approved.

"The house is a big help. I don't see a problem with you or Duncan visiting. Give me the address. I'll arrange security. If you're picking up pizza, save some for me. It's been eighteen hours since I had a bite."

I reported back to my family conclave. "Agent Weaver thanks you for the house, May. She's doubling the number of FBI agents on the Olsen security detail, and she plans to personally spend the night holding hands with Darlene and Julie."

I took a deep breath. "Darlene needs her friends more than ever. I'll spend the night, too. It'll be fine."

"Fine?" May threw up her hands. "From what I can tell, FBI agents are about as helpful as vampires. They never die, but folks around them have the life expectancy of a fruit fly. If you have so much faith in the FBI, you're not needed."

"Strictly moral support. You'd do the same for a friend."

Concern for Darlene's fragile mental state factored into my decision. And so did Agent Weaver's throwaway comment about my personal safety. I didn't intend to bring harm to May's doorstep. Better to board with Darlene tonight. Tomorrow I'd decide if I should move out of May's house—which would prompt my aunt to throw one doozy of a fit.

I walked Ross off for a private word about Weaver's scheme to trap the killer. Since the plan didn't endanger his mom, he readily agreed to his part in the subterfuge.

When Ross left to retrieve the car, Duncan and I headed to Sam Larsson's private office to tell our beleaguered friends about their new digs.

I smiled at Darlene. "I told Weaver we'd pick up pizza, but I have a better idea. We'll cook our own, like old times. Nothing like the smell of pizza baking to forget your cares for a spell."

Darlene glanced over at her daughter. "Thank God. Only one more night to get through. Tomorrow I'm putting Julie on a plane. I want her out of here until they catch the murderer. I tried to get her to leave tonight. She refused. Said the FBI might not let her go. I say bullshit. She doesn't need their permission to take off."

"Are you kidding?" Julie piped up. She'd caught the tail end of her mother's rant. "Before they found Glaston's journal, the Feds were a nanosecond away from arresting me. While his scribbling makes it clear I didn't plan the Jolbiogen theft, I'm still a prime suspect. I had motive, means and opportunity for the Glaston murders."

Julie snaked an arm around Darlene's waist. "Mom, I won't go anywhere without you."

A brainstorm struck. Better late than never. "Why don't both of you stay at my place in South Carolina? I'll be here another week. You'd have my house to yourself. It's on a private island so there's a smidgeon of built-in security, and we could arrange more. Let's talk about it tonight."

Duncan and I walked out of Sam's office together. "Hold on, a minute." I scooted over to Jake's tribute and palmed the photo Nancy added. Maybe the faded black-and-white print had a story to tell.

As we reached the porch, Ross tooted his car horn. May and Eunice sat buckled into their seats.

Duncan kissed my cheek. "See you in a bit."

"Sounds good," I answered.

We both had assignments. I'd change clothes and pack all my toys—stun gun, pepper spray, gas mask, night goggles. Duncan would purchase the list of groceries I'd prepared on the fly, then swing by to pick me up.

Ross met my gaze in the rearview mirror as I slid into the Chevy Blazer's backseat. "That pizza idea doesn't sound half bad, Mom. What's say we order one, too? The three of us can watch a movie at your house. There's a Cary Grant tribute tonight on AMC."

God bless Ross. When May worked herself into a tizzy, she liked her family gathered round. With Ross and Eunice keeping her company tonight, she'd be less inclined to fret.

While I packed, my cousin shifted the conversation from murder to his mom's eightieth bash and his fast-approaching antique boat show.

Duncan knocked and announced himself through the closed door. I crossed the room to kiss May goodbye.

"You call me," she ordered. "Ten o'clock sharp. I'd like to know you're still breathing before I head to bed."

"I will, May, Scout's honor. I'll be back here by eight in the morning. Count on it."

May doffed her glasses, pulled a hanky from her purse and started polishing. "You know I still talk with your mom, just like

I do with Uncle John. So don't you go getting yourself killed, kid. Sis would never, ever forgive me."

I hugged May once more and whispered. "Not to worry. I'm too ornery."

❧

The garage door of May's "for-sale" house sat open, just like Weaver promised. Duncan pulled the car in. We walked up three stairs to the landing of the out-of-sight mudroom entry. He hit a switch and the garage door lowered.

Duncan pulled me to him. His arms tightened. My head nestled against his chest.

"Since it's group activity night, I don't know when I'll get another chance." Duncan's warm lips seemed mighty insistent, and who was I to argue? If that man's kisses didn't wriggle a girl's toes, her shoes were too tight.

"Maybe we can stop at your place for breakfast?" I attempted to mimic Cousin Ross's exaggerated eyebrow waggle.

Duncan grinned. "Sounds perfect. I stocked up on Wheaties—good for stamina."

An FBI agent flung the mudroom door open, gun in hand. We leapt apart. So much for canoodling.

With a curt apology, the agent patted us down and pawed through our belongings. I wasn't sure he knew what to look for—fake foot powder? Meticulously he inspected every ration in Duncan's grocery bags. In addition to fixings for pizzas, the sacks held all essentials of the slumber-party food pyramid—namely potato chips, French onion dip, cashews, chocolate chip cookies and ice cream.

My defensive weapons—pepper spray et al—were the man's most provocative find. He extracted the contraband from my gym bag before returning it. He also confiscated Duncan's cell phone.

"I'll hold onto these till Agent Weaver gets here and gives an okay," he said. "I expect her within the hour. I was told anyone who arrives stays. You will not be allowed to leave without an FBI escort, and any phone conversations will be monitored."

Okay, prisoner status? Weaver took her protection responsibilities seriously.

As soon as we were cleared, Darlene rushed to hug me. "I'm so glad to see you."

Julie took the grocery bags from Duncan and set them on the counter.

Darlene motioned toward a hallway. "You two can put your stuff in the first bedroom on the left. I assume you want to share."

Heat crept up my neck. I hoped no one construed my goodwill gesture to spend the night as respectable cover for a roll in the hay. Duncan tossed our overnight bags on the king bed, while I dumped my purse on a chest of drawers.

He caught my arm and spun me for another kiss. "That agent and his gun kept me from finishing." His marauding hands felt good, his probing tongue even better.

We came up for air. "I think they expect us to return," I whispered.

As we walked toward the kitchen, I considered the rustic cottage's layout. A long, scarred pine table filled a dining alcove. Scratches on the galley kitchen's cabinets revealed multiple layers of paint. The vintage stove and refrigerator dated from the sixties. Quite a come down from the Olsen's stainless steel Mecca.

Yet the house radiated charm. The picture window framed a pretty beach scene, and French doors led to a weathered screened porch with comfortable wicker furniture.

By rote, we headed toward the long pine table. Since Friday, I'd spent more time sitting at kitchen tables with Darlene than visiting with my aunt. Was it only Tuesday night? The days and nights blurred.

"Weaver called," Darlene said. "Olivia passed away. Now there's one more Olsen house roped off as a crime scene. I hope she has better news for us at dinner—like a lead on the killer. She said to expect her by seven."

Hunger prodded us to start our pizza making. As we rolled

dough, we argued over which ingredients would grace the entire surface of our pies and which should be confined to personalized taste zones. Onions, mushrooms and green peppers proved common denominators. Pepperoni, anchovies and hot peppers made the restricted substance list.

As we worked, Darlene and I bumped behinds in what Mom would have called a "one-butt kitchen." Duncan announced the action as if it were a hockey game. Laughter and the aroma of baking pizza made the evening seem deceptively normal. Our FBI minders stayed out of sight.

Weaver arrived about ten minutes before the pizzas were due out of the oven. Darlene wasted no time asking permission for her and Julie to leave town. One of our babysitters had allowed Darlene to call one of Jake's long-time friends, who'd agreed to put a private jet at her disposal. It would arrive at the local airfield at six the next morning. Barring any objections from the FBI, the plane would touch down at the Beaufort County Airport by nine o'clock, just in time for a late breakfast at my island home. Though islanders nicknamed our local airfield Frogmore International, my pilot friends told me it was a decent place to land.

After Weaver blessed the escape plan, she accompanied me to the bedroom and monitored my calls to smooth the way. The head of island security agreed to hire some off-duty folks to provide added protection for my houseguests. My neighbor Janie, who has a spare key, volunteered to meet Darlene and Julie's plane and ferry them to the island.

By the time the oven bell dinged, Darlene and Julie's departure plans were set.

Darlene hugged me, tears in her eyes. "What a relief. I don't know how to thank you."

I snuck a glance at Weaver. She appeared happy, too. Two potential victims—or possible killers—would soon be subtracted from the confusing Spirit Lake arithmetic. Would the new math help solve the murder equation?

With the Olsens in hiding, there were no butlers, maids or

other functionaries. No one seemed to mind or even notice. We helped ourselves to plates, paper towels and soda pop.

"I seldom say grace," Darlene said, "but I need to offer a little prayer tonight. Let's hold hands."

Those of us already grabbing for slices withdrew our greedy mitts. Duncan, seated on my left, squeezed my hand. On my right, Weaver accepted my hand with the same enthusiasm she might have shown a request to fondle a rattlesnake. Handholding wasn't one of her preferred customs.

"Thank you Lord," Darlene began, "for providing good friends to see us through bad times. Please let no more evil befall this family or the friends who join us tonight. Amen."

"Amen," we somberly echoed.

Once blessed, our supper chatter turned unexpectedly cheerful. It began with critiques of recent movies, then Julie asked me to tell her more about what her mom was like when we first met.

"Darlene was a few years younger than you…" My Spirit Resort yarns—censored for explicit sexual content—entertained the gathering. Julie especially liked the farting contest in which contestants used a cigarette lighter to flare gaseous emissions. Darlene indignantly protested that my memories were clouded.

"I didn't compete. Only judged," she countered with a laugh. "Marley must have been smoking wacky-baccie."

Weaver, a straight arrow except for her lesbian proclivities, frowned.

"She's kidding," I assured her. "Like President Clinton, I never inhaled."

As we pushed our plates away, I remembered the photo I'd pilfered from Jake's tribute. I retrieved it from my bag and passed it round the table, starting with Duncan to my left.

"Speaking of old times, does anyone know who's standing beside Jake in this picture?"

Everyone answered "no" until the photo reached Weaver at the end of the line.

"Don't you see the resemblance, Marley? Imagine him with a few more years under his belt. I'd bet anything it's Hamilton."

"Quentin Hamilton, no way," I interrupted. "If the man in this photo's still alive, he's what—seventy-five or eighty?"

Weaver rolled her eyes. "Listen up, it's Quentin's father. Can't you see the family resemblance? I figured you met Ansley Hamilton during your stint at the Pentagon. He died last year. His obituary earned several inches in the 'Washington Post'."

The mention jogged my memory. How had I missed the likeness?

Weaver tipped her chair back and rocked. "He got a lot of media coverage during hearings on Capitol Hill when he defended that billionaire CEO charged with insider trading. Ansley must have been a good lawyer—his client walked away with two-hundred-million dollars even though thousands of investors lost their pensions."

She handed the photo back to me. "Where did you get this, Marley? What's it have to do with this case?"

"Honestly, I don't know." I described how Nancy snuck it onto the display. "It may have no significance. Maybe it's just a happy memory of her time with Jake."

"Given what my husband told me about that bitch, she's not the sentimental type." Darlene's eyes narrowed. "I'd sooner believe she meant to give Jake the proverbial finger at his final send-off."

"How so?" I asked.

Darlene scrunched her face in a moue of distaste. "I don't know. Maybe she entertained a lover while the men took Kyle off to drown worms. I don't think she considered any lover off limits. Jake caught her screwing his business partner, you know. He knew she had multiple affairs."

Clearly my friend held no truck with philanderers.

"Did you run a background check on Nancy?" I asked Weaver. "Say, I just realized I don't even know the woman's last name. Does she go by Olsen?"

"No, she remarried—twice," Darlene answered. "Her last husband was a Pike. That's the surname she's using. Kept it after the last divorce."

"I'll see what we can dig up on her," the FBI agent promised. "Probably nothing. But it's not as if we have tons of leads. I'll crosscheck information on Ansley Hamilton, too. See how, where and why he crossed paths with Jake."

"Don't bother." Darlene balled up her paper napkin and stood. "That's no secret. Ansley and Jake were college roommates at Harvard, lifelong friends. Ansley's law firm handled all Jolbiogen's legal work. Ansley visited Jake just before the cancer did him in. I wish they hadn't been such good friends." She shuddered. "That's why Jake hired Quentin Hamilton—because that prick was Ansley's son."

Nineteen

After dinner, we moved to the cottage's well-worn sofas and oversized La-Z-Boys. Outside the drizzle turned into a driving rain. Every time a northerly gust picked up the tempo, splatters smacked the large windows. The barrages sounded like spinouts on a gravel road.

Duncan inspected the old stone fireplace and discovered gas logs. He flipped a switch and flames danced merrily. While the fire wasn't needed for heat, its warming blaze provided a psychic balm.

Our conversation veered to the topic of scientific advances and their potential for good and evil. The chatter reminded me of the DNA report hidden in Glaston's floor vault. Undecided if Weaver wanted it mentioned, I dosey-doed with a roundabout inquiry.

"Is Jolbiogen doing any pioneering DNA research?" I asked Julie. "Let me rephrase that. Is the company doing anything you can talk about?"

"Sure. There's plenty of work going on that's public domain. In fact, Jolbiogen regularly puts out press releases on our progress. This may interest you, Agent Weaver. We've developed new DNA screening kits for crime-scene and paternity. Both huge markets. We're in the final testing phase now and expect to begin sales before year-end.

"Our portable kit separates DNA source material into sequences, then uploads to a high-speed mainframe programmed for this work. The kit can be plugged into any phone jack and delivers results in a couple of hours. So if a murder victim got a few licks in before she died, police can determine if blood under the victim's fingernails matches a suspect."

"I read about that," Weaver commented. "When we went through Dr. Glaston's papers, we found a Jolbiogen header on a DNA report dated May 10. Could it be related to testing for the kit? We didn't find any test data with the same date on the Jolbiogen computers."

"That's odd." Julie frowned. "If it was a Jolbiogen printout, the information should be there. One of Dr. Glaston's labs is handling quality control studies. For each test, DNA samples are taken from a dozen volunteers—employees, relatives, lab visitors, whoever wanders by. Each test includes two relatives, say a mother and son or a brother and sister. All the rest are control blinds to make sure the kits don't give false positives. In fact, Jake and I both donated skin scrapes for a test."

Weaver twirled the pencil she'd been holding. "Our missing report showed two distinct DNA matches—one for siblings, one for a father and son. Perhaps they included multiple relatives in that test."

Julie shrugged. "That doesn't sound right. You could ask Jim Jacobs. He set up the protocols and supervised all of the studies until a couple of weeks ago. Jim's no longer at Jolbiogen though. A headhunter lured him away to Boston."

My skin tingled. Were we onto something? "Julie, what if one of the tests turned up an unanticipated DNA match?"

"Jim would have reported it to Dr. Glaston and asked permission to contact the folks involved for added testing. He'd want to determine if the test kit delivered a false positive or if the people were truly related. A ticklish situation. Who'd be eager to ask a woman, 'Could this young man be the kid you put up for adoption twenty years ago?'"

Aha. Potential blackmail.

"Glaston's printout identified patients by number, not name," Weaver added. "How could we identify the people who took part in that particular study? Our computer forensics team turned up zilch. Either the study was never input or an expert wiped the computer. Our guys found none of the electronic footprints that are usually left behind when people erase files."

Duncan leaned forward. "A lot of wills have a standard phrase that divides an estate between named heirs and any other living issue." His voice hummed with excitement. "Some attorneys are looking to use DNA tests as a means to claim inheritances for illegitimate children. Maybe we have a motive."

The FBI agent excused herself. "I need to leave. I'll be back in a couple of hours."

I stood. "Too many Cokes," I fibbed.

I caught up with Weaver in the mudroom as she slipped on a rain slicker. "Would you ask the folks at Jolbiogen to compare DNA samples from all Olsen blood relatives—Jake included— plus everyone who's visited Julie's lab in the past three weeks?"

"You think Glaston blackmailed someone about an illegitimate kid? Could be. We have hair samples from every family member—gathered to help us sift through trace evidence."

"Can you get a sample from Hamilton, too?"

Weaver's eyebrows shot up and she laughed. "Are you kidding? Why?"

"Let's call it a hunch."

Weaver shrugged. "I'll try. Maybe I'll stick a pin in him to see if his blood's really blue."

While her suggestion sounded appealing, I had a better idea. "Vacuum the chair in the office Hamilton uses at Jolbiogen. Despite the hair gel, I'll bet he sheds."

Duncan smiled when I reclaimed my chair. "Well, there's one subject we've studiously avoided," he said, "even though it's on everyone's mind. The murders. Let's brainstorm, try to make sense of what's happened."

No one objected but silence reigned. What the hell? I had something to say.

"We know Dr. Glaston's our thief, but I'm convinced the doctor's accomplice is our serial killer. Glaston certainly didn't kill himself. So who did? Jake, the Glastons, Olivia—all were murdered by someone with estate access and toxin know-how."

"Thanks, Marley. You're describing me," Julie complained.

"True. But Kyle fits the bill just as well. He comes and goes as he pleases at Jolbiogen. He has a degree in chemistry, knows his way around a lab. The Glastons welcomed him into their home. They didn't invite you over for cocktails. Plus Kyle could have walked into his wife's dressing room whenever he pleased."

"But he was in Omaha when Jake died," Darlene interrupted.

"True, but who's to say he didn't switch the eyedrops days before Jake used it?"

Duncan leaned back in his chair. "So what's the son's motive?"

"He's plain evil." Julie shuddered. "That man makes my skin crawl. I heard how he talked about his dad—not exactly a loving son. He's been cheating on his wife for years, too. I think even dimwitted Olivia knew."

"Julie, I don't like Kyle either, but that's malicious gossip," Darlene jumped in.

"Oh, Mom, it isn't," Julie snapped. "Remember Celia Riley, the friend I met at Camp Foster when we were twelve? In junior high, Celia told me Kyle regularly spent the night with her mother, Vivian. Celia hated Kyle."

"So what if Kyle was bonking Vivian?" Darlene asked. "That doesn't give him any reason to kill Jake, the Glastons or Olivia."

"Celia said she used to eavesdrop on Kyle and her mom. Kyle talked trash about his father. Called Jake a mean, stingy tyrant who sent him to boarding school because he didn't want him around. He described Gina's mom as the wicked stepmother personified."

Until the woman conveniently died in a boating accident with Kyle at the wheel.

"Kyle's second favorite topic was how much he hated his wife," Julie added. "He claimed he'd married her to please his father and the shrew couldn't even bear children to carry on the glorious Olsen family name."

"Oh what hogwash!" Darlene piped up. "Jake only wanted him to be happy."

Duncan held up his hands. "How about Eric? Sure, his image is one of a druggie unable to hatch a plot, but the boy's not stupid, and he put in time at Jolbiogen. Jake told me he has a one-forty IQ. Maybe his zonked-out demeanor's an act. He was mad at Jake, and he hated Dr. Glaston."

"Which is why Eric would never have teamed up with Glaston," Darlene objected. "Don't forget, that's the other part of the equation. We're looking for someone who collaborated with the doctor. You know how a cat toys with a cockroach, that's how Dr. Glaston played with his stepson. Nothing could have compelled Eric to help him."

My friend shook her head. "No. Eric wouldn't kill Jake, or his mother. He's unbalanced. But the boy loved Jake. His granddad was one of the few people who showed the kid affection."

"Why not add Nancy to the suspect list?" I asked. "When did she first turn up in Spirit Lake?"

"The day before Jake died," Duncan answered. "Jake called the gate to let her in. I checked the log."

"What!" Darlene exploded. "Jake said nothing about a visit. He hated the woman."

"Mom, don't go ballistic. Why would Nancy want to kill Jake now, after they'd been divorced what—more than forty years? An ex who wants revenge would have acted a lot sooner."

"You know what they say about revenge being a dish best served cold," Duncan tossed in. "But I think Julie's right."

"Yeah, Mom. Nancy's grudge isn't cold, it's permafrost. Even if we invent a motive for Nancy, how could she get cyclogel and know it would kill Jake? Plus she'd have needed a supply of phalloidin to murder Olivia and Gina."

I jumped in. "The murderer didn't have to kill these folks with his—or her—own hands. No one in this family is exactly strapped for cash. Any one of them would have enough dough or promised inheritance to pay a creative hit man. Dozens of people visited the estate before that wedding reception. A paid killer could have waltzed in with the caterers, the florists, pest control, hell, any service company."

Duncan nodded. "There's another group with unlimited access to the estate—Thrasos International Security. Those guards share a lot of skills with hit men. They know plenty of criminals, too. Maybe one of the Thrasos guards was hard up for cash."

I glanced at my watch. Almost ten. Time for a reassuring chat with Aunt May.

"I need to ask one of our babysitters to dial Aunt May. If I don't check in, she'll have my hide."

When I returned from my brief conversation with May, all signs of bonhomie had vanished. Darlene and Duncan sat silent, eyes glued to a hallway where an FBI agent stood at parade rest. Where had Julie gone?

"What's happened?" I asked.

"Weaver walked in with a funny look on her face and another agent in tow," Duncan answered. "She asked Julie to come with her. Very formal and told us to wait. They disappeared into that last bedroom down the hall and closed the door."

"Probably routine," I lied. Had it been routine Weaver wouldn't have asked another agent to join her nor would she have cut Julie from the herd.

I sat beside Duncan. He reached over and squeezed my hand.

Julie burst through the watched door and barreled down the hall toward us. "Oh, Mom," she sobbed and collapsed in her mother's arms.

Her grown-up composure had crumbled. Her sobs stretched into a child's long wracking cries of misery. Too distraught to talk.

Weaver and her fellow agent emerged. Faces somber.

"What did you do to her?" Duncan demanded.

"CSI investigators found new evidence at Kyle's house." Weaver spoke like an automaton, all emotion buried. "The tampered foot powder container was wiped clean—just the victim's prints. But the techs found Julie's prints on an Advil bottle nearby. Strands of Julie's hair were caught on a dresser hinge. She can't explain the fingerprints or hair."

"I never set foot in that house," Julie wailed. "That's why I can't explain it. I didn't even know Olivia. And if I'd killed her, I sure as hell would have worn gloves. Yes, I'm guilty of taking Advil, but that's all. Somebody must have taken that bottle from my purse and planted it. My hair, too."

Duncan glared at Weaver. "For Christ's sake, don't you see the pattern? This isn't the first time someone's manufactured evidence to make Julie look guilty. Remember the fake emails and mysterious UPS package. Glaston's journal made it clear those clues were bogus. Someone's trying to let Julie take the rap."

"Yes, I remember. I have no plans to arrest Julie. But the fake emails designed to implicate Julie in the theft were probably put there by Glaston. Since he's dead, who's framing her now? I can't ignore this. I'm afraid I'll need to confer with my boss again before allowing Julie to leave town.

"Right now, I'm headed to Kyle's house to talk with the crime scene techs. I've asked Agent Rickard"—she nodded in the direction of the man who'd joined her for the interrogation—"to stay with you."

Julie's crying jag collapsed into soft hiccups. Tears trickled down her cheeks. While Darlene cradled her daughter in her arms, Duncan and I offered platitudes. Everything would turn out okay.

We sank into silence. The room seemed to shrink, sucking all life from its dejected inhabitants. Bruise-like smudges reappeared under Darlene's eyes. How I wished I'd stayed at May's.

A slumber party first. Regret.

Exhaustion—physical and emotional—finally overtook us and we dozed. The thunk of a closing door startled us awake. We never made it to bed.

When I moved, my joints crackled like a just-milked bowl of Rice Krispies. No light through the blinds. I squinted at my watch. Four-thirty. Duncan yawned, and I began to ascend from brain dead to groggy.

Did everyone feel as scruffy and crotchety as me? My teeth

wore little fur coats—accessorized with cookie crumbs.

"Morning," Weaver said softly. "Sorry I woke you. Figured you'd be in bed by now."

"We were waiting for you. More bad news?" Darlene mumbled.

"No, though you won't like everything I have to say. My boss has agreed to hold off on charging Julie, and he'll permit both of you to go to South Carolina. You have to surrender your passports, however."

So far, so good. Dear Island, my home, may have some strange customs, but it's part of the good old U.S. of A.

"I asked one of our agents in Omaha to check Julie's desk at Jolbiogen," she continued. "He also rousted one of Julie's coworkers in the middle of the night. She confirmed the young researcher always kept an Advil bottle in her top drawer. No bottle. The absence doesn't prove tampering, but it raises questions."

"That took all night?" Duncan asked.

"No," Weaver answered. "About midnight Eric called the sheriff claiming that Nancy was drugging him. The boy also claimed he heard Nancy say she was thrilled Jake and that blackmailing son-of-a-bitch Glaston were dead. Then Eric screamed, 'She's going to kill me just like Grandpa.' The sheriff immediately called us."

"That bitch," Darlene spat. "Did you arrest her?"

Weaver shook her heard. "The kid was ranting. Probably high. There's zero evidence to support his claims. Naturally we checked on the boy. Since Kyle refused FBI protection, we didn't have anyone at the house. When our agent arrived, Eric was in bed. Passed out."

Darlene stood, hands on hips. "So that's it? You're not going to do anything to protect Eric?"

"Simmer down. I talked to Kyle in person, suggested hospitalizing Eric. He wouldn't hear of it—not without a court order. He claims Eric's been through hell so he sought refuge in drugs. Kyle characterized Eric's phone call as a bad trip. Said institutionalizing Eric would make things worse. I'm going after that court order."

"Maybe Doc Johnson can help you show cause," Duncan said. "He treated Eric before and after he went into a drug program in Omaha."

"Eric should go back to Omaha," he added. "Kyle should leave, too. With Jake's memorial service postponed, there's no reason for any of Jake's heirs to hang around and wait for a new death."

Weaver nodded. "I made a similar recommendation. Kyle rejected it. He intends to stay in Spirit Lake until the coroner releases all three bodies—Olivia and the two Glastons." Weaver cast an apologetic glance at Darlene and Julie "As long as the FBI sits on top of you, Kyle says he doesn't need protection.

"The bodies will be released Friday. Then, he'll head to Omaha for services and burial. Meanwhile, Kyle and Eric are staying put. So your visit to South Carolina is a good plan. Puts a couple thousand miles between you. I'll see you to your plane."

TWENTY

While Duncan gathered our belongings from our unused bedroom, I pulled Weaver aside. "You promise to de-bug Aunt May's condo after this morning's play, right?"

"It's a deal. Just make sure you and Ross pull this off."

"When will I hear from you again?" I asked.

"I don't know. Sorry, but if our planned script stirs up the killers, I may be a little busy. I'll contact you as soon as I can."

Darlene and Julie waited for Weaver at the door.

"Guess it's time to say goodbye." I hugged Darlene. Until last week, my old friend had been little more than a wisp of memory. Now she felt like a sister. Tears matted my eyelashes.

She clung to me and wept. Her shoulders shook. "This will be over soon." I patted her back. "We won't lose track of each other so easily this time. You'll love Dear Island. Stay as long as you like. When I return, we'll sip rum and Cokes and drive the natives nuts. A few weeks and this soap opera will be just another chapter from our colorful pasts."

"I hope so." Darlene straightened. "Thanks for everything, Marley...Duncan. I couldn't have gotten through the last few days without the two of you."

Duncan took my hand as we watched them drive away. When the car disappeared, he kissed my tear-stained cheek. "You are absolutely right," he whispered. "This nightmare will end soon."

At a little after five a.m., he walked me to Aunt May's door, all last night's bawdy talk about breakfast nookie long forgotten.

In the doorway, we whispered, making plans for the next couple of days. Not surprisingly, sleep, sleep, and deep sleep topped my immediate agenda. Dozing fitfully in a chair hadn't improved my disposition.

Since Duncan had cleared his morning calendar for Jake's memorial, now a non-event, he decided to take advantage of the hiatus to get some shuteye and wade through stacks of accumulated paperwork.

"Want to come over to May's for supper?" I asked. "I'll spend the afternoon doing her bidding to atone for last night's desertion. But I'm sure my aunt would love your charming company tonight."

"It's tempting." Duncan smiled. "But I'd suck as a companion. Think I'll cart home Chinese takeout, park in front of the TV and watch anything that flickers across the screen. Don't worry. I bounce back quickly. I'll be up to snuff by tomorrow. That's Wednesday, right? God, I'm losing my damn marbles."

A vivid flashback to a marbles game convinced me my mental equilibrium had slipped, too. My prized cat's eye rolled straight for one of our cast-iron floor registers and tumbled through the grate. I listened as it pinged its way down the metal chute to our cellar's coal-burning behemoth. It's never good to lose your marbles.

"I'm not sure I have any left to lose."

Duncan awarded me a smile and placed a chaste kiss on my forehead.

❖

The strange noise put me on alert. Then I laughed.

My aunt's snores, louder than a buzz saw, had no difficulty piercing her bedroom door and echoing down the hall. The homey sound comforted. When she woke, May would be well rested and ready to verbally kick my butt.

Today I could promise my aunt in all good conscience that the Olsen murderfest wouldn't impinge on our time together. Too bad I couldn't say how or when the ordeal would end for Darlene and Julie.

Weaver had dismissed my fears for May's welfare. She theorized that Darlene and Julie's departure took me out of danger as well. "Who are the killers going to blame if there are more attacks? Darlene and Julie can't be framed if they're a thousand miles away."

After Ross and I did our shtick this morning, my family's involvement would end.

At seven o'clock, Aunt May woke and spouted off as expected. Once she decided I was appropriately contrite, she forgave my pigheadedness. We breakfasted on her patio. The sunshine painfully bright. I squinted at the new day.

While I didn't divulge all of the evening's surprises, I did reveal Darlene and Julie had flown the coop. Since I knew someone might be listening, I professed ignorance of the destination. May didn't care. She was simply delighted they wouldn't be drawing fire in my vicinity.

"I must say I never get bored when you visit." May harrumphed. "I didn't give birth to girls of my own, but you and Kay are like daughters. You know I love you. I just naively assumed my girls would play with dolls not guns."

Though bed called to me with a siren's song, naptime had to wait for May to exit for a date with real estate prospects and Ross to drop by at nine o'clock for our pre-scripted chat.

My cousin's job was to ask questions. I mentally rehearsed my responses. Weaver reckoned panic about new evidence should prompt the murderer to act rashly. She reasoned our playacting would give the killer—or killers—a single target: Weaver. I'd paint a big bulls-eye on her back when I identified her as the sole possessor of Jake's pretend second riddle.

The doorbell rang.

"Ross, you just missed May," I said. "But come on in and have a cup of coffee."

After three minutes of what we gauged to be sufficient chitchat, we got to the meat of our play. "So, Cuz, what's new on the murder front? You didn't trip over any new bodies last night, did you?"

"No, but the evening didn't lack for drama," I answered. "Turns out Darlene found yet another note from the beyond. Guess Jake figured multiple clues would ensure at least one of his evidence packets surfaced."

"So was this new note a carbon copy of the one that led us on our Tipsy House wild goose chase?"

"Nope. According to Agent Weaver, Jake left a clue for a different hiding place."

"What's the clue, maybe I can figure this one out, too?"

I chuckled. "I'm sure you could have, but Weaver's playing this one close to the vest. Darlene is the only person besides Weaver who's seen the clue, and Darlene's been whisked out of town and placed under guard."

"Weaver didn't even give you a hint?"

"No, and she claimed she wasn't going to show the note to anyone else in the FBI either. She thinks there's a leak so she's going this one alone."

"Well, good luck to her," Ross said. "Hope she finds the hidden treasure. Oh, man, look at the time. I need to run. See you at the museum later?"

"Yep. See you this afternoon."

I grinned conspiratorially at my cousin and patted myself on the back for our flawless performance. God, how I hoped our listeners tumbled into Weaver's trap.

Mission accomplished, I practically shoved Ross out the door. Sleep was my sole objective.

I pulled the covers over my head and slept like a baby.

Aunt May shook me awake with more gusto than my throbbing head deemed necessary. Two cups of caffeine didn't halt the pounding hooves in my mental carousel. Morbid thoughts circled in lazy repetition. Maybe the sugar lift of a sin cookie would help. I munched.

Inside an hour, I climbed the evolutionary ladder to humanoid, and Aunt May suggested a drive. For the next two hours, we circled blue lakes and chatted about real estate and relatives.

May left her cell phone switched off. What peace.

My aunt checked her answering machine as soon as we walked into the house. It had logged loads of hang-ups. "Probably pesky reporters," May decided. Friends and family members tended to leave cranky messages, rather than stony silences, to discourage phone possum.

Weaver hadn't phoned. No surprise. I'd be very happy when the agent terminated all listening devices tuned to May's condo and had no further need to phone me. I wanted life to return to normal. Boring has its virtues.

We spent the rest of the afternoon indoors. I fired up my laptop to help my internet-challenged aunt update real estate listings with photos I'd snapped on my digital camera. I'd taken a portrait of May for the site, too, but she nixed it, claiming it would "frighten a horse."

Next we collaborated on the genealogy tree. It showed all our family nuts and fruits hanging from appropriate branches using hundreds of heirloom pictures Ross scanned last winter as a stay-indoors, frozen-lake project. For her likeness, May selected her wedding photo. A little arithmetic told me she was not yet twenty when it was taken. Her gleaming dark hair curled softly. Her eyes sparkled with pleasure. She wore a creamy satin dress and held a bouquet of calla lilies.

"Want to use your wedding portrait on your real estate site?" I teased.

"No." May snorted. "I'm better looking now. You just haven't captured my beauty."

The genealogy artwork would decorate the walls at May's birthday party and we'd handout legal-sized copies as party favors. Working on the family tree brought to mind Mom's cautionary tale of skeletons in the closet.

"Remember Mom's initiation into genealogy?"

May frowned. "Not really."

"When she retired, Mom decided to trace our roots. After retrieving her parents' birth and death certificates, she searched for their marriage license. Couldn't find it. Finally Mom asked Aunt Julia if she had the marriage location wrong. Julia told her to stop looking because the records had burned in a fire at an Illinois courthouse.

"A year later, Mom stumbled across the marriage license. She'd been looking in the wrong year, not the wrong county. Aunt Julia fibbed because she didn't want Mom to learn about her parents' shotgun wedding. Like Mom would be shocked by that news at the tender age of sixty-two."

May laughed. "I remember now. Your mom was fit to be tied. Couldn't believe she'd wasted all that time combing records because Julia felt honor-bound to protect her sister's 'shameful' secret. People sure have funny notions about what's proper for children of any age to know about their parents. Parents are people."

May's comment reminded me of Darlene's pledge to keep Kyle from finding out he wasn't Jake's biological child. Silently I asked my friend's forgiveness for urging Weaver to test the DNA of all Olsen family members. Technically I'd kept my promise. I hadn't told a soul Kyle was a bastard. Tactically I'd forfeited the confidence.

My suggested DNA screening would cause more people to learn Jake didn't contribute to Kyle's genetic code. I hoped the FBI would be discrete if that finding didn't relate to the case. Maybe Kyle would die believing Jake was his natural father.

Glaston's mystery DNA report highlighted two DNA matches—a father-and-child and siblings. Jake and Kyle weren't the father and son match, and they certainly weren't siblings. But I figured either might have fathered an out-of-wedlock child. If the FBI stumbled across an unexpected genetic link, it might offer a clue about blackmail possibilities.

Could blackmail have triggered all the murders?

At six o'clock, May and I warmed our leftover chicken divan and settled in to watch the evening news. Winding up a *special report* on the Olsen tragedy, the anchor closed with her juiciest tidbit. "WYZK just learned that Olivia Olsen, daughter-in-law of billionaire Jake Olsen, is the latest biotech murder victim. Knowledgeable sources confirm her death was caused by the same exotic research toxin that killed Olsen's daughter, Gina Glaston, two days ago."

I choked on a forkful of chicken. Who'd leaked the information?

The anchor wasn't finished. Her mascara-enhanced eyes widened as she credited confidential informants. "The same sources tell us Darlene Olsen, the billionaire's widow, and her daughter, Julie Nauer, left Spirit Lake this morning in a private jet. Destination unknown. It's believed the FBI continues to consider Ms. Nauer, a person of interest in the high-tech murders."

The reporter's facial calisthenics produced a frown. "No one knows the mother and daughter's destination or if they plan a return to Spirit Lake."

I wondered if Weaver might be the anchor's source. Maybe she wanted the world to know Darlene and Julie weren't in residence.

May and I called our yawnfest quits at nine o'clock. I tried to read several pages in my mystery but my mind went AWOL. It continually drifted back to four murders.

Twenty-One

Vowing not to subject any new morning visitors to my crumb-decorated wardrobe or peanut butter breath, I set my alarm for seven a.m. Plenty of time to imbibe java and brush my teeth before a doorbell rang.

My precaution proved unnecessary. I woke at six thirty and started coffee. A peek into May's bedroom confirmed she still slept. I eased the door shut and called first dibs on our hot water supply. The steamy shower felt heavenly.

By the time I dressed, May presided in her easy chair, coffee cup in one hand, "Des Moines Register" in the other.

"Morning," I greeted.

"Good morning." A chipper reply. "It's sure nice having coffee ready. Why don't you set an alarm every morning? Six or six-thirty would be dandy."

"Fat chance. I'll put a new coffeepot on your Christmas list, one with auto start. What's on your agenda, May? Is this your day for office duty?"

"Yeah, my turn to answer phones." She wrinkled her nose. "Nine until two. Every now and again, office duty pays with a lucrative walk-in, but mostly, it's boring. One reason I'm thinking of retiring. My eightieth birthday's right around the corner. Why the heck should I dance to someone else's tune?"

I grinned. "Pardon me for contradicting, but you're allergic to retirement. Remember, you tried it and it didn't take? You love to crank up your charm-o-meter and schmooze with strangers.

Besides your real estate broker's wrapped around your little finger. Tell him to jump and he'll ask how high. Ask him to take you off office rotation."

"I could," my aunt admitted. "Truth is, I'm not as sharp as I used to be. Sometimes I look at numbers—offers or real estate comps—and I can't remember why they're there, what they mean. Your mom confessed the same unease, and less than a year later, whamo! Alzheimer's hit sis like a Mack truck. Remember? That's when she started hallucinating about machine guns in the mall and started calling cops on neighbors she swore stole her pocketbook."

I remembered. Oh, how I remembered. Nevertheless, May's forgetfulness and occasional mental lapses had a very different character, and I told her so. For better or worse, May's personality showed no sign of change.

"May, none of us is at the top of our game when we're tired," I offered. "You just get weary a bit more easily. With one word, I can tell you why Alzheimer's isn't a worry. That word is bridge. You've been top dog in your bridge club for six months running. No way could you win consistently if Alzheimer's were creeping up.

"Mom loved cards and never missed a trick. About two years before other symptoms surfaced, she started forgetting cards, losing count," I added. "That was our first hint of trouble. You're fine. Trust me."

I crossed the room, hugged May and kissed her cheek. God, I prayed my layman's diagnosis was correct. I couldn't stand to see another bright woman—a woman I loved—mentally wither.

"Where are you playing bridge tonight?" I asked.

"At Gertie's. June's picking me up at six-thirty. Say, kid, want to come? The ladies wouldn't mind a little kibitzing. You could even sit in on a hand or three."

"Thanks, May, but I made plans with Duncan. Dinner and Okoboji Summer Theater. He has season tickets."

May closed her eyes. A smile played on her lips. "Duncan reminds me of Bob. We had lots of fun. Maybe you'll get all prickly when I say this, but I get damn tired of spending all my time with women. They jabber about the same nonsense. It's nice to go out to dinner with a man...to have a man pay you a compliment... to have a man hold your hand."

I sighed. "I understand. You know, I've always been a little puzzled why you never married Bob."

May had "dated" Bob for ten years, starting at age sixty-five. The relationship ended when he died of cancer. The two had golfed together in a senior couples' league, played in a weekly bridge group, and dined out every Tuesday and Friday. Even my doting male cousins approved of May's charming suitor.

I smiled when I realized I'd never allowed my mind to wander to May's sex life. Why is it that we imagine our elders live in sexless purgatory until we start to approach the same stage of life?

May raised her coffee cup, took a sip. "Bob asked, I considered. I think he popped the question because he felt obligated. I doubt he wanted to marry me any more than I wanted to marry him. We liked our arrangement. I could spend time alone whenever I pleased, but I was never lonely. With my own bank account, I could splurge on anything—antiques, my boys, grandkids—without fretting I'd be chastised for going overboard. Plus, if I got a hankering to visit my far-flung chicks, I could hop on a plane. Bob had children, too, a tight-knit family. Neither of us needed a new spouse. We needed a friend—a special friend of the opposite sex."

Was that what I wanted from a relationship? No children complicated my equation. Like May, I treasured my independence and relished occasional solitude.

A doorbell interrupted my mental meandering.

"Morning," I greeted Weaver before she could push the bell a second time.

"Hello, Marley." She strode across the room to greet May. "A pleasure to see you again, Mrs. Carr. Sorry your family's been dragged into the Olsen troubles. I'm sure you've been worried about Marley. I'm pleased to report we should have this business wrapped up soon. Would you two like to join me for breakfast?"

Clearly Weaver played to hidden microphones. She knew May's schedule.

"Wish I could," May replied. "You two go ahead. I have to leave for my office shortly and won't be back till after two. Marley, that means you won't have wheels. You'll have to call Eunice or Ross to play taxi driver if you need to go somewhere."

"Not a problem, May. Have a great day."

With a round of waves, we parted.

Weaver speed-walked toward her government-issued sedan. I stayed on her heels. She shot out of the parking lot. I assumed we were headed for what had become "our spot"—the Kettleson Hogs Back Wildlife Refuge.

The FBI agent swiveled her head my way. "Wait till we get there."

The cleared straightaway leading to the refuge made it impossible for a tail to go unnoticed. Our empty rearview mirror bolstered Weaver's confidence we were alone. The rendezvous spot's only inhabitants were perhaps a hundred squawking trumpeter swans.

She climbed out of the car. I joined her. "Jolbiogen ran the DNA tests," she began without preamble. "Your hunch was right, we found a genetic shocker. Kyle Olsen and Quentin Hamilton are half brothers, and Jake Olsen didn't come up as daddy for either. How on earth did you know?"

"What! I didn't. Kyle and Quentin Hamilton are brothers? You're kidding. There's no resemblance beyond some nasty personality traits. I knew Jake wasn't Kyle's biological father. I thought there was a remote possibility Hamilton had an illegitimate kid working at Jolbiogen. Who do you think Glaston blackmailed?"

"My bet's on Kyle. He had the most to lose," Weaver replied. "Maybe Kyle enlisted his half-brother's help. They were friendly even before the DNA test. I assume Ansley Hamilton was our indiscriminate sperm donor. The notion that Kyle and Quentin are both bastards with the same phantom father is too big a stretch."

I shook my head, mystified. "I don't see this as fodder for blackmail. What's the big deal? The sons aren't at fault. Neither was Jake. Ansley Hamilton's the jerk, and he's dead. Who cares? Ancient history not even worthy of a reality show."

"I'll bet Kyle and Hamilton care—maybe enough to kill over it," Weaver countered. "We're talking money and prestige. Maybe Kyle figured Jake would disown a *son* who was the issue of a friend's traitorous fling. Hamilton wouldn't want his precious family name besmirched either. He revels in his blue-blood genealogy and lofty perch among Washington's elite."

I shoved my hands in my pocket. "Too bad Hamilton's vulnerability to blackmail seems iffy. He's a better candidate for criminal mastermind. He knows how to stage crimes, manufacture evidence and hire black-op types. Since Thrasos protects big shots from rock stars to foreign royalty, he can access Interpol and other intelligence on the world's top assassins."

It was hard for me to imagine Kyle pulling off the complicated murders alone. "The sad part is Jake knew from the get-go that Kyle was his 'adopted' son. He kept it secret because he wanted to protect their relationship. Jake loved him."

The FBI agent jingled the keys in her pocket. "Sad but irrelevant. What Kyle believed is all that matters. He probably figured the DNA report would devastate his old man."

"I guess," I admitted reluctantly.

Weaver straightened from her slouch. "How about this?" Her choppy hand gestures communicated excitement. "Let's say Jake discovered Glaston was the thief and gave his son-in-law a small window to turn himself in. Instead Glaston blackmailed Kyle into helping him kill Jake. Then, once he had one murder under his belt, Kyle decided murder wasn't all that difficult and whacked Glaston."

I wasn't buying. "Glaston I can see. But would Kyle murder his own sister and wife in cold blood?"

"Hey, he'd just received a news flash that Gina Glaston wasn't even a half-sister. The drunk would take millions out of his pocket if she lived longer than Jake. Remember the terms of the will? And Kyle was boinking this Vivian woman, a classic reason to off the missus.

"Or maybe Olivia listened in on the wrong conversation. We do know that Kyle didn't waste any time shacking up with Vivian Riley, his long-time lover."

"Any evidence to support your theories?"

"Not a shred," she admitted. "Just my gut. We'll find evidence. Kyle isn't as smart as he thinks. Hamilton either, if he's in the mix."

Now that we'd moved from speculation to evidence gathering, I asked why Weaver hadn't tried to locate and capture May's eavesdropper. "Even if it's a hired hand, couldn't you tie him to Kyle or Hamilton?"

"Our equipment tells us the receiver's located inside a five-mile radius. Doesn't narrow things down much. It could be in a rented house, a hotel room or a vacant unlocked cabin. Dozens of second homes sit empty, especially during the week."

"What's your next move?"

Weaver kicked at some gravel. "I'm disappointed your chat with Ross about new evidence didn't panic our targets. We'll pull the plug on this phase of the operation. This afternoon we'll do a sweep and electronically block the eavesdropper who's tuning into your aunt's condo."

My relief wasn't complete. "I'd feel better if you had concrete proof Kyle's your killer."

"Me, too. Guess I'd better get to work and make that happen. I'll stay in Spirit Lake one more day. If we don't get a break here, I'll head to Omaha and follow other leads. I'll contact you when I have something new to share."

"I hope that's soon. Darlene must be going crazy, wondering if and when she and Julie can reclaim their lives."

❖

I checked our refrigerator bulletin board and, sure enough, found a scribbled note from May: "Be home three p.m. latest. Call 555-1875 if you need me."

Poised in front of the refrigerator, I opened the freezer and helped myself to a Dairy Queen Dilly Bar, my favorite summer breakfast.

Having decided to run ten miles to atone for recent caloric transgressions, I snagged a tourist map from May's hoard of real estate giveaways and calculated a Spine Trail route that would deposit me close to Ross and Eunice's doorstep. They'd given me a key so I could shower and change clothes at my alternate vacation base.

Hmm, wonder if Eunice might want to join me for a late lunch at Arnolds Park. Using May's speed dialer, I punched the button labeled with my cousin's name. Eunice picked up on the fourth ring. A yawn preceded her response.

"You know how I hate mornings, breakfast and cooking. One o'clock sounds perfect. You sure you want to run over here on the Spine Trail?"

"Yep, I need the exercise. I'll change at your house."

"Okay, I'll let Ross know we're coming. You know how he is on the first day of a show. The big parade isn't till Saturday, but all the boats go on display at noon. He practically needs a towel to mop up his drool."

The boat show offered a fun finish line for my run. My first post-Tipsy House visit to Arnolds Park would be in broad daylight. Good. On this sunny June day, there'd be no shadows to hide imaginary bogeymen.

My jog generated more than a few extra huffs and puffs, payback for a few days' layoff. The exertion performed its usual mind-scrubbing magic, allowing me to think clearly about the merits of Weaver's hypotheses.

I had trouble imagining a well-off executive—filthy rich by my yardstick—killing four people to protect an inheritance. Yet the half-brothers appeared to have inherited the same arrogance gene. Maybe Kyle considered himself too intelligent to be caught.

Were Kyle and Hamilton in cahoots? Hamilton's company hired plenty of ex-CIA and FBI agents. Corporations called on

Thrasos to salvage computer records deleted by embezzlers. If Hamilton wanted files to permanently disappear, he only needed to reverse the process.

An unholy alliance between the half-brothers made a certain sick sense. The pair had opportunity with a capital O.

Weaver's problem. Like it or not, I was out of the fray. Truth was I liked it. I was ready to enjoy my relatives—and Duncan, lust willing—for the remainder of my "vacation."

I rounded a corner and saw a man in the distance. He stood perfectly still. Not a runner. After a few more steps, recognition dawned. General Irvine.

"General." My greeting came between pants. I'd been running flat out.

"We can walk and talk," he said. "Looks like you're ready for a cool down."

I squinted at him in the bright sunlight. "How did you know where to find me?"

"Weaver told me. The bug was still operational when you made the lunch date with your cousin. I figured you had to run down this section of path, and I wanted to see you in private."

"Have you identified the terrorists who bought from Glaston?"

"Yes, thank God. Knowing Glaston was the seller was a big help. The doctor flirted with right-wing groups for decades. I feared the buyers were Middle East terrorists targeting our troops with deadly diseases. Given Glaston's profile, we started poking at different viper nests and got lucky. We traced a Glaston email to a Bo Quigley disciple. Bo's a racist nutcase—a very charismatic one. Homeland Security's been watching his group a couple of years."

"Have you recovered the stolen materials or made any arrests?"

The general shook his head. "That's why I'm here. Homeland Security arrested the man we believe is responsible for infecting those farm workers. They're sweating him, and we're getting close to having enough evidence for a raid. I'm contacting you because he had a scrap of paper with your name on it and your aunt's address."

My stomach dropped and the sweat on my arms turned to ice. "Do you think I'm a target? I'm not about to spend a minute more with May or my cousins if it puts them in danger."

General Irvine seized my shoulders and held tight. "Don't overreact. We're watching May's condo. My guess is Glaston's co-conspirators enlisted the terrorists to monitor conversations in May's condo. That's why the guy had your name and May's address. They're not interested in you, just in tracking down any evidence Jake scared up."

I wrapped my arms tight to my body to ward off a wave of chills.

"Weaver still thinks her trap will work? That they'll come after her?"

"Yes. We just figured you ought to have the complete picture. It doesn't look as if any of the villains are foreigners. They're WASPs who'd blend in anywhere."

My head reeled. "So what does this Bo character want with a targeted virus? And where's his money coming from? Glaston's journal indicated he was getting ten million for the theft."

"Hispanics are Bo's newest focus for hatred. The recent downturn in the economy helped his recruitment big time. He blames illegals for stealing jobs, grabbing freebies that bankrupt our government, and sabotaging the American way of life. Bo has a pile of money and he's mad as a hatter."

"That's why the field test targeted seasonal farm workers?"

"If we're right, yes. We think the grand plan was to 'cleanse' the American population by releasing a virus targeted to kill Hispanics in cities across the country."

"My God. These people are crazy. Are they even human? Their plan would kill millions of innocent civilians, bona fide citizens as well as undocumented workers."

Before we parted, the general promised he or Weaver would contact me if they made progress or any change suggested my family might be in danger. "My purpose wasn't to frighten you," he added. "I just believe forewarned is forearmed."

Walking up the path to Ross and Eunice's house, the silence felt ominous. Typically, Queenie and Empress—my cousin's Shelties named for excursion boats—get so wound up they hurl themselves against the low picture window and yap with ecclesiastic fervor when anyone approaches. Tomblike silence, never.

My heart hammered. Sweet Jesus, the general had made me jumpy.

I tapped out a "Shave and a Haircut" jingle on the doorbell to alert Eunice. A Chevy Blazer parked out front indicated Eunice hadn't motored away. Walking the dogs?

I strolled around back to claim an Adirondack chair and enjoy the view from the high bluff while my sweaty body cooled. Once I rounded the bend, I spied Eunice and her Shelties on the dock. Simultaneously, the dogs spotted me and brayed like lunatics as they raced up and down the boardwalk's narrow confine. For once their racket was music to my ears.

"Be right down," I bellowed. Since the dock was too far for shouted conversation, I trucked down the hillside's sixty-one stone steps. Ross claimed there were sixty-one steps going down, two hundred and one coming back up.

Eunice held what looked like toddler life jackets.

"Expecting youngsters?" I asked.

"They're for Queenie and Empress. The UPS man just brought them."

I laughed. "You're kidding."

Eunice didn't crack a smile. "You know Ross. He gets in the water and teases the dogs until they jump in. He can't stand it if he doesn't have playmates. But the girls are getting up there. One day they won't be able to paddle to shore."

I stifled my grin and helped Velcro Queenie into a stylish lifejacket decorated with racing stripes.

"Okay, Queenie, honey." Eunice leaned over the dock to immerse Sheltie number one. "Let's see how this works."

The straggly-haired dog flipped and bobbed like a cork—upside down. Her wee feet pedaled with madcap frenzy above water. "Oh, no!" A swell threatened to carry the submerged dog away from Eunice's outstretched arms.

Already soaked from my run, I jumped in to right the feisty mutt. Queenie rewarded my valor with a nip. Eunice heaped more praise on me than a Medal of Honor winner.

She cradled the writhing mop in her arms. "How's my baby? Don't you fret."

"I'd say that lifejacket needs a little refining." Eunice ignored the hint of amusement in my voice.

Before we left, I noticed a sleek cabin cruiser anchored perhaps two-hundred feet offshore. No one on deck. How odd.

❖

Volunteer handyman Nels had outdone himself. The museum's entry showcased three classic wooden boats on raised platforms. Two 1950s-era Chris-Crafts leaned like fancy struts at thirty-degree angles to the passageway's sides, while a locally built 1932 Hafer claimed top billing above the archway. Ross had tipped the runabout on its side so everyone could covet its cherry red leather seats, gleaming mahogany decking, and shiny brass trim.

"Wow, impressive. Who did Ross coax into hoisting the Hafer up there?"

"Don Henderson," Eunice replied. "He's building a three-story timeshare on East Okoboji and Ross sweet-talked him into burning a little midnight oil with his crane."

"Looks terrific." I marveled as always at what Ross accomplished through jocularity. Everyone who meets my cousin—men and women, young and old—are eager to find ways to bask in his hundred-watt smile. Ross is the exception to the rule that good guys finish last.

Unfortunately, his bonhomie seems nontransferable. This week alone, I could name a dozen folks who hadn't taken a shine to me. For some reason, the Hamiltons, Kyles and Olivias of this world have little affinity for lippy broads.

As Eunice and I craned our necks to admire the boat show's come-hither arch, one of the museum's part-time workers greeted us. "I'm heading over to Godfather's Pizza for a little breather. Wait'll you see what Ross is up to now!" She rolled her eyes in mock exasperation.

The tinkling sound of children's laughter greeted us inside the museum proper. Ross had donned a tattered, old-time canvas dive suit, complete with a bell helmet that looked as if it were bolted—and rusted—in place.

It had to be one hundred degrees inside. Ross didn't seem to notice. He'd recorded "Monster Mash" as background music and performed a lurching jig in the sand surrounding the Miss Lively—the 1928 recovered wreck displayed near the museum's entrance. Ross's merry blue eyes danced with more zeal than his clunky dive boots could manage.

Two-dozen six- to eight-year-olds wearing bright aqua T-shirts from a lakeside church camp giggled, wriggled and clapped to the music. They gasped en masse as Ross plucked two giant bones from the wreck's interior.

Once he had them spellbound, the curator-showman doffed his heavy bubble helmet. "These aren't human bones. They're buffalo bones unearthed at the bottom of West Okoboji. This takes us back to a time when Indians called our region home. Believing Big Spirit Lake had evil demons waiting to destroy them if they ventured upon the waters, they never risked crossing any of our Okoboji lakes. No boats, canoes or rafts of Indian origin have ever been found—"

Having all but memorized the upcoming segment of Ross's history lesson, we waved farewell and sauntered down the center aisle of the airplane-hangar sized museum. Ross had scootched around permanent exhibits to make room for the most valuable and fragile participants in this year's Antique and Classic Boat Show. A red carpet runner and an overhead banner proclaimed we'd entered the realm of wooden boat royalty.

As a nonconnoisseur, a person who wouldn't know a 1940 Chris-Craft from a 1958 Resorter, I still was impressed with the proud craftsmanship and timeless style. "These boats really are beautiful."

"Thank you." The man's voice startled me. "Now what would you like to know about my 'Wet Dream'?"

"Pardon me," Eunice said.

The speaker, whose gleaming dentures were the centerpiece of a puckish grin, looked almost as old as the 1938 twenty-four-foot Sportsman he stroked with proprietary pride. *Wet Dream* was the name the old prankster had gilded on her prow.

Neither Eunice nor I had the heart to abandon the devilish oldster without giving him an opportunity to brag. So we asked about the boat and listened to his discourse on its pedigree. The speedboat was one of only two models built during 1937 with a Scripps/Ford flathead engine. The elderly gent claimed he'd personally applied fifteen coats of varnish to the gleaming deck.

Escaping the garrulous showman, we wandered through one of the museum's overhead garage-style doors to an outside area. Each hydraulic door opens wide enough for a small airplane to taxi through without clipping her wings. A godsend for moving boats with six-foot beams in and out of the museum.

The open bay led to a loading and storage zone Ross had temporarily converted into a showroom annex. Jerry-rigged canvas awnings borrowed from regional funeral homes and lashed together with boat lines provided spots of shade and limited protection from the elements.

We ambled through the exhibit. "I do like to look, but I'm happy we no longer have a wooden boat—or, rather, pieces of one—strewn across our basement. When Ross was restoring his Hafer, I had a recurring nightmare someone would strike a match and our house would blow. Those resin fumes can bowl you over. Once Ross started captaining the Queen, he no longer had time to putter. Now that he's museum director, he plays with his toys at work."

"I resemble that remark." Ross had snuck up behind us. Though he'd exchanged his diving suit for a short-sleeved seersucker shirt and lightweight khakis, he still mopped copious amounts of sweat from his forehead. "Let's get something to drink. I must've sweat off five pounds in that diving suit. Don't think I'll wear that thing again before February."

At the boardwalk Godfather's Pizza, we traded money for high-test calories and claimed a café table in the mild afternoon sunshine. As we lunched, we watched antique boat enthusiasts ogle and salivate. In addition to the boats showcased in dry dock, three-dozen vintage vessels were moored in Arnolds Park anchorages. Owners of these seaworthy boats, prepped to lead the weekend's stately water parade, gave short rides to tourists. Ticket revenue from the excursions contributed to the show's prize money.

"Just wait till you see the harbor at night," Ross enthused. "Prettier than Disneyworld. Colored lights drape all of these classics. They twinkle like fairy dust."

After we polished off our late lunch, Eunice checked her watch. "Three o'clock. Ye gods, I have to run. Marley, I can drop you at May's, but you'll have to join me for a few errands first."

"Don't let her hijack you." My heart sped up. The voice belonged to Duncan. "I just got here. Stay awhile and I'll take you home."

Ross pumped Duncan's hand. "Hey, nice shirt."

His knit polo shirt's red pocket was embroidered with a white Queen II logo. The rest of the package wasn't shabby either. Crisp chinos, polished loafers and a big smile.

"Our board meeting starts in a few minutes, but it'll be over quickly," Duncan added. "We're going to tell the rest of the board about Jake's bequest. Why don't you stay, Marley? You can come straight home with me. It'll give us time for a boat ride before dinner."

"If slacks are fine, it sounds like a plan. I'll call May so she won't worry. Ross, can I use your computer to check emails?"

"Help yourself."

In Ross's office, I dialed May's home phone. Her answering machine picked up on the fourth ring. She'd probably latched onto some poor walk-in schlemiel. I left a message.

To pass the time, I checked emails and piddled around on

the Web. A little after four, I tried May's home again. No pick up. After debating a few minutes, I dialed her work number. Though reluctant to bother her at the office, I wanted to suggest she bring her bridge club to Arnolds Park tonight after the final rubber. Let the ladies enjoy the harbor light show her son had planned.

"Robinson Realty," a perky voice answered. "This is Donna."

"Hi, Donna. This is May's niece, Marley. Could I please speak with my aunt—or is she with a customer?"

The pause was lengthy. "May's not here." Donna sounded puzzled. "Isn't she with you? She left about noon, after that fellow called to say you'd had an accident while you were jogging. We figured May would come back to work or call after she picked you up. When she didn't phone, we decided she was playing nursemaid."

My stomach lurched and my head started pounding. I wanted to scream at the real estate agent, pummel her with questions until her blathering made sense. There'd been no accident.

Calm down. Panic won't help.

A sick hunch told me to reach Weaver pronto. If May'd been kidnapped, it would be counter-productive to spread the alarm and stir up a media hornet's nest.

"Sorry, Donna," I stammered. "I'm a little confused."

"That's okay," Donna answered. "Hope you feel better soon. Why don't you drop by the office tomorrow? Say, the other phone is ringing. Bye."

Twenty-Two

Why the hell would someone harm—or kidnap—May? Did they think she could help them get their mitts on that damned nonexistent riddle?

Though my body stayed rooted in Ross's computer chair, my mind raced like a hyped-up gerbil scrabbling on a wheel. The telephone on Ross's desk rang and I jumped. Not sure why I answered. It wasn't my phone. Habit, I guess.

"Maritime Museum," I mumbled.

"You're doing well, Colonel Clark," a distorted voice commented. "You haven't lost your head. That's good. Very good—if you hope to see your aunt alive again. We tapped all the museum phone lines. So I know you just hung up from Robinson Realty. Your aunt ran straight into our arms when she thought you'd been hurt."

"Bastard." In my head, I screamed. The actual sound I made came closer to a whimper. Breathe, I told myself. Concentrate on every word. Listen to background noises, to his accent.

"We can listen in on every phone call—cell or hard-wired," the voice continued in mechanical singsong. "Don't think about phoning for help or emailing. We have that covered, too. Plus we have observers inside the museum. They paid admission. More money for your cousin's coffers. Look out the door at those happy tourists. Care to guess which ones have you under surveillance?"

My hand tightened on the receiver. "Why are you doing this?" I worked hard to keep my volume under control. "I'll kill you myself if you harm May."

I figured the disembodied voice belonged to either Kyle or Hamilton. But sharing my conviction could only make things worse.

"A touching, foolhardy threat," my tele-tormentor replied. "We hold all the cards. You haven't been dealt a hand. So let's not waste time on theatrics, shall we? You asked what we want. The answer is simple—Weaver. And, you, Colonel Clark, will acquire her for us. Just telephone and ask her to meet you at the museum. Tonight at eight-thirty, half an hour after closing. Tell her you can't say more over the phone. Instruct her to come alone. We'll listen to every word.

"If you try to warn Weaver, we kill your aunt," he continued. "If you speak to anyone besides your cousin, we kill your aunt. Clear enough? Until the museum closes, you and Captain Ross will confine yourselves to his office. You won't talk to another soul. I'll call with more instructions at eight o'clock, after the museum doors are locked."

"What you're asking is impossible," I objected. "Ross is in a board meeting with Duncan James. Duncan's expecting me to go home with him. I have to speak to him at least long enough to beg off."

"Well, well, guess you've turned this into a party for three. When the gentlemen join you, tell both of them our arrangement. I hope Captain Ross's office has three chairs. Or maybe you'd prefer to sit on Mr. James's lap."

The accompanying noise sounded more like a hyena's bray than a laugh.

"How do I know May is alive? I won't do a thing until I speak to her."

"Oh, I expected that and arranged a little party-line call. I'm not with her, but my colleagues say she's very spirited for her advanced age. My associates will now let Mrs. Carr say a few words—a very few."

"Marley," Aunt May croaked, her voice hoarse and low. "I'm fine, kid. Just be brave—like your Grandpa Brown. Keep your fears at bay. We'll make it through this."

"May, are you really okay? Have they hurt you?"

"That's it." My nemesis cut May off. "I may let you speak with her later—if you behave. Remember, your aunt is family. Weaver is an FBI agent. This is her battle, not an old woman's war. Consider carefully where your loyalties lie.

"Your aunt told my friends she wasn't afraid to die, that she's lived a good life. The question is will she be awarded a good death. If you force my associates to kill her, I promise this old woman won't die peacefully in her sleep. Similar unpleasant finales will also await Captain Ross and your Mr. James. Do as you are told, and you'll all be around to celebrate your aunt's birthday."

A click. Disconnect. I couldn't seem to loosen my grip on the phone. Static buzzed in my ear. Somehow it seemed that returning the receiver to its cradle would end my connection to May forever.

Finally, I hung up, grabbed pencil and paper, and started writing. First, I made notes about the call—time, instructions, voice, stray noises, May's words. Next I penned a script for my call to Weaver. I didn't trust myself to vocalize without a cheat sheet. The caller had one thing right: this was Weaver's war. She'd orchestrated our play to trigger a reaction. Surely, she'd be on red alert.

I believed the caller would kill May if I failed to follow orders. What was one more body? I also was certain he meant to murder May, Ross, Duncan, Weaver and me, as soon as he discovered the FBI agent had no new evidence. Stalling would buy a little time. There wasn't another play.

I took several deep breaths, exhaled, and dialed Weaver's cell. She answered immediately. I read from my notes, swallowed repeatedly trying to keep my voice neutral. I hoped any distress in my tone would seem natural, given my message. "Something's come up and I can't discuss it over the phone. Can you meet Ross and me at the Maritime Museum tonight? Around eight thirty? It's urgent."

"Marley, how about toning down the drama? I'll come get you now. Where are you?"

"No, please," I countered. "There's a traitor in the FBI. Come alone. It's a matter of life and death. Yours. I can't say more. Please come at eight-thirty."

I hung up. Sweat trickled down my back. Weaver's alarm bells had to be clanging. Unfortunately, I couldn't count on those bells leading the agent to the proper conclusion.

What else could I do? An inkling of an answer stirred in my brain.

Ross and Duncan sauntered into the office at five after five. Absorbed in an animated discussion, my angst didn't register until they turned to say howdy.

"What's wrong, Marley?" Ross demanded. "Are you sick? You're white as a jib sheet."

"Close the door, please."

Standing in the office threshold, Duncan raised an eyebrow but did as he was bid.

My gaze locked on Ross. "I am so sorry. I never intended to put either of you in danger."

I didn't sob. No hysteria. Tears gently rolled down my cheeks. I could tell my demeanor scared Ross and Duncan. It couldn't be helped. My fright—the suffocating kind you feel when your actions, or inaction, might harm a loved one—held me tight in its grip.

I blurted out the news. "May's been kidnapped." Ross reacted as if he'd been punched in the gut. He sagged like a deflating beach toy. He would have sunk to the floor if his desk hadn't served as a supporting pillar.

"Let's hear it," he said stoically. "All of it."

I'd never seen such an expression of hatred cross my cousin's face. While I hoped his rage was focused on the kidnapper, I wouldn't fault him if his broad brush of anger tarred me with equal blame. My guilt at dragging May, Ross and Duncan into this quagmire squeezed my chest in a vise.

I couldn't change the past. My only hope—our only hope—was to affect the future.

I gave a bare-bones synopsis of my phone calls, repeated

Donna's account of May's disappearance, outlined the caller's demands, and reported my monologue with Weaver.

"Are you certain the kidnapper's monitoring all the phones?" Duncan asked.

"Given that he could repeat my entire conversation with Donna, I don't think he's bluffing," I answered. "And his claim of email omniscience isn't much of a stretch if he has a worthwhile hacker in his employ."

Ross put his finger to his lips and motioned us in. "Is there a bug?"

I'd conducted a thorough search—a skill acquired while stationed in Turkey—and found none.

"I'm relatively confident there's no bug in this office," I whispered. "If we talk softly, I think it's safe enough. And I may have figured out where they're holding May."

Ross's head snapped up.

I consulted my notes. "Aunt May urged me to be 'brave like Grandpa Brown.' Ross, I don't have a Grandpa Brown, and, if memory serves, there's no such relative on the Woods family tree either."

Ross shook his head. "No." His forehead creased.

"Next May said to 'keep fear at bay.' Could she be telling us she's in Brown's Bay? When Eunice and I were down on your dock, I spotted a cabin cruiser anchored offshore. Maybe they picked that location in case they needed to grab Eunice as a backup hostage if anything went wrong."

Ross's face turned red. His hands balled into fists. "You're grabbing at straws. Hell, that Grandpa Brown clue could mean anything. There's a Brown Street in Spirit Lake. Or maybe Mom was telling us her kidnapper's named Brown. She's nearly eighty and someone's holding a gun to her head!"

I sensed Ross was desperate to reject the notion Eunice might be in danger, too. "I could be wrong. But while we were talking, I heard a distinctive clink of metal rigging against a mast. They were on or near a sailboat, like that large catamaran tied to your neighbor's dock. Plus I heard the Queen's air horn—it sounded really loud. The man called about four-thirty."

Ross sank into a chair. "The Queen would have been near Brown's Bay. How many times did the horn blow?"

"Three," I replied.

"They're in Brown's Bay." Ross dropped his head into his hands. "When I piloted the Queen, I gave three blasts on the horn every time we entered the bay to say howdy to Eunice. The younger captains continued the tradition. God, we have to warn Eunice and figure out a way to rescue Mom."

"Could one of us sneak out?" Duncan wondered.

"Too risky—at least before the museum closes. The caller may be blowing smoke about surveillance. Then again, it could be true. Look at all those people wandering about." I pointed at the gawkers clearly visible through the office door's sidelight windows.

"Phone calls and emails seem equally chancy," I added. "But maybe we can use the Maritime Museum's website. Ross, you built your own site to save money. Do you still maintain it and host it on a local server?"

Ross looked at me. "Yes. I use the Mac on my desk for updates. What do you have in mind?"

"Could you add a big banner to your home page—immediately? Promise the first fifty people who call Weaver's number a free pass to Arnolds Park and eligibility for a grand prize drawing.

"To qualify, callers must repeat a phrase as soon as their calls are answered. I seriously doubt the killer's monitoring your website. I only hope someone in cyberspace visits your site within the next couple of hours."

Ross rubbed his hands together. Having something to do recharged his optimism. "Our hosting service claims we average fifteen thousand click-throughs a month. We only need one person. If we don't take a chance, we're all dead. I have no illusions this guy will let Mom—or any of us—go, even if we follow him like sheep."

With a decision made, we debated the banner's message. We

considered listing two phone numbers for contestants—Ross's home phone plus Weaver's private line. After my cousin pointed out Eunice was likely to be in the garden and callers might get an answering machine, we nixed that option.

We had to count on Weaver. She'd answer her phone. She had the resources to react.

Next we struggled with wording. Finally, Ross fired up his Macintosh, typed the copy and pulled in eye-catching graphics. In less than five minutes, he posted a red banner across the top third of the museum's website. A pulsing Queen icon drew the eye directly to our headline:

BECOME AN INSTANT WINNER! QUALIFY FOR A $5,000 GRAND PRIZE!

In slightly smaller type, the banner promised the first fifty callers would receive a season's pass to Arnolds Park good for their entire family—Duncan's idea—plus eligibility for a $5,000 drawing. To become instant winners, cyber visitors simply needed to dial Weaver's number and read a paragraph of promotional copy:

"Prepare to be ambushed! Our museum is full of surprises! Heart-stopping moments for every family member. So, even if your aunt claims she's tied up in Brown's Bay, insist on bringing the whole clan. Drag your spouse out of that house on the hill. Plan on having a blast!"

If Weaver didn't get the overall picture, we figured more words wouldn't help—they'd just make callers think the banner was a hoax or too weird to comply. Message posted, we crossed our fingers. Time to brainstorm ways to seize the offensive.

At eight o'clock, a museum guide walked by the office. Noticing Ross's closed door, an anomaly, she frowned. Ross pasted on a smile and saluted her, but didn't open the door. The museum volunteer took the hint and pantomimed inserting a key in a lock and turning it. Ross nodded assent.

We heard the motorized doors at the rear grind closed. At five after eight, Ross, Duncan and I were alone.

"Let's open the door. It won't feel quite as much like prison."

Duncan moved from his perch on the edge of Ross's cluttered desk. He swung the door open. Simultaneously the phone rang. Could they still see us?

"What?" Ross answered and punched the telephone's speaker option.

"Ah, the sound quality tells me I'm on speaker. Excellent. It's best if you all hear this. We think Weaver will comply with Marley's request. So far, the three of you have behaved prudently. No phone calls or emails. We have one final request. Unlock the side door, the one that brings visitors into the Chamber offices."

"I can't," Ross replied.

"I was led to believe you're rather fond of your mother, Captain," the voice hummed with menace.

"The Chamber has its own alarm system." A vein danced a peripatetic jig in my cousin's temple but his voice remained calm. "I don't know the code to deactivate it. The door between Chamber offices and our museum is locked when the last employee leaves. Any attempt to get in will trigger an alarm at the sheriff's office. Our insurance company insisted on separate alarms. That way, if there's a theft, the insider suspect list is halved."

"Why should I believe you?" the voice growled.

"As you said, I love my mother."

"Then open the overhead door at the back," the kidnapper demanded.

"Happy to," Ross replied. "But it's clearly visible from the boardwalk and people can hear the gears gnashing half a mile away."

Silence. We'd evidently thrown the villain an unexpected curve. Good.

Our pre-scripted answers were designed to buy either extra time or advantage. We didn't want our captor to know we could escape through the Chamber offices.

Our other comments were partially true. Guards had been added and the giant garage-style doors groaned louder than a rusty drawbridge.

"If you want us to keep cooperating, let me speak to my mother," Ross demanded.

"Hold on while my associates put Mrs. Carr on our party line. We've warned Mrs. Carr what will happen if she tries to get clever."

"Ross, Marley?" May whispered. Her voice thready, weak. "Whatever happens, I've had a wonderful life. I'm not afraid. I love you."

No clues. May's words conveyed a mix of defiance, melancholy and resignation.

"That's it folks." Our tormentor was back on line. Was he the mastermind or a hired gun? "After we give Agent Weaver a fitting reception at the museum, we'll let Mrs. Carr go. For now, your only job is to follow my rules. No phone calls, no emails, no warnings."

The moment the line went dead a surge of anger had the three of us tripping over our tongues as we rushed to vent our fury with a torrent of swear words.

"Do you think they've harmed May?" I asked. "That goon's comment about hurting her if she tried anything clever worries me."

Ross sighed. "I've never heard Mom sound so dejected. Not even when she was headed for her triple bypass."

"I know you're beside yourselves with worry about May," Duncan interrupted. "But getting sidetracked won't help. She's alive. He'll keep her that way until he has his grubby mitts on Weaver. So let's get busy."

Confident we couldn't be watched inside the museum's empty and windowless interior, we raced to arm ourselves. During our interminable wait, Ross listed every conceivable weapon in the antique treasure trove. Our weapons came courtesy of generations of boaters, fishermen and hunters who'd left a legacy of prickly tools and clever devices. After debating their lethal merits and portability, we called dibs on items matching our individual strengths.

Duncan, a hunter, picked a modern flare gun and a silver-plated shotgun—the 1908 sportsman's choice for dove hunting. A stickler for accuracy, Ross kept all the antiques oiled and in working order with ammo displayed in the same locked case. Duncan quickly loaded the over and under gun with two 20-ought shells and pocketed a dozen more.

Staying with his underwater diving theme, Ross ransacked the museum's spear gun collection. His chosen weapon—including loaded spear—weighed less than three pounds.

I studied the weapon's pistol-like grip. "Do you fire that thing like a gun? What's your range?"

"Yeah, it operates like a handgun," he answered. "Shooting in air, I should be able to hit a target ten to fifteen feet away with so-so accuracy. Underwater, I'd attach a shockline to retrieve spears that go astray.

"These spears are particularly nasty." My cousin's smile didn't reach his eyes. "After they pierce a target, these little barbed flippers open like a molly bolt. If I nail any of these bastards, they're not going to get the spear back out."

Ross bent to retrieve an all-purpose serrated knife—superb for filleting fish and sharp enough to whack off a finger.

My first armament choice was a grappling hook—the kind used to drag lake bottoms for drowning victims. The nightmarish device looked like an anchor but bristled with sharp hooks. Tied to a six-foot length of rope, it was probably too heavy for me to use like a bola. But I could imagine other uses. Pirates used grappling hooks to haul over and board ships. An interesting possibility.

Next I picked up a nasty-looking gaff attached to a thick wooden pole. Some old-timer had probably used the gaff's razor-edged barb to hoist fifty-pound walleyes into his dinghy. I wondered if the handle's rusty discoloration was blood.

For good measure, I bundled up a large fishnet and wound several strands of clear fishing line around my waist. Might come in handy if I got the chance to use a snare or hog-tie someone's hands and feet.

Our plunder included the museum's retail section. We needed

wind suits, tee shirts and caps. We selected blend-into-gloom shades of black and navy. Cheap plastic pool shoes completed our stealth ensembles. We bypassed the display of life jackets. Neon orange and day-glow yellow would advertise our presence. I hoped Duncan was as strong a swimmer as Ross and me.

We didn't speak as we dressed and crammed most of our weapons in over-the-shoulder book bags. Last of all, Ross cracked open a laser printer toner cartridge lifted from his desktop printer. We'd finally found a use for that nasty black matte powder that clings so readily to moist fingertips. We smeared the powder on our shiny—and sweating—white faces. The camouflage would help us blend in with the deepening twilight.

I laughed when I glanced over at Ross. He'd tried to comb toner through his white moustache. It looked as if a tiny skunk hovered above his lip. The grim look in Ross's eyes suffocated my transitory amusement.

"Ready?" Ross asked.

"Yes." Duncan and I answered in unison.

Though we doubted the museum's industrial strength walls would give our movements away, we crept in stealth mode toward the side door we'd claimed was inaccessible. Fearing a telltale light leak through Chamber windows, we didn't switch on a single overhead as we tiptoed through the adjacent offices. We prayed the murderer's attention was riveted on the museum's front door, waiting for Weaver. That gave our lakeside sortie a fair chance of going undetected.

After mulling over alternatives, we agreed we'd done all we could for Weaver with our website warning. Saving May and safeguarding Eunice would be our focus. We counted on our enemy dismissing us as demoralized and cowed patsies. Not the type to try a nighttime break out.

Yes, the risks were high. Watchdogs might spot us. Or the kidnapper—Kyle or Hamilton?—could dial with a new demand and wonder why we didn't answer.

We took the chance.

We slipped out the door and ducked behind shrubs planted between the museum-Chamber complex and the employee parking lot. In full summer bloom, the fragrant roses scratched my hands and snagged my clothes. Still the limited cover delighted me.

Total darkness inside the Chamber offices had adjusted our eyes to gloom. Outside the golden twilight seemed bright as the noonday sun. I blinked, feeling as though I'd stepped into a spotlight. My heart hammered. I imagined hoodlums pointing guns and laughing at my minstrel-blackened face.

As seconds ticked by without shouts or shots, my confidence increased and my heartbeat slowed. For the moment, no one looked our way. I scanned the surrounding area. No sign of predators lurking behind the lonely oak sentinels that dotted the grassy park to our right. Scattered trees provided the only cover in that sector.

The pier housed two idle Lakes Patrol wave runners. Our goal. Ross had spare keys so Queen helmsmen could commandeer the craft if lake emergencies arose when deputies weren't on duty.

My cousin groused often about the detrimental influence of "personal watercraft" on lake aesthetics and ecology. In his opinion, the moment teenaged boys saddled up and felt throbbing engines rumble between their thighs, testosterone surges drowned all traces of reason in their brains.

Tonight we were all glad that Lakes Patrol officers—like highway patrolmen—pony up money for machines designed to outrun offenders. The authorities had purchased models capable of rocketing from a stand still to sixty miles per hour in under six seconds. We prayed that power would help us catch the cruiser serving as May's prison.

When Lakes Patrol first acquired the craft, Ross teased the drivers mercilessly when they bragged their bright yellow and black machines had won some sort of shootout. Now we were happy to be mounting such champion steeds.

To reach the wave runners, we had to cross one hundred feet of open space. Ross knew the territory best and led the way.

Forgoing a madcap dash across the main thoroughfare, he led us in a slow stealthy crouch. As we inched along, the urge to run proved almost irresistible. I knew fast movement was more likely to catch a watcher's eye.

Safely across the road separating the museum complex from the main boardwalk, we picked our way among the shadows cast by the shops and cafés that cater to boardwalk strollers. With every step, my ragged breathing echoed in my ears. Adrenaline, not exertion, made each gasp feel like an indigestible solid. A cool breeze caressed my face. My wind suit stymied its relief from reaching any other part of my anatomy. Rivers of sweat trickled down my sides, back and legs with no escape hatch in the sticky confines.

One more hurdle. We needed to traverse the boardwalk to reach the pier.

"Ready?" Ross whispered. "I'll take the first Sea-Doo and Marley will ride with me. Duncan, you take the second. Here's the key. Untie her and paddle into open water. Make sure she's ready to roar before you fire up the engine. The minute we start these suckers, someone's bound to hear. They make more noise than a Cuisinart in a phone booth."

There was nothing sexist in the decision to have Ross and Duncan pilot. Both knew lake landmarks and were used to navigating West Okoboji at night. I wasn't. Worse, I'd never been on a wave runner in my life. That put me only slightly behind Ross and Duncan, who'd together logged less than an hour on the floating equivalent of a Harley-Davidson. I hoped I'd be able to stay on—if we weren't shot before we launched.

Duncan and I gave Ross a thumbs up. The three of us hightailed it across the boardwalk. We crouched on the pier by our commandeered Sea-Doos and breathed a communal sigh of relief. The bulk of the two-story Queen—in a parallel berth—would help screen us from anyone who looked our way.

Ross slid onto a wave runner and I slipped behind him. As the machine sank beneath our weight, cold lake water sloshed against my calves. Icy prickles penetrated the mesh of my pool shoes. Now the sweat that coated my body felt like dry ice, so cold it burned. My teeth chattered violently.

The wave runner rocked beneath us. It seemed to lurch with electric-shock suddenness at the least provocation—like batting an eyelash. I wrapped my arms tightly around my cousin's chest, determined to hold on for all I was worth.

Ross shoved us away from the dock and maneuvered into open water. "I know you're nervous," he wheezed, "but you have to let up. I can't breathe."

"Sorry." I loosened my death grip.

Ross started the engine, and the peaceful twilight exploded. For a mind-numbing second, I thought our miniature gas tank blew. Why was I still in one piece?

I caught fireworks in my peripheral vision as all hell broke loose near the front of the museum. Bursts of machinegun fire began a rat-tat-tat rhythm.

Good. The warlike cacophony at our back would mask our exit. Why didn't Ross go?

He fumbled in his wind suit pocket and pulled out the radiophone he used on the Queen.

"Now that the fight's begun, I'm calling Eunice. Warn her to get out of the house."

Duncan slipped beside us on his idling wave runner. "Why are we waiting?"

I explained while Ross yelled into his phone. The fireworks at our back escalated.

Relief lit Ross's cherubic face as he pocketed the phone. "Eunice's fine. A website visitor called Weaver and she deciphered our warning. Our FBI friend's getting her licks in now, and agents are protecting Eunice."

"What about May?" I asked.

"The agents set up in my study to monitor that cabin cruiser in our bay. Based on body-heat signatures, they presume May's locked in the cuddy cabin below deck."

"What's the rescue plan?" Duncan asked.

"Not yet underway," Ross answered. "The FBI feared someone was inside the museum with us. Now that they know we're out, they'll try to capture the boat. We've been ordered to stay put. I say no way. I'm heading to Brown's Bay. If either of you want to stay, fine."

"I'm with you," I said.

"Me, too," Duncan yelled. His last words were almost swallowed in a roar as Ross revved our wave runner like a lunatic teenager.

Twenty-Three

We torpedoed onto the gunmetal lake. Maybe we didn't reach sixty miles per hour in six seconds, but it felt like I was pulling G's.

Had I been curled in a rocker instead of rocketing over West Okoboji's surface, the evening might have seemed inspired. The sinking sun lit a layer of high white clouds from beneath, painting them lavender, pink, red and purple. The clouds shimmered with an inner glow as the twilight deepened. To our left, the harbor's antique boats twinkled, the colored lights winking as the boats bounced in our wake.

The beauty served as contrast. Nature's antonym to our terrifying reality.

We seemed to pick up speed with each skip over the choppy water. A persistent nor'easter churned the water. Whitecaps threatened.

I felt like I rode a bucking bronco. In Alaska. Cold, stinging pellets of lake seeded the whistling wind scouring my face. With eyes scrunched into protective slits, searching West Okoboji's dark eddies for tree stumps or rocks proved impossible. At our speed, any half-submerged object could fling us into oblivion. Would our riderless Sea-Doo lurch on? No, a "dead man" feature would cut the motor instantly if we both flew overboard.

We rose and slapped down on an endless series of cresting waves. Frenzied musicians beating a tambourine. My bottom wasn't as well padded as I'd thought.

Off to port, I recognized a white-pillared mansion bathed in spotlights. We'd passed Pillsbury Point. Thank God. We'd safely skirted its treacherous rock piles.

A snaggletoothed branch surfaced directly ahead. Ross veered sharply to avoid contact. Oh, God, we were headed straight for Duncan.

My heart slammed in my chest. My gaze focused on Duncan's leg, which I was certain we'd crush in an instant. Somehow he dodged in tandem. We sliced by one another with a teaspoon of water to spare.

We'd pledged at the outset to stick together—the nautical three musketeers. If we reached the boat before the FBI, we figured a two-pronged attack would stand a better chance of success than a solo kamikaze run.

Through the cold spray, a smoke-like mist rose from the lake. Glowing lights in a smattering of cottages provided the only sign of habitation. The shore appeared as a blur of trees and rocks. For safety, Ross gave the land a fifty-yard berth.

The darkening landscape's contours suggested we'd passed the modest rises of Sunset, Gilley's and Wheeler's Beach. Steeper embankments signaled the hilltop neighborhoods of Bayview Beach and Maywood. Ross's house and the moored kidnap cruiser were less than a minute ahead.

Abruptly Ross rolled us ninety degrees right. I held on for dear life.

"What are you doing?" I screamed.

Duncan had been cruising slightly behind us, allowing Ross to set the pace. Dammit. We'd need more than the luck of the Irish to avoid a collision this time. I gritted my teeth, braced for impact.

A high-pitched whine signaled Duncan's shift into reverse. Hallelujah, maybe we'd make it. We zoomed diagonally across his path. We'd lucked out again. I let out my breath.

I swiveled, searching the water behind us. Our churning wake fused with a large wave. Duncan's wave runner rode its crest, then slammed on its side with casual fury. The gymnastics hurled Duncan into the air. With a loud splash, he vanished in the gray-green depths. Flailing arms. A head bobbed.

"Go back," I yelled. "Duncan's down!"

"I know," Ross screamed in reply. "These bastards are going to run him over."

Now I saw why Ross had changed direction. A white Stingray. The sleek twenty-four-foot cruiser would have mowed us down or swamped us if Ross hadn't altered course. Its driver either hadn't seen us or didn't care. The boat's prow, moving at what seemed mach speed, took aim at Duncan's head.

"It's them!" Ross yelled over the deafening roar of wind and screeching engines. "Eunice told me they had a Stingray 240."

The cruiser zoomed toward Duncan. Not a damned thing we could do.

Ross boomeranged us into a U-turn. He'd decided to play chicken, force the boat to flinch and alter course before it creamed Duncan.

We'd lost momentum wallowing in our turn, and our target had gained speed. The cruiser planed—her bow jacked high above the dark, churning water. The upright posture wouldn't prevent her knife-like propellers from slicing into Duncan's unprotected body.

A second boat sprang into view. The FBI. The villains had turned tail. Unfortunately the FBI's nondescript deck boat had been chosen for its fade-into-the-scenery façade. It was outclassed in this race.

With no time to influence the unfolding drama, Ross idled our wave runner. Our only play was rescue. He edged closer to Duncan's runaway wave runner. Ross captured it and fastened a towrope to its nose.

I scanned the water where we'd last spotted Duncan. The cruiser and chase boat would intersect the area in seconds. I frantically searched for some sign of Duncan. Nothing. No hint of a head or arm breaking the churning surface. The boats roared by.

Afraid to look, I forced myself to dissect every dark, oily smudge that might be blood. The chop churned the water into a witch's cauldron. Seconds ticked by. The dual wakes flattened like the dying line on a heart monitor. Nothing. Then Duncan surfaced less than six feet away. He gasped like a landed trout.

"Are you hurt?" I yelled.

Duncan hadn't enough breath to answer, but shook his head. "I dived," he choked out. "Damned glad I wasn't wearing a lifejacket. Any extra buoyancy and I'd never have kicked deep enough. My weapons pack is gone."

Ross coaxed the riderless wave runner into Duncan's reach. With trembling arms, he draped his wheezing body over the seat.

"Will you be okay?" Ross asked. "We have to go. The FBI will never catch that cruiser. It's got a 280-horsepower motor and a top speed of around fifty miles per hour. If we go flat out, we might run them down."

"Go," Duncan said. "I'll follow in a minute."

"No, no. Go to Ross's house," I yelled. "You don't have any weapons. Tell the FBI what we know."

Ross blasted off. Had Duncan heard my entreaty? I wasn't sure. We retraced our course from Arnolds Park. Why would the kidnappers head there? The flight seemed nonsensical. By now, they surely knew any Arnolds Park cohorts were dead or engaged in a losing battle.

Night fell. The boats we shadowed were harder and harder to see. No running lights. Even the arctic white of the villain's cruiser disappeared with regularity, a ghostly moon that played hide and seek in twilight's murky mist. When I again caught sight of our quarry, the cruiser looked bigger. We were gaining.

The icy lake spray had ceased to rule my body. I no longer shivered. The goose bumps that had marched up and down my spine were at parade rest. Numbness has its rewards. The constant spank of our ride had deadened my behind.

We closed on the FBI boat. Silhouettes of gun-toting men crowded the deck. Losers in the drag race. A widening gap between the speedboats neutralized the FBI guns. The kidnap boat pulled out of range. Of course, even eyeball to eyeball, the FBI agents would be reluctant to fire from their jouncing platform. An errant shot could hit Aunt May.

Hang in there, May.

We rocketed past the FBI. The on-deck agents gestured wildly, mouthing commands we couldn't hear. Soundless and meaningless appeals. We sped forward. "Catch the bastards." My scream merged with the whine of our maritime motorcycle.

The skeletal frame of the amusement park's roller coaster and the Queen's shadowy majesty grew distinct. Our adversaries would ram the pier if they didn't change course or slow.

Tethered at irregular intervals, the antique flotilla created a formidable obstacle course. The haphazard deployment of vessels would normally be no more than an inconvenience in a No Wake Zone. For a boat approaching at fifty miles per hour, the twinkling boats could prove the ultimate no wake zone.

Was this the plan? Did the kidnappers want to crash and die in a cataclysmic explosion? Were they choosing a fiery death over jail?

Please God, no. In what seemed an answer to my silent prayers, the cruiser slowed.

The first muzzle flash dashed any hope they'd surrender. They weren't going to say adios without a final firefight. A bevy of bullets whizzed past me. Tiny geysers erupted nearby as bullets peppered the lake's surface. I tightened my grip as Ross zigged our wave runner one way, then zagged another.

We were at a definite disadvantage. Even if we'd had firearms, we wouldn't have used them—not with May aboard. Our paltry weaponry required proximity. We'd also need luck or surprise for our odd armament assortment to yield any success.

I picked out the shadowy silhouettes of at least three bad guys. We were outnumbered. Well, well. On shore, I picked up bustling activity. What looked like a full platoon of agents scurried about the boardwalk. Unfortunately none of them had water wings. The FBI wouldn't be joining our boating party for awhile.

A bright flash lit the sky. An explosion bloomed. An antique boat blew sky high. Chunks of fiery debris rained down like hail from a virulent thunderstorm. Though outside the inferno's radius, shockwaves lifted us heavenward, then plummeted us toward hell. Ross slipped sideways. I grabbed his jacket, yanked with fury. He scrambled back into position.

"Dammit. That was Gus Swenson's 1933 Chris-Craft. He'll be sick."

Only Ross could expend mental energy mourning a boat owner's loss with bullets flying.

A new roar drowned out my response. More lethal pyrotechnics. Somehow the kidnappers were blasting the antiques to smithereens.

"God damn!" Ross yelled. "That was Harry Johnson's 1920 Weekender!"

"Well, Harry and Gus won't be the only losers if we don't do something fast."

What were these idiots trying to pull? The anchored oldies were empty—God, at least I hoped they were. Were the pyrotechnics simply intended to add confusion? Or had their shots gone awry? Did they think FBI agents were swimming toward them?

The destruction did something more than distract us. It narrowed everyone's field of vision—theirs as well as ours. Oily smoke billowed from the sinking wrecks and added a layer of inky fog to the night sky. The sharp contrast between blazing timbers and the surrounding gloom was enough to make anyone's retinas act like out-of-control auto-focus lenses. Pinpoints of light danced in my vision. I couldn't see anything beyond the fires.

Where had the cruiser gone? There she was. Inching our way and maneuvering for a clear shot at open water. Her captain must have decided landing here wasn't such a hot idea after all. The lake offered many dark, unpopulated coves that promised far better opportunities for a getaway.

So why didn't they take off?

Suddenly it dawned on me. The bad guys had ceased firing at us. Since I could barely see them, maybe we'd become invisible as well. We presented a much more compact target, and our water-hugging profile had to help. While a sliver of our wave runner's bumblebee color scheme rode above the chop, how visible could it be from above? Especially with two people in Batman costumes draped over the frame?

"Can you sneak around and sidle up behind them?" I asked. "I don't think they have a clue where we went after the fireworks started. If you can get close, we can board her—use my grappling hook to lever ourselves up to her deck. They won't expect that."

"Forget the grappling hook," Ross chuckled. "The dummies picked a Stingray with a swim platform. We can step onto that sucker from our wave runner. Or swim in and roll onto the ledge if push comes to shove."

Playing cat and mouse, we made a do-si-do maneuver around a moored antique, keeping it between us and our prey. The Stingray appeared to be using the same relic to screen its movements from the land-locked FBI. The cruiser huddled so close to the old powerboat their beams almost kissed.

"I've got an idea to put the brakes on that Stingray, if she tries to zoom out of here," I whispered. "I can use the grappling hook to make these boats Siamese twins. Tie the bad guys' Stingray to the anchored Chris-Craft."

"Might work," Ross allowed. "The line won't hold forever, but it'll sure give 'em a few seconds' pause."

Within six feet, Ross cut our idling motor. Dipping our feet below the lake surface, we finned our way toward the Stingray's swim platform. No one was visible in the boat's stern. I prayed all three men were in the bow, eyes trained forward to scan the horizon for the FBI boat pursuing them and, possibly, us. Elimination of their water-based pursuers would dramatically improve their odds of escape.

With hand motions, I signaled Ross to wait. I tied the grappling hook's line through a cleat on the Stingray—the one usually reserved for a ski tow line. Then I grabbed hold of trim on the old Chris-Craft and heaved myself upright. I wobbled like a crazed first-time rollerblader. As I hefted the grappling hook over the antique's gunnels, my feet scooted out from under me.

Crap. The jig was up. The hook dropped onto the Chris-Craft's deck with a loud metallic thwack. I entered the water with a splash grand enough to rival my best-ever cannonball.

As the cold lake baptized me, I said a final prayer. My face broke the lake's surface. Aboard the Stingray, a solo giant ran toward me. What the heck?

Ross steadied the Sea-Doo and aimed his spear gun. I held my breath as his spear arced over the stern and pierced the man's torso. The target dropped his gun and clutched at the spear. Trying to extract its imbedded barbs would only increase his agony.

Fine by me. One down. The man grunted and collapsed.

"Gary?" a gruff voice bellowed from the Stingray's bow. In seconds, Gary's failure to answer would send another villain charging our way.

Somehow Ross managed a world-class dismount to the Stingray swim platform. With an outstretched hand, he yanked me from my ice-water bath. Together we scrambled over the fiberglass knee wall separating us from the deck.

Now we were onboard but ill prepared. Ross needed time to load another spear. Downing the next kidnapper would be up to me. I grabbed the gaff I'd planned to use as a club and sprinted ahead. I hunkered down in shadows to the left of Gary's body, held my breath...and prayed the sight of a spear protruding from a colleague would rattle our enemy. Coupled with a background image of Ross and his spear gun, the visual confusion might provide an opening for me to whomp him upside the head.

The new kidnapper hustled into view, then stalled as he tried to absorb the scene. I took my one chance. Winding up as if there were runners on all bases, I had to hit one out of the ballpark. The man's gun swiveled toward me. I swung my bat-gaff. A sickening thwonk confirmed contact. A second later, a sharp sting and burning sensation told me he'd landed a blow, too. I'd been shot.

My bleeding left arm hung dead and useless at my side. My adversary looked even worse. While the gaff missed his temple, it tore a hole through his cheek and impaled his tongue.

Ross retrieved the man's dropped gun and pointed it at his chest. "Move an eyelash and I'll shoot."

Despite gagging on his own blood, the man grabbed a seat and attempted to lever himself upright.

Someone stomped on the gas. The Stingray leapt forward. Guess the survivor figured to shake things up. The boat snapped back like an enraged pit bull stymied by a choke chain. The grappling hook-as-anchor blocked the attempted getaway. The bucking knocked Ross and me flat.

Our bleeding enemy recovered his balance quicker than we did. He made for the bow. We pursued. Ross led as we bolted up the step to the raised captain's platform. I stared at the captain's handgun aimed directly at us. Ross squeezed off a shot. He'd kept his finger on the trigger of the captured gun.

The captain screamed and toppled overboard. One less threat in our equation. Now the odds favored us. Two versus one hemorrhaging villain. Except he'd disappeared. Feeling vulnerable without a weapon, I used my still-working right arm to extract the only thing left in my backpack—a wadded up fish net.

"Where'd he go?" I whispered.

"Dammit, he crawled into the cuddy cabin. Down with Mom. Only one way in. He's got a definite advantage."

"Yeah, but he doesn't have a gun. The faster we move the better off we are."

Cradling my injured arm, I ran like hell to beat Ross to the cuddy cabin door. I knew the first person in would take the brunt of any counterattack. I figured that should be me since I'd gotten us into this mess.

As I burst headfirst into the cabin, I threw the net clutched in my left hand.

"Marley!" Aunt May screamed. "He has a knife."

As the lunatic pulled his dagger from a leg holster, my fishnet snared him. I pushed off the stairs. The fishnet snagged my legs. Thrashing arms and legs kicked at our shared straitjacket. Out of the corner of my eye, I glimpsed something red and shiny. A cylinder? I heard a pop and a loud whoosh.

The last thing I remembered.

Twenty-Four

Stretched out on an operating table, I bit my lip as a doctor pulled another stitch through my upper arm. It hurt like hell, even though my arm felt tingly from the shoulder down.

"If you leave a scar, you'll answer to me," Aunt May warned. "I want those stitches harder to see than tits on a boar hog!"

I wanted to laugh. My hallucination was funny. The deja vu dialogue was lifted straight from my teenage follies—my infamous après car wreck visit to Dickinson County Hospital's ER. Aunt May sure was bossy back then.

Her voice sounded so real, so close.

Lazily, I opened my eyes. A doctor. I could smell his Brut aftershave and count individual follicles in his five o'clock shadow. He bent close, frowning in concentration. A needle popped into my flesh. I squinted. Aunt May hovered on the sidelines. Her snow-white hair a dead giveaway I wasn't in some trance. I blinked.

"Lookey who's decided to join the party," May crowed. "About time. Didn't want you to miss all the fun."

"You're okay? And Ross?" Words tumbled like cotton balls on my sandpaper tongue.

"Fine and fine." May smiled.

"Okay, May." The doctor looming over me made a shooing motion. "Out with you. No need to excite our patient. We'll have her out of here in no time—if you'll let us be."

"Humph." May toddled away. I slipped back into never-never land.

❖

What a nice dream. Duncan kissed me. One of those deep, lingering numbers that make my knees go weak, not arthritic. He bent to kiss my breast. Not good. His lips felt like ice.

I awoke with a start and stared into the face of a white-on-white nurse—pasty skin, gray hair, white uniform. Her cold metal stethoscope pressed against my chest.

Why don't they ever let you sleep in hospitals? Uh-oh, why was I in the hospital?

It started to come back. I scanned my field of vision for added clues. Duncan rose from a bedside chair to take my hand. "Hi."

I squinted to make his smile swim into clearer focus.

"How are you feeling?"

I felt grouchy and anxious despite his devilish grin. "What the hell happened?"

"You got shot and you have a concussion. The doctors say you'll be fine but they kept you for observation because of the knock on your head. Ross and May fared better—not a scratch. Your aunt's wrists and ankles are a little irritated from being tied up. She'll probably outlive us all."

"What happened to that guy in the cabin with May? I don't remember a thing after I tackled him. How did Ross take him down?"

"He didn't." Duncan laughed. "May did. They tied her hands in front of her. Didn't think a pipsqueak eighty-year-old could do much damage. She hopped around the cabin, found a compact fire extinguisher, and hid it under a blanket. She planned to foam the bastard. Blind him with a high-pressure nozzle in the face.

"Then you dropped in—so to speak—and snagged the kidnapper in the fishnet. Since you had the guy's head pinned securely to the ground, May stuck the nozzle right in his ear and pulled the trigger. Might as well have shot him with a .22 caliber. He died instantly. But the explosion jackknifed his body and drove your head into a cabin beam."

"Dammit, I can't believe it. All three guys on the kidnap boat are dead?"

"No. The driver—the fellow Ross shot—lived," said Duncan.

"The FBI arrived about the time May extinguished the last fellow, picked the wounded captain out of the brink and medevaced him to a hospital. Weaver hopes he'll talk, though he may not know much. He was one of Bo Quigley's disciples. He never communicated with anyone in Spirit Lake."

"What about Bo Quigley and his bioterrorism plans?"

"I can answer that." The new voice came from the door to my room. General Irvine looked tired but pleased.

"Homeland Security raided Quigley's camp in Montana. He's done for and the genie's back in the bottle—at least this time around. All the stolen research has been secured. The lab making the bioterrorism cocktails was destroyed and the workers are in jail."

"Is Weaver okay?"

The general walked over to a small table and set down a vase of roses. "Yes. She sends her thanks. You have mine, too. She's busy with some mop-up details or she'd be here."

Duncan chimed in. "Your idea for a website warning gave Weaver ample time to set up her own ambush. The FBI bagged four homegrown terrorists in the Arnolds Park skirmish. All dead."

The general nodded. "Too bad her only hope of nailing Kyle and Hamilton rests with the guy your cousin hospitalized, plus any evidence they inadvertently left behind."

"You're kidding." My head pounded. "She can't put Kyle or Hamilton at Arnolds Park? There's no proof one or both of them were behind this?"

Duncan put a hand on my shoulder, trying to pin me to the bed. "Calm down."

My eyes pleaded with the general. "I know this is Hamilton's scheme. He hired those thugs. Kyle wouldn't have the contacts, the know-how. Can't Weaver trace payments... or phone calls?"

General Irvine played with the cuff of his jacket. His eyes didn't meet mine. "Agent Weaver and the FBI will follow the money trail. Let her do her work. I'm sure all the guilty parties will pay. In time."

"In time," I repeated with disgust. "Okay, now it's time for me to go home."

"Let's ask the doctor," Duncan said.

A namby-pamby answer if I ever heard one. "Let's not," I snapped. "I have to see Ross and May with my own eyes, convince myself they're okay."

The general laughed. "It's a wonder the colonel lasted in the Army. She doesn't like to follow orders."

He gave a jaunty salute. "I have to leave. Just wanted to say thanks."

When the general exited, Duncan took my hand again. "May and Ross sat vigil with you most of the night, until the doctors insisted they leave. Doc Johnson worried May's health would suffer if she didn't get some sleep. He gave her a sedative and sent her home with Ross. They'll both be asleep for hours. So there's no rush."

"I still want to go. Please."

Duncan helped me dress—a strange reversal of roles. Despite the strenuous objections of the nurse on duty, I signed myself out without a doctor's blessing. As usual, the hospital triumphed with its final humiliation, insisting Duncan roll me away in a wobbly wheelchair. It was early morning, seven a.m.

Duncan drove us straight to Eunice and Ross's house. Queenie and Empress yelped as soon as our feet hit the front path. Some things had returned to normal. The barking hubbub made the doorbell superfluous. Eunice greeted us instantly and hugged me tight.

I winced at the pressure on my newly upholstered arm.

"Oh, sorry. I'm so glad to see you. I'm up early for me, but I wanted to make sure no one bothered Ross and May. They need their sleep."

"I just want to see them." The tears I'd been holding back sprang a leak. "I promise I won't wake them."

Eunice nodded and led me to a ground-floor master bedroom where Ross hugged a pillow. A smile tugged at my sleeping cousin's puckered mouth. He looked about five years old—and cuddly—though he'd refute the adjective.

Next I followed Eunice upstairs, where she carefully opened a guestroom door. May's snoring confirmed her presence before her fluffy white perm came into view. Her lips gently puffed open with each exhale.

"Thank you." I hugged Eunice again then headed down the staircase.

Duncan waited in the hall, patiently petting the Shelties. They'd attached themselves like Velcro to his pant legs. As a rule, Queenie and Empress regard men with disdain. Their acceptance of Duncan seemed a good sign. Or maybe not, since the dogs were none too fond of me.

I caught a glimpse of myself in the hallway mirror and shuddered. No one had mentioned my black eye or the nasty bruises coloring a fair percentage of my body.

"Why don't you stay?" Eunice suggested. "Sleep here. I'll make up another guestroom."

"Thanks but no thanks," I answered. "Think I'll head to May's and soak out some of this soreness in a hot bubble bath. Clean clothes and hot coffee sound wonderful."

I'd actually gotten a fair night's sleep at the hospital, even though my slumber was the pharmacologically-induced kind that leaves me groggy for days.

I smiled. "Please, please call as soon as Ross and May wake up. I'll come running."

"Of course."

"I love you." I kissed my cousin's cheek as we left.

"Love you, too."

Though Duncan offered to keep me company, I sent him away with a kiss and a promise of more to come. His cool head and pluck under pressure impressed me. His willingness to pull sentry duty for a hospitalized friend added brownie points. Of course, Duncan's superb performance ratings in other areas didn't hurt my overall fondness for the man.

Yet I wasn't anxious for anyone's company. Duncan needed

sleep; I craved a little self-pampering and solitude. A few hours to relax without a single demand.

But first I figured I'd wrangle an update from Weaver. Surely she'd figured some new avenue to prove Hamilton and Kyle pulled the strings.

Weaver answered my call on the first ring. "Marley, I can't talk. I'm at Vivian Riley's house. Kyle's dead. So are Nancy and Vivian. All three shot in the head with a nine-millimeter Glock. Eric, our presumed shooter, is missing."

"What!"

"Later." Weaver hung up before I could digest her news.

Kyle Olsen, another of my mastermind candidates, lay dead. Why would Eric kill all three of them? Had to be some drug-induced psychotic rage.

It felt like I had ten-pound sacks of potatoes tied to each appendage. My drooping eyelids also signaled defeat. I dragged myself to May's bathroom and turned the faucets to fill her oversized spa tub then added a generous dollop of lavender bubble bath. Steam filled the room as the hot water ran. The tub sloshed a little water on the tiled floor as I slid in.

I'm a shower person. Baths are too much trouble, too time consuming. Yet this felt wonderful. What's more, the nurse had given stern instructions to keep my stitches dry for at least forty-eight hours. With my left arm draped on the tub ledge, I submerged all other body parts except for a small breathing oval of eyes, nose and mouth. The bubbles tingled. The lilac scent soothed; the heat consoled.

Eyes closed, I let my mind drift. Would Darlene and Julie ever feel safe enough to come home? I was convinced Kyle and Hamilton were behind all the deaths. Still Weaver theorized the killers had little to gain by pursuing a vendetta against Darlene and Julie. They'd been convenient scapegoats, not targets.

If I were Darlene, I'd feel uneasy until the bloodthirsty half-brothers traded pinstripes for prison stripes.

And now Eric was shooting folks.

Twenty-Five

I have generous ears. You can pick any Carr relative out of a lineup—me, my sister, my cousins—solely by the size and shape of our ears. This time, my submerged, plus-sized hearing appendages failed me.

My eyes popped open when the bathroom door swung wide and ushered in a cool breeze. An apparition stared down at me. Paralyzed with fear, my scream caught in my throat.

Had anyone—even Aunt May—entered, I'd have shrieked in shock. But Eric, oh, God, what did he plan to do?

Jake's orphaned grandson loomed in the doorway. He wheezed. His face ruddy from rage, exertion or both. His light blue eyes looked wild. Their crazed, shifting focus scared me shitless.

He was the spitting image of every murdering maniac conjured up by film noir. My total vulnerability didn't help. You can't get much more vulnerable than reclining naked in a tub.

His right hand grasped a large butcher knife. It swung to and fro like a shiny pendulum on a grandfather clock. At least the sharp blade wasn't dripping blood.

Inexplicably, his weapon transformed my fear into righteous—I'm sure some would say menopausal—wrath. I refused to cower in front of this deranged, wet-behind-the-ears killer. The past twenty-four hours overloaded my nervous system with one too many shocks. The gleaming blade cut it.

"Okay, Eric," I screamed. "Stab me. Just get it over with, punk. Nothing I can do. But you'll kill me without the satisfaction of hearing me beg. What are you waiting for, you frigging idiot? Afraid you'll miss a vital organ because you can't see through the suds? Well, how's this—I'll help you decide where to aim?"

I violently pushed off the tub's ledge and levered my nude body fully erect to its five-foot-seven-inch height. A tidal wave of soapy water splashed over the tub and rolled like an ocean breaker across the floor. The bathroom tsunami inundated Eric's running shoes, then retreated in a wash of muddy detritus. Would this be the last sight I'd see?

The twenty-year-old spun, turning his back on my naked body. He blubbered like a baby. Not exactly the expected reaction.

"I don't want to kill you," he whimpered. "I tried to shoot him, but I couldn't. My hands shook too much. Uncle Kyle's blood made me dizzy. I guess I dropped the gun."

Full-body sobs jerked the kid's shoulders up and down. "I don't even remember grabbing this knife. Musta seen it when I ran through the kitchen."

My adrenaline-soaked brain wobbled from thought to thought. What in the hell was this boy saying? Could I snatch that knife from his hand?

"Who did you shoot? Your uncle?"

Eric slumped against the doorjamb. "A mistake. He's coming for me. I gotta kill him before he kills me. He doesn't scare you. I heard him talk about you. Help me. Please."

Gingerly, I climbed out of the tub and slipped behind him. My wet hand closed over his trembling fingers. Miniature soap bubbles burst on my skin as I guided his arm toward May's aqua commode and unwrapped his fingers. No resistance. The blade splashed into the toilet bowl. Step one.

Step two. Calm him down. Had the boy truly blocked out the fact that he'd killed Kyle Olsen? "Why did your uncle want to kill you?"

While waiting for an answer, I snagged a towel wrapper and nudged Eric ahead of me out of the bathroom. The young man hadn't quit crying long enough to speak.

"Sit on the bed," I ordered.

He sat, head in hands, and rocked. His sobs came in anguished waves.

"Eric, your uncle can't kill you. He's dead. You have to turn yourself in."

The kid's head snapped up. "What?"

"I just talked to Agent Weaver. She's at Vivian's house. Kyle Olsen is dead. So are Vivian and Nancy. Do you remember shooting? Maybe it was an accident."

Eric leapt toward me. Not good. The chords in his neck stood out. "He killed them all. I didn't do it."

"Sit. Back. Down." I made it a command, no choice but to submit.

His lanky frame folded in on itself. Maybe I'd get out of this alive.

"Why would your uncle kill Vivian and Nancy and then kill himself?"

"Not Uncle Kyle. That other man. He taunted him. Told him he had to do it." Eric's blubbering made his next words unintelligible.

"Snap out of it!" The notion of slapping Eric to stop his hysterics held a certain appeal. But that meant letting go of my towel cover. I snagged May's pink robe on a nearby hook and shimmied it over my head.

"In the living room." I pointed the way.

Eric staggered to a couch. "I rang the bell. When no one answered, I broke in to wait for you. Then I heard water running."

The front door stood ajar, a sidelight window broken. Time to get the kid back on track. "You mentioned another man. What man?" If Eric meant Hamilton, I wanted him to say so without coaching.

My fingers itched to dial 911 while Eric appeared docile. Yet this might be my one chance to get him to talk. Traumatized, the not-quite-grownup seemed willing to spill his guts. Whatever Eric wanted to get off his chest might lighten Darlene's load. Not often does one land a blubbering, voluble defector from the enemy camp.

"That Hamilton fellow. The security guy."

Bingo. We were getting somewhere.

"Did I hear my name?"

The oily voice made my bowels shrivel. I turned toward May's front door as Hamilton nudged it closed with his backside. His right hand, encased in thin surgeon's gloves, held a Glock aimed squarely at my chest.

Eric leapt up from the couch.

"Sit down or you'll have another death on your conscience," Hamilton barked. "One more step and I shoot Marley. Behave and she might live."

Yeah, right. I willed Eric to rush Hamilton. With the gun pointed at me, he had a chance. I'd be dead either way.

My mental telepathy failed. The kid collapsed on the couch in defeat.

"Good boy." Hamilton glanced at Eric. "Those last three murders are all your fault. If you'd kept swallowing your pills, you'd never have overheard your uncle and me."

Hamilton hadn't ordered me to sit. I stood maybe eight feet away. Too far to down him before a bullet ended a tackle. I held my breath and inched one foot forward. Hamilton's head snapped in my direction. His glare pinned me. "Don't get cute, Colonel. Sit. Now."

I backed up. May's recliner sat directly behind me. I veered left and gingerly lowered myself onto a cane-bottomed chair, one of May's recent antique finds. The wooden chair was heavy yet light enough to lift. Could I swing it like a club?

"I assume you plan to kill me and blame it on Eric." My calm tone seemed to surprise and irritate my captor. "Let the boy live. No one will believe him if he accuses you."

Hamilton's smug smile chilled me. "You're right about that. My alibi's airtight."

"So why track Eric down?"

He shrugged. "I wiped the gun clean. No fingerprints. That didn't quite jibe with a drug-crazed killer. So much neater if the FBI found Eric holding the proverbial smoking gun.

"I wondered where the sniveling brat might run. His shiny red car advertised he'd come calling. Killing you, Colonel, wasn't part of my plan. Just a nice bonus."

I maintained direct eye contact. I didn't want him to notice my fingers. My aunt had plans to repair the loose chair arm. As my fingers pried at it, I thanked heaven she'd procrastinated. Free of its pegs, the dense wood would make a solid club.

"So why kill your half-brother and the women? Wouldn't it have been easier to do away with Eric?"

Keep Hamilton talking.

He chuckled. While his right hand trained the Glock on me, his left pulled a syringe from his pocket. "A heroin overdose for Eric would have been a tidy solution, but Kyle had a sudden bout of conscience. While we argued, dopehead here found a gun and fired at me." Hamilton smiled. "Dopey dropped the pistol after he winged Kyle. When I settled down, I realized Kyle had become a liability. So I set up an alibi and doubled back to finish him off. Nancy and Vivian blundered in. Bad timing."

I nodded, willing Hamilton to keep his eyes locked on mine. Eric stirred. Was he going to rush Hamilton?

"Handing over military secrets to homegrown terrorists didn't bother you? You knew they planned to kill thousands, maybe millions, of innocents."

The chair's arm came free. I settled it lightly on its dowel and scooted my hand further back until I reached a narrow section I could grip like a bat handle.

Hamilton bared his white teeth in what passed for a smile. "We both know no one's really innocent, don't we? I had sympathy with the cause. I figured Bo's clowns would get caught after they killed off a few thousand wetbacks. My contribution to solving our immigration problems."

"They'll catch you," I growled.

"No, they won't. That two million Glaston transferred to a Swiss bank is sitting in my account, got ten million more from Bo after his successful field tests."

Hamilton's eyes traveled down my body. He snickered. "Your death costume adds an extra touch of humiliation. You look like a bag lady who stole a smaller kid's clothes."

Eric sprang. Hamilton's taunt morphed into a grunt. He crashed to the floor, Eric on top. The gun boomed, and plaster rained from the ceiling. Hamilton dropped the syringe, but not the pistol. I jumped to my feet, solid armrest in hand.

The twenty-year-old straddled his adversary, pinning one of the older man's wrists in each hand. Too bad a steady diet of drugs had sapped the kid's strength. His hold wasn't enough to keep Hamilton from steadily inching the Glock upward. In a minute, it would tuck under Eric's chin.

The men rolled. Positions flipped. Hamilton claimed the top. Time to act.

I sprinted and swung my makeshift club. Hamilton saw it coming and ducked. The armrest connected with floor not flesh. A jarring wave of pain shot from my wrist to my shoulder.

The gun coughed, and May's Tiffany lamp exploded.

I refocused on the squirming men. When Hamilton coiled to escape my club, the kid seized the distraction, pinning the corrupt exec's gun arm beneath his body. But the experienced older man had a new weapon. He'd recovered the hypodermic syringe. A weapon just as lethal as the gun. Using his teeth, he plucked the plastic cover off the syringe. Armed and ready.

Eric gripped the man's forearm, wrestling to keep the hypodermic needle away. He was losing the battle. Hamilton scissored his legs in an attempt to heave Eric off. I threw myself across his whipsawing legs, anchoring them in place. It was like riding side-by-side bucking broncos.

The deadly needle moved closer to the young man's face. I slid further up Hamilton's legs. His knees battered my ribs, but I'd gained a clear shot at his groin. Rising up, I dropped all my weight on my elbow between Hamilton's legs. His whole body arched, accompanied by a scream that climbed two octaves.

Eric's arm rose. He'd seized the syringe. Blood spurted as

the needle plunged into Hamilton's eye. Eric's fingers pressed the plunger. The legs beneath me bucked in a wild frenzy. When they stilled, the only sounds were my labored pants and Eric's gasps for air.

The kid rolled off Hamilton and lay spread-eagled on the rug. His chest heaved with every intake of air.

I attempted to stagger up. My body felt limp, boneless. Get up, call the police.

A shriek coaxed me to hoist my body up on one elbow. Had some new enemy come to murder us?

May's elderly upstairs neighbors swayed in the doorway, a twin portrait of fear. A blue-veined hand covered the woman's open mouth. Her stooped husband held her up by her elbow.

"We called 911," he said. "A bullet came through our floor. Scared us silly. Are you okay, Marley?" His gaze swept over the still body and Eric gasping for oxygen.

"Yes," I answered. "Thanks."

Sirens blared nearby. Just the tonic I needed to prompt action. I wobbled to my feet and pulled the hem of my borrowed pink robe to cover my still-soapy thighs.

❖

Sheriff's deputies swarmed the condo and stood guard over the scene until Agent Weaver arrived with her team. She ushered Eric and me into the guest bedroom for a chat while the crime scene techs combed May's living room, and Gertie examined another dead body. I hoped all evidence of the bloody melee could be erased before my aunt returned to the condo she viewed as her quiet, safe haven.

I tuned in as Weaver questioned Eric. The boy reported that his Uncle Kyle had been feeding him pharmaceuticals like popcorn to keep him out of the way. Feeling ill, Eric began spitting out pills as soon as his caretakers left the room. He'd wandered down to the kitchen for a snack and was foraging in the walk-in pantry when he heard his Uncle Kyle and Hamilton having a heated argument.

"Hamilton insisted I had to die," Eric said. "Kyle found the stash of pills I'd been spitting up so they weren't sure how much I knew. Hamilton suggested a drug overdose, but Uncle Kyle claimed it was too risky. He said even if I talked, no one would believe a druggie."

Eric stopped talking and stared at the hands folded in his lap. Weaver patted his shoulder. "What happened then?"

"Hamilton called my uncle a coward. That made Uncle Kyle mad. He said he wished he'd never asked Hamilton for help when Dr. Glaston put the squeeze on him. Hamilton told Uncle Kyle to suck it up or he'd just be another loser bastard."

As Weaver peppered Eric with a new question, his eyes seemed to focus.

"I knew Kyle kept a Glock by his bed. So I snuck into his room and stole it. I crept downstairs, saw Hamilton standing in the doorway. A stair squeaked just when I took aim. Hamilton dove behind Uncle Kyle and ran out the front door."

Eric stopped talking. Weaver asked an agent to go to May's kitchen and get him a glass of water. He gulped it down.

"So you shot Kyle?"

"I didn't mean to. The bullet hit his arm. All that blood made me feel sick. I ran back through the kitchen. Then I came here."

Eric hiccupped.

I was convinced the young man told the truth. He wasn't a killer though it would have been easy for Hamilton to convince a jury otherwise. "Ladies and gentlemen, the boy is out of his skull. He shot his uncle and two women during a black-out episode." Given gunpowder on the young man's hands, and his verbal threats at the funeral parlor, a guilty verdict was a slam-dunk. Not a living soul could have disputed Hamilton's twisted version of the facts.

The phone rang. I jumped a foot. Guess I was still wound a tad tight. I looked over at the FBI agent. "Can I answer that?"

She nodded and I walked into May's bedroom.

"May and Ross are awake," Eunice reported. "Come on over.

I called Mrs. Lady's and ordered takeout. Stop on your way and bring lunch. I ordered hot tamales for you."

"I'll be along as soon as I can."

Weaver herded Eric toward the living room. "I'm taking him into custody," she said. "I have to until we check out all the facts. He'll be under guard in a hospital. First job is getting him clean of whatever chemicals they've been pumping into him."

"You don't need anything else from me now, right? That was Eunice. Ross and May are awake. I want to go see them. Plus I'm hoping I can convince May to stay at Ross's house until I can get her condo looking like it did when she last saw it."

After Weaver gave me her blessing, I dressed and headed to Mrs. Lady's to pick up the lunches. I wasn't quite sure how to tell them about all the fun they'd missed while they slept. If they were up for a spicy lunch, I'd deliver.

My relatives were all gathered around the kitchen table when I arrived. I dished out our entrees and waited until everyone had dug in before I began my tale.

May wasn't exactly happy about losing a Tiffany lamp and the damage to her ceiling and door. I didn't even mention the blood on the rug. She agreed to stay at Ross's until her home was back in order.

After I burped my last tamale, Weaver called. "Thought you might want to know how Hamilton planned to set up an alibi. You'll love this. He called the FBI just after he finished shooting Kyle, Vivian and Nancy. He knew we'd triangulate the call to see where it originated."

"So, wouldn't it show he called from the murder scene?"

"No," Weaver answered. "He used a two-way radio. Taped one radio to his cell phone in a rental house across the lake from the murder scene. He used a voice command to initiate the call. Then talking into his radio, he carried on a conversation while he tidied up the crime scene."

"Thank heaven, he didn't get away with it," I answered.

As soon as I hung up, I dialed my home on Dear Island. It

was time to share some good news with Darlene and Julie. "How can I thank you, Marley? Now we can come home. Now we can come home and I can give Jake a proper farewell. I won't feel right until Reverend Schmidt says the final prayer."

❁

"Now my mother isn't one to brag, but she's quite the baker." Ross chuckled, a warm-up exercise for his audience. "A week after Mom and Dad married, Mom was determined to bake an apple pie that compared favorably with Grandma Carr's famous pastries. So when the crust burnt on her first attempt, she hid her disaster on the roof…"

Arms gesturing, Ross owned the dais, his grin broader than a beaver prepared to smile down an oak. The audience loved his storytelling, almost as much as May's. There wasn't a single frown among the kin gathered to celebrate May's entry into her ninth decade.

After two days of lake jollity, this was our final evening bash. The banquet at Village West. What a grand night. May preened like a peacock at a table with her three sons. The roast couldn't have pleased her more. My cousins Ed and Woods already had done their shtick to heavy applause. May's daughters-in-law laughed their heads off.

May beamed and wagged a scolding finger at Ross. My aunt could dish it out, but she could take it, too—especially since adulation so clearly laced the ribbing.

Our large table accommodated my sister, brother-in-law, nephew and nieces and their spouses. Duncan had earned an honorary slot by my side. That ensured I'd be grilled about our intentions. Was our romance serious?

At the moment, I didn't care. In fact, I was carefree.

I looked at the table next to us, delighted that Darlene, Julie, General Irvine and Agent Weaver had joined in the merriment. Darlene and Julie, returned from their unscheduled vacation at my island home, had bravely soldiered through Jake's memorial. Their lives were returning to normal.

To her credit, Darlene arranged and attended the funerals for Kyle and Olivia Olsen, Robert and Gina Glaston, and Vivian Riley. She paid for Nancy's funeral, too—somewhere in Texas—but opted not to attend.

Of course, the expense didn't really matter. In good taste, I never mentioned how the terms of her husband's will and the deaths of Gina and Kyle made Darlene richer than Midas.

Since May's kidnapping, there'd been more unexpected—and beneficial—fallout. In response to emails from Ross, wooden boat lovers around the country had sent contributions to replace the antique boats lost in the shootout. My cousin found two replacement antiques that could be restored to the same pristine condition. He'd also organized a fall boating extravaganza-tribute. He expected it to bring wooden boat lovers from around the U.S. to the unveiling of Gus and Harry's born-again boats.

I tuned back into Ross's familiar story just as he regaled the audience with Uncle John's climb onto the roof as he followed the apple pie scent.

Peals of laughter echoed through the banquet hall as Ross delivered his punch line. I joined in. She who laughs last...

Under the tablecloth, Duncan's hand crept over and his fingers began a merry tap-dance on my thigh.

Life is full of surprises. Ain't it grand?

Don't miss Marley's next adventure in:

With Neighbors Like These

Marley Clark's free-spirited friend Janie has gone entrepreneur, launching Helping Hollis HOAs, a Lowcountry management company that serves homeowner associations (HOAs) across Hollis County, South Carolina. Unfortunately, DOA—dead on arrival—threatens to become the acronym most associated with Janie's start-up firm as neighborhood fights turn lethal and Board members wind up wearing toe tags.

Braden Mann, Marley's former flame, is back in the Lowcountry and eager to stoke their relationship fire. But conflict develops when Marley answers Janie's plea to help end the mayhem. Braden owns the firm contracted to provide security to the HOAs Janie manages, and he's doesn't cotton to anyone nosing around his turf. Marley's life becomes even more complicated when she finds a link between the neighborhood bloodbaths and a powerful group's resolve to seek revenge against an enemy in Witness Protection.

If you didn't read Marley's first outing, it's a crackling good read:

Dear Killer

Marley Clark, a retired military intelligence officer, works security for the Dear Island community simply to keep busy. A single night patrol transforms the feisty widow's yawner of a job into a deadly battle of wits when she finds an islander drowned and bobbing naked amid a potpourri of veggies in a Jacuzzi.

Asked to serve as the lead investigator's liaison, the 52-year-old heroine is startled to discover she's become Deputy Braden Mann's target as well—for romance. Yet their steamy attraction doesn't deter the pair from sorting through a viper's nest of suspects as the body count grows and the pun-loving killer plans a grizzly epitaph for Marley.

AUTHOR LINDA LOVELY

A journalism major, Linda has always made her living as a writer. Mostly nonfiction. Well, except for advertising copy. Now she concentrates on her first love—fiction. Her stories dish up a main course of suspense, action and mystery with a generous side of romance.

The detail-rich settings for her Marley Clark Mystery series—Spirit Lake, Iowa, and the South Carolina Lowcountry—clearly reflect her love for the Midwest and South. An Iowa native, Linda currently lives beside a South Carolina lake with her husband of thirty-six years.

A member of Romance Writers of America (RWA), Sisters in Crime and the South Carolina Writers Workshop, she feels lucky to have found close friends and exceptional critique partners—snarky, funny, talented and generous—through these writer organizations.

Her manuscripts have made the finals in 15 contests, including RWA's prestigious Golden Heart and Daphne du Maurier competitions, and mystery contests such as Deadly Ink, Murder in the Grove, and Malice Domestic.

In addition to reading, she enjoys swimming, walking/hiking, kayaking, tennis and gardening.

For more information about the author, visit her website: www.lindalovely.com